THE ROMAN HAT MYSTERY

THE ROMAN HAT MYSTERY

Ellery Queen

MYSTERIOUSPRESS.COM

Cover design by Mumtaz Mustafa

978-1-4976-9518-4

This edition published in 2015 by MysteriousPress.com/Open Road Integrated Media
345 Hudson Street
New York, NY 10014
www.mysteriouspress.com
www.openroadmedia.com

Grateful acknowledgment
is made to
PROFESSOR ALEXANDER GOETTLER
Chief Toxicologist of the City of New York
for his friendly offices
in the preparation of this tale

THE ROMAN HAT MYSTERY

FOREWORD

I have been asked by both publisher and author to write a cursory preface to the story of Monte Field's murder. Let me say at once that I am neither a writer nor a criminologist. To make authoritative remarks, therefore, anent the techniques of crime and crime fiction is obviously beyond my capacity. Nevertheless, I have one legitimate claim to the privilege of introducing this remarkable story, based as it is upon perhaps the most mystifying crime of the past decade. . . . If it were not for me, *The Roman Hat Mystery* would never have reached the fiction-reading public. I am responsible for its having been brought to light; and there my pallid connection with it ends.

During the past winter I shook off the dust of New York and went a-traveling in Europe. In the course of a capricious roving about the corners of the Continent (a roving induced by that boredom which comes to every Conrad in quest of his youth)—I found myself one August day in a tiny Italian mountain village. How I got there, its location and its name do not matter; a promise is a promise, even when it is made by a stockbroker. Dimly I remembered that this toy hamlet perched on the lip of a sierra harbored two old friends whom I had not seen for two years. They had come from the seething sidewalks of New York to bask in the brilliant peace of an Italian countryside—well, perhaps it was as much curiosity about their regrets as anything else, that prompted me to intrude upon their solitude.

My reception at the hands of old Richard Queen, keener and grayer than ever, and of his son Ellery was cordial enough. We had been more than friends in the old days; perhaps, too, the vinous air of Italy was too heady a cure for their dust-choked Manhattan memories. In any case, they seemed profoundly glad to see me. Mrs. Ellery Queen—Ellery was now the husband of a glorious creature and the startled father of an infant who resembled his grandfather to an extraordinary degree—was as gracious as the name she bore. Even Djuna, no longer the scapegrace I had known, greeted me with every sign of nostalgia.

Despite Ellery's desperate efforts to make me forget New York and appreciate the lofty beauties of his local scenery, I had not been in their tiny villa for many days before a devilish notion took possession of me and I began to pester poor Ellery to death. I have something of a reputation for persistence, if no other virtue; so that before I left, Ellery in despair agreed to compromise. He took me into his library, locked the door and attacked an old steel filing cabinet. After a slow search he managed to bring out what I suspect was under his fingers all the time. It was a faded manuscript bound Ellery-like in blue legal paper.

The argument raged. I wished to leave his beloved Italian shores with the manuscript in my trunk, whereas he insisted that the sheaf of contention remain hidden in the cabinet. Old Richard was wrenched away from his desk, where he was writing a treatise for a German magazine on "American Crime and Methods of Detection," to settle the affair. Mrs. Queen held her husband's arm as he was about to close the incident with a workmanlike fist; Djuna clucked gravely; and even Ellery, Jr., extracted his pudgy hand from his mouth long enough to make a comment in his gurgle-language.

The upshot of it all was that *The Roman Hat Mystery* went back to the States in my luggage. Not unconditionally, however—Ellery is a peculiar man. I was forced solemnly and by all I held dear to swear the identities of my friends and of the important characters concerned in the story be veiled by pseudonyms; and that, on pain of instant annihilation, their names be permanently withheld from the reading public.

Consequently "Richard Queen" and "Ellery Queen" are not the true names of those gentlemen. Ellery himself made the selections; and I might add at once that his choices were contrived to baffle the reader who might endeavor to ferret the truth from some apparent clue of anagram.

The Roman Hat Mystery is based on actual records in the police archives of New York City. Ellery and his father, as usual, worked hand-in-hand on the case. During this period in his career Ellery was a detective-story writer of no mean reputation. Adhering to the aphorism that truth is often stranger than fiction, it was his custom to make notes of interesting investigations for possible use in his murder tales. The affair of the Hat so fascinated him that he kept unusually exhaustive notes, intending to publish it. Immediately after, however, he was plunged into another investigation which left him scant opportunity for business; and when this last case was successfully closed, Ellery's father, the Inspector, consummated a lifelong ambition by retiring and moving to Italy, bag and baggage. Ellery, who had in this affair found the lady of his heart, was animated by a painful desire to do something "big" in letters, Italy sounded idyllic to him; he married with his father's blessing and the three of them, accompanied by Djuna, went off to their new European home. The manuscript was utterly forgotten until I rescued it.

On one point, before I close this painfully unhandsome preface, I should like to make myself clear.

I have always found it extremely difficult to explain to strangers the peculiar affinity which bound Richard to Ellery Queen, as I must call them. For one thing, they are persons of by no means uncomplicated natures. Richard Queen, sprucely middle-aged after thirty-two years' service in the city police, earned his Inspector's chevrons not so much through diligence as by an extraordinary grasp of the technique of criminal investigation. It was said, for example, at the time of his brilliant detectival efforts during the now-ancient Barnaby Ross murder case, that "Richard Queen by this feat firmly establishes his fame beside such masters of crime detection as Tamaka Hiero, Brillon the Frenchman, Kris Oliver, Renaud, and James Redix the Younger."

Queen, with his habitual shyness toward newspaper eulogy, was the first to scoff at this extravagant statement; although Ellery maintains that for many years the old man secretly preserved a clipping of the story. However that may be—and I like to think of Richard Queen in terms of human personality, despite the efforts of imaginative journalists to make a legend of him—I cannot emphasize too strongly the fact that he was heavily dependent upon his son's wit for success in many of his professional achievements.

This is not a matter of public knowledge. Some mementoes of their careers are still reverently preserved by friends: the small bachelor establishment maintained during their American residence on West 87th Street, and now a semiprivate museum of curios collected during their productive years; the really excellent portrait of father and son, done by Thiraud and hanging in the art gallery of an anonymous millionaire; Richard's precious snuffbox, the Florentine antique which he had picked up at an auction and which he therefore held dearer than rubies, only to succumb to the blandishments of a charming old lady whose name he cleared of slander; Ellery's enormous collection of books on violence, perhaps as complete as any in the world, which he regretfully discarded when the Queens left for Italy; and, of course, the many as yet unpublished documents containing records of cases solved by the Queens and now stored away from prying eyes in the City's police archives.

But the things of the heart—the spiritual bonds between father and son—have until this time remained secret from all except a few favored intimates, among whom I was fortunate enough to be numbered. The old man, perhaps the most famous executive of the Detective Division in the last half-century, overshadowing in public renown, it is to be feared, even those gentlemen who sat briefly in the Police Commissioner's suite—the old man, let me repeat, owed a respectable portion of his reputation to his son's genius.

In matters of pure tenacity, when possibilities lay frankly open on every hand, Richard Queen was a peerless investigator. He had a crystal-clear mind for detail; a retentive memory for complexities of motive and plot; a cool viewpoint when the obstacle seemed insuperable. Give him a hundred facts, bungled and torn, out of proportion and sequence, and he had them assembled in short order. He was like a blood-hound who follows the true scent in the clutter of a hopelessly tangled trail.

But the intuitive sense, the gift of imagination, belonged to Ellery Queen, the fiction writer. The two might have been twins possessing abnormally developed faculties of mind, impotent by themselves but vigorous when applied one to the other. Richard Queen, far from resenting the bond which made his success so spectacularly possible—as a less generous nature might have done—took pains to make it plain to his friends. The slender, gray old man whose name was anathema to contemporary lawbreakers, used to utter his "confession," as he called it, with a naïveté explicable only on the score of his proud fatherhood.

One word more. Of all the affairs pursued by the two Queens this, which Ellery has titled *The Roman Hat Mystery* for reasons shortly to be made clear, was surely the crowning case of them all. The dilettante of criminology, the thoughtful reader of detective literature, will understand as the tale unfolds why Ellery considers the murder of Monte Field worthy of study. The average murderer's motives and habits are fairly accessible to the criminal specialist. Not so, however, in the case of the Field killer. Here the Queens dealt with a person of delicate perception and extraordinary finesse. In fact, as Richard pointed out shortly after the dénouement, the crime planned was as nearly perfect as human ingenuity could make it. As in so many "perfect crimes," however, a small mischance of fate coupled with Ellery's acute deductive analyses gave the hunting Queens the single clue which led ultimately to the destruction of the plotter.

J. J. McC.
New York
March 1, 1929

LEXICON OF PERSONS CONNECTED WITH THE INVESTIGATION

Note: The complete list of individuals, male and female, brought into the story of Monte Field's murder and appended below is given solely for the convenience of the reader. It is intended to simplify rather than mystify. In the course of perusing mysterio-detective literature the reader is, like as not, apt to lose sight of a number of seemingly unimportant characters who eventually prove of primary significance in the solution of the crime. The writer therefore urges a frequent study of this chart during the reader's pilgrimage through the tale, if toward no other end than to ward off the inevitable cry of "Unfair!"—the consolation of those who read and do not reason.

ELLERY QUEEN

Monte Field, an important personage indeed—the victim.
William Pusak, clerk. Cranially a brachycephalic.
Doyle, a *gendarme* with brains.
Louis Panzer, a Broadway theatre manager.
James Peale, the Don Juan of "Gunplay."
Eve Ellis. The quality of friendship is not strained.
Stephen Barry. One can understand the perturbation of the juvenile lead.
Lucille Horton, the "lady of the streets"—in the play.
Hilda Orange, a celebrated English character actress.
Thomas Velie, Detective-Sergeant who knows a thing or two about crime.
Hesse, Piggoff, Flint, Johnson, Hagsfrom, Ritter, gentlemen of the Homicide Squad.
Dr. Samuel Prouty, Assistant to the Chief Medical Examiner.
Madge O'Connell, usherette on the fatal aisle.
Dr. Stuttgard. There is always a doctor in the audience.
Jess Lynch, the obliging orangeade boy.
John Cazzanelli, alias "Parson Johnny," naturally takes a professional interest in "Gunplay."
Benjamin Morgan. What do you make of him?
Frances Ives-Pope. Enter the society interest.
Stanford Ives-Pope, man-about-town.
Harry Neilson. He revels in the sweet uses of publicity.
Henry Sampson, for once an intelligent District Attorney.
Charles Michaels, the fly—or the spider?
Mrs. Angela Russo, a lady of reputation.

Timothy Cronin, a legal ferret.
Arthur Stoates, another.
Oscar lewin, the Charon of the dead man's office.
Franklin Ives-Pope. If wealth meant happiness.
Mrs. Franklin Ives-Pope, a maternal hypochondriac.
Mrs. Phillips. Middle-aged angels have their uses.
Dr. Thaddeus Jones, toxicologist of the City of New York.
Edmund Crewe, architectural expert attached to the Detective Bureau.
Djuna, an Admirable Crichton of a new species.

The Problem Is—
Who Killed Monte Field?
Meet the astute gentlemen whose business
it is to discover such things—
Mr. Richard Queen *Mr. Ellery Queen*

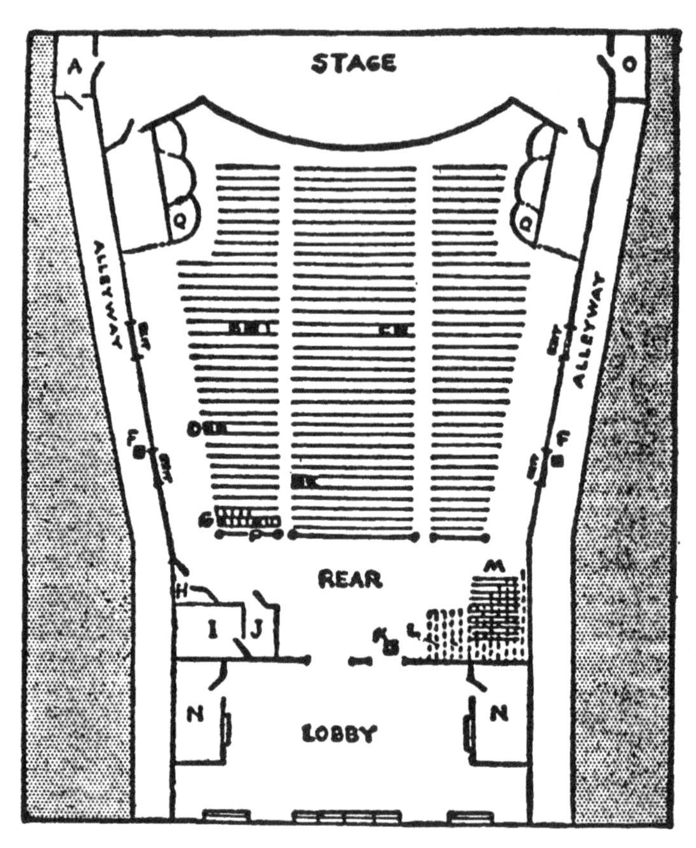

Map of the Roman Theatre
Drawn by Ellery Queen

EXPLANATION FOR THE MAP OF THE ROMAN THEATRE

A: Actors' dressing-rooms.

B: Frances Ives-Pope's seat.

C: Benjamin Morgan's seat.

D: Aisle seats occupied by "Parson Johnny" Cazzanelli and Madge O'Connell.

E: Dr. Stuttgard's seat.

F, F: Orangeade boys' stands (only during intermissions).

G: Area in vicinity of crime. Black square represents seat occupied by Monte Field. Three white squares to the right and four white squares directly in front represent vacant seats.

H: Publicity office, occupied by Harry Neilson.

I: Manager Louis Panzer's private office.

J: Anteroom to manager's office.

K: Ticket-taker's box.

L: Only stairway leading to the balcony.

M: Stairway leading downstairs to General Lounge.

N, N: Cashiers' offices.

O: Property Room.

P: William Pusak's seat.

Q, Q: Orchestra boxes.

PART ONE

"The policeman must oft follow the precept of the 'baka-dori'—those fool-birds who, though they know disaster awaits them at the hands and clubs of the beachcombers, brave ignominious death to bury their eggs in the sandy shore. . . . So the policeman. All Nippon should not deter him from hatching the egg of thoroughness."

—*from* A THOUSAND LEAVES

by Tamaka Hiero

1

IN WHICH ARE INTRODUCED A THEATRE AUDIENCE AND A CORPSE

The dramatic season of 192– began in a disconcerting manner. Eugene O'Neill had neglected to write a new play in time to secure the financial encouragement of the *intelligentsia;* and as for the "low-brows," having attended play after play without enthusiasm, they had deserted the legitimate theatre for the more ingenuous delights of the motion picture palaces.

On the evening of Monday, September 24th, therefore, when a misty rain softened the electric blaze of Broadway's theatrical district, it was viewed morosely by house managers and producers from 37th Street to Columbus Circle. Several plays were then and there given their walking papers by the men higher up, who called upon God and the weather bureau to witness their discomfiture. The penetrating rain kept the play-going public close to its radios and bridge tables. Broadway was a bleak sight indeed to those few who had the temerity to patrol its empty streets.

The sidewalk fronting the Roman Theatre, on 47th Street west of the "White Way," however, was jammed with a mid-season, fair-weather crowd. The title "Gunplay" flared from a gay marquee. Cashiers dextrously attended the chattering throng lined up at the "Tonight's Performance" window. The buff-and-blue doorman, impressive with the dignity of his uniform and the placidity of his years, bowed the evening's top-hatted and befurred customers into the orchestra with an air of satisfaction, as if inclemencies of weather held no terrors for those implicated in "Gunplay's" production.

Inside the theatre, one of Broadway's newest, people bustled to their seats visibly apprehensive, since the boisterous quality of the play was public knowledge. In due time the last member of the audience ceased rustling his program; the last latecomer stumbled over his neighbor's feet; the lights dimmed and the curtain rose. A pistol coughed in the silence, a man screamed . . . the play was on.

"Gunplay" was the first drama of the season to utilize the noises customarily associated with the underworld. Automatics, machine guns, raids on night-clubs, the lethal sounds of gang vendettas—the entire stock-in-trade of the romanticized crime society was jammed into three swift acts. It was an exaggerated reflection of the times—a bit raw, a bit nasty and altogether satisfying to the theatrical public. Consequently it played to packed houses in rain and shine. This evening's house was proof of its popularity.

The performance proceeded smoothly. The audience was thrilled at the thunderous climax to the first act. The rain having stopped, people strolled out into the side alley for a breath of air during the first ten-minute intermission. With the rising of the curtain on Act II, the detonations on the stage increased in volume. The second act hurtled to its big moment as explosive dialogue shot across the footlights. A slight commotion at the rear of the theatre went unnoticed, not unnaturally, in the noise and the darkness. No one seemed aware of anything amiss and the play crashed on. Gradually, however, the commotion increased in volume. At this point a few spectators at the rear of the left section squirmed about in their seats, to assert their rights in angry whispers. The protest was contagious. In an incredibly short time scores of eyes turned toward that section of the orchestra.

Suddenly a sharp scream tore through the theatre. The audience, excited and fascinated by the swift sequence of events on the stage, craned their necks expectantly in the direction of the cry, eager to witness what they thought was a new sensation of the play.

Without warning the lights of the theatre snapped on, revealing puzzled, fearful, already appreciative faces. At the extreme left, near a closed exit door, a large policeman stood holding a slight nervous man by the arm. He fended off a group of inquisitive people with a huge hand, shouting in stentorian tones, "Everybody stay right where he is! Don't get out of your seat, any of you!"

People laughed.

The smiles were soon wiped away. For the audience began to perceive a curious hesitancy on the part of the actors. Although they continued to recite their lines behind the footlights they were casting puzzled glances out into the orchestra. People, noting this, half-rose from their seats, panicky in the presence of a scented tragedy. The officer's Jovian voice continued to thunder, "Keep your seats, I say! Stay where you are!"

The audience suddenly realized that the incident was not playacting but reality. Women shrieked and clutched their escorts. Bedlam broke loose in the balcony, whose occupants were in no position to see anything below.

The policeman turned savagely to a stocky, foreign-looking man in evening clothes who was standing by, rubbing his hands together.

"I'll have to ask you to close every exit this minute and see that they're kept closed, Mr. Panzer," he growled. "Station an usher at all the doors and tell 'em to hold everybody tryin' to get in or out. Send somebody outside to cover the alleys, too, until help comes from the station. Move fast, Mr. Panzer, before hell pops!"

The swarthy little man hurried away, brushing aside a number of excited people who had disregarded the officer's bellowed admonition and had jumped up to question him.

The bluecoat stood wide-legged at the entrance to the last row of the left section, concealing with his bulk the crumpled figure of a man in full evening dress, lying slumped in a queer attitude on the floor between rows. The policeman looked up, keeping a firm grip on the arm of the cowering man at his side, and shot a quick glance toward the rear of the orchestra.

"Hey, Neilson!" he shouted.

A tall tow-headed man hurried out of a small room near the

main entrance and pushed his way through to the officer. He looked sharply down at the inert figure on the floor.

"What's happened here, Doyle?"

"Better ask this feller here," replied the policeman grimly. He shook the arm of the man he was holding. "There's a guy dead, and Mr."—he bent a ferocious glance upon the shrinking little man—"Pusak, W-William Pusak," he stammered—"this Mr. Pusak," continued Doyle, "says he heard him whisper he'd been croaked."

Neilson stared at the dead body, stunned.

The policeman chewed his lip. "I'm in one sweet mess, Harry," he said hoarsely. "The only cop in the place, and a pack of yellin' fools to take care of. . . . I want you to do somethin' for me."

"Say the word. . . . This is one hell of a note!"

Doyle wheeled in a rage to shout to a man who had just risen three rows ahead and was standing on his seat, peering at the proceedings. "Hey you!" he roared. "Get down offa there! Here—get back there, the whole bunch o' you. Back to your seats, now, or I'll pinch the whole nosey mob!"

He turned on Neilson. "Beat it to your desk, Harry, and give headquarters a buzz about the murder," he whispered. "Tell 'em to bring down a gang—make it a big one. Tell 'em it's a theatre—they'll know what to do. And here, Harry—take my whistle and toot your head off outside. I gotta get some help right away."

As Neilson fought his way back through the crowd, Doyle shouted after him: "Better ask 'em to send old man Queen down here, Harry!"

The tow-headed man disappeared into the office. A few

moments later a shrill whistle was heard from the sidewalk in front of the theatre.

The swarthy theatre manager whom Doyle had commanded to place guards at the exits and alleys came scurrying back through the press. His dress shirt was slightly rumpled and he was mopping his forehead with an air of bewilderment. A woman stopped him as he wriggled his way forward. She squeaked,

"Why is this policeman keeping us here, Mr. Panzer? I've a right to leave, I should like you to know! I don't care if an accident *did* happen—I had nothing to do with it—that's your affair—please tell him to stop this silly disciplining of innocent people!"

The little man stammered, trying to escape. "Now, madam, please. I'm sure the officer knows what he is doing. A man has been killed here—it is a serious matter. Don't you see. . . . As manager of the theatre I must follow his orders. . . . Please be calm—have a little patience. . . ."

He wormed his way out of her grasp and was off before she could protest.

Doyle, his arms waving violently, stood on a seat and bellowed: "I told you to sit down and keep quiet, the pack o' you! I don't care if you're the Mayor himself, you—yeah, you there, in the monocle—stay down or I'll shove you down! Don't you people realize what's happened? Pipe down, I say!" He jumped to the floor, muttering as he wiped the perspiration from his capband.

In the turmoil and excitement, with the orchestra boiling like a huge kettle, and necks stretched over the railing of the balcony as the people there strove vainly to discover the cause of the confusion, the abrupt cessation of activity on the stage was forgotten by the audience. The actors had stammered their way through lines rendered meaningless by the drama before the footlights. Now the slow descent of the curtain put an end to the evening's entertainment. The actors, chattering, hurried toward the stagestairs. Like the audience they peered toward the nucleus of the trouble in bewilderment.

A buxom old lady, in garish clothes—the very fine imported actress billed in the character of Madame Murphy, "keeper of the public house"—her name was Hilda Orange; the slight, graceful figure of "the street waif, Nanette"—Eve Ellis, leading-lady of the piece; the tall robust hero of "Gunplay," James Peale, attired in a rough tweed suit and cap; the juvenile, smart in evening clothes, portraying the society lad who had fallen into the clutches of the "gang"—Stephen Barry; Lucille Horton, whose characterization of the "lady of the streets" had brought down a shower of adjectives from the dramatic critics, who had little enough to rant about that unfortunate season; a vandyked old man whose faultless evening clothes attested to the tailoring genius of M. Le Brun, costumer extraordinary to the entire cast of "Gunplay"; the heavy-set villain, whose stage scowl was dissolved in a foggy docility as he surveyed the frantic auditorium; in fact, the entire personnel of the play, bewigged and powdered, rouged and painted—some wielding towels as they hastily removed their make-up—scampered in a body under the lowering curtain and trooped down the stage steps into the orchestra, where they elbowed their way up the aisle toward the scene of the commotion.

Another flurry, at the main entrance, caused many people despite Doyle's vigorous orders to rise in their seats for a clearer view. A group of bluecoats were hustling their way inside, their night sticks ready. Doyle heaved a gargantuan sigh of relief as he saluted the tall man in plainclothes at their head.

"What's up, Doyle?" asked the newcomer, frowning at the pandemonium raging about them. The bluecoats who had entered with him were herding the crowd to the rear of the orchestra, behind the seat section. People who had been standing tried to slip back to their seats; they were apprehended and made to join the angry cluster jammed behind the last row.

"Looks like this man's been murdered, Sergeant," said Doyle.

"Uh-huh." The plainclothes man looked incuriously down at the one still figure in the theatre—lying at their feet, a black-sleeved arm flung over his face, his legs sprawled gawkily under the seats in the row before.

"What is it—gat?" asked the newcomer of Doyle, his eyes roving.

"No, sir—don't seem to be," said the policeman. "Had a doctor from the audience look him over the very first thing—thinks it's poison."

The Sergeant grunted. "Who's this?" he rapped, indicating the trembling figure of Pusak by Doyle's side.

"Chap who found the body," returned Doyle. "He hasn't moved from the spot since."

"Good enough." The detective turned toward a compact group huddled a few feet behind them and asked, generally: "Who's the manager here?"

Panzer stepped forward.

"I'm Velie, detective-sergeant from headquarters," said the plainclothes man abruptly. "Haven't you done anything to keep this yelling pack of idiots quiet?"

"I've done my best, Sergeant," mumbled the manager, wringing his hands. "But they all seem incensed at the way this officer"—he indicated Doyle apologetically—"has been storming at them. I don't know how I can reasonably expect them to keep sitting in their seats as if nothing had happened."

"Well, we'll take care of that," snapped Velie. He gave a rapid order to a uniformed man nearby. "Now"—he turned back to Doyle—"how about the doors, the exits? Done anything yet in that direction?"

"Sure thing, Sergeant," grinned the policeman. "I had Mr. Panzer here station ushers at every door. They've been there all night, anyway. But I just wanted to make sure."

"You were right. Nobody try to get out?"

"I think I can vouch for that, Sergeant," put in Panzer meekly. "The action of the play necessitates having ushers posted near every exit, for atmosphere. This is a crook play, with a good deal of shooting and screaming and that sort of thing going on, and the presence of guards around the doors heightens the general effect of mystery. I can very easily find out for you if . . ."

"We'll attend to that ourselves," said Velie. "Doyle, who'd you send for?"

"Inspector Queen," answered Doyle. "I had the publicity man, Neilson, phone him at headquarters."

Velie allowed a smile to crease his wintry face. "Thought of everything, didn't you? Now how about the body? Has it been touched at all since this fellow found it?"

The cowering man held in Doyle's hard grasp broke out, half-crying. "I—I only found him, officer—honest to God, I—"

"All right, all right," said Velie coldly. "You'll keep, won't you? What are you blubbering about? Well, Doyle?"

"Not a finger was laid on the body since I came over," replied Doyle, with a trace of pride in his voice. "Except, of course, for a Dr. Stuttgard. I got him out of the audience to make sure the man was dead. He was, and nobody else came near."

"You've been busy, haven't you, Doyle? I'll see you won't suffer by it," said Velie. He wheeled on Panzer, who shrank back. "Better trot up to the stage and make an announcement, Mr. Manager. The whole crew of 'em are to stay right where they are until Inspector Queen lets them go home—understand? Tell them it won't do any good to kick—and the more they kick the longer they'll be here. Make it plain, too, that they're to stick to their seats, and any suspicious move on anybody's part is going to make trouble."

"Yes. Yes. Good Lord, what a catastrophe!" groaned Panzer as he made his way down the aisle toward the stage.

At the same moment a little knot of people pushed open the big door at the rear of the theatre and stepped across the carpet in a body.

2

IN WHICH ONE QUEEN WORKS AND ANOTHER QUEEN WATCHES

There was nothing remarkable in either the physique or the manner of Inspector Richard Queen. He was a small, withered, rather mild-appearing old gentleman. He walked with a little stoop and an air of deliberation that somehow accorded perfectly with his thick gray hair and mustaches, veiled gray eyes and slender hands.

As he crossed the carpet with short, quick steps Inspector Queen was far from impressive to the milling eyes that observed his approach from every side. And yet, so unusual was the gentle dignity of his appearance, so harmless and benevolent the smile that illumined his lined old face, that an audible rustle swept over the auditorium, preceding him in a strangely fitting manner.

In his own men the change was appreciable. Doyle retreated into a corner near the left exits. Detective-Sergeant Velie, poised over the body—sardonic, cold, untouched by the near-hysteria about him—relaxed a trifle, as if he were satisfied to relinquish his place in the sun. The bluecoats guarding the aisles saluted with alacrity. The nervous, muttering, angry audience sank back with an unreasoning relief.

Inspector Queen stepped forward and shook hands with Velie.

"Too bad, Thomas, my boy. I hear you were going home when this happened," he murmured. To Doyle he smiled in a fatherly fashion. Then, in a mild pity, he peered down at the man on the floor. "Thomas," he asked, "are all the exits covered?" Velie nodded.

The old man turned back and let his eyes travel interestedly about the scene. He asked a low-voiced question of Velie, who nodded his head in assent; then he crooked his finger at Doyle.

"Doyle, where are the people who were sitting in these seats?" He pointed to three chairs adjoining the dead man's and four directly to the front of them in the preceding row.

The policeman appeared puzzled. "Didn't see anybody there, Inspector. . . ."

Queen stood silent for a moment, then waved Doyle back with the low remark to Velie, "In a crowded house, too. . . . Remember that." Velie raised his eyebrows gravely. "I'm cold on this whole business," continued the Inspector genially. "All I can see right now are a dead man and a lot of perspiring people making noise. Have Hesse and Piggott direct traffic for a while, eh, son?"

Velie spoke sharply to two of the plainclothes men who had entered the theatre with the Inspector. They wriggled their way toward the rear and the people who had been crowding around found themselves pushed aside. Policemen joined the two detectives. The group of actors and actresses were ordered to move back. A section was roped off behind the central tier of seats and some fifty men and women packed into the small space. Quiet men circulated among them, instructing them to show their tickets and return to their seats one by one. Within five minutes not a member of the audience was left standing. The actors were cautioned to remain within the rope enclosure for the time being.

In the extreme left aisle Inspector Queen reached into his topcoat pocket, carefully extracted a brown carved snuffbox and took a pinch with every evidence of enjoyment.

"That's more like it, Thomas," he chuckled. "You know how fussy I am about noises. . . . Who is the poor chap on the floor—do you know?"

Velie shook his head. "I haven't even touched the body, Inspector," he said. "I got here just a few minutes before you did. A man on the 47th Street beat called me up from his box and reported Doyle's whistle. Doyle seems to have been doing things, sir. . . . His lieutenant reports favorably on his record."

"Ah," said the Inspector, "ah, yes. Doyle. Come here, Doyle."

The policeman stepped forward and saluted.

"Just what," went on the little gray man, leaning comfortably against a seat back, "just what happened here, Doyle?"

"All I know about it, Inspector," began Doyle, "is that a couple of minutes before the end of the second act this man"—he pointed to Pusak, who stood wretchedly in a corner—"came running up to me where I was standin' in the back, watchin' the show, and he says, 'A man's been murdered, officer! . . . A man's murdered!' He was blubberin' like a baby and I thought he was pie-eyed. But I stepped mighty quick and came over here—the place was dark and there was a lot of shootin' and screamin' on the stage—and I took a look at the feller on the floor. I didn't move him, but I felt his heart and there wasn't anything to feel. To make sure he was croaked I asked for a doctor and a gent by the name of Stuttgard answered my call. . . ."

Inspector Queen stood pertly, his head cocked on a side like a parrot's. "That's excellent," he said. "Excellent, Doyle. I'll question Dr. Stuttgard later. Then what happened?" he went on.

"Then," continued the policeman, "then I got the usherette on this aisle to beat it back to the manager's office for Panzer. Louis Panzer—that's the manager right over there. . . ."

Queen regarded Panzer, who was standing a few feet to the rear talking to Neilson, and nodded. "That's Panzer, you say. All right, all right . . . Ellery! You got my message?"

He darted forward, brushing aside Panzer, who fell back apologetically, and clapped the shoulder of a tall young man who had slipped through the main door and was slowly looking about the scene. The old man passed his arm through the younger man's.

"Haven't inconvenienced you any, son? What bookstore did you haunt tonight? Ellery, I'm mighty glad you're here!"

He dipped into his pocket, again extracted the snuffbox, sniffed deeply—so deeply that he sneezed—and looked up into his son's face.

"As a matter of fact," said Ellery Queen, his eyes restlessly roving,

"I can't return the compliment. You just lured me away from a perfect book-lover's paradise. I was at the point of getting the dealer to let me have a priceless Falconer first edition, intending to borrow the money from you at headquarters. I telephoned—and here I am. A Falconer—Oh, well. Tomorrow will do, I suppose."

The Inspector chuckled. "Now if you told me you were picking up an old snuffbox I might be interested. As it is—trot along. Looks as if we have some work tonight."

They walked toward the little knot of men on the left, the old man's hand grasping his son's coatsleeve. Ellery Queen towered six inches above his father's head. There was a square cut to his shoulders and an agreeable swing to his body as he walked. He was dressed in oxford gray and carried a light stick. On his nose perched what seemed an incongruous note in so athletic a man—a rimless pince-nez. But the brow above, the long delicate lines of the face, the bright eyes were those of a man of thought rather than action.

They joined the group at the body. Ellery was greeted respectfully by Velie. He bent over the seat, glanced earnestly at the dead man, and stepped back.

"Go on, Doyle," said the Inspector briskly. "You looked at the body, detained the man who found it, got the manager. . . . Then what?"

"Panzer at my orders closed all the doors at once and saw that no one either came in or went out," answered Doyle. "There was a lot of fuss here with the audience, but nothing else happened."

"Right, right!" said the Inspector, feeling for his snuffbox. "You did a mighty good job. Now—that gentleman there."

He gestured in the direction of the trembling little man in the corner, who stepped forward hesitantly, licked his lips, looked about him with a helpless expression, and then stood silent.

"What's your name?" asked the Inspector, in a kindly tone.

"Pusak—William Pusak," said the man. "I'm a bookkeeper, sir. I was just—"

"One at a time, Pusak. Where were you sitting?"

Pusak pointed eagerly to the sixth seat from the aisle, in the last row. A frightened young girl in the fifth seat sat staring in their direction.

"I see," said the Inspector. "Is that young lady with you?"

"Yes, sir—yes, sir. That's my fiancée, sir. Her name is Esther—Esther Jablow. . . ."

A little to the rear a detective was scribbling in a notebook. Ellery stood behind his father, glancing from one exit to another. He began to draw a diagram on the flyleaf of a small book he had taken from his topcoat pocket.

The Inspector scrutinized the girl, who immediately averted her eyes. "Now, Pusak, I want you to tell me just what happened."

"I—I didn't do a thing out of the way, sir."

Inspector Queen patted his arm. "Nobody is accusing you of anything, Pusak. All I want is your story of what happened. Take your time—tell it your own way. . . ."

Pusak gave him a curious glance. Then he moistened his lips and began. "Well, I was sitting there in that seat with my—with Miss Jablow—and we were enjoying the show pretty much. The second act was kind of exciting—there was a lot of shooting and yelling on the stage—and then I got up and started to go out the row to the aisle. This aisle—here." He pointed nervously to the spot of carpet on which he was standing. Queen nodded, his face benign.

"I had to push past my—Miss Jablow, and there wasn't anybody except one man between her and the aisle. That's why I went that way. I didn't sort of like to"—he hesitated apologetically—"to bother people going out that way in the middle of the most exciting part. . . ."

"That was very decent of you, Pusak," said the Inspector, smiling.

"Yes, sir. So I walked down the row, feeling my way, because it was pretty dark in the theatre, and then I came to—to this man." He shuddered, and continued more rapidly. "He was sitting in a funny way, I thought. His knees were touching the seat in front of him and I couldn't get past. I said, 'I'm sorry,' and tried again, but his knees hadn't moved an inch. I didn't know what to do, sir—I'm not nervy, like some fellows, and I was going to turn around and go back when all of a sudden I felt the man's body slip to the floor—I was still pressed up close to him. Of course, I got kind of scared—it was only natural. . . ."

"I should say," said the Inspector, with concern. "It must have given you quite a turn. Then what happened?"

"Well, sir. . . . Then, before I realized what was happening, he fell clean out of his seat and his head bumped against my legs. I didn't know what to do. I couldn't call for help—I don't know why, but I couldn't somehow—and I just naturally bent over him, thinking he was drunk or sick or something, and meant to lift him up. I hadn't figured on what I'd do after that. . . ."

"I know just how you felt, Pusak. Go on."

"Then it happened—the thing I told this policeman about. I'd just got hold of his head when I felt his hand come up and grab mine, just like he was trying awfully hard to get a grip on something, and he moaned. It was so low I could hardly hear it, but sort of horrible. I can't quite describe it exactly. . . ."

"Now, we're getting on," said the Inspector. "And?"

"And then he talked. It wasn't really talking—it was more like a gurgle, as if he was choking. He said a few words that I didn't catch at all, but I realized that this was something different from just being sick or drunk, so I bent even lower and listened hard. I heard him gasp, 'It's murder. . . . Been murdered . . .' or something like that. . . ."

"So he said, 'It's murder,' eh?" The Inspector regarded Pusak with severity. "Well, now. That must have given you a shock, Pusak." He snapped suddenly, "Are you certain this man said 'murder'?"

"That's what I heard, sir. I've got good hearing," said Pusak doggedly.

"Well" Queen relaxed, smiling again. "Of course. I just wanted to make sure. Then what did you do?"

"Then I felt him squirm a little and all of a sudden go limp in my arms. I was afraid he'd died and I don't know how—but next thing I knew I was in the back telling it all to the policeman—this policeman here." He pointed to Doyle, who rocked on his heels impersonally.

"And that's all?"

"Yes, sir. Yes, sir. That's all I know about it," said Pusak, with a sigh of relief.

Queen grasped him by the coat front and barked, "That isn't all, Pusak. You forgot to tell us why you left your seat in the first place!" He glared into the little man's eyes.

Pusak coughed, teetered back and forth a moment, as if uncertain of his next words, then leaned forward and whispered into the Inspector's astonished ear.

"Oh!" Queen's lips twitched in the suspicion of a smile, but he said gravely, "I see, Pusak. Thank you very much for your help. Everything is all right now—you may go back to your seat and leave with the others later on." He waved his hand in a gesture of dismissal. Pusak, with a sickly glance at the dead man on the floor, crept around the rear wall of the last row and reappeared by the girl's side. She immediately engaged him in a whispered but animated conversation.

As the Inspector with a little smile turned to Velie, Ellery made a slight movement of impatience, opened his mouth to speak, appeared to reconsider, and finally moved quietly backwards, disappearing from view.

"Well, Thomas," sighed the Inspector, "let's have a look at this chap."

He bent nimbly over the dead man, on his knees in the space between the last row and the row directly before it. Despite the brilliant sparkle of light from the fixtures overhead, the cramped space near the floor was dark. Velie produced a flashlight and stooped over the Inspector, keeping its bright beam on the corpse, shifting it as the Inspector's hands roved about. Queen silently pointed to an ugly ragged brown stain on the otherwise immaculate shirtfront.

"Blood?" grunted Velie.

The Inspector sniffed the shirt cautiously. "Nothing more dangerous than whisky," he retorted.

He ran his hands swiftly over the body, feeling over the heart and at the neck, where the collar was loosened. He looked up at Velie.

"Looks like a poisoning case, all right, Thomas. Get hold of this Dr. Stuttgard for me, will you? I'd like to have his professional opinion before Prouty gets here."

Velie snapped an order and a moment later a medium-sized man in evening clothes, olive-skinned and wearing a thin black mustache, came up behind a detective.

"Here he is, Inspector," said Velie.

"Ah, yes." Queen looked up from his examination. "How do you do, Doctor? I am informed that you examined the body almost immediately after it was discovered. I see no obvious sign of death—what is your opinion?"

"My examination was necessarily a cursory one," said Dr. Stuttgard carefully, his fingers brushing a phantom speck from his satin lapel. "In the semidark and under these conditions I could not at first discern any abnormal sign of death. From the construction of the facial muscles I thought that it was a simple case of heart failure, but on closer examination I noticed that blueness of the face—it's quite clear in this light, isn't it? That combined with the alcoholic odor from the mouth seems to point to some form of alcoholic poisoning. Of one thing I can assure you—this man did not die of a gunshot wound or a stab. I naturally made sure of that at once. I even examined his neck—you see I loosened the collar—to make sure it was not strangulation."

"I see." The Inspector smiled, "Thank you very much, Doctor. Oh, by the way," he added, as Dr. Stuttgard with a muttered word turned aside, "do you think this man might have died from the effects of wood alcohol?"

Dr. Stuttgard answered promptly. "Impossible," he said. "It was something much more powerful and quick-acting."

"Could you put a name to the exact poison which killed this man?"

The olive-skinned physician hesitated. Then he said stiffly, "I am very sorry, Inspector; you cannot reasonably expect me to be more precise. Under the circumstances . . ." His voice trailed off, and he backed away.

Queen chuckled as he bent again to his grim task.

The dead man sprawled on the floor was not a pleasant sight. The Inspector gently lifted the clenched hand and stared hard at the contorted face. Then he looked under the seat. There was nothing there. However, a black silk-lined cape hung carelessly over the back of the chair. He emptied all of the pockets of both dress suit and cape, his hands diving in and out of the clothing. He extracted a few letters and papers from the inside breast pocket, delved into the vest pockets and trouser pockets, heaping his discoveries in two piles—one containing papers and letters, the other coins, keys and miscellaneous material. A silver flask initialed "M. F." he found in one of the hip pockets. He handled the flask gingerly, holding it by the neck, and scanning the gleaming surface as if for fingerprints. Shaking his head, he wrapped the flask with infinite care in a clean handkerchief, and placed it aside.

A ticket stub colored blue and bearing the inscription "LL32 Left," he secreted in his own vest pocket.

Without pausing to examine any of the other objects individually, he ran his hands over the lining of the vest and coat, and made a rapid pass over the trouser legs. Then, as he fingered the coat-tail pocket, he exclaimed in a low tone, "Well, well, Thomas—here's a pretty find!" as he extracted a woman's evening bag, small, compact and glittering with rhinestones.

He turned it over in his hands reflectively, then snapped it open, glanced through it and took out a number of feminine accessories. In a small compartment, nestling beside a lipstick, he found a tiny cardcase. After a moment, he replaced all the contents and put the bag in his own pocket.

The Inspector picked up the papers from the floor and swiftly glanced through them. He frowned as he came to the last one—a letterhead.

"Ever hear of Monte Field, Thomas?" he asked, looking up.

Velie tightened his lips. "I'll say I have. One of the crookedest lawyers in town."

The Inspector looked grave. "Well, Thomas, this is Mr. Monte Field—what's left of him." Velie grunted.

"Where the average police system falls down," came Ellery's voice over his father's shoulder, "is in its ruthless tracking down of gentlemen who dispose of such fungus as Mr. Monte Field."

The Inspector straightened, dusted his knees carefully, took a pinch of snuff, and said, "Ellery, my boy, you'll never make a policeman. I didn't know you knew Field."

"I wasn't exactly on terms of intimacy with the gentleman," said Ellery. "But I remember having met him at the Pantheon Club, and from what I heard at the time I don't wonder somebody has removed him from our midst."

"Let's discuss the demerits of Mr. Field at a more propitious time," said the Inspector gravely. "I happen to know quite a bit about him, and none of it is pleasant."

He wheeled and was about to walk away when Ellery, gazing curiously at the dead body and the seat, drawled, "Has anything been removed, Dad—anything at all?"

Inspector Queen turned his head. "And why do you ask that bright question, young man?"

"Because," returned Ellery, with a grimace, "unless my eyesight fails me, the chap's tophat is not under the seat, on the floor beside him, or anywhere in the general vicinity."

"So you noticed that too, did you, Ellery?" said the Inspector grimly. "It's the first thing I saw when I bent down to examine him—or rather the first thing I didn't see." The Inspector seemed to lose his geniality as he spoke. His brow wrinkled and his gray mustache bristled fiercely. He shrugged his shoulders. "And no hat check in his clothes, either. . . . Flint!"

A husky young man in plain clothes hurried forward.

"Flint, suppose you exercise those young muscles of yours by getting down on your hands and knees and hunting for a tophat. It ought to be somewhere around here."

"Right, Inspector," said Flint cheerfully, and he began a methodical search of the indicated area.

"Velie," said Queen, in a businesslike tone, "suppose you find

Ritter and Hesse and—no, those two will do—for me, will you?" Velie walked away.

"Hagstrom!" shouted the Inspector to another detective standing by.

"Yes, Chief."

"Get busy with this stuff"—he pointed to the two small piles of articles he had taken from Field's pockets and which lay on the floor—"and be sure to put them safely away in my own bags."

As Hagstrom knelt by the body, Ellery quietly bent over and opened the coat. He immediately jotted a memorandum on the flyleaf of the book in which he had drawn a diagram some time before. He muttered to himself, patting the volume, "And it's a Stendhause private edition, too!"

Velie returned with Ritter and Hesse at his heels. The Inspector said sharply, "Ritter, go to this man's apartment. His name is Monte Field, he was an attorney, and he lived at 113 West 75th Street. Stick around until you're relieved. If any one shows up, nab him."

Ritter, touching his hat, mumbled, "Yes, Inspector," and turned away.

"Now Hesse, my lad," continued the Inspector to the other detective, "hurry down to 51 Chambers Street, this man's office, and wait there until you hear from me. Get inside if you can, otherwise park outside the door all night."

"Right, Inspector." Hesse disappeared.

Queen turned about and chuckled as he saw Ellery, broad shoulders bent over, examining the dead man.

"Don't trust your father, eh, Ellery?" the Inspector chided. "What are you snooping for?"

Ellery smiled, straightening up. "I'm merely curious, that's all," he said. "There are certain things about this unsavory corpse that interest me hugely. For example, have you taken the man's head measurement?" He held up a piece of string, which he had slipped from a wrapped book in his coat pocket, and offered it for his father's inspection.

The Inspector took it, scowled and summoned a policeman from the rear of the theatre. He issued a low-voiced order, the string exchanged hands and the policeman departed.

"Inspector."

Queen looked up. Hagstrom stood by his elbow, eyes gleaming.

"I found this pushed way back under Field's seat when I picked up the papers. It was against the back wall."

He held up a dark-green bottle, of the kind used by gingerale manufacturers. A gaudy label read, "Paley's Extra Dry Ginger Ale." The bottle was half-empty.

"Well, Hagstrom, you've got something up your sleeve. Out with it!" the Inspector said curtly.

"Yes, sir! When I found this bottle under the dead man's seat, I knew that he had probably used it tonight. There was no matinee today and the cleaning women go over the place every twenty-four hours. It wouldn't have been there unless this man, or somebody connected with him, had used it and put it there tonight. I thought, 'Maybe this is a clue,' so I dug up the refreshment boy who had this section of the theatre and I asked him to sell me a bottle of ginger ale. He said"—Hagstrom smiled—"he said they don't sell ginger ale in this theatre!"

"You used your head that time, Hagstrom," said the Inspector approvingly. "Get hold of the boy and bring him here."

As Hagstrom left, a stout little man in slightly disarranged evening clothes bustled up, a policeman doggedly holding his arm. The Inspector sighed.

"Are you in charge of this affair, sir?" stormed the little man, drawing himself up to five feet two inches of perspiring flesh.

"I am," said Queen gravely.

"Then I want you to know," burst out the newcomer, "—here, you, let go of my arm, do you hear?—I want you to know, sir . . ."

"Detach yourself from the gentleman's arm, officer," said the Inspector, with deepening gravity.

". . . that I consider this entire affair the most vicious outrage! I have been sitting here with my wife and daughter since the interruption to the play for almost an hour, and your officers refuse to allow us even to stand up. It's a damnable outrage, sir! Do you think you can keep this entire audience waiting at your leisure? I've been watching you—don't think I haven't. You've been dawdling around while we sat and suffered. I want you to know, sir—I want you to know!—that unless you permit my party to leave at once, I shall get in touch with my very good friend District Attorney Sampson and lodge a personal complaint against you!"

Inspector Queen gazed distastefully into the empurpled face of the stout little man. He sighed and said with a note of sternness, "My dear man, has it occurred to you that at this moment, while you stand beefing about a little thing like being detained an hour or so, a person who has committed murder may be in this very audience—perhaps sitting next to your wife and daughter? He is just as anxious as you to get away. If you wish to make a complaint to the District Attorney, your very good friend, you may do so after you leave this theatre. Meanwhile, I'll trouble you to return to your seat and be patient until you are permitted to go. . . . I hope I make myself clear."

A titter arose from some spectators nearby, who seemed to be enjoying the little man's discomfiture. He flounced away, with the policeman stolidly following. The Inspector, muttering "Jackass!" turned to Velie.

"Take Panzer with you to the box office and see if you can find complete tickets for these numbers." He bent over the last row and the row before it, scribbling the numbers LL30 Left, LL28 Left, LL26 Left, KK32 Left, KK30 Left, KK28 left, and KK26 Left on the back of an old envelope. He handed the memorandum to Velie, who went away.

Ellery, who had been leaning idly against the rear wall of the last row, watching his father, the audience, and occasionally restudying the geography of the theatre, murmured in the Inspector's ear: "I was just reflecting on the unusual fact that with such a popular bit of dramatic trash as 'Gunplay,' seven seats in the direct vicinity of the murdered man's seat should remain empty during the performance."

"When did you begin to wonder, my son?" said Queen, and while Ellery absently tapped the floor with his stick, barked, "Piggott!"

The detective stepped forward.

"Get the usherette who was on this aisle and the outside doorman—that middle-aged fellow on the sidewalk—and bring 'em here."

As Piggott walked off, a disheveled young man appeared by Queen's side, wiping his face with a handkerchief.

"Well, Flint?" asked Queen instantly.

"I've been over this floor like a scrubwoman, Inspector. If you're looking for a hat in this section of the theatre, it's mighty well hidden."

"All right, Flint, stand by."

The detective trudged off. Ellery said slowly, "Didn't really think your young Diogenes would find the tophat, did you, dad?"

The Inspector grunted. He walked down the aisle and proceeded to lean over person after person, questioning each in low tones. All heads turned in his direction as he went from row to row, interrogating the occupants of the two aisle seats successively. As he walked back in Ellery's direction, his face expressionless, the policeman whom he had sent out with the piece of string saluted him.

"What size, officer?" asked the Inspector.

"The clerk in the hat store said it was exactly 7⅛," answered the bluecoat. Inspector Queen nodded, dismissing him.

Velie strode up, with Panzer trailing worriedly behind. Ellery leaned forward with an air of keen absorption to catch Velie's words. Queen grew tense, the light of a great interest on his face.

"Well, Thomas," he said, "what did you find in the box office?"

"Just this, Inspector," reported Velie unemotionally. "The seven tickets for which you gave me the numbers are not in the ticket rack. They were sold from the box office window, what date Mr. Panzer has no way of knowing."

"The tickets might have been turned over to an agency, you know, Velie," remarked Ellery.

"I verified that, Mr. Queen," answered Velie. "Those tickets were not assigned to any agency. There are definite records to prove it."

Inspector Queen stood very still, his gray eyes gleaming. Then he said, "In other words, gentlemen, it would seem that at a drama which has been playing to capacity business ever since its opening, seven tickets in a group were bought—and then the purchasers conveniently forgot to attend the performance!"

3

IN WHICH A 'PARSON' CAME TO GRIEF

There was a silence as the four men regarded each other with a dawning conviction. Panzer shuffled his feet and coughed nervously; Velie's face was a study in concentrated thought; Ellery stepped backward and fell into a rapt contemplation of his father's gray-and-blue necktie.

Inspector Queen stood biting his mustache. He shook his shoulders suddenly and turned on Velie.

"Thomas, I'm going to give you a dirty job," he said. "I want you to marshal a half-dozen or so of the uniformed men and set 'em to a personal examination of every soul in this place. All they have to do is get the name and address of each person in the audience. It's quite a job, and it will take time, but I'm afraid it's absolutely necessary. By the way, Thomas, in your scouting around, did you question any of the ushers who take care of the balcony?"

"I got hold of the very man to give me information," said Velie. "He's the lad who stands at the foot of the stairs in the orchestra, directing holders of balcony tickets to the upper floor. Chap by the name of Miller."

"A very conscientious boy," interposed Panzer, rubbing his hands.

"Miller is ready to swear that not a person in this theatre either went upstairs from the orchestra or came downstairs from the moment the curtain went up on the second act."

"That sort of cuts down your work, Thomas," remarked the Inspector, who had been listening intently. "Have your men go through the orchestra boxes and orchestra only. Remember I want the name and address of every person here—every single one. And Thomas—"

"Yes, Inspector?" said Velie, turning back.

"While they're at it, have 'em ask these people to show the ticket stubs belonging to the seats in which they are sitting. Every case of loss of stub should be noted beside the name of the loser; and in cases—it is a bare possibility—where a person holds a stub which does not agree with the seat number of the chair in which he's sitting, a notation is also to be made. Think you can get all that done, my boy?"

"Sure thing!" Velie grunted as he strode away.

The Inspector smoothed his gray mustache and took a pinch of snuff, inhaling deeply.

"Ellery," he said, "there's something worrying you. Out with it, son!"

"Eh?" Ellery started, blinking his eyes. He removed his

pince-nez, and said slowly, "My very revered father, I am beginning to think that—Well, there's little peace in this world for a quiet book-loving man." He sat down on the arm of the dead man's seat, his eyes troubled. Suddenly he smiled. "Take care that you don't repeat the unfortunate error of that ancient butcher who, with his twoscore apprentices, sought high and low for his most treasured knife when all the time it reposed quietly in his mouth."

"You're very informative these days, my son," said the Inspector petulantly. "Flint!"

The detective came forward.

"Flint," said Queen, "you've had one pleasant job tonight and I've another for you. Think your back could stand a little more bending? Seems to me I remember you took a weightlifting contest in the Police Games when you were pounding a beat."

"Yes, sir," said Flint, grinning broadly. "I guess I can stand the strain."

"Well, then," continued the Inspector, jamming his hands into his pockets, "here's your job. Get a squad of men together—good Lord, I should have brought the Reserves along with me!—and make an exhaustive search of every square foot of the theatre property, inside and out. You'll be looking for ticket stubs, do you understand? Anything resembling half a ticket has to be in my possession when you're through. Search the theatre floor particularly, but don't neglect the rear, the steps leading up to the balcony, the lobby outside, the sidewalk in front of the theatre, the alleyways at both sides, the lounge downstairs, the men's room, the ladies' room—Here, here! That'll never do. Call up the nearest precinct for a matron and have her do that Thoroughly clear?"

Flint was off with a cheerful nod.

"Now, then." Queen stood rubbing his hands. "Mr. Panzer, would you step this way a minute? Very kind of you, sir. I'm afraid we're making unholy nuisances of ourselves tonight, but it can't be helped. I see the audience is on the verge of rebellion. I'd be obliged if you would trot up to the stage and announce that they will be held here just a little while longer, to have patience, and all that sort of thing. Thank you!"

As Panzer hurried down the center aisle, people clutching at his coat to detain him, Detective Hagstrom, standing a few feet away, caught the Inspector's eye. By his side was a small slim youth of nineteen, chewing gum with vehement motions of his jaw, and obviously quite nervous at the ordeal he was facing. He was clad in a black-and-gold uniform, very ornate and resplendent, and incongruously fitted out with a starched shirt front and a wing collar and bow tie. A cap resembling the headgear of a bellboy perched on his blond head. He coughed deprecatingly as the Inspector motioned him forward.

"Here is the boy who says they don't sell ginger ale in this theatre," said Hagstrom severely, grasping the lad's arm in a suggestive grip.

"You don't, eh, son?" asked Queen affably. "How is that?"

The boy was plainly in a funk. His eyes rolled alarmingly as they sought the broad face of Doyle. The policeman patted him encouragingly on the shoulder and said to the Inspector, "He's a little scared, sir—but he's a good boy. I've known him since he was a shaver. Grew up on my beat. Answer the Inspector, Jessie. . . ."

"Well, I—I don't know, sir," stammered the boy, shuffling his feet. "The only drinks we're allowed to sell during the intermissions is orangeade. We got a contract with the-----"—he mentioned the name of a well-known manufacturer of the concoction—"people and they give us a big discount if we sell their stuff and nobody else's. So—"

"I see," said the Inspector. "Are drinks sold only during intermissions?"

"Yes, sir," answered the boy, more naturally. "As soon as the curtain goes down the doors to the alleys on both sides are opened, and there we are—my partner and me, with our stands set up, and the cups filled ready to serve."

"Oh, so there are two of you, eh?"

"No, sir, three all together. I forgot to tell you—one feller is downstairs in the main lounge, too."

"Ummmm." The Inspector fixed him with a large and kindly eye. "Now, son, if the Roman Theatre sells nothing but orangeade, do you think you could explain how this ginger-ale bottle got here?"

His hand dove down and reappeared brandishing the dark-green bottle discovered by Hagstrom. The boy paled and began to bite his lips. His eyes roved from side to side as if they sought a quick avenue of escape. He inserted a large and dirty finger between his neck and collar and coughed.

"Why—why . . ." He had some difficulty in speaking.

Inspector Queen put down the bottle and rested his wiry length against the arm of a seat. He folded his arms sternly.

"What's your name?" he demanded.

The boy's color changed from blue-white to a pasty yellow. He furtively eyed Hagstrom, who had with a flourish taken a notebook and pencil from his pocket and was waiting forbiddingly.

The boy moistened his lips. "Lynch—Jess Lynch," he said hoarsely.

"And where is your station between acts, Lynch?" said the Inspector balefully.

"I'm—I'm right here, in the left-side alley, sir," stuttered the boy.

"Ah!" said the Inspector, knitting his brows ferociously. "And were you selling drinks in the left alley tonight, Lynch?"

"Why, why—yes, sir."

"Then you know something about this ginger-ale bottle?"

The boy peered about, saw the stout small form of Louis Panzer on the stage, about to make an announcement, and leaning forward, whispered, "Yes, sir—I do know about that bottle. I—I didn't want to tell before because Mr. Panzer's a strict guy when it comes to breaking rules, and he'd fire me in a minute if he knew what I did. You won't tell, sir?"

The Inspector started, then smiled. "Shoot, son. You've got something on your conscience—might as well get it off." He relaxed and at a flick of a finger Hagstrom unconcernedly walked away.

"This is how it happened, sir," began Jess Lynch eagerly. "I'd set my stand up in the alley here about five minutes before the end of the first act, like we're supposed to. When the girl on this aisle opened the doors after the first act, I began to give the people comin' out a nice refined selling chatter. We all do. A lot of people bought drinks and I was so busy I didn't have time to notice anything going on around me. In a little while I had a breathing spell, and then a man came up to me and said, 'Let me have a bottle of ginger ale, boy.' I looked up and saw he was a ritzy feller in evening dress, actin' kind of tipsy. He was laughing to himself and he looked pretty happy. I says to myself, 'I bet I know what *he* wants ginger ale for!' and sure enough he taps his back pocket and winks. Well—"

"Just a minute son," interrupted Queen. "Ever see a dead man before?"

"Why—why, no, sir, but I guess I could stand it once," said the boy nervously.

"Fine! Is this the man who asked you for the ginger ale?" The Inspector took the boy by the arm and made him bend over the dead body.

Jess Lynch regarded it with awed fascination. He bobbed his head vigorously.

"Yes, sir. That's the gentleman."

"You're sure of that now, Jess?" The boy nodded. "By the way, is that the outfit he was wearing when he accosted you?"

"Yes, sir."

"Anything missing, Jess?" Ellery, who had been nestling in a dark corner, leaned forward a little.

The boy regarded the Inspector with puzzlement on his face, looking from Queen to the body and back again. He was silent for a full minute, while the Queens hung on his words. Then his face lit up suddenly and he cried, "Why—yes, sir! He was wearin' a hat—a shiny topper—when he spoke to me!"

Inspector Queen looked pleased. "Go on, Jess—Doc Prouty! It's taken you a long time getting here. What held you up?"

A tall lanky man had come striding across the carpet, a black bag in his hand. He was smoking a vicious-looking cigar with no apparent concern for local fire rules, and appeared in something of a hurry.

"You said something there, Inspector," he said, setting down the bag and shaking hands with both Ellery and Queen. "You know we just moved and I haven't got my new phone yet. I had a hard day today and I was in bed anyway. They couldn't get hold of me—had to send a man around to my new place. I rushed down here as fast as I could. Where's the casualty?"

He dropped to his knees in the aisle as the Inspector indicated the body on the floor. A policeman was summoned to hold a flashlight as the Assistant Medical Examiner worked.

Queen took Jess Lynch by the arm and walked him off to one side. "What happened after he asked you for the ginger ale, Jess?"

The boy, who had been staring at the proceedings, gulped and continued. "Well, sir, of course I told him that we didn't sell ginger ale, only orangeade. He leaned a little closer, and then I could smell the booze on his breath. He says confidentially, 'There's a half dollar in it for you if you get me a bottle, kid! But I want it right away!' Well—you know how it is—they don't give tips nowadays. . . . Anyway, I said I couldn't get it that minute but that I'd duck out and buy a bottle for him right after the second act started. He walked away—after tellin' me where he was sitting—I saw him go back into the theatre. As soon as the intermission ended and the usherette closed the doors, I left my stand in the alleyway and hopped across the street to Libby's ice-cream parlor. I—"

"Do you usually leave your stand in the alley, Jess?"

"No, sir. I always hop inside the doors with the stand just before she locks the doors, and then take it downstairs to the lounge. But the man said he wanted the ginger ale right away, so I figured I'd save time by getting the bottle for him first. Then I thought I'd go back into the alley, get my stand, and bring it into the theatre through the front door. Nobody'd say anything. . . . Anyway, I left the stand in the alley and ran over to Libby's. I bought a bottle of Paley's ginger ale, sneaked it inside to this man, and he gave me a buck. Pretty nice of him, I thought, seeing as how he'd only promised me four bits."

"You told that very nicely, Jess," said the Inspector with approval. "Now, a few things more. Was he sitting in this seat—was this the seat he told you to come to?"

"Oh, yes, sir. He said LL32 Left, and sure enough that's where I found him."

"Quite right." The Inspector, after a pause, asked casually, "Did you notice if he was alone, Jess?"

"Sure thing, sir," returned the boy in a cheerful tone. "He was sittin' all alone on this end seat. The reason I noticed it was that the show's been packed ever since it opened, and I thought it was queer that there should be so many seats empty around here."

"That's fine, Jess. You'll make a detective yet. . . . You couldn't tell me how many seats were empty, I suppose?"

"Well, sir, it was kind of dark and I wasn't payin' much

attention. I guess it was about half a dozen all told—some next to him in the same row and some right in the row in front."

"Just a moment, Jess." The boy turned, licking his lips in honest fright at the sound of Ellery's low cool voice. "Did you see anything more of that shiny topper when you handed him the bottle of ginger ale?" asked Ellery, tapping the point of his neat shoe with his stick.

"Why, yes—yes, sir!" stammered the boy. "When I gave him the bottle he was holding the hat in his lap, but before I left I saw him stick it underneath his seat."

"Another question, Jess." The boy sighed with relief at the sound of the Inspector's reassuring voice. "About how long, do you reckon, did it take you to deliver the bottle to this man after the second act started?"

Jess Lynch thought gravely for a moment, and then said with finality, "It was just about ten minutes, sir. We got to keep pretty close tabs on the time, and I know it was ten minutes because when I came into the theatre with the bottle it was just the part on the stage when the girl is caught in the gang's hangout and is being grilled by the villain."

"An observant young Hermes!" murmured Ellery, smiling suddenly. The orangeade boy caught the smile and lost the last vestige of his fear. He smiled back. Ellery crooked his finger and bent forward. "Tell me, Jess. Why did it take you ten minutes to cross the street, buy a bottle of ginger ale and return to the theatre? Ten minutes is a long time, isn't it?"

The boy turned scarlet as he looked appealingly from Ellery

to the Inspector. "Well, sir—I guess I stopped to talk for a few minutes with my girl. . . ."

"Your girl?" The Inspector's voice was mildly curious.

"Yes, sir. Elinor Libby—her old man owns the ice-cream parlor. She—she wanted me to stay there in the store with her when I went for the ginger ale. I told her I had to deliver it in the theatre, so she said all right but wouldn't I come right back. And I did. We stayed there a couple of minutes and then I remembered the stand in the alley. . . ."

"The stand in the alley?" Ellery's tone was eager. "Quite so, Jess—the stand in the alley. Don't tell me that, by some remarkable whim of fortune, you went back to the alley!"

"Sure I did!" rejoined the boy, in surprise. "I mean—we both did, Elinor and me."

"Elinor and you, eh, Jess?" said Ellery softly. "And how long were you there?"

The Inspector's eyes flashed at Ellery's question. He muttered approvingly to himself and listened intently as the boy answered.

"Well, I wanted to take the stand right away, sir, but Elinor and me—we got to talking there—and Elinor said why not stay in the alley till the next intermission. . . . I figured that was a good idea. I'd wait till a few minutes before 10:05, when the act ends, and I'd duck down for some more orangeade, and then when the doors opened for the second intermission, I'd be all ready. So we stayed there, sir. . . . It wasn't wrong, sir. I didn't mean anything wrong."

Ellery straightened and fixed the boy with his eyes. "Jess, I want you to be very careful now. At exactly what time did you and Elinor get to the alley?"

"Well. . . ." Jess scratched his head. "It was about 9:25 when I gave that man the ginger ale. I went across for Elinor, stayed a few minutes and then came over to the alley. Musta been just about 9:35—just about—when I went back for my orangeade stand."

"Very good. And what time exactly did you leave the alley?"

"It was just ten o'clock, sir. Elinor looked at her wrist watch when I asked her if it was time to go in for my orangeade refills."

"You didn't hear anything going on in the theatre?"

"No, sir. We were too busy talking, I guess. . . . I didn't know anything had happened inside until we walked out of the alley and I met Johnny Chase, one of the ushers, standing there, like he was on guard. He told me there was an accident inside and Mr. Panzer had sent him to stand outside the left alley."

"I see. . . ." Ellery removed his pince-nez in some agitation and flourished it before the boy's nose. "Carefully now, Jess. Did anyone go in or out of the alley all the time you were there with Elinor?"

The boy's answer was immediate and emphatic. "No, sir. Not a soul."

"Right, my lad." The Inspector gave the boy a spanking slap on the back and sent him off grinning. Queen looked around sharply, spied Panzer, who had made his announcement on the stage with ineffectual results, and beckoned with an imperative finger.

"Mr. Panzer," he said abruptly, "I want some information about the time schedule of the play. . . . At what times does the curtain go up on the second act?"

"The second act begins at 9:15 sharp and ends at 10:05 sharp," said Panzer instantly.

"Was tonight's performance run according to this schedule?"

"Certainly. We must be on the dot because of cues, lights, and so on," responded the manager.

The Inspector muttered some calculations to himself. "That makes it 9:25 the boy saw Field alive," he mused. "He was found dead at. . ."

He swung about and called for Officer Doyle. The man came running.

"Doyle," asked the Inspector, "Doyle, do you remember exactly at what time this fellow Pusak approached you with his story of the murder?"

The policeman scratched his head. "Why, I don't remember exactly, Inspector," he said. "All I do know is that the second act was almost over when it happened."

"Not definite enough, Doyle," said Queen irritably. "Where are the actors now?"

"Got 'em herded right over there back of the center section, sir," said Doyle. "We didn't know what to do with 'em except that."

"Get one of them for me!" snapped the Inspector.

Doyle ran off. Queen beckoned to Detective Piggott, who was standing a few feet to the rear between a man and a woman.

"Got the doorman there, Piggott?" asked Queen. Piggott nodded and a tall, corpulent old man, cap trembling in his hand, uniform shrunken on his flabby body, stumbled forward.

"Are you the man who stands outside the theatre—the regular doorman?" asked the Inspector.

"Yes, sir," the doorman answered, twisting the cap in his hands.

"Very well. Now think hard. Did anyone—anyone, mind you—leave the theatre by the front entrance during the second act?" The Inspector was leaning forward, like a small greyhound.

The man took a moment before replying. Then he said slowly, but with conviction, "No, sir. Nobody went out of the theatre. Nobody, I mean, but the orangeade boy."

"Were you there all the time?" barked the Inspector.

"Yes, sir."

"Now then. Do you remember anybody *coming in* during the second act?"

"We-e-ll . . . Jessie Lynch, the orangeade boy, came in right after the act started."

"Anybody else?"

There was silence as the old man made a frenzied effort at concentration. After a moment he looked helplessly from one face to another, eyes despairing. Then he mumbled, "I don't remember, sir."

The Inspector regarded him irritably. The old man seemed sincere in his nervous way. He was perspiring and frequently looked sidewise at Panzer, as if he sensed that his defection of memory would cost him his position.

"I'm awfully sorry, sir," the doorman repeated. "Awfully sorry. There might've been someone, but my memory ain't as good as it used to be when I was younger. I—I just can't seem to recall."

Ellery's cool voice cut in on the old man's thick accents.

"How long have you been a doorman?"

The old man's bewildered eyes shifted to this new inquisitor. "Nigh onto ten years, sir. I wasn't always a doorman. Only when I got old and couldn't do nothin' else—"

"I understand," said Ellery kindly. He hesitated a moment, then added inflexibly, "A man who has been a doorman for as many years as you have might forget something about the first act. But people do not often come into a theatre during the second act. Surely if you think hard enough you can answer positively, one way or the other?"

The response came painfully. "I—I don't remember, sir. I could say no one did, but that mightn't be the truth. I just can't answer."

"All right." The Inspector put his hand on the old man's shoulder. "Forget it. Perhaps we're asking too much. That's all for the time being." The doorman shuffled away with the pitiful alacrity of old age.

Doyle clumped toward the group, a tall handsome man dressed in rough tweeds in his wake, traces of stage make-up streaking his face.

"This is Mr. Peale, Inspector. He's the leading man of the show," reported Doyle.

Queen smiled at the actor, offering his hand. "Pleased to

make your acquaintance, Mr. Peale. Perhaps you can help us out with a little information."

"Glad to be of service, Inspector," replied Peale, in a rich baritone. He glanced at the back of the Medical Examiner, who was busy over the dead man; then looked away with repugnance.

"I suppose you were on the stage at the time the hue-and-cry went up in this unfortunate affair?" pursued the Inspector.

"Oh, yes. In fact, the entire cast was. What is it you would like to know?"

"Could you definitely place the time that you noticed something wrong in the audience?"

"Yes, I can. We had just about ten minutes before the end of the act. It was at the climax of the play, and my role demands the discharge of a pistol. I remember we had some discussion during rehearsals of this point in the play, and that is how I can be so sure of the time."

The Inspector nodded. "Thank you very much, Mr. Peale. That's exactly what I wanted to know. . . . Incidentally, let me apologize for having kept you people crowded back here in this fashion. We were quite busy and had no time to make other arrangements. You and the rest of the cast are at liberty to go backstage now. Of course, make no effort to leave the theatre until you are notified."

"I understand completely, Inspector. Happy to have been able to help." Peale bowed and retreated to the rear of the theatre.

The Inspector leaned against the nearest seat, absorbed in thought, Ellery, at his side, was absently polishing the lenses of his pince-nez. Father motioned significantly to son.

"Well, Ellery?" Queen asked in a low voice.

"Elementary, my dear Watson," murmured Ellery. "Our respected victim was last seen alive at 9:25, and he was found dead at approximately 9:55. Problem: What happened between times? Sounds ludicrously simple."

"You don't say?" muttered Queen. "Piggott!"

"Yes, sir."

"Is that the usherette? Let's get some action."

Piggott released the arm of the young woman standing at his side. She was a pert and painted lady with even white teeth and a ghastly smile. She minced forward and regarded the Inspector brazenly.

"Are you the regular usherette on this aisle, Miss—?" asked the Inspector briskly.

"O'Connell, Madge O'Connell. Yes, I am!"

The Inspector took her arm gently. "I'm afraid I'll have to ask you to be as grave as you are impertinent, my dear," he said. "Step over here for a moment." The girl's face was deathly white as they paused at the LL row. "Pardon me a moment, Doc. Mind if we interrupt your work?"

Dr. Prouty looked up with an abstracted scowl. "No, go right ahead, Inspector. I'm nearly through." He stood up and moved aside, biting the cigar between his teeth.

Queen watched the girl's face as she stooped over the dead man's body. She drew her breath in sharply.

"Do you remember ushering this man to his seat tonight, Miss O'Connell?"

The girl hesitated. "Seems like I do. But I was very busy

tonight, as usual, and I must have ushered two hundred people all told. So I couldn't say positively."

"Do you recall whether these seats which are empty now"—he indicated the seven vacant chairs—"were unoccupied all during the first and second acts?"

"Well . . . I do seem to remember noticing them that way as I walked up and down the aisle. . . . No, sir. I don't think anybody sat in those seats all night."

"Did anyone walk up or down this aisle during the second act, Miss O'Connell? Think hard, now; it's important that you answer correctly."

The girl hesitated once more, flashing bold eyes at the impassive face of the Inspector. "No—I didn't see anybody walk up or down the aisle." She quickly added, "I couldn't tell you much. I don't know a thing about this business. I'm a hard-working girl, and I—"

"Yes, yes, my dear, we understand that. Now—where do you generally stand when you're not ushering people to their seats?"

The girl pointed to the head of the aisle.

"Were you there all during the second act, Miss O'Connell?" asked the Inspector softly.

The girl moistened her lips before she spoke. "Well—yes, I was. But, honest, I didn't see anything out of the way all night."

"Very well." Queen's voice was mild. "That's all." She turned away with quick, light steps.

There was a stir behind the group. Queen wheeled to confront Dr. Prouty, who had risen to his feet and was closing his bag. He was whistling dolefully.

"Well, Doc—I see you're through. What's the verdict?" asked Queen.

"It's short and snappy, Inspector. Man died about two hours ago. Cause of death puzzled me for a while but it's pretty well settled in my mind as poison. The signs all point to some form of alcoholic poisoning—you've probably noticed the sallow blue color of the skin. Did you smell his breath? Sweetest odor of bum booze I ever had the pleasure of inhaling. He must have been drunk as a lord. At the same time, it couldn't have been ordinary alcoholic poisoning—he wouldn't have dropped off so fast. That's all I can tell you right now." He paused, buttoning his coat.

Queen took Field's kerchief-wrapped flask from his pocket and handed it to Dr. Prouty. "This is the dead man's flask, Doc. Suppose you analyze the contents for me. Before you handle it, though, let Jimmy down at the laboratory look it over for fingerprints. And—but wait a minute." The Inspector peered about and picked up the half-empty ginger-ale bottle where it stood in a corner on the carpet. "You can analyze this ginger ale for me, too, Doc," he added.

The Assistant Medical Examiner, after stowing the flask and bottle into his bag, tenderly adjusted the hat on his head.

"Well, I'll be going, Inspector," he drawled. "I'll have a fuller report for you when I've performed the autopsy. Ought to give you something to work on. Incidentally, the morgue-wagon must be outside—I phoned for one on my way down. So long." He yawned and slouched away.

As Dr. Prouty disappeared, two white-garbed orderlies

hurried across the carpet, bearing a stretcher between them. At a sign from Queen they lifted the inert body, deposited it on the stretcher, covered it with a blanket and hustled out. The detectives and policemen around the door watched with relief as the grisly burden was borne away—the main work of the evening for them was almost over. The audience—rustling, shifting, coughing, murmuring—twisted about with a renewal of interest as the body was unceremoniously carted off.

Queen had just turned to Ellery with a weary sigh when from the extreme right-hand side of the theatre came an ominous commotion. People everywhere popped out of their seats staring while policemen shouted for quiet. Queen spoke rapidly to a uniformed officer nearby. Ellery slipped to one side, eyes gleaming. The disturbance came nearer by jerky degrees. Two policemen appeared hauling a struggling figure between them. They dragged their capture to the head of the left aisle and hustled the man to his feet, holding him up by main force.

The man was short and ratlike. He wore cheap storeclothes of a sombre cut. On his head was a black hat of the kind sometimes worn by country dominies. His mouth writhed in an ugly manner; imprecations issued from it venomously. As he caught the eye of the Inspector fixed upon him, however, he ceased struggling and went limp at once.

"Found this man tryin' to sneak out the alley door on the other side of the buildin', Inspector," panted one of the bluecoats, shaking the captive roughly.

The Inspector chuckled, took his brown snuffbox from his

pocket, inhaled, sneezed his habitual joyful sneeze, and beamed upon the silent cowering man between the two officers.

"Well, well, Parson," he said genially. "Mighty nice of you to turn up so conveniently!"

4

IN WHICH MANY ARE CALLED AND TWO ARE CHOSEN

Some natures, through peculiar weakness, cannot endure the sight of a whining man. Of all the silent, threatening group ringed about the abject figure called "Parson," Ellery alone experienced a sick feeling of disgust at the spectacle the prisoner was making of himself.

At the hidden lash in Queen's words, the Parson drew himself up stiffly, glared into the Inspector's eyes for a split second, then with a resumption of his former tactics began to fight against the sturdy arms which encircled him. He writhed and spat and cursed, finally becoming silent again. He was conserving his breath. The fury of his threshing body communicated itself to his captors; another policeman joined the melee and helped pin the prisoner to the floor. And suddenly he wilted and shrank like a pricked balloon. A policeman hauled him roughly to his feet, where he stood, eyes downcast, body still, hat clutched in his hand.

Ellery turned his head.

"Come now, Parson," went on the Inspector, just as if the man had been a balky child at rest after a fit of temper, "you know that sort of business doesn't go with me. What happened when you tried it last time at the Old Slip on the riverfront?"

"Answer when you're spoken to!" growled a bluecoat, prodding him in the ribs.

"I don't know nothin' and besides I got nothin' to say," muttered the Parson, shifting from one foot to the other.

"I'm surprised at you, Parson," said Queen gently. "I haven't asked you what you know."

"You got no right to hold an innocent man!" shouted the Parson indignantly. "Ain't I as good as anybody else here? I bought a ticket and I paid for it with real dough, too! Where do you get that stuff—tryin' to keep me from goin' home!"

"So you bought a ticket, did you?" asked the Inspector, rocking on his heels. "Well, well! Suppose you snap out the old stub and let Papa Queen look it over."

The Parson's hand mechanically went to his lower vest pocket, his fingers dipping into it with a quite surprising deftness. His face went blank as he slowly withdrew his hand, empty. He began a search of his other pockets with an appearance of fierce annoyance that made the Inspector smile.

"Hell!" grunted the Parson. "If that ain't the toughest luck. I always hangs onto my ticket stubs, an' just tonight I have to go and throw it away. Sorry, Inspector!"

"Oh, that's quite all right," said Queen. His face went bleak and hard. "Quit stalling, Cazzanelli! What were you doing in this theatre tonight? What made you decide to duck out so suddenly? Answer me!"

The Parson looked about him. His arms were held very securely by two bluecoats. A number of hard-looking men surrounded him. The prospect of escape did not seem particularly bright. His face underwent another change. It assumed a priestly, outraged innocence. A mist filmed his little eyes, as if he were truly the Christian martyr and these tyrants his pagan inquisitors. The Parson had often employed this trick of personality to good purpose.

"Inspector," he said, "you know you ain't got no right to grill me this way, don't you, Inspector? A man's got a right to his lawyer, ain't he? Sure he's got a right!" And he stopped as if there were nothing more to be said.

The Inspector eyed him curiously. "When did you see Field last?" he asked.

"Field? You don't mean to say—Monte Field? Never heard of him, Inspector," muttered the Parson, rather shakily. "What are you tryin' to put over on me?"

"Not a thing, Parson, not a thing. But as long as you don't care to answer now, suppose we let you cool your heels for a while. Perhaps you'll have something to say later. . . . Don't forget, Parson, there's still that little matter of the Bonomo Silk robbery to go into." He turned to one of the policemen. "Escort our friend to that anteroom off the manager's office, and keep him company for a while, officer."

Ellery, reflectively watching the Parson being dragged toward the rear of the theatre, was startled to hear his father say, "The Parson isn't too bright, is he? To make a slip like that—!"

"Be thankful for small favors," smiled Ellery. "One error breeds twenty more."

The Inspector turned with a grin to confront Velie, who had just arrived with a sheaf of papers in his hand.

"Ah, Thomas is back," chuckled the Inspector, who seemed in good spirits. "And what have you found, Thomas?"

"Well, Inspector," replied the detective, ruffling the edges of his papers, "it's hard to say. This is half of the list—the other half isn't ready yet. But I think you'll find something interesting here."

He handed Queen a batch of hastily written names and addresses. They were the names which the Inspector had ordered Velie to secure by interrogation of the audience.

Queen, with Ellery at his shoulder, examined the list, studying each name carefully. He was halfway through the sheaf when he stiffened. He squinted at the name which had halted him and looked up at Velie with a puzzled air.

"Morgan," he said thoughtfully. "Benjamin Morgan. Sounds mighty familiar, Thomas. What does it suggest to you?"

Velie smiled frostily. "I thought you'd ask me that, Inspector. Benjamin Morgan was Monte Field's law partner until two years ago."

Queen nodded. The three men stared into each other's eyes. Then the old man shrugged his shoulders and said briefly. "Have to see some more of Mr. Morgan, I'm afraid."

He turned back to the list with a sigh. Again he studied each name, looking up at intervals reflectively, shaking his head, and going on. Velie, who knew Queen's reputation for memory even more thoroughly than Ellery, watched his superior with respectful eyes.

Finally the Inspector handed the papers back to the detective. "Nothing else, there, Thomas," he said. "Unless you caught something that escaped me. Did you?" His tone was grave.

Velie stared at the old man wordlessly, shook his head and started to walk away.

"Just a minute, Thomas," called Queen. "Before you get that second list completed, ask Mr. Morgan to step into Panzer's office will you? Don't scare him. And by the way, see that he has his ticket stub before he goes to the office." Velie departed.

The Inspector motioned to Panzer, who was watching a group of policemen being marshaled by detectives for Queen's work. The stout little manager hurried up.

"Mr. Panzer," inquired the Inspector, "at what time do your scrubwomen generally start cleaning up?"

"Why, they've been here for quite a while now, Inspector, waiting to get to work. Most theatres are tidied early in the morning, but I've always had my employees come immediately after the evening performance. Just what is on your mind?"

Ellery, who had frowned slightly when the Inspector spoke, brightened at the manager's reply. He began to polish his pince-nez with satisfaction.

"Here's what I want you to do, Mr. Panzer," continued Queen evenly. "Arrange to have your cleaning women make a particularly thorough search tonight, after everybody is gone. They must pick up and save everything—everything, no matter how seemingly trivial—and they're to watch especially for ticket stubs. Can you trust these people?"

"Oh, absolutely, Inspector. They've been with the theatre ever since it was built. You may be sure that nothing will be overlooked. What shall I do with the sweepings?"

"Wrap them carefully, address them to me and send them by a trustworthy messenger to headquarters tomorrow morning." The Inspector paused. "I want to impress upon you, Mr. Panzer, the importance of this task. It's much more important than it seems. Do you understand?"

"Certainly, certainly!" Panzer hastened away.

A detective with grizzled hair walked briskly across the carpet, turned down the left aisle and touched his hat to Queen. In his hand was a sheaf of papers resembling the one which Velie had presented.

"Sergeant Velie had asked me to give you this list of names. He says that it's the rest of the names and addresses of the people in the audience, Inspector."

Queen took the papers from the detective's hand with a sudden show of eagerness. Ellery leaned forward. The old man's eyes traveled slowly from name to name as his thin finger moved down each sheet. Near the bottom of the last one he smiled, looked at Ellery triumphantly, and finished the page. He turned and whispered into his son's ear. A light came over Ellery's face as he nodded.

The Inspector turned back to the waiting detective. "Come here, Johnson," he said. Queen spread out the page he had been studying for the man's scrutiny. "I want you to find Velie and have him report to me at once. After you've done that, get hold of this woman"—his finger pointed to a name and a row and seat number next to it—"ask her to step into the manager's office with you. You'll find a man by the name of Morgan there. Stay with both of them until you hear from me. Incidentally, if there's any conversation between them keep your ears open—I want to know what is said. Treat the woman courteously."

"Yes, sir. Velie also asked me to tell you," continued Johnson, "that he has a group of people separated from the rest of the audience—they're the ones who have no ticket stubs. He'd like to know what you want done with them."

"Do their names appear on both lists, Johnson?" asked Queen, handing him the second sheaf for return to Velie.

"Yes, sir."

"Then tell Velie to let them leave with the others, but not before he makes a special list of their names. It won't be necessary for me to see or speak to them."

Johnson saluted and disappeared.

Queen turned to converse in low tones with Ellery, who seemed to have something on his mind. They were interrupted by the reappearance of Panzer.

"Inspector?" The manager coughed politely.

"Oh, yes, Panzer!" said the Inspector, whirling about "Everything straight with regard to the cleaning women?"

"Yes, sir. Is there anything else you would like me to do . . .? And, Inspector, I hope you will pardon me for asking, but how much longer will the audience have to wait? I have been receiving most disturbing inquiries from many people. I am hoping no trouble comes of this affair." His dark face was glistening with perspiration.

"Oh, don't worry about that, Panzer," said the Inspector

casually. "Their wait is almost over. In fact I am ordering my men to get them out of here in a few minutes. Before they leave, however, they'll have one thing more to complain about," he added with a grim smile.

"Yes, Inspector?"

"Oh, yes," said Queen. "They're going to submit to a search. No doubt they'll protest, and you'll hear threats of lawsuits and personal violence, but don't worry about it. I'm responsible for everything done here tonight, and I'll see that you're kept out of trouble. . . . Now, we'll need a woman searcher to help our men. We have a police matron here, but she's busy downstairs. Do you think you could get me a dependable woman—middle-aged preferably—who won't object to a thankless job and will know how to keep her mouth shut?"

The manager pondered for a moment. "I think I can get you the woman you want. She's a Mrs. Phillips, our wardrobe mistress. She's well on in years and as pleasant as anyone you could get for such a task."

"Just the person," said Queen briskly. "Get her at once and station her at the main exit. Detective-Sergeant Velie will give her the necessary instructions."

Velie had come up in time to hear the last remark. Panzer bustled down the aisle toward the boxes.

"Morgan set?" asked Queen.

"Yes, Inspector."

"Well, then, you have one more job and you'll be through for the night, Thomas. I want you to superintend the departure of the people seated in the orchestra and boxes. Have them leave one by one, and overhaul them as they go out. No one is to leave by any exit except the main door, and just to make sure tell the men at the side exits to keep 'em moving toward the rear." Velie nodded. "Now, about the search. Piggott!" The detective came on the run. "Piggott, you accompany Mr. Queen and Sergeant Velie and help search every man who goes out the main door. There'll be a matron there to search the women. Examine every parcel. Go over their pockets for anything suspicious; collect all the ticket stubs; and watch especially for *an extra hat.* The hat I want is a silk topper. But if you find any other kind of extra hat, nab the owner and be sure he's nabbed properly. Now, boys, get to work!"

Ellery, who had been lounging against a pillar, straightened up and followed Piggott. As Velie stalked behind, Queen called, "Don't release the people in the balcony until the orchestra is empty. Send somebody up there to keep them quiet."

With his last important instruction given the Inspector turned to Doyle, who was standing guard nearby, and said quietly, "Shoot downstairs to the cloakroom, Doyle, my lad, and keep your eyes open while the people are getting their wraps. When they're all gone, search the place with a fine comb. If there is anything left in the racks, bring it to me."

Queen leaned back against the pillar which loomed, a marble sentinel, over the seat in which murder had been done. As he stood there, eyes blank, hands clutching his lapels, the broad-shouldered Flint hurried up with a gleam of excitement in his eyes. Inspector Queen regarded him critically.

"Found something, Flint?" he asked, fumbling for his snuffbox.

The detective silently offered him a half-ticket, colored blue, and marked "LL30 Left."

"Well, well!" exclaimed Queen. "Where did you find that?"

"Right inside the main door," said Flint. "Looked as if it was dropped just as the owner came into the theatre."

Queen did not answer. With a swooping dip of his fingers he extracted from his vest pocket the blue-colored stub he had found on the dead man's person. He regarded them in silence—two identically colored and marked stubs, one with the inscription LL32 Left, the other LL30 Left.

His eyes narrowed as he studied the innocent-appearing pasteboards. He bent closer, slowly turning the stubs back to back. Then, with a puzzled light in his gray eyes, he turned them front to front. Still unsatisfied, he turned them back to front.

In none of the three positions did the torn edges of the tickets coincide!

5

IN WHICH INSPECTOR QUEEN CONDUCTS SOME LEGAL CONVERSATIONS

Queen made his way across the broad red carpet covering the rear of the orchestra, his hat pulled down over his eyes. He was searching the recesses of his pocket for the inevitable snuffbox. The Inspector was evidently engaged in a weighty mental process, for his hand closed tightly upon the two blue ticket stubs and he grimaced, as if he were not at all satisfied with his thoughts.

Before opening the green-speckled door marked "Manager's Office," he turned to survey the scene behind him. The stir in the audience was businesslike. A great chattering filled the air; policemen and detectives circulated among the rows, giving orders, answering questions, hustling people out of their seats, lining them up in the main aisles to be searched at the huge outer door. The Inspector noticed absently that there was little protest from the audience at the ordeal they were facing. They seemed too tired to resent the indignity of a search. A long queue of half-angry, half-amused women was lined up at one side being examined rapidly, one by one, by a motherly woman dressed in black. Queen glanced briefly at the detectives blocking the door. Piggott with the experience of long practice was making rapid passes over the clothing of the men. Velie, at his side, was studying the reaction of the various people undergoing examination. Occasionally he searched a man himself. Ellery stood a little apart, hands in his capacious topcoat pockets smoking a cigarette and seeming to be thinking of nothing more important than the first edition he had missed buying.

Queen sighed, and went in.

The anteroom to the main office was a tiny place, fitted out in bronze and oak. On one of the chairs against the wall, burrowed into the deep leather cushions, sat Parson Johnny, puffing at a cigarette with a show of unconcern. A policeman stood by the chair, one massive hand on the Parson's shoulder.

"Trail along, Parson," said Queen casually, without stopping. The little gangster lounged to his feet, spun his cigarette butt deftly into a shining brass cuspidor, and slouched after the Inspector, the policeman treading on his heels.

Queen opened the door to the main office, glancing quickly about him as he stood on the threshold. Then he stepped aside, allowing the gangster and the bluecoat to precede him. The door banged shut behind them.

Louis Panzer had an unusual taste in office appointments. A clear green lightshade shone brilliantly above a carved desk. Chairs and smoking stands; a skillfully wrought clothes-tree; silk-covered divan—these and other articles were strewn tastefully about the room. Unlike most managers' offices, Panzer's did not exploit photographs of stars, managers, producers and "angels." Several delicate prints, a huge tapestry, and a Constable oil painting hung on the wall.

But Inspector Queen's scrutiny at the moment was not for the artistic quality of Mr. Panzer's private chamber. It was rather for the six people who faced him. Beside Detective Johnson sat a middle-aged man inclining to corpulence, with shrewd eyes and a puzzled frown. He wore faultless evening clothes. In the next chair sat a young girl of considerable beauty, attired in a simple evening gown and wrap. She was looking up at a handsome young man in evening clothes, hat in hand, who was bending over her chair and talking earnestly in an undertone. Beside them were two other women, both leaning forward and listening intently.

The stout man held aloof from the others. At Inspector Queen's entrance he immediately got to his feet with an inquiring look. The little group became silent and turned solemn faces on Queen.

With a deprecating cough Parson Johnny, accompanied by his escort, sidled across the rug into a corner. He seemed overwhelmed by the splendor of the company in which he found himself. He shuffled his feet and cast a despairing look in the direction of the Inspector.

Queen moved over to the desk and faced the group. At a motion of his hand Johnson came quickly to his side.

"Who are the three extra people, Johnson?" he asked in a tone inaudible to the others.

"The old fellow there is Morgan," whispered Johnson, "and the good-looker sitting near him is the woman you told me to get. When I went for her in the orchestra I found the young chap and the other two women with her. The four of 'em were pretty chummy. I gave her your message, and she seemed nervous. But she stood up and came along like a major—only the other three came, too. I didn't know but what you'd like to see 'em, Inspector. . . ."

Queen nodded. "Hear anything?" he asked in the same low tone.

"Not a peep, Inspector. The old chap doesn't seem to know any of these people. The others have just been wondering why you could possibly want *her.*"

The Inspector waved Johnson to a corner and addressed the waiting group.

"I've summoned two of you," he said pleasantly, "for a little chat. And since the others are here, too, it will be all right for them to wait. But for the moment I must ask you all to step into the anteroom while I conduct a little business with this gentleman." He inclined his head toward the gangster, who stiffened indignantly.

With a flutter of excited conversation the two men and three women departed, Johnson closing the door behind them.

Queen whirled on Parson Johnny.

"Bring that rat here!" he snapped to the policeman. He sat down in Panzer's chair and drew the tips of his fingers together. The gangster was jerked to his feet and marched across the carpet, to be pushed directly in front of the desk.

"Now, Parson," said Queen menacingly. "I've got you where I want you. We're going to have a nice little talk with nobody to interrupt. Get me?"

The Parson was silent, his eyes liquid with distrust.

"So you won't say anything, eh, Johnny? How long do you think I'll let you get away with that?"

"I told you before—I don't know nothin' and besides I won't say nothin' till I see my lawyer," the gangster said sullenly.

"Your lawyer? Well, Parson, who *is* your lawyer?" asked the Inspector in an innocent tone.

The Parson bit his lip, remaining silent. Queen turned to Johnson.

"Johnson, my boy, you worked on the Babylon stickup, didn't you?" he asked.

"Sure did, Chief," said the detective.

"That," explained Queen gently, to the gangster, "was when you were sent up for a year. Remember, Parson?"

Still silence.

"And Johnson," continued the Inspector, leaning back in his chair, "refresh my memory. Who was the lawyer defending our friend here?"

"Field. By—" Johnson exclaimed, staring at the Parson.

"Exactly. The gentleman now lying on one of our unfeeling slabs at the morgue. Well, what about it? Cut the comedy! Where do you come off saying you don't know Monte Field? You knew his first name, all right, when I mentioned only his last. Come clean, now!"

The gangster had sagged against the policeman, a furtive despair in his eyes. He moistened his lips and said, "You got me there, Inspector. I—I don't know nothin' about this, though, honest I ain't seen Field in a month. I didn't—my

Gawd, you're not tryin' to tie this croakin' around my neck, are you?"

He stared at Queen in anguish. The policeman jerked him straight.

"Parson, Parson," said Queen, "how you do jump at conclusions. I'm merely looking for a little information. Of course, if you want to confess to the murder I'll call my men in and we can get your story all straight and go home to bed. How about it?"

"No!" shouted the gangster, thrashing out suddenly with his arm. The officer caught it deftly and twisted it behind the squirming back. "Where do you get that stuff? I ain't confessin' nothin'. I don't know nothin'. I didn't see Field tonight an' I didn't even know he was here! Confess. . . . I got some mighty influential friends, Inspector—you can't pull that stuff on me, I'll tell you!"

"That's too bad, Johnny," sighed the Inspector. He took a pinch of snuff. "All right, then. You didn't kill Monte Field. What time did you get here tonight, and Where's your ticket?"

The Parson twisted his hat in his hands. "I wasn't goin' to say nothin' before, Inspector, because I figured you was tryin' to railroad me. I can explain when and how I got here all right. It was about half past eight, and I got in on a pass, that's how. Here's the stub to prove it." He searched carefully in his coat pocket and produced a perforated blue stub. He handed it to Queen, who glanced at it carefully and put it in his pocket.

"And where," he asked, "and where did you get the pass, Johnny?"

"I—my girl give it to me, Inspector," replied the gangster nervously.

"Ah—the woman enters the case," said Queen jovially. "And what might this young Circe's name be, Johnny?"

"Who?—why, she's—hey, Inspector, don't get her in no trouble, will you?" burst out Parson Johnny. "She's a reg'lar kid, an' she don't know nothin' either. Honest, I—"

"Her name?" snapped Queen.

"Madge O'Connell," whined Johnny. "She's an usher here."

Queen's eyes lit up. A quick glance passed between him and Johnson. The detective left the room.

"So," continued the Inspector, leaning back again comfortably, "so my old friend Parson Johnny doesn't know a thing about Monte Field. Well, well, well! We'll see how your lady-friend's story backs you up." As he talked he looked steadily at the hat in the gangster's hand. It was a cheap black fedora, matching the sombre suit which the man was wearing. "Here, Parson," he said suddenly. "Hand over that hat of yours."

He took the head piece from the gangster's reluctant hand and examined it. He pulled down the leather band inside, eyed it critically and finally handed it back.

"We forgot something, Parson," he said. "Officer, suppose you frisk Mr. Cazzanelli's person, eh?"

The Parson submitted to the search with an ill grace, but he was quiescent enough. "No gat," said the policeman briefly, and continued. He put his hand into the man's hip pocket, extracting a fat wallet. "Want this, Inspector?"

Queen took it, counted the money briskly, and handed it back to the policeman, who returned it to the pocket.

"One hundred and twenty-two smackers, Johnny," the old

man murmured. "Seems to me I can smell Bonomo silk in these bills. However!" He laughed and said to the bluecoat, "No flask?" The policeman shook his head. "Anything under his vest or shirt?" Again a negative. Queen was silent until the search was completed. Parson Johnny relaxed with a sigh.

"Well, Johnny, mighty lucky night this is for you—Come in!" Queen said at a knock on the door. It opened to disclose the slender girl in usherette's uniform whom he had questioned earlier in the evening. Johnson came in after her and closed the door.

Madge O'Connell stood on the rug and stared with tragic eyes at her lover, who was thoughtfully studying the floor. She flashed a glance at Queen. Then her mouth hardened and she snapped at the gangster. "Well? So they got you after all, you sap! I told you not to try to make a break for it!" She turned her back contemptuously on the Parson and began to ply a powderpuff with vigor.

"Why didn't you tell me before, my girl," said Queen softly, "that you got a pass for your friend John Cazzanelli?"

"I ain't telling everything, Mr. Cop," she answered pertly. "Why should I? Johnny didn't have anything to do with this business."

"We won't discuss that," said the Inspector, toying with his snuffbox. "What I want you to tell me now, Madge, is whether your memory has improved any since I spoke to you."

"What d'ya mean?" she demanded.

"I mean this. You told me that you were at your regular station just before the show started—that you conducted a lot of people to their seats—that you didn't remember whether you ushered Monte Field, the dead man, to his row or not—and that you were standing up at the head of the left aisle all during the performance. *All* during the performance, Madge. Is that correct?"

"Sure it is, Inspector. Who says I wasn't?" The girl was growing excited, but Queen glanced at her fluttering fingers and they became still.

"Aw, cut it out, Madge," snapped the Parson unexpectedly. "Don't make it no worse than it is. Sooner or later he'll find out we were together anyways, and then he'd have something on you. You don't know this bird. Come clean, Madge!"

"So!" said the Inspector, looking pleasantly from the gangster to the girl. "Parson, you're getting sensible in your old age. Did I hear you say you two were together? When, and why, and for how long?"

Madge O'Connell's face had gone red and white by turns. She favored her lover with a venomous glance, then turned back to Queen.

"I guess I might as well spill it," she said disgustedly, "after this halfwit shows a yellow streak. Here's all I know, Inspector—and Gawd help you if you tell that little mutt of a manager about it!" Queen's eyebrows went up, but he did not interrupt her. "I got the pass for Johnny all right," she continued defiantly, "because—well, Johnny kind of likes blood-and-thunder stuff, and it was his off-night. So I got him the pass. It was for two—all the passes are—so that the seat next to Johnny was empty all the time. It was an aisle seat on the left—best I could get for that loud-mouthed shrimp!

During the first act I was pretty busy and couldn't sit with him. But after the first intermission, when the curtain went up on Act II, things got slack and it was a good chance to sit next to him. Sure, I admit it—I was sittin' next to him nearly the Whole act! Why not—don't I deserve a rest once in a while?"

"I see." Queen bent his brows. "You would have saved me a lot of time and trouble, young lady, if you'd told me this before. Didn't you get up at all during the second act?"

"Well, I did a couple of times, I guess," she said guardedly. "But everything was okay, and the manager wasn't around, so I went back."

"Did you notice this man Field as you passed?"

"No—no, sir."

"Did you notice if anybody was sitting next to him?"

"No, sir. I didn't know he was there. Wasn't—wasn't looking that way, I guess."

"I suppose, then," continued Queen coldly, "you don't remember ushering somebody into the last row, next to the last seat, during the second act?"

"No, sir. . . . Aw, I know I shouldn't have done it, maybe, but I didn't see a thing wrong all night." She was growing more nervous at each question. She furtively glanced at the Parson, but he was staring at the floor.

"You're a great help, young lady," said Queen, rising suddenly. "Beat it."

As she turned to go, the gangster with an innocent leer slid across the rug to follow her. Queen made a sign to the policeman. The Parson found himself yanked back to his former position.

"Not so fast, Johnny," said Queen icily. "O'Connell!" The girl turned, trying to appear unconcerned. "For the time being I shan't say anything about this to Mr. Panzer. But I'd advise you to watch your step and learn to keep your mouth clean when you talk to your superiors. Get on now, and if I ever hear of another break on your part God help *you!*"

She started to laugh, wavered and fled from the room.

Queen whirled on the policeman. "Put the nippers on him, officer," he snapped, jerking his finger toward the gangster, "and run him down to the station!"

The policeman saluted. There was a flash of steel, a dull click, and the Parson stared stupidly at the handcuffs on his wrists. Before he could open his mouth he was hustled out of the room.

Queen made a disgusted motion of his hand, threw himself into the leather-covered chair, took a pinch of snuff, and said to Johnson in an entirely different tone, "I'll trouble you, Johnson my boy, to ask Mr. Morgan to step in here."

Benjamin Morgan entered Queen's temporary sanctum with a firm step that did not succeed entirely in concealing a certain bewildered agitation. He said in a cheerful, hearty baritone, "Well, sir, here I am," and sank into a chair with much the same air of satisfaction that a man exhales when he seats himself in his clubroom after a hard day. Queen was not taken in. He favored Morgan with a long, earnest stare, which made the paunchy grizzled man squirm.

"My name is Queen, Mr. Morgan," he said in a friendly voice, "Inspector Richard Queen."

"I suspected as much," said Morgan, rising to shake hands. "I think you know who I am, Inspector. I was under your eye more than once in the Criminal Court years ago. There was a case—do you remember it?—I was defending Mary Doolittle when she was being tried for murder. . . ."

"Indeed, yes!" exclaimed the Inspector heartily. "I wondered where I'd seen you before. You got her off, too, if I'm not mistaken. That was a mighty nice piece of work, Morgan—very, very nice. So *you're* the fellow! Well, well!"

Morgan laughed. "Was pretty nice, at that," he admitted. "But those days are over, I'm afraid, Inspector. You know—I'm not in the criminal end of it any more."

"No?" Queen took a pinch of snuff. "I didn't know that. Anything"—he sneezed—"anything go wrong?" he asked sympathetically.

Morgan was silent. After a moment he crossed his legs and said, "Quite a bit went wrong. May I smoke?" he asked abruptly. On Queen's assent he lit a fat cigar and became absorbed in its curling haze.

Neither man spoke for a long time. Morgan seemed to sense that he was under a rigid inspection, for he crossed and uncrossed his legs repeatedly, avoiding Queen's eyes. The old man appeared to be ruminating, his head sunk on his breast.

The silence became electric, embarrassing. There was not a sound in the room, except the ticking of a floor-clock in a corner. From somewhere in the theatre came a sudden burst of conversation. Voices were raised to a high pitch of indignation or protest. Then even this was cut off.

"Come now, Inspector. . . ." Morgan coughed. He was enveloped in a thick rolling smoke from his cigar, and his voice was harsh and strained. "What is this—a refined third degree?"

Queen looked up, startled. "Eh? I beg your pardon, Mr. Morgan. My thoughts went wool-gathering, I guess. Been rubbing it in, have I? Dear me! I must be getting old." He rose and took a short turn about the room, his hands clasped loosely behind his back. Morgan's eyes followed him.

"Mr. Morgan"—the Inspector pounced on him with one of his habitual conversational leaps—"do you know why I've asked you to stay and talk to me?"

"Why—I can't say I do, Inspector. I suppose, naturally, that it has to do with the accident here tonight. But what connection it can possibly have with me, I'll confess I don't know." Morgan puffed violently at his weed.

"Perhaps, Mr. Morgan, you will know in a moment," said Queen, leaning back against the desk. "The man murdered here tonight—it wasn't any accident, I can assure you of that—was a certain Monte Field."

The announcement was placid enough but the effect upon Morgan was astounding. He fairly leaped from his chair, eyes popping, hands trembling, breath hoarse and heavy. His cigar dropped to the floor. Queen regarded him with morose eyes.

"Monte—Field!" Morgan's cry was terrible in its intensity. He stared at the Inspector's face. Then he collapsed in the chair, his whole body sagging.

"Pick up your cigar, Mr. Morgan," said Queen. "I shouldn't like to abuse Mr. Panzer's hospitality." The lawyer stooped mechanically and retrieved the cigar.

"My friend," thought Queen to himself, "either you are one of the world's greatest actors or you just got the shock of your life!" He straightened up. "Come now, Mr. Morgan—pull yourself together. Why should the death of Field affect you in this way?"

"But—but, man! Monte Field . . . Oh, my God!" And he threw back his head and laughed—a wild humor that made Queen sit up alertly. The spasm continued, Morgan's body rocking to and fro in hysteria. The Inspector knew the symptoms. He slapped the lawyer in the face, pulling him to his feet by his coat collar.

"Don't forget yourself, Morgan!" commanded Queen. The rough tone had its effect Morgan stopped laughing, regarded Queen with a blank expression, and dropped heavily into the chair—still shaken, but himself.

"I'm—I'm sorry, Inspector," he muttered, dabbing his face with a handkerchief. "It was—quite a surprise."

"Evidently," said Queen dryly. "You couldn't have acted more surprised if the earth had opened under your feet. Now, Morgan, what's this all about?"

The lawyer continued to wipe the perspiration from his face. He was shaking like a leaf, his jowls red. He gnawed at his lip in indecision.

"All right, Inspector," he said at last. "What do you want to know?"

"That's better," said Queen approvingly. "Suppose you tell me when you last saw Monte Field?"

The lawyer cleared his throat nervously. "Why—why, I haven't seen him for ages," he said in a low voice. "I suppose you know that we were partners once—we had a successful legal practice. Then something happened and we broke up. I—I haven't seen him since."

"And that was how long ago?"

"A little over two years."

"Very good." Queen leaned forward. "I'm anxious to know, too, just why the two of you broke up your partnership."

The lawyer looked down at the rug, fingering his cigar. "I—well, I guess you know Field's reputation as well as I. We didn't agree on ethics, had a little argument and decided to dissolve."

"You parted amicably?"

"Well—under the circumstances, yes."

Queen drummed on the desk. Morgan shifted uneasily. He was evidently still laboring under the effects of his astonishment.

"What time did you get to the theatre tonight, Morgan?" asked the Inspector.

Morgan seemed surprised at the question. "Why—about a quarter after eight," he replied.

"Let me see your ticket stub, please," said Queen.

The lawyer handed it over after fumbling for it in several pockets. Queen took it, extracted from his own pocket the three stubs he had secreted there, and lowered his hands below the level of the desk. He looked up in a moment, his eyes expressionless as he returned the four bits of pasteboard to his own pocket.

"So you were sitting in M2 Center, were you? Pretty good seat, Morgan," he remarked. "Just what made you come to see 'Gunplay' tonight, anyway?"

"Why, it *is* a rum sort of show, isn't it, Inspector?" Morgan appeared embarrassed. "I don't know that I would ever have thought of coming—I'm not a theatre-going man, you know—except that the Roman management was kind enough to send me a complimentary ticket for this evening's performance."

"Is that a fact?" exclaimed Queen ingenuously. "Quite nice of them, I'd say. When did you receive the ticket?"

"Why, I got the ticket and the letter Saturday morning, Inspector, at my office."

"Oh, you got a letter too, eh? You don't happen to have it around you, do you?"

"I'm—pretty—sure I—have," grunted Morgan as he began to search his pockets. "Yes! Here it is."

He offered the Inspector a small, rectangular sheet of paper, deckle-edged and of crushed bond stock. Queen handled it gingerly as he held it up to the light. Through the few typewritten lines on it a watermark was distinctly visible. His lips puckered, and he laid the sheet cautiously on the desk blotter. As Morgan watched, he opened the top drawer of Panzer's desk and rummaged about until he found a piece of notepaper. It was large, square, and heavily glazed with an ornate theatre insignia engraved on an upper quarter. Queen put the two pieces of paper side by side, thought a moment, then sighed and picked up the sheet which Morgan had handed him. He read it through slowly.

> The Management of the Roman Theatre cordially invites the attendance of Mr. Benjamin Morgan at the Monday evening, September twenty-fourth performance of GUNPLAY. As a leading figure of the New York bar, Mr.

Morgan's opinion of the play as a social and legal document is earnestly solicited. This, however, is by no means obligatory; and the Management wishes further to assure Mr. Morgan that the acceptance of its invitation entails no obligation whatsoever.
(Signed)THE ROMAN THEATRE
Per: S.

The "S" was a barely decipherable ink scrawl.

Queen looked up, smiling. "Mighty nice of the Theatre, Mr. Morgan. I just wonder now—" Still smiling, he signalled to Johnson, who had been sitting in a corner chair, silent spectator to the interview.

"Get Mr. Panzer, the manager, for me, Johnson," said Queen. "And if the publicity man—chap by the name of Bealson, or Pealson, or something—is around, have him step in here, too."

He turned to the lawyer after Johnson left.

"Let me trouble you for your gloves a moment, Mr. Morgan," he said lightly.

With a puzzled stare, Morgan dropped them on the desk in front of Queen, who picked them up curiously. They were of white silk—the conventional gloves for eveningwear. The Inspector pretended to be very busy examining them. He turned them inside out, minutely scrutinized a speck on the tip of one finger, and even went so far as to try them on his own hands, with a jesting remark to Morgan. His examination concluded, he gravely handed the gloves back to the lawyer.

"And—oh, yes, Mr. Morgan—that's a mighty spruce-looking tophat you've got there. May I see it a moment?"

Still silently, the lawyer placed his hat on the desk. Queen picked it up with a carefree air, whistling in a slightly flat key, "The Sidewalks of New York." He turned the hat over in his hand. It was a glistening affair of extremely fine quality. The lining was of shimmering white silk, with the name of the maker, "James Chauncey Co.," stamped in gold. Two initials, "B.M.," were similarly inlaid on the band.

Queen grinned as he placed the hat on his own head. It was a close fit. He doffed it almost immediately and returned it to Morgan.

"Very kind of you to allow me these liberties, Mr. Morgan," he said as he hastily scribbled a note on a pad which he took from his pocket.

The door opened to admit Johnson, Panzer and Harry Neilson. Panzer stepped forward hesitantly and Neilson dropped into an armchair.

"What can we do for you, Inspector?" quavered Panzer, making a valiant attempt to disregard the presence of the grizzled aristocrat slumped in his chair.

"Mr. Panzer," said Queen slowly, "how many kinds of stationery are used in the Roman Theatre?"

The manager's eyes opened wide. "Just one, Inspector. There's a sheet of it on the desk in front of you."

"Ummmm." Queen handed Panzer the slip of paper which he had received from Morgan. "I want you to examine that sheet very carefully, Mr. Panzer. To your knowledge, are there any samples of it in the Roman?"

The manager looked it over with an unfamiliar stare. "No, I don't think so. In fact, I'm sure of it. What's this?" he exclaimed as his eye caught the first few typewritten lines. "Neilson!" he cried, whirling on the publicity man. "What's this—your latest publicity stunt?" He waved the sheet in Neilson's face.

Neilson snatched it from his employer's hand and read it quickly. "Well, I'll be switched!" he said softly. "If that doesn't beat the nonstop exploitation record!" He reread it, an admiring look on his face. Then, with four pairs of eyes trained accusingly on him, he handed it back to Panzer. "I'm sorry I have to deny any share in this brilliant idea," he drawled. "Why the deuce didn't *I* think of it?" And he retreated to his corner, arms folded on his chest.

The manager turned to Queen in bewilderment. "This is very peculiar, Inspector. To my knowledge the Roman Theatre has never used this stationery, and I can state positively that I never authorized any such publicity stunt. And if Neilson denies a part in it—" He shrugged his shoulders.

Queen placed the paper carefully in his pocket. "That will be all, gentlemen. Thank you." He dismissed the two men with a nod.

He looked appraisingly at the lawyer, whose face was suffused with a fiery color that reached from his neck to the roots of his hair. The Inspector raised his hand and let it drop with a little bang on the desk.

"What do you think of *that,* Mr. Morgan?" he asked simply.

Morgan leaped to his feet. "It's a damned frame-up!" he shouted, shaking his fist in Queen's face. "I don't know any more about it than—than *you* do, if you'll pardon a little impertinence! What's more, if you think you can scare me by this hocus-pocus searching of gloves and hats and—and, by God, you haven't examined my underwear yet, Inspector!" He stopped for lack of breath, his face purple.

"But, my dear Morgan," said the Inspector mildly, "why do you upset yourself so? One would think I've been accusing you of Monte Field's murder. Sit down and cool off, man; I asked you a simple question."

Morgan collapsed in his chair. He passed a quivering hand over his forehead and muttered, "Sorry, Inspector. Lost my temper. But of all the rotten deals—" He subsided, mumbling to himself.

Queen sat staring quizzically at him. Morgan was making a great to-do with his handkerchief and cigar. Johnson coughed deprecatingly, looking up at the ceiling. Again a burst of sound penetrated the walls, only to be throttled in mid-air.

Queen's voice cut sharply into the silence. "That's all, Morgan. You may go."

The lawyer lumbered to his feet, opened his mouth as if to speak, clamped his legs together and, clapping his hat on his head, walked out of the room. Johnson innocently lounged forward to help him with the door, on a signal from the Inspector. Both men disappeared.

Queen, left alone in the room, immediately fell into a fierce preoccupation. He took from his pockets the four stubs, the letter Morgan had given him and the woman's rhinestone evening bag which he had found in the dead man's pocket. This last article he opened for the second time that evening and spread its contents on the desk before him. A few calling cards, with the name "Frances Ives-Pope" neatly engraved; two dainty lace handkerchiefs; a vanity case filled with powder, rouge and lipstick; a small change purse containing twenty dollars in bills and a few coins; and a housekey. Queen fingered these articles thoughtfully for a moment, returned them to the handbag and putting bag, stubs and letter back into his pocket once more, rose and looked slowly about. He crossed the room to the clothestree, picked up the single hat, a derby, hanging there and examined its interior. The initials "L.P." and the head-size "6⅞," seemed to interest him.

He replaced the hat and opened the door.

The four people sitting in the anteroom jumped to their feet with expressions of relief. Queen stood smiling on the threshold, his hands jammed into his pockets.

"Here we are at last," he said. "Won't you all please step into the office?"

He politely stood aside to let them pass—the three women and the young man. They trooped in with a flurry of excitement, the women sitting down as the young man busied himself setting chairs for them. Four pairs of eyes gazed earnestly at the old man by the door. He smiled paternally, took one quick glance into the anteroom, closed the door and marched in a stately way to the desk, where he sat down, feeling for his snuffbox.

"Well!" he said genially. "I must apologize for having kept you people waiting so long—official business, you know. . . . Now, let's see. Hmmm. Yes. . . . Yes, yes. I must—All right! Now, in the first place, ladies and gentleman, how do we stand?" He turned his mild gaze on the most beautiful of the three women. "I believe, miss, that your name is Frances Ives-Pope, although I haven't had the pleasure of being introduced. Am I correct?"

The girl's eyebrows went up. "That's quite correct, sir," she said in a vibrant musical voice. "Although I don't quite understand how you know my name."

She smiled. It was a magnetic smile, full of charm and a certain strong womanliness that was extremely attractive. A full-bodied creature in the bloom of youth, with great brown eyes and a creamy complexion, she radiated a wholesomeness that the Inspector found refreshing.

He beamed down at her. "Well, Miss Ives-Pope," he chuckled, "I suppose it is mysterious to a layman. And the fact that I am a policeman no doubt heightens the general effect. But it's quite simple. You are by no means an unphotographed young lady—I saw your picture in the paper today, as a matter of fact, on the society page."

The girl laughed, a trifle nervously. "So that's how it was!" she said. "I was beginning to be frightened. Just what is it, sir, that you want of me?"

"Business—always business," said the Inspector ruefully. "Just when I'm getting interested in someone I'm brought bang-up against my profession. . . . Before we conduct our inquisition, may I ask who your friends are?"

An embarrassed coughing arose from the three people on whom Queen bent his eyes. Frances said charmingly, "I'm sorry—Inspector, is it? Allow me to introduce Miss Hilda Orange and Miss Eve Ellis, my very dear friends. And this is Mr. Stephen Barry, my fiancé."

Queen glanced at them in some surprise. "If I'm not mistaken—aren't you members of the cast of 'Gunplay'?"

There was a unanimous nodding of heads.

Queen turned to Frances. "I don't want to seem too officious, Miss Ives-Pope, but I want you to explain something. . . . Why are you accompanied by your friends?" he asked with a disarming smile. "I know it sounds impertinent, but I distinctly recall ordering my man to summon you—alone. . . ."

The three thespians rose stiffly. Frances turned from her companions to the Inspector with a pleading look.

"I—please forgive me, Inspector," she said swiftly. "I—I've never been questioned by the police before. I was nervous and—and I asked my fiancé and these two ladies, who are my most intimate friends, to be present during the interview. I didn't realize that I was going against your wishes. . . ."

"I understand," returned Queen, smiling. "I understand completely. But you see—" He made a gesture of finality.

Stephen Barry leaned over the girl's chair. "I'll stay with you, dear, if you give the word." He glared at the Inspector belligerently.

"But, Stephen, dear—" Frances cried helplessly. Queen's face was adamant. "You—you'd better all go. But please wait for me outside. It won't take long, will it, Inspector?" she asked, her eyes unhappy.

Queen shook his head. "Not so very long." His entire attitude had changed. He seemed to be growing truculent. His audience sensed the metamorphosis in him and in an intangible manner grew antagonistic.

Hilda Orange, a large buxom woman of forty, with traces of a handsome youth in her face, now brutally shorn of its make-up in the cold light of the room, leaned over Frances and glared at the Inspector.

"We'll be waiting outside for you, my dear," she said grimly. "And if you feel faint, or something, just screech a little and you'll see what action means." She flounced out of the room. Eve Ellis patted Frances' hand. "Don't worry, Frances," she said in her soft, clear voice. "We're with you." And taking Barry's arm, she followed Hilda Orange. Barry looked back with a mixture of anger and solicitude, shooting a vitriolic glance at Queen as he slammed the door.

Queen was instantly on his feet, his manner brisk and impersonal. He gazed fully into Frances' eyes, his palms pressed against the top surface of the desk. "Now, Miss Frances Ives-Pope," he said curtly, "this is all the business I have to transact with you. . . ." He dipped into his pocket and produced with something of the stage-magician's celerity the rhinestone bag. "I want to return your bag."

Frances half-rose to her feet, staring from him to the shimmering purse, the color drained from her face. "Why, that's—that's my evening bag!" she stammered.

"Precisely, Miss Ives-Pope," said Queen. "It was found in the theatre—tonight."

"Of course!" The girl dropped back into her seat with a little nervous laugh. "How stupid of me! And I didn't miss it until now. . . ."

"But, Miss Ives-Pope," the little Inspector continued deliberately, "the finding of your purse is not nearly so important as the place in which it was found." He paused. "You know that there was a man murdered here this evening?"

She stared at him open-mouthed, a wild fear gathering in her eyes. "Yes, I heard so," she breathed.

"Well, your bag, Miss Ives-Pope," continued Queen inexorably, "was found in the murdered man's pocket!"

Terror gleamed in the girl's eyes. Then, with a choked scream, she toppled forward in the chair, her face white and strained.

Queen sprang forward, concern and sympathy instantly apparent on his face. As he reached the limp form, the door burst open and Stephen Barry, coat tails flying, catapulted into the room. Hilda Orange, Eve Ellis and Johnson, the detective, hurried in behind him.

"What in hell have you done to her, you damned snooper!" the actor cried, shouldering Queen out of the way. He gathered Frances' body tenderly in his arms, pushing aside the wisps of black hair tumbled over her eyes, crooning desperately in her ear. She sighed and looked up in bewilderment as she saw the flushed young face close to hers. "Steve, I—fainted," she murmured, and dropped back in his arms.

"Get some water, somebody," the young man growled, chafing her hands. A tumbler was promptly pushed over his shoulder by Johnson. Barry forced a few drops down Frances' throat and she choked, coming back to consciousness. The two actresses pushed Barry aside and brusquely ordered the men to leave. Queen meekly followed the protesting actor and the detective.

"You're a fine cop, you are!" said Barry scathingly, to the Inspector. "What did you do to her—hit her over the head with the policeman's usual finesse?"

"Now, now, young man," said Queen mildly, "no harsh words, please. The young lady simply received a shock."

They stood in a strained silence until the door opened and the actresses appeared supporting Frances between them. Barry flew to her side. "Are you all right now, dear?" he whispered, pressing her hand.

"Please—Steve—take me—home," she gasped, leaning heavily on his arm.

Inspector Queen stood aside to let them pass. There was a mournful look in his eyes as he watched them walk slowly to the main door and join the short line going out.

6

IN WHICH THE DISTRICT ATTORNEY TURNS BIOGRAPHER

Inspector Richard Queen was a peculiar man. Small and wiry, thatched with gray and wrinkled in fine lines of experience, he might have been a business executive, a night watchman, or what he chose. Certainly, in the proper raiment, his quiet figure would mold itself to any disguise.

This ready adaptability was carried out in his manner as well. Few people knew him as he was. To his associates, to his enemies, to the forlorn scraps of humanity whom he turned over to the due processes of the law, he remained ever a source of wonder. He could be theatrical when he chose, or mild, or pompous, or fatherly, or bulldogging.

But underneath, as someone had said with an overemphatic sentimentality, the Inspector had "a heart of gold." Inside he was harmless, and keen, and not a little hurt by the cruelties of the world. It was true that to the people who officially came under his eye he was never twice the same. He was constantly whirling into some new facet of personality. He found this to be good business; people never understood him, never knew what he was going to do or say, and consequently they were always a little afraid of him.

Now that he was alone, back in Panzer's office, the door shut tight, his investigations temporarily halted, the true character of the man shone from his face. At this moment it was an old face—old physically, old and wise spiritually. The incident of the girl he had startled into unconsciousness was uppermost in his mind. The memory of her drawn, horrified face made him wince. Frances Ives-Pope seemed to personify everything a man of years could hope for in his own daughter. To see her shrink under the lash pained him. To see her fiancé turn fiercely in her defense made him blush.

Abstemious except for his one mild dissipation, the Inspector reached for his snuffbox with a sigh and sniffed freely. . . .

When there came a peremptory knock on the door, he was the chameleon again—a detective-inspector sitting at a desk and no doubt thinking clever and ponderous thoughts. In truth, he was wishing that Ellery would come back.

At his hearty "Come in!" the door swung open to admit a thin, bright-eyed man dressed in heavy overclothes, a woolen muffler wound about his neck.

"Henry!" exclaimed the Inspector, starting to his feet "What the dickens are you doing here? I thought the doctor had ordered you to stay in bed!"

District Attorney Henry Sampson winked as he slumped into an armchair.

"Doctors," he said didactically, "doctors give me a pain in the neck. How are tricks?"

He groaned and felt his throat gingerly. The Inspector sat down again.

"For a grown man, Henry," he said decisively, "you're the most unruly patient I've ever seen. Man alive, you'll catch pneumonia if you don't watch out!"

"Well," grinned the District Attorney, "I carry a lot of insurance, so I should worry. . . . You haven't answered my question."

"Oh, yes," grunted Queen. "Your question. How's tricks, I think you asked? Tricks, my dear Henry, are at present in a state of complete nullity. Does that satisfy you?"

"Kindly be more explicit," said Sampson. "Remember, I'm a sick man and my head is buzzing."

"Henry," said Queen, leaning forward earnestly, "I warn you that we're in the midst of one of the toughest cases this department has ever handled. . . . Is *your* head buzzing? I'd hate to tell you what's happening in mine!"

Sampson regarded him with a frown. "If it's as you say—and I suppose it is—this comes at a rotten time. Election's not so far off—an unsolved murder handled by the improper parties. . . ."

"Well, that's one way of looking at it," remarked Queen, in a low voice. "I wasn't exactly thinking of this affair in terms of votes, Henry. A man's been killed—and at the moment I'll be frank enough to admit that I haven't the slightest idea who did the job or how."

"I accept your well-meant rebuke, Inspector," said Sampson,

in a lighter tone. "But if you'd heard what I did a few moments ago—over the telephone . . ."

"One moment, my dear Watson, as Ellery would say," chuckled Queen, with that startling change of temperament so characteristic of him. "I'll bet I know what happened. You were at home, probably in bed. Your telephone rang. A voice began to crab, protest, gurgle, and do all the other things a voice does when its owner is excited. The voice said, 'I won't stand for being cooped up by the police, like a common criminal! I want that man Queen severely reprimanded! He's a menace to personal liberty!' And so on, in words of that general tenor. . . ."

"My dear fellow!" said Sampson, laughing.

"This gentleman, the owner of the protesting voice," continued the Inspector, "is short, rather stout, wears goldrimmed eyeglasses, has an exceedingly disagreeable feminine voice, displays a really touching concern for his 'very good friend, District Attorney Sampson.' Correct?"

Sampson sat staring at him. Then his keen face creased into a smile.

"Perfectly astounding, my dear Holmes!" he murmured. "Since you know so much about my friend, perhaps it would be child's play for you to give me his name?"

"Er—but that was the fellow, wasn't it?" said Queen, his face scarlet. "I—Ellery, my boy! I'm glad to see you!"

Ellery had entered the room. He shook hands cordially with Sampson, who greeted him with a pleasure born of long association, and made a remark about the dangers of a District Attorney's life, briskly setting down on the desk a huge container of coffee and a paper bag pleasantly suggestive of French pastry.

"Well, gentlemen, the great search is finished, over, *kaput*, and the perspiring detectives will now partake of midnight tiffin." He laughed and slapped his father affectionately on the shoulder.

"But, Ellery!" cried Queen delightedly. "This is a welcome surprise! Henry, will you join us in a little celebration?" He filled three paper cups with the steaming coffee.

"I don't know what you're celebrating, but count me in," said Sampson and the three men fell to with enthusiasm.

"What's happened, Ellery?" asked the old man, sipping his coffee contentedly.

"Gods do not eat, neither do they drink," murmured Ellery from behind a cream puff. "I am not omnipotent, and suppose you tell me what happened in your impromptu torture chamber. . . . I can tell you one thing you don't know, however. Mr. Libby, of Libby's ice-cream parlor, whence came these elegant cakes, confirms Jess Lynch's story about the ginger ale. And Miss Elinor Libby nicely corroborated the alley story."

Queen wiped his lips daintily with a huge handkerchief. "Well, let Prouty make sure about the ginger ale, anyway. As for me, I interviewed several people and now I have nothing to do."

"Thank you," remarked Ellery dryly. "That was a perfect recitation. Have you acquainted the D. A. with the events of this tumultuous evening?"

"Gentlemen," said Sampson, setting down his cup, "here's what I know. About a half-hour ago I was telephoned by 'one of my very good friends'—who happens to wield a little power behind the scenes—and he told me in no uncertain terms that during tonight's performance a man was murdered. Inspector Richard Queen, he said, had descended upon the theatorium like a whirlwind, accompanied by his minor whirlwinds, and had proceeded to make everybody wait over an hour—an inexcusable, totally unwarranted procedure, my friend charged. He further deposed that said Inspector even went so far as to accuse him personally of the crime, and had domineering policemen search him and his wife and daughter before they were allowed to leave the theatre.

"So much for my informant's story—the rest of his conversation, being rather profane, is irrelevant. The only other thing I know is that Velie told me outside who the murdered man was. And *that*, gentlemen, was the most interesting part of the whole story."

"You know almost as much about this case as I do," grunted Queen. "Probably more, because I have an idea you are thoroughly familiar with Field's operation. . . . Ellery, what happened outside during the search?"

Ellery crossed his legs comfortably. "As you might have guessed, the search of the audience was entirely without result. Nothing out of the way was found. Not one solitary thing. Nobody looked guilty, and nobody took it upon himself to confess. In other words, it was a complete fiasco."

"Of course, of course," said Queen. "There's somebody almighty clever behind this business. I suppose you didn't even come across the suspicion of an extra hat?"

"That, Dad," remarked Ellery, "was what I was decorating the lobby for. No—no hat."

"Are they all through out there?"

"Just finished when I strolled across the street for the refreshments," said Ellery. "There was nothing else to do but allow the angry mob in the gallery to file downstairs and out into the street. Everybody's out now—the galleryites, the employees, the cast. . . . Queer species, actors. All night they play God and then suddenly they find themselves reduced to ordinary street clothes and the ills that flesh is heir to. By the way, Velie also searched the five people who came out of this office. Quite a motor that young lady possesses. Miss Ives-Pope and her party, I gathered. . . . Didn't know but that you might have forgotten them," he chuckled.

"So we're up a tree, eh?" muttered the Inspector. "Here's the story, Henry." And he gave a concise résumé of the evening's events to Sampson, who sat silently throughout, frowning.

"And that," concluded Queen, after describing briefly the scenes enacted in the little office, "is that. Now, Henry, you must have something to tell us about Monte Field. We know that he was a slick article—but that's all we do know."

"That would be putting it mildly," said Sampson savagely. "I can give you almost by rote the story of his life. It looks to me as if you're going to have a difficult time and some incident in his past might give you a clue.

"Field first came under the scrutiny of my office during my predecessor's regime. He was suspected of negotiating a swindle connected with the bucket-shop scandals. Cronin, an assistant D. A. at the time, couldn't get a thing on him. Field had covered his operations well. All we had was the telltale story, which might or might not have been true, of a 'stool pigeon' who had been kicked out of the mob. Of course, Cronin never let on to Field directly or indirectly that he was under suspicion. The affair blew over and although Cronin was a bulldog, every time he thought he had something he found that he had nothing after all. Oh, no question about it—Field was slick."

"When I came into office, on Cronin's fervent suggestion we began an exhaustive investigation of Field's background. On the q. t., of course. And this is what we discovered: Monte Field came of a blue-blood New England family—the kind that doesn't brag about its Mayflower descendants. He had private tutoring as a kid, went to a swanky prep school, got through by the skin of his teeth and then was sent to Harvard by his father as a sort of last despairing gesture. He seems to have been a pretty bad egg even as a boy. Nothing criminal, but just wild. On the other hand, he must have had a grain of pride because when the blow-up came he actually shortened his name. The family name was Fielding—and he became Monte Field."

Queen and Ellery nodded, Ellery's eyes introspective, Queen staring steadily at Sampson.

"Field," resumed Sampson, "wasn't a total loss, understand. He had brains. He studied law brilliantly at Harvard. He seemed to have a flair for oratory that was considerably aided by his profound knowledge of legal technology. But just after graduation, before his family could get even the bit of pleasure out of his scholastic career that should have been theirs, he was mixed up in a dirty deal with a girl. His father cut him off in jigtime. He was through—out—he'd disgraced the family name—you know the sort of thing. . . .

"Well, this friend of ours didn't let grief overwhelm him, evidently. He made the best of being done out of a nice little legacy, and decided to go out and make some money on his own. How he managed to get along during this period we couldn't find out, but the next thing we hear of him is that he has formed a partnership with a fellow by the name of Cohen. One of the smoothest shysters in the business. What a partnership that was! They cleaned up a fortune between them establishing a select clientele chosen from among the biggest crooks in crookdom. Now, you know as well as I just how hard it is to 'get' anything on a bird who knows more about the loopholes of the law than the Supreme Court judges. They got away with everything—it was a golden era for crime. Crooks considered themselves top-notch when Cohen & Field were kind enough to defend them."

"And then Mr. Cohen, who was the experienced man of the combination, knowing the ropes, making the 'contacts' with the firm's clients, fixing the fees—and he could do that beautifully in spite of his inability to speak untainted English—Mr. Cohen, I say, met a very sad end one winter night on the North River waterfront. He was found shot through the head, and although it's twelve years since the happy event, the murderer is still unknown. That is—unknown in the legal sense. We had grave suspicions as to his identity. I shouldn't be at all surprised if Mr. Field's demise this evening removed the Cohen case from the register."

"So that's the kind of playboy he was," murmured Ellery. "Even in death his face is most disagreeable. Too bad I had to lose my first edition on his account."

"Forget it, you bookworm," growled his father. "Go on, Henry."

"Now," said Sampson, taking the last piece of cake from the desk and munching it heartily, "now we come to a bright spot in Mr. Field's life. For after the unfortunate decease of his partner, he seemed to turn over a new leaf. He actually went to work—real legal work—and of course he had the brains to pull it through. For a number of years he worked alone, gradually effacing the bad reputation he had built up in the profession and even gaining a little respect now and then from some of our hoity-toity legal lights.

"This period of apparent good behavior lasted for six years. Then he met Ben Morgan—a solid man with a spotless record and a good reputation, although perhaps lacking the vital spark which makes the great lawyer. Somehow Field persuaded Morgan to join him in partnership. Then things began to hum."

"You'll remember that in that period some highly shady things were happening in New York. We got faint inklings of a gigantic criminal ring, composed of 'fences,' crooks, lawyers, and in some cases politicians. Some smashing big robberies were pulled off; bootlegging got to be a distinct art in the city environs; and a number of daring hold-ups resulting in murder put the department on its toes. But you know that as well as I do. You fellows 'got' some of them; but you never broke the ring, and you never reached the men higher up. And I have every reason to believe that our late friend Mr. Monte Field was the brains behind the whole business."

"See how easy it was for a man of his talents. Under the tutelage of Cohen, his first partner, he had become thoroughly familiar with the underworld moguls. When Cohen outlived his usefulness, he was conveniently bumped off. Then Field—remember, I am working now on speculation chiefly, because the evidence is practically nil—then Field, under the cloak of a respectable legal business, absolutely aboveboard, quietly built up a far-flung criminal organization. How he accomplished this we have no way of knowing, of course. When he was quite ready to shoot the works, he tied up with a well-known respectable partner, Morgan, and now secure in his legal position, began to engineer most of the big crooked deals pulled off in the last five years or so. . . ."

"Where does Morgan come in?" asked Ellery idly.

"I was coming to that. Morgan, we have every reason to believe, was absolutely innocent of any connection with Field's undercover operations. He was as straight as a die and in fact had often refused cases in which the defendant was a shady character. Their relations must have become strained when Morgan got a hint of what was going on. Whether this is so or not I don't know—you could easily find out from Morgan himself. Anyway, they broke up. Since the dissolution, Field has operated a little more in the open, but still not a shred of tangible evidence which would count in a court of law."

"Pardon me for interrupting, Henry," said Queen reflectively, "but can't you give me a little more information on their break-up? I'd like to use it as a check on Morgan when I talk to him again."

"Oh, yes!" replied Sampson grimly. "I'm glad you reminded me. Before the last word was written in the dissolving of the partnership, the two men had a terrific blow-up which almost resulted in tragedy. At the Webster Club, where they were lunching, they were heard quarreling violently. The argument increased until it was necessary for the bystanders to interfere. Morgan was beside himself with rage and actually threatened Field's life right then and there. Field, I understand, was quite calm."

"Did any of the witnesses get an inkling of the cause of the quarrel?" asked Queen.

"Unfortunately, no. The thing blew over soon enough; they dissolved quietly and that was the last anybody ever heard of it. Until, of course, tonight."

There was a pregnant silence when the District Attorney stopped talking. Ellery whistled a few bars of a Schubert air, while Queen frankly took a pinch of snuff with a ferocious vigor.

"I'd say, offhand," murmured Ellery, looking off into space, "that Mr. Morgan is in deucedly hot water."

His father grunted. Sampson said seriously, "Well, that's your affair, gentlemen. I know what my job is. Now that Field is out of the way, I'm going to have his files and records gone over with a fine comb. If nothing else, his murder will accomplish eventually, I hope, the complete annihilation of his gang. I'll have a man at his office in the morning."

"One of my men is camping there already," remarked Queen absently. "So you think it's Morgan, do you?" he asked Ellery, with a flash of his eyes.

"I seem to recall making a remark a minute ago," said Ellery calmly, "to the effect that Mr. Morgan is in hot water. I did not commit myself further. I admit that Morgan seems to be the logical man—except, gentlemen, for one thing," he added.

"The hat," said Inspector Queen instantly.

"*No,*" said Ellery, *"the other hat."*

7

THE QUEENS TAKE STOCK

"Let's see where we stand," continued Ellery without pausing. "Let's consider this thing in its most elementary light.

"These, roughly, are the facts: A man of shady character, Monte Field, probable head of a vast criminal organization, with undoubtedly a host of enemies, is found murdered in the Roman Theatre ten minutes before the end of the second act, at precisely 9:55 o'clock. He is discovered by a man named William Pusak, a clerk of an inferior type of intelligence, who is sitting five seats away in the same row. This man, attempting to leave, pushes his way past the victim who before he dies mutters, 'Murder! Been murdered!' or words to that effect."

"A policeman is called and to make sure the man is dead, secures the services of a doctor in the audience, who definitely pronounces the victim killed by some form of alcoholic poisoning. Subsequently Dr. Prouty, the Assistant Medical Examiner, confirms this statement, adding that there is only one disturbing factor—that a man would not die so soon from lethal alcohol. The question of the cause of death, therefore, we must leave for the moment, since only an autopsy can definitely determine it."

"With a large audience to attend to, the policeman calls for help, officers of the vicinity come in to take charge and subsequently the headquarters men arrive to conduct the immediate investigation. The first important issue that arises is the question of whether the murderer had the opportunity to leave the scene of the crime between the time it was committed and the time it was discovered. Doyle, the policeman who was first on the scene, immediately ordered the manager to station guards at all exits and both alleys."

"When I arrived, I thought of this point the very first thing and conducted a little investigation of my own. I went around to all the exits and questioned the guards. I discovered that there was a guard at every door of the auditorium during the entire second act, with two exceptions which I shall mention shortly. Now, it had been determined from the testimony of the orangeade boy, Jess Lynch, that the victim was alive not only during the intermission between Act I and Act II—when he saw and talked to Field in the alleyway—but that Field was also in apparently good health ten minutes after the raising of the curtain for Act II. This was when the boy delivered a bottle of ginger ale to Field at the seat in which he was later found dead. Inside the theatre, an usher stationed at the foot of the stairs leading to the balcony swore that no one had either gone up or come down during the second act. This eliminates the possibility that the murderer had access to the balcony."

"The two exceptions I noted a moment ago are the two doors on the extreme left aisle, which should have been guarded but were not because the usherette, Madge O'Connell, was sitting in the audience next to her lover. This presented to my mind the possibility that the murderer might have left by one of these two doors, which were conveniently placed for an escape should the murderer have been so inclined. However, even this possibility was eliminated by the statement of the O'Connell girl, whom I hunted up after she was questioned by Dad."

"You talked to her on the sly, did you, you scalawag?" roared Queen, glaring at Ellery.

"I certainly did," chuckled Ellery, "and I discovered the one important fact that seems pertinent to this phase of the investigation. O'Connell swore that before she left the doors to sit down next to Parson Johnny she stepped on the inside floorlock that latches them top and bottom. When the commotion began the girl sprang from the Parson's side and finding the doors locked as she had left them, unlatched them while Doyle was attempting to quiet the audience. Unless she was lying—and I don't think she was—this proves that the murderer did not leave by these doors, since at the time the body was found they were still locked from the inside."

"Well, I'll be switched!" growled Queen. "She didn't tell me a thing about that part of it, drat her! Wait till I get my hands on her, the little snip!"

"Please be logical, *M. le Gardien de la Paix,*" laughed Ellery.

"The reason she didn't tell you about bolting the doors was that you didn't ask her. She felt that she was in enough of an uncomfortable position already.

"At any rate, that statement of hers would seem to dispose of the two side doors near the murdered man's seat. I will admit that all sorts of possibilities enter into the problem—for example, Madge O'Connell might have been an accomplice. I mention this only as a possibility, and not even as a theory. At any rate, it seems to me that the murderer would not have run the risk of being seen leaving from side doors. Besides, a departure in so unusual a manner and at so unusual a time would have been all the more noticeable especially since few people leave during a second act. And again—the murderer could have no foreknowledge of the O'Connell girl's dereliction in duty—if she were not an accomplice. As the crime was carefully planned—and we must admit that from all indications it was—the murderer would have discarded the side doors as a means of escape."

"This probe left, I felt, only one other channel of investigation. That was the main entrance. And here again we received definite testimony from the ticket-taker and the doorman outside to the effect that no one *left* the building during the second act by that route. Except, of course, the harmless orangeade boy."

"All the exits having been guarded or locked, and the alley having been under constant surveillance from 9:35 on by Lynch, Elinor, Johnny Chase—the usher—and after him the police—these being the facts, all my questioning and checking, gentlemen," continued Ellery in a grave tone, "lead to the inevitable conclusion that, from the time the murder was discovered and all the time thereafter while the investigation was going on, *the murderer was in the theatre!*"

A silence followed Ellery's pronouncement. "Incidentally," he added calmly, "it occurred to me when I talked to the ushers to ask if they had seen anyone leave his seat after the second act started, and they can't recall anyone changing seats!"

Queen idly took another pinch of snuff. "Nice work—and a very pretty piece of reasoning, my son—but nothing, after all, of a startling or conclusive nature. Granted that the murderer was in the theatre all that time—how could we possibly have laid our hands on him?"

"He didn't say you could," put in Sampson, smiling. "Don't be so sensitive, old boy; nobody's going to report you for negligence in the performance of your duty. From all I've heard tonight you handled the affair well."

Queen grunted. "I'll admit I'm a little peeved at myself for not following up that matter of the doors more thoroughly. But even if it were possible for the murderer to have left directly after the crime, I nevertheless would have had to pursue the inquiry as I did, on the chance that he was still in the theatre."

"But Dad—of course!" said Ellery seriously. "You had so many things to attend to, while all I had to do was stand around and look Socratic."

"How about the people who have come under the eye of the investigation so far?" asked Sampson curiously.

"Well, what about them?" challenged Ellery. "We certainly can draw no definite conclusions from either their conversation or their actions. We have Parson Johnny, a thug, who was there apparently for no other reason than to enjoy a play giving some interesting sidelights on his own profession. Then there is Madge O'Connell, a very doubtful character about whom we can make no decision at this stage of the game. She might be an accomplice—she might be innocent—she might be merely negligent—she might be almost anything. Then there is William Pusak, who found Field. Did you notice the moronic cast of his head? And Benjamin Morgan—here we strike fallow ground in the realm of probability. But what do we know of his actions tonight? True, his story of the letter and the complimentary ticket sounds queer, since anyone could have written the letter, even Morgan himself. And we must always remember the public threat against Field; and also the enmity, reason unknown, which has existed between them for two years. And, lastly, we have Miss Frances Ives-Pope. I'm exceedingly sorry I was absent during that interview. The fact remains—and isn't it an interesting one?—that her evening bag was found in the dead man's pocket. Explain that if you can.

"So you see where we are," Ellery continued ruefully. "All we have managed to derive from this evening's entertainment is a plethora of suspicions and a poverty of facts."

"So far, son," said Queen casually, "you have kept on mighty safe ground. But you've forgotten the important matter of the suspiciously vacant seats. Also the rather startling fact that Field's ticket stub and the only other stub that could be attributed to the murderer—I refer to the LL30 Left stub found by Flint—that these two stubs do not coincide. That is to say, that the torn edges indicate they were gathered by the ticket-taker at different times!"

"Check," said Ellery. "But let's leave that for the moment and get on to the problem of Field's tophat."

"The hat—well, what do you think of it?" asked Queen curiously.

"Just this. In the first place, we have fairly established the fact that the hat is not missing through accident. The murdered man was seen by Jess Lynch with the hat in his lap ten minutes after Act II began. Now—for the moment, let's forget the problem of where the hat is now. The immediate conclusion to draw is that the hat was taken away for one of two reasons: first, that it was in some way incriminating in itself, so that if it were left behind it would point to the murderer's identity. What the nature of this incriminating indication is we cannot even guess at the moment. Second, the hat may have contained something which the murderer wanted. You will say: Why couldn't he take this mysterious object and leave the hat? Probably, if this supposition is true, because he either had not sufficient time to extract it, or else did not know *how* to extract it and therefore took the hat away with him to examine it at his leisure. Do you agree with me so far?"

The District Attorney nodded slowly. Queen sat still, his eyes vaguely troubled.

"Let us for a moment consider what the hat could possibly have contained," resumed Ellery, as he vigorously polished his glasses. "Due to its size, shape and cubic content our field of speculation is not a broad one. What could be hidden in a tophat? The only things that present themselves to my mind are: papers of some sort, jewelry, banknotes, or any other small object of value which could not easily be detected in such a place.

Obviously, this problematical object would not be carried merely in the crown of the hat since it would fall out whenever the wearer uncovered his head. We are led to believe therefore that, whatever the object was, it was concealed in the lining of the hat. This immediately narrows our list of possibilities. Solid objects of bulk must be eliminated. A jewel might have been concealed; banknotes or papers might have been concealed. We can, I think, discard the jewel, from what we know of Monte Field. If he was carrying anything of value, it would probably be connected in some way with his profession.

"One point remains to be considered in this preliminary analysis of the missing tophat. And, gentlemen, it may very well become a pivotal consideration before we are through. It is of paramount importance for us to know whether the murderer knew in advance of his crime that it would be necessary for him to take away Monte Field's tophat. In other words, did the murderer have *foreknowledge* of the hat's significance, whatever it may prove to be? I maintain that the facts prove deductively, as logically as facts *can* prove deductively, that the murderer had no foreknowledge."

"Follow me closely. . . . Since Monte Field's tophat is missing, and since no other tophat has been found in its place, it is an undeniable indication that it was essential that it be taken away. You must agree that, as I pointed out before, the murderer is most plausibly the remover of the hat. Now! Regardless of *why* it had to be taken away, we are faced with two alternatives: one, that the murderer knew in advance that it had to be taken away; or two, that he did *not* know in advance. Let us exhaust the possibilities in the former case. If he knew in advance, it may be surely and logically assumed that he would have brought with him to the theatre a hat to replace Field's, rather than leave an obvious clue by the provocative absence of the murdered man's hat. To bring a replacement hat would have been the safe thing to do. The murderer would have had no difficulty in securing a replacement hat, since knowing its importance in advance, he could certainly have armed himself with a further knowledge of Field's head-size, style of tophat, and other minor details. *But there is no replacement hat.* We have every right to expect a replacement hat in a crime so carefully concocted as this one. There being none, our only conclusion can be that the murderer did not know beforehand the importance of Field's hat; otherwise he would assuredly have taken the intelligent precaution of leaving another hat behind. In this way the police would never know that Field's hat had any significance at all."

"Another point in corroboration. Even if the murderer didn't desire, for some dark reason of his own, to leave a replacement hat, he certainly would have arranged to secure what was in the hat by cutting it out. All he had to do was to provide himself in advance with a sharp instrument—a pocket knife, for example. The *empty* hat, though cut, would not have presented the problem of disposal that the *missing* hat would. Surely the murderer would have preferred this procedure, had he foreknowledge of the hat's contents. But he did not do even this. This, it seems to me, is strong corroborative evidence that he did not know before he came to the Roman Theatre that he would have to take away a hat or its contents. *Quod erat demonstrandum.*"

The District Attorney gazed at Ellery with puckered lips. Inspector Queen seemed sunk in a lethargy. His hand hovered midway between his snuffbox and his nose.

"Just what's the point, Ellery?" inquired Sampson. "Why is it important for you to know that the murderer had no foreknowledge of the hat's significance?"

Ellery smiled. "Merely this. The crime was committed after the beginning of the second act. I want to be sure in my own mind that the murderer, by not knowing in advance of the hat's significance, could not have used the first intermission in any manner whatsoever as an essential element of his plan. . . . Of course, Field's hat may turn up somewhere on the premises, and its discovery would invalidate all these speculations. But—I don't think it will. . . ."

"That analysis of yours might be elementary, boy, but it sounds quite logical to me," said Sampson approvingly. "You should have been a lawyer."

"You can't beat the Queen brains," chuckled the old man suddenly, his face wreathed in a wide smile. "But I'm going to get busy on another tack that ought to jibe somewhere with this puzzle of the hat. You noticed, Ellery, the name of the clothier sewed into Field's coat?"

"No sooner said than done," grinned Ellery. Producing one of the small volumes which he carried in his topcoat pocket, he opened it and pointed to a notation on the flyleaf. "Browne Bros., gentlemen—no less."

"That's right; and I'll have Velie down there in the morning to check up," said the Inspector. "You must have realized that

Field's clothing is of exceptional quality. That evening-suit cost three hundred dollars, if it cost a penny. And Browne Bros. are the artists to charge such fashionable prices. But there's another point in this connection: every stitch of clothing on the dead man's body had the same manufacturer's mark. That's not uncommon with wealthy men; and Browne's made a specialty of outfitting their customers from head to foot. What more probable to assume—"

"Than that Field bought his hats there, too!" exclaimed Sampson, with an air of discovery.

"Exactly, Tacitus," said Queen, grinning. "Velie's job is to check up on this clothing business and if possible secure an exact duplicate of the hat Field wore tonight. I'm mighty anxious to look it over."

Sampson rose with a cough. "I suppose I really ought to get back to bed," he said. "The only reason I came down here was to see that you didn't arrest the Mayor. Boy, that friend of mine was sore! I'll never hear the end of it!"

Queen looked up at him with a quizzical smile. "Before you go, Henry, suppose you tell me just where I stand on this thing. I know that I used a pretty high hand tonight, but you must realize how necessary it was. Are you going to put one of your own men on the case?"

Sampson glared at him. "When did you get the idea I wasn't satisfied with your conduct of the investigation, you old canary bird!" he growled. "I've never checked you up yet, and I'm not going to start now. If you can't bring this thing to a successful conclusion, I certainly don't think any of my men can. My dear

Q, go ahead and detain half of New York if you think it's necessary. I'll back you up."

"Thanks, Henry," said Queen. "I just wanted to be sure. Add now, since you're so nice about it, watch my smoke!"

He ambled across the room into the anteroom, stuck his head past the doorway into the theatre, and shouted, "Mr. Panzer, will you come here a moment?"

He came back smiling grimly to himself, the swarthy theatre manager close on his heels.

"Mr. Panzer, meet District Attorney Sampson," said Queen. The two men shook hands. "Now, Mr. Panzer, you've got one more job and you can go home and go to sleep. I want this theatre shut down so tight a mouse couldn't get into it!"

Panzer grew pale. Sampson shrugged his shoulders, as if to indicate that he washed his hands of the entire affair. Ellery nodded sagely in approval.

"But—but Inspector, just when we're playing to capacity!" groaned the little manager. "Is it absolutely necessary?"

"So necessary, my dear man," answered the Inspector coolly, "that I'm going to have two men here patrolling the premises all the time."

Panzer wrung his hands, looking furtively at Sampson. But the District Attorney was standing with his back to them, examining a print on the wall.

"This is terrible, Inspector!" wailed Panzer. "I'll never hear the end of it from Gordon Davis, the producer. . . . But of course—if you say so, it will be done."

"Heck, man, don't look so blue," said Queen, more kindly.

"You'll be getting so much publicity out of this that when the show reopens you'll have to enlarge the theatre. I don't expect to have the theatre shut down more than a few days, anyway. I'll give the necessary orders to my men outside. After you've transacted your routine business here tonight, just tip off the men I've left and go home. I'll let you know in a few days when you can reopen."

Panzer waggled his head sadly, shook hands all around and left. Sampson immediately whirled on Queen and said, "By the Lord Harry, Q, that's going some! Why do you want the theatre closed? You've milked it dry, haven't you?"

"Well, Henry," said Queen slowly, "the hat hasn't been found. All those people filed out of the theatre and were searched—and each one had just one hat. Doesn't that indicate that the hat we're looking for is still here somewhere? And if it's still here, I'm not giving anybody a chance to come in and take it away. If there's any taking to be done, I'll do it."

Sampson nodded. Ellery was still wearing a worried frown as the three men walked out of the office into the almost deserted orchestra. Here and there a busy figure was stooping over a seat, examining the floor. A few men could be seen darting in and out of the boxes up front. Sergeant Velie stood by the main door, talking in low tones to Piggott and Hagstrom. Detective Flint, superintending a squad of men, was working far to the front of the orchestra. A small group of cleaning women operated vacuum cleaners tiredly here and there. In one corner, to the rear, a buxom police matron was talking with an elderly woman—the woman Panzer had called Mrs. Phillips.

The three men walked to the main door. While Ellery and Sampson were silently surveying the always depressing scene of an untenanted auditorium, Queen spoke rapidly to Velie, giving orders in an undertone. Finally he turned and said, "Well, gentlemen, that's all for tonight. Let's be going."

On the sidewalk a number of policemen had roped off a large space, behind which a straggling crowd of curiosity-seekers was gaping.

"Even at two o'clock in the morning these nightbirds patrol Broadway," grunted Sampson. With a wave of the hand he entered his automobile after the Queens politely refused his offer of a "lift." A crowd of businesslike reporters pushed through the lines and surrounded the two Queens.

"Here, here! What's this, gentlemen?" asked the old man, frowning.

"How about the lowdown on tonight's job, Inspector?" asked one of them urgently.

"You'll get all the information you want, boys, from Detective-Sergeant Velie—inside." He smiled as they charged in a body through the glass doors.

Ellery and Richard Queen stood silently on the curb, watching the policemen herd back the crowd. Then the old man said with a sudden wave of weariness, "Come on, son, let's walk part of the way home."

PART TWO

". . . To illustrate: Once young Jean C. ----- came to me after a month of diligent investigation on a difficult assignment. He wore a forlorn expression. Without a word he handed me a slip of official paper. I read it in surprise. It was his resignation."

"'Here, Jean!' I cried. 'What is the meaning of this?'

"'I have failed, M. Brillon,' he muttered. 'A month's work gone to the devil. I have been on the wrong track. It is a disgrace.'

"'Jean, my friend,' said I solemnly, 'this for your resignation.' Wherewith I tore it to bits before his astonished eyes. 'Go now,' I admonished him, 'and begin from the beginning. For remember always the maxim: He who would know right must first know wrong!'"

—*from* REMINISCENCES OF A PREFECT

by Auguste Brillon

8

IN WHICH THE QUEENS MEET MR. FIELD'S VERY BEST FRIEND

The Queens' apartment on West 87th Street was a man's domicile from the piperack over the hearth to the shining sabers on the wall. They lived on the top floor of a three-family brownstone house, a relic of late Victorian times. You walked up the heavily carpeted stairs through seemingly endless halls of dismal rectitude. When you were quite convinced that only mummified souls could inhabit such a dreary place, you came upon the huge oaken door marked, "The Queens"—a motto lettered neatly and framed. Then Djuna grinned at you from behind a crack and you entered a new world.

More than one individual, exalted in his own little niche, had willingly climbed the uninviting staircases to find sanctuary in this haven. More than one card bearing a famous name had been blithely carried by Djuna through the foyer into the living room.

The foyer was Ellery's inspiration, if the truth were told. It was so small and so narrow that its walls appeared unnaturally towering. With a humorous severity one wall had been completely covered by a tapestry depicting the chase—a most appropriate appurtenance to this medieval chamber. Both Queens detested it heartily, preserving it only because it had been presented to them with regal gratitude by the Duke of—, the impulsive gentleman whose son Richard Queen had saved from a noisome scandal, the details of which have never been made public. Beneath the tapestry stood a heavy mission table, displaying a parchment lamp and a pair of bronze bookends bounding a three-volume set of the Arabian Nights' Entertainment.

Two mission chairs and a small rug completed the foyer.

When you walked through this oppressive place, always gloomy and almost always hideous, you were ready for anything except the perfect cheeriness of the large room beyond. This study in contrast was Ellery's private jest, for if it were not for him the old man would long since have thrown the foyer and its furnishings into some dark limbo.

The living room was lined on three sides with a bristling and leathern-reeking series of bookcases, rising tier upon tier to the high ceiling. On the fourth wall was a huge natural fireplace, with a solid oak beam as a mantel and gleaming ironwork spacing the grate. Above the fireplace were the famous crossed sabers, a gift from the old fencing master of Nuremberg with whom Richard had lived in his younger days during his studies in Germany. Lamps winked and gleamed all over the great sprawling room; easychairs, armchairs, low divans, footstools, bright-colored leather cushions were everywhere. In a word, it was the most comfortable room two intellectual gentlemen of luxurious tastes could devise for their living quarters. And where such a place might after a time have become stale through sheer variety, the bustling person of Djuna, man-of-work, general factotum, errand boy, valet and mascot prevented such a dénouement.

Djuna had been picked up by Richard Queen during the period of Ellery's studies at college, when the old man was very much alone. This cheerful young man, nineteen years old, an orphan for as long as he could remember, ecstatically unaware of the necessity for a surname—slim and small, nervous and joyous, bubbling over with spirit and yet as quiet as a mouse when the occasion demanded—this Djuna, then, worshipped old Richard in much the same fashion as the ancient Alaskans bowed down to their totempoles. Between him and Ellery, too, there was a shy kinship which rarely found expression except in the boy's passionate service. He slept in a small room beyond the bedroom used by father and son and, according to Richard's own chuckling expression, "could hear a flea singing to its mate in the middle of the night."

On the morning after the eventful night of Monte Field's murder, Djuna was laying the cloth for breakfast when the telephone rang. The boy, accustomed to early morning calls, lifted the receiver:

"This is Inspector Queen's man Djuna talking. Who is calling, please?"

"Oh, it is, is it?" growled a bass voice over the wire. "Well, you son of a gypsy policeman, wake the Inspector for me and be quick about it!"

"Inspector Queen may not be disturbed, sir, unless his man Djuna knows who's calling." Djuna, who knew Sergeant Velie's voice especially well, grinned and stuck his tongue in his cheek.

A slim hand firmly grasped Djuna's neck and propelled him halfway across the room. The Inspector, fully dressed, his nostrils quivering appreciatively with his morning's first ration of snuff, said into the mouthpiece, "Don't mind Djuna, Thomas. What's up? This is Queen talking."

"Oh, that you, Inspector? I wouldn't have buzzed you so early in the morning except that Ritter just phoned from Monte Field's apartment. Got an interesting report," rumbled Velie.

"Well, well!" chuckled the Inspector. "So our friend Ritter's bagged someone, eh? Who is it, Thomas?"

"You guessed it, sir," came Velie's unmoved voice. "He said he's got a lady down there in an embarrassing state of deshabille and if he stays alone with her much longer his wife will divorce him. Orders, sir?"

Queen laughed heartily. "Sure enough, Thomas. Send a couple of men down there right away to chaperon him. I'll be there myself in two shakes of a lamb's tail—which is to say, as soon as I can drag Ellery out of bed."

He hung up, grinning. "Djuna!" he shouted. The boy's head popped out from behind the kitchenette door immediately. "Hurry up with the eggs and coffee, son!" The Inspector turned toward the bedroom to find Ellery, collarless but unmistakably on the road to dress, confronting him with an air of absorption.

"So you're really up?" grumbled the Inspector, easing himself into an armchair. "I thought I'd have to drag you out of bed, you sluggard!"

"You may rest easy," said Ellery absently. "I most certainly am up, and I am going to stay up. And as soon as Djuna replenishes the inner man I'll be off and out of your way." He lounged into the bedroom, reappearing a moment later brandishing his collar and tie.

"Here! Where d'ye think you're going, young man?" roared Queen, starting up.

"Down to my bookshop, Inspector darling," replied Ellery judicially. "You don't think I'm going to allow that Falconer first edition to get away from me? Really—it may still be there, you know."

"Falconer fiddlesticks," said his father grimly. "You started something and you're going to help finish it. Here—Djuna—where in time is that kid?"

Djuna stepped briskly into the room balancing a tray in one hand and a pitcher of milk in the other. In a twinkling he had the table ready, the coffee bubbling, the toast browned; and father and son hurried through their breakfast without a word.

"Now," remarked Ellery, setting down his empty cup, "now that I've finished this Arcadian repast, tell me where the fire is."

"Get your hat and coat on and stop asking pointless questions, son of my grief," growled Queen. In three minutes they were on the sidewalk hailing a taxicab.

The cab drew up before a monumental apartment building. Lounging on the sidewalk, a cigarette drooping from his lips, was Detective Piggott. The Inspector winked and trotted into the lobby. He and Ellery were whisked up to the fourth floor where Detective Hagstrom greeted them, pointing to an apartment door numbered 4-D. Ellery, leaning forward to catch the inscription on the nameplate, was about to turn on his father with an amused expostulation when the door swung open at Queen's imperious ring and the broad flushed face of Ritter peered out at them.

"Morning, Inspector," the detective mumbled, holding the door open. "I'm glad you've come, sir."

Queen and Ellery marched inside. They stood in a small foyer, profusely furnished. Directly in their line of vision was a living room, and beyond that a closed door. A frilled feminine slipper and a slim ankle were visible at the edge of the door.

The Inspector stepped forward, changed his mind and quickly opening the hall door called to Hagstrom, who was sauntering about outside. The detective ran up.

"Come inside here," said Queen sharply. "Got a job for you."

With Ellery and the two plainclothesmen following at his heels, he strode into the living room.

A woman of mature beauty, a trifle worn, the pastiness of a ruined complexion apparent beneath heavily applied rouge, sprang to her feet. She was dressed in a flowing flimsy negligée and her hair was tousled. She nervously crushed a cigarette underfoot.

"Are you the big cheese around here?" she yelled in a strident fury to Queen. He stood stock still and examined her impersonally. "Then what the hell do you mean by sending one o' your flatfoots to keep me locked up all night, hey?"

She jumped forward as if to come to grips with the old man. Ritter lumbered swiftly toward her and squeezed her arm. "Here you," he growled, "shut up until you're spoken to."

She glared at him. Then with a tigerish twist she was out of his grasp and in a chair, panting, wild-eyed.

Arms akimbo, the Inspector stood looking her up and down with unconcealed distaste. Ellery glanced at the woman briefly and began to putter about the room, peering at the wall hangings and Japanese prints, picking up a book from an end table, poking his head into dark corners.

Queen motioned to Hagstrom. "Take this lady into the next room and keep her company for a while," he said. The detective unceremoniously hustled the woman to her feet. She tossed her head defiantly and marched into the next room, Hagstrom following.

"Now, Ritter, my boy," sighed the old man, sinking into an easychair, "tell me what happened."

Ritter answered stiffly. His eyes were strained, bloodshot. "I followed out your orders last night to the dot. I beat it down here in a police car, left it on the corner because I didn't know but what somebody might be keeping a lookout, and strolled up to this apartment Everything was quiet—and I hadn't noticed any lights either, because before I went in I beat it down to the court and looked up at the back windows of the apartment. So I gave 'em a nice short ring on the bell and waited."

"No answer," continued Ritter, with a tightening of his big jaw. "I buzzed again—this time longer and louder. This time I got results. I heard the latch on the inside rattle and this woman yodels, 'That you, honey? Where's your key?' Aha—thinks I—Mr. Field's lady friend! So I shoved my foot in the door and grabbed her before she knew what was what. Well, sir, I got a surprise. Sort of expected," he grinned sheepishly, "sort of expected to find the woman dressed, but all I grabbed was a thin piece o' silk nightgown. I guess I must have blushed. . . ."

"Ah, the opportunities of our good minions of the law!" murmured Ellery, head bent over a small lacquered vase.

"Anyway," continued the detective, "I got my hands on her and she yelped—plenty. Hustled her into the living room here where she'd put on the light, and took a good look at her. She was scared blue but she was kind of plucky, too, because she began to cuss me and she wanted to know who in hell I was, what I was tryin' to do in a woman's apartment at night, and all that sort of stuff. I flashed my badge. And Inspector, that hefty Sheba—the minute she sees the badge, she shuts up tight like a bluepoint and won't answer a question I ask her!"

"Why was that?" The old man's eyes roved from floor to ceiling as he looked over the appointments of the room.

"Hard to tell, Inspector," said Ritter. "First she seemed scared, but when she saw my badge she bucked up wonderful. And the longer I was here the more brazen she became."

"You didn't tell her about Field, did you?" queried the Inspector, in a sharp, low tone.

Ritter gave his superior a reproachful glance. "Not a peep out o' me, sir," he said. "Well, when I saw it was no go tryin' to get anything out of her—all she'd yell was, 'Wait till Monte gets home, you bozo!'—I took a look at the bedroom. Nobody there, so I shoved her inside, kept the door open and the light on and stayed all night. She climbed into bed after a while and I guess she went to sleep. At about seven this morning she popped out and started to yell all over again. Seemed to think that Field had been grabbed by headquarters. Insisted on having a newspaper. I told her nothin' doin' and then phoned the office. Not another thing happened since."

"I say, Dad!" exclaimed Ellery suddenly, from a corner of the room. "What do you think our legal friend reads—you'll never guess. 'How to Tell Character from Handwriting'!"

The Inspector grunted as he rose. "Stop fiddling with those eternal books," he said, "and come along."

He flung open the bedroom door. The woman was sitting cross-legged on the bed, an ornate affair of a bastard French period style, canopied and draped from ceiling to floor with heavy damask curtains. Hagstrom leaned stolidly against the window.

Queen looked quickly about. He turned to Ritter. "Was that bed mussed up when you came in here last night—did it look as if it had been slept in?" he whispered aside.

Ritter nodded. "All right, then, Ritter," said Queen in a genial tone. "Go home and get some rest. You deserve it. And send up Piggott on your way out." The detective touched his hat and departed.

Queen turned on the woman. He walked to the bed and sat down beside her, studying her half-averted face. She lit a cigarette defiantly.

"I am Inspector Queen of the police, my dear," announced the old man mildly. "I warn you that any attempt to keep a stubborn silence or lie to me will only get you into a heap of trouble. But there! Of course you understand."

She jerked away. "I'm not answering any questions, Mr. Inspector, until I know what right you have to ask 'em. I haven't done anything wrong and my slate's clean. You can put that in your pipe and smoke it!"

The Inspector took a pinch of snuff, as if the woman's reference to the vile weed had reminded him of his favorite vice. He said: "That's fair enough," in dulcet tones. "Here you are, a lonely woman suddenly tumbled out of bed in the middle of the night—you *were* in bed, weren't you—?"

"Sure I was," she flashed instantly, then bit her lip.

"—and confronted by a policeman. . . . I don't wonder you were frightened, my dear."

"I was not!" she said shrilly.

"We'll not argue about it," rejoined the old man benevolently. "But certainly you have no objection to telling me your name?"

"I don't know why I should but I can't see any harm in it," retorted the woman. "My name is Angela Russo—Mrs. Angela Russo—and I'm, well, I'm engaged to Mr. Field."

"I see," said Queen gravely. "Mrs. Angela Russo and you are engaged to Mr. Field. Very good! And what were you doing in these rooms last night, Mrs. Angela Russo?"

"None of your business!" she said coolly. "You'd better let me go now—I haven't done a thing out of the way. You've got no right to jabber at me, old boy!"

Ellery, in a corner peering out of the window, smiled. The Inspector leaned over and took the woman's hand gently.

"My dear Mrs. Russo," he said, "believe me—there is every reason in the world why we should be anxious to know what you were doing here last night. Come now—tell me."

"I won't open my mouth till I know what you've done with Monte!" she cried, shaking off his hand. "If you've got him, why are you pestering me! I don't know anything."

"Mr. Field is in a very safe place at the moment," snapped the Inspector, rising, "I've given you plenty of rope, madam. Monte Field is dead."

"Monte—Field—is—" The woman's lips moved mechanically. She leaped to her feet, clutching the negligee to her plump figure, staring at Queen's impassive face.

She laughed shortly and threw herself back on the bed. "Go on—you're taking me for a ride," she jeered.

"I'm not accustomed to joking about death," returned the old man with a little smile. "I assure you that you may take my word for it—Monte Field is dead." She was staring up at him, her lips moving soundlessly. "And what is more, Mrs. Russo, he has been murdered. Perhaps now you'll deign to answer my questions. Where were you at a quarter to ten last night?" he whispered in her ear, his face close to hers.

Mrs. Russo relaxed limply on the bed, a dawning fright in her large eyes. She gaped at the Inspector, found little comfort in his face and with a cry whirled to sob into the rumpled pillow. Queen stepped back and spoke in a low tone to Piggott, who had come into the room a moment before. The woman's heaving sobs subsided suddenly. She sat up, dabbing her face with a lace handkerchief. Her eyes were strangely bright.

"I get you now," she said in a quiet voice. "I was right here in this apartment at a quarter to ten last night."

"Can you prove that, Mrs. Russo?" asked Queen fingering his snuffbox.

"I can't prove anything and I don't have to," she returned dully. "But if you're looking for an alibi, the doorman downstairs must have seen me come into the building at about nine-thirty."

"We can easily check that up," admitted Queen. "Tell me—why did you come here last night at all?"

"I had an appointment with Monte," she explained lifelessly. "He called me up at my own place yesterday afternoon and we made a date for last night. He told me he'd be out on business until about ten o'clock, and I was to wait here for him. I come up"—she paused and continued brazenly—"I come up quite often like that. We generally have a little 'time' and spend the evening together. Being engaged—you know."

"Ummm. I see, I see." The Inspector cleared his throat in some embarrassment. "And then, when he didn't come on time—?"

"I thought he might've been detained longer than he'd figured. So I—well, I felt tired and took a little nap."

"Very good," said Queen quickly. "Did he tell you where he was going, or the nature of his business?"

"No."

"I should be greatly obliged to you, Mrs. Russo," said the Inspector carefully, "if you would tell me what Mr. Field's attitude was toward theatre-going."

The woman looked at him curiously. She seemed to be recovering her spirits. "Didn't go very often," she snapped. "Why?"

The Inspector beamed. "Now, that's a question, isn't it?" he asked. He motioned to Hagstrom, who pulled a notebook out of his pocket.

"Could you give me a list of Mr. Field's personal friends?" resumed Queen. "And any business acquaintances you might know of?"

Mrs. Russo put her hands behind her head, coquettishly. "To tell the truth," she said sweetly, "I don't know any. I met Monte about six months ago at a masque ball in the Village. We've kept our engagement sort of quiet, you see. In fact, I've never met his friends at all. . . . I don't think," she confided, "I don't think Monte had many friends. And of course I don't know a thing about his business associates."

"What was Field's financial condition, Mrs. Russo?"

"Trust a woman to know those things!" she retorted, completely restored to her flippant manner. "Monte was always a good spender. Never seemed to run out of cash. He's spent five hundred a night on me many a time. That was Monte—a damned good sport. Tough luck for him!—poor darling." She wiped a tear from her eye, sniffling hastily.

"But—his bank account?" pursued the Inspector firmly.

Mrs. Russo smiled. She seemed to possess an inexhaustible fund of shifting emotions. "Never got nosey," she said. "As long as Monte was treating me square it wasn't any of my business. At least," she added, "he wouldn't tell me, so what did I care?"

"Where were you, Mrs. Russo," came Ellery's indifferent tones, "*before* nine-thirty last night?"

She turned in surprise at the new voice. They measured each other carefully, and something like warmth crept into her eyes. "I don't know who you are, mister, but if you want to find out ask the lovers in Central Park. I was taking a little stroll in the Park—all by my lonesome—from about half-past seven until the time I reached here."

"How fortunate!" murmured Ellery. The Inspector hastily went to the door, crooking his finger at the other three men. "We'll leave you now to dress, Mrs. Russo. That will be all for the present." She watched quizzically as they filed out. Queen, last, shut the door after a fatherly glance at her face.

In the living room the four men proceeded to make a hurried but thorough search. At the Inspector's command Hagstrom and Piggott went through the drawers of a carved desk in one corner of the room. Ellery was interestedly rifling the pages of the book on character through handwriting. Queen prowled restlessly about, poking his head into a clothes closet just inside the room, off the foyer. This was a commodious storage compartment for clothes—assorted topcoats, capes and the like hung from a rack. The Inspector rifled the pockets. A few miscellaneous articles—handkerchiefs, keys, old personal letters, wallets—came to light. These he put to one side. A top shelf held several hats.

"Ellery—hats," he grunted.

Ellery quickly crossed the room, stuffing into his pocket

the book he had been reading. His father pointed out the hats meaningly; together they reached up to examine them. There were four—a discolored Panama, two fedors, one gray and one brown, and a derby. All bore the imprint of Browne Bros.

The two men turned the hats over in their hands. Both noticed immediately that three of them had no linings—the Panama and the two fedoras. The fourth hat, an excellent derby, Queen examined critically. He felt the lining, turned down the leather sweatband, then shook his head.

"To tell the truth, Ellery," he said slowly, "I'll be switched if I know why I should expect to find clues in these hats. We know that Field wore a tophat last night and obviously it would be impossible for that hat to be in these rooms. According to our findings the murderer was still in the theatre when we arrived. Ritter was down here by eleven o'clock. The hat therefore *couldn't* have been brought to this place. For that matter, what earthly reason would the murderer have for such an action, even if it were physically possible for him to do it? He must have realized that we would search Field's apartment at once. No, I guess I'm feeling a little offcolor, Ellery. There's nothing to be squeezed out of these hats." He threw the derby back onto the shelf disgustedly.

Ellery stood thoughtful and unsmiling. "You're right enough, Dad; these hats mean nothing. But I have the strangest feeling. . . . By the way!" He straightened up and took off his pince-nez. "Did it occur to you last night that something else belonging to Field might have been missing besides the hat?"

"I wish they were all as easy to answer as that," said Queen grimly. "Certainly—a walking stick. But what could I do about that? Working on the premise that Field brought one with him—it would have been simple enough for someone who had entered the theatre without a walking stick to leave the theatre with Field's. And how could we stop him or identify the stick? So I didn't even bother thinking about it. And if it's still on the Roman premises, Ellery, it will keep—no fear about that."

Ellery chuckled. "I should be able to quote Shelley or Wordsworth at this point," he said, "in proof of my admiration for your prowess. But I can't think of a more poetical phrase than 'You've got one over on me.' Because I didn't think of it until just now. But here's the point: there is no cane of any kind in the closet. A man like Field, had he possessed a swanky halberd to go with evening dress, would most certainly have owned other sticks to match other costumes. That fact—unless we find sticks in the bedroom closet, which I doubt, since all the overclothes seem to be here—that fact, therefore, eliminates the possibility that Field had a stick with him last night *Ergo*—we may forget all about it."

"Good enough, El," returned the Inspector absently. "I hadn't thought of that. Well—let's see how the boys are getting on."

They walked across the room to where Hagstrom and Piggott were rifling the desk. A small pile of papers and notes had accumulated on the lid.

"Find anything interesting?" asked Queen.

"Not a thing of value that I can see, Inspector," answered Piggott. "Just the usual stuff—some letters, chiefly from this

Russo woman, and pretty hot too!—a lot of bills and receipts and things like that. Don't think you'll find anything here."

Queen went through the papers. "No, nothing much," he admitted. "Well, let's get on." They restored the papers to the desk. Piggott and Hagstrom rapidly searched the room. They tapped furniture, poked beneath cushions, picked up the rug—a thorough, workmanlike job. As Queen and Ellery stood silently watching, the bedroom door opened. Mrs. Russo appeared, saucily appareled in a brown walking suit and toque. She paused at the door, surveying the scene with wide, innocent eyes. The two detectives proceeded with their search without looking up.

"What are they doing, Inspector?" she inquired in a languid tone. "Looking for pretty-pretties?" But her eyes were keen and interested.

"That was remarkably rapid dressing for a female, Mrs. Russo," said the Inspector admiringly. "Going home?"

Her glance darted at him. "Sure thing," she answered, looking away.

"And you live at—?"

She gave an address on MacDougal Street in Greenwich Village.

"Thank you," said Queen courteously, making a note. She began to walk across the room. "Oh, Mrs. Russo!" she turned. "Before you go—perhaps you could tell us something about Mr. Field's convivial habits. Was he, now, what you would call a heavy drinker?"

She laughed merrily. "Is that all?" she said. "Yes and no. I've seen Monte drink half a night and be sober as a—as a parson.

And then I've seen him at other times when he was pickled silly on a couple of tots. It all depended—don't you know?" She laughed again.

"Well, many of us are that way," murmured the Inspector. "I don't want you to abuse any confidences, Mrs. Russo—but perhaps you know the source of his liquor supply?"

She stopped laughing instantly, her face reflecting an innocent indignation. "What do you think I am, anyway?" she demanded. "I don't know, but even if I did I wouldn't tell. There's many a hard-working bootlegger who's head and shoulders above the guys who try to run 'em in, believe me!"

"The way of all flesh, Mrs. Russo," said Queen soothingly. "Nevertheless, my dear," he continued softly, "I'm sure that if I need that information eventually, you will enlighten me. Eh?" There was a silence. "I think that will be all, then, Mrs. Russo. Just stay in town, won't you? We may require your testimony soon."

"Well—so long," she said, tossing her head. She marched out of the room to the foyer.

"Mrs. Russo!" called Queen suddenly, in a sharp tone. She turned with her gloved hand on the front-door knob, the smile dying from her lips. "What's Ben Morgan been doing since he and Field dissolved partnership—do you know?"

Her reply came after a split second of hesitation. "Who's he?" she asked, her forehead wrinkled into a frown.

Queen stood squarely on the rug. He said sadly, "Never mind. Good day," and turned his back on her. The door slammed. A moment later Hagstrom strolled out, leaving Piggott, Queen and Ellery in the apartment.

The three men, as if inspired by a single thought, ran into the bedroom. It was apparently as they had left it. The bed was disordered and Mrs. Russo's nightgown and negligee were lying on the floor. Queen opened the door of the bedroom clothes closet. "Whew!" said Ellery. "This chap had a quiet taste in clothes, didn't he? Sort of Mulberry Street Beau Brummell." They ransacked the closet with no results. Ellery craned his neck at the shelf above. "No hats—no canes; that settles *that!*" he murmured with an air of satisfaction. Piggott, who had disappeared into a small kitchen, returned staggering under the burden of a half-empty case of liquor bottles.

Ellery and his father bent over the case. The Inspector removed a cork gingerly, sniffed the contents, then handed the bottle to Piggott, who followed his superior's example critically.

"Looks and smells okay," said the detective. "But I'd hate to take a chance tasting this stuff—after last night."

"You're perfectly justified in your caution," chuckled Ellery. "But if you should change your mind and decide to invoke the spirit of Bacchus, Piggott, let me suggest this prayer: O wine, if thou hast no name to be known by, let us call thee Death."[1]

"I'll have the firewater analyzed," growled Queen. "Scotch and rye mixed, and the labels look like the real thing. But then you never can tell. . . ." Ellery suddenly grasped his father's arm, leaning forward tensely. The three men stiffened.

---

1 Ellery Queen was here probably paraphrasing the Shakespearian quotation: "O thou invisible spirit of wine, if thou hast no name to be known by, let us call thee devil."

A barely audible scratching came to their ears, proceeding from the foyer.

"Sounds as if somebody is using a key on the door," whispered Queen. "Duck out, Piggott—jump whoever it is as soon as he gets inside!"

Piggott darted through the living room into the foyer. Queen and Ellery waited in the bedroom, concealed from view.

There was utter silence now except for the scraping on the outer door. The newcomer seemed to be having difficulty with the key. Suddenly the rasp of the lock tumblers falling back was heard and an instant later the door swung open. It slammed shut almost immediately.

A muffled cry, a hoarse bull-like voice, Piggott's half-strangled oath, the frenzied shuffling of feet—and Ellery and his father were speeding across the living room to the foyer.

Piggott was struggling in the arms of a burly, powerful man dressed in black. A suitcase lay on the floor to one side, as if it had been thrown there during the tussle. A newspaper was fluttering through the air, settling on the parquet just as Ellery reached the cursing men.

It took the combined efforts of the three to subdue their visitor. Finally, panting heavily, he lay on the floor, Piggott's arm jammed tightly across his chest.

The Inspector bent down, gazed curiously into the man's red, angry features and said softly, "And who are you, mister?"

9

IN WHICH THE MYSTERIOUS MR. MICHAELS APPEARS

The intruder rose awkwardly to his feet. He was a tall, ponderous man with solemn features and blank eyes. There was nothing distinguishing in either his appearance or his manner. If anything unusual could be said of him at all, it was that both his appearance and manner were so unremarkable. It seemed as if, whoever he was or whatever his occupation, he had made a deliberate effort to efface all marks of personality.

"Just what's the idea of the strong-arm stuff?" he said in a bass voice. But even his tones were flat and colorless.

Queen turned to Piggott. "What happened?" he demanded, with a pretense of severity.

"I stood behind the door, Inspector," gasped Piggott, still winded, "and when this wildcat stepped in I touched him on the arm. He jumped me like a trainload o' tigers, he did. Pushed me in the face—he's got a wallop, Inspector. . . . Tried to get out the door again."

Queen nodded judicially. The newcomer said mildly, "That's a lie, sir. He jumped me and I fought back."

"Here, here!" murmured Queen. "This will never do. . . ."

The door swung open suddenly and Detective Johnson stood on the threshold. He took the Inspector to one side. "Velie sent me down the last minute on the chance you might need me, Inspector. . . . And as I was coming up I saw that chap there. Didn't know but what he might be snooping around, so I followed him up." Queen nodded vigorously. "Glad you came—I can use you," he muttered and motioning to the others, he led the way into the living room.

"Now, my man," he said curtly to the big intruder, "the show is over. Who are you and what are you doing here?"

"My name is Charles Michaels—sir. I am Mr. Monte Field's valet." The Inspector's eyes narrowed. The man's entire demeanor had in some intangible manner changed. His face was blank, as before, and his attitude seemed in no way different. Yet the old man sensed a metamorphosis; he glanced quickly at Ellery and saw a confirmation of his own thought in his son's eyes.

"Is that so?" inquired the Inspector steadily. "Valet, eh? And where are you going at this hour of the morning with that traveling bag?" He jerked his hand toward the suitcase, a cheap black affair, which Piggott had picked up in the foyer and carried into the living room. Ellery suddenly strolled away in the direction of the foyer. He bent over to pick up something.

"Sir?" Michaels seemed upset by the question. "That's mine, sir," he confided. "I was just going away this morning on my vacation and I'd arranged with Mr. Field to come here for my salary check before I left."

The old man's eyes sparkled. He had it! Michaels' expression and general bearing had remained unchanged, but his voice and enunciation were markedly different.

"So you arranged to get your check from Mr. Field this morning?" murmured the Inspector. "That's mighty funny now, come to think of it."

Michaels permitted a fleeting amazement to scud across his features. "Why—why, where is Mr. Field?" he asked.

"'Massa's in de cold, cold ground,'" chuckled Ellery, from the foyer. He stepped back into the living room, flourishing the newspaper which Michaels had dropped during the fracas with Piggott. "Really, now, old chap, that's a bit thick, you know. Here is the morning paper you brought in with you. And the first thing I see as I pick it up is the nice black headline describing Mr. Field's little accident. Smeared over the entire front page. And—er, you failed to see the story?"

Michaels stared stonily at Ellery and the paper. But his eyes fell as he mumbled, "I didn't get the opportunity of reading the paper this morning, sir. What has happened to Mr. Field?"

The Inspector snorted. "Field's been killed, Michaels, and you knew it all the time."

"But I didn't, I tell you, sir," objected the valet respectfully.

"Stop lying!" rasped Queen. "Tell us why you're here or you'll get plenty of opportunity to talk behind bars!"

Michaels regarded the old man patiently. "I've told you the truth, sir," he said. "Mr. Field told me yesterday that I was to come here this morning for my check. That's all I know."

"You were to meet him here?"

"Yes, sir."

"Then why did you forget to ring the bell? Used a key as if you didn't expect to find anyone here, my man," said Queen.

"The bell?" The valet opened his eyes wide. "I always use my key, sir. Never disturb Mr. Field if I can help it."

"Why didn't Field give you a check yesterday?" barked the Inspector.

"He didn't have his checkbook handy, I think, sir."

Queen's lip curled. "You haven't even a fertile imagination, Michaels. At what time did you last see him yesterday?"

"At about seven o'clock, sir," said Michaels promptly. "I don't live here at the apartment. It's too small and Mr. Field likes—liked privacy. I generally come early in the morning to make breakfast for him and prepare his bath and lay out his clothes. Then when he's gone to the office I clean up a bit and the rest of the day is my own until dinnertime. I return about five, prepare dinner unless I've heard from Mr. Field during the day that he is dining out, and get his dinner or evening clothes ready. Then I am through for the night. . . . Yesterday after I laid out his things he told me about the check."

"Not an especially fatiguing itinerary," murmured Ellery. "And what things did you lay out last evening, Michaels?"

The man faced Ellery respectfully. "There was his underwear, sir, and his socks, his evening shoes, stiff shirt, studs, collar, white tie, full evening dress, cape, hat—"

"Ah, yes—his hat," interrupted Queen. "And what kind of hat was it, Michaels?"

"His regular tophat, sir," answered Michaels. "He had only one, and a very expensive one it was, too," he added warmly. "Browne Bros., I think."

Queen drummed lazily on the arm of his chair. "Tell me, Michaels," he said, "what did you do last night after you left here—that is, after seven o'clock?"

"I went home, sir. I had my bag to pack and I was rather fatigued. I went right to sleep after I'd had a bite to eat—it must have been near nine-thirty when I climbed into bed, sir," he added innocently."

"Where do you live?" Michaels gave a number of East 146th Street, in the Bronx section. "I see. . . . Did Field have any regular visitors here?" went on the Inspector.

Michaels frowned politely. "That's hard for me to say, sir. Mr. Field wasn't what you would call a friendly person. But then I wasn't here evenings, so I can't say who came after I left. But—"

"Yes?"

"There was a lady, sir. . . ." Michaels hesitated primly. "I dislike mentioning names under the circumstances—"

"Her name?" said Queen wearily.

"Well, sir—it isn't sort of right—Russo. Mrs. Angela Russo, her name is," answered Michaels.

"How long did Mr. Field know this Mrs. Russo?"

"Several months, sir. I think he met her at a party in Greenwich Village somewhere."

"I see. And they were engaged, perhaps?"

Michaels seemed embarrassed. "You might call it that, sir, although it was a little less formal. . . ."

Silence. "How long have you been in Monte Field's employ, Michaels?" pursued the Inspector.

"Three years next month."

Queen switched to a new line of questioning. He asked Michaels about Field's addiction to theatre-going, his financial condition and his drinking habits. In these particulars Michaels corroborated Mrs. Russo's statements. Nothing of a fresh nature was disclosed.

"A few moments ago you said you have been working for Field a matter of three years," continued Queen, settling back in his chair. "How did you get the job?"

Michaels did not answer immediately. "I followed up an ad in the papers, sir."

"Quite so. . . . If you have been in Field's service for three years, Michaels, you should know Benjamin Morgan."

Michaels permitted a proper smile to cross his lips. "Certainly I know Mr. Benjamin Morgan," he said heartily. "And a very fine gentleman he is, too, sir. He was Mr. Field's partner, you know, in their law business. But then they separated about two years ago and I haven't seen much of Mr. Morgan since."

"Did you see him often before the split?"

"No, sir," returned the burly valet, in a tone which implied regret. "Mr. Field was not Mr. Mogan's—ah—type, and they didn't mix socially. Oh, I remember seeing Mr. Morgan in this apartment three or four times, but only when it was a matter of most urgent business. Even then I couldn't say much about it since I didn't stay all evening. . . . Of course, he hasn't been here, so far as I know, since they broke up the firm."

Queen smiled for the first time during the conversation. "Thank you for your frankness, Michaels. . . . I'm going to be an old gossip—do you recall any unpleasantness about the time they dissolved?"

"Oh, no, sir!" protested Michaels. "I never heard of a quarrel or anything like that. In fact, Mr. Field told me immediately after the dissolution that he and Mr. Morgan would remain friends—very good friends, he said."

Michaels turned with his politely blank expression at a touch of his arm. He found himself face to face with Ellery. "Yes, sir?" he asked respectfully.

"Michaels, dear man," said Ellery with severity, "I detest raking up old coals, but why haven't you told the Inspector about the time you were in jail?"

As if he had stepped on an exposed live-wire Michaels' body stiffened and grew still. The ruddy color drained out of his face. He stared open-mouthed, aplomb swept away, into Ellery's smiling eyes.

"Why—why—how did you find that out?" gasped the valet, his speech less soft and polished. Queen appraised his son with approval. Piggott and Johnson moved closer to the trembling man.

Ellery lit a cigarette. "I didn't know it at all," he said cheerfully.

"That is, not until you told me. It would pay you to cultivate the Delphic oracles, Michaels."

Michaels' face was the color of dead ashes. He turned, shaking, toward Queen. "You—you didn't ask me about that, sir," he said weakly. Nevertheless his tone had again become taut and blank. "Besides, a man doesn't like to tell things like that to the police. . . ."

"Where did you do time, Michaels?" asked the Inspector in a kindly voice.

"Elmira Reformatory, sir," muttered Michaels. "It was my first offense—I was up against it, starving, stole some money. . . . I got a short stretch, sir."

Queen rose. "Well, Michaels, of course you understand that you are not exactly a free agent at present. You may go home and look for another job if you want to, but stay at your present lodgings and be ready for a call at any time. . . . Just a moment, before you go." He strode over to the black suitcase and snapped it open. A jumbled mass of clothing—a dark suit, shirts, ties, socks—some clean, some dirty—was revealed. Queen rummaged swiftly through the bag, closed it and handed it to Michaels, who was standing to one side with an expression of sorrowful patience.

"Seems to me you were taking mighty few duds with you, Michaels," remarked Queen, smiling. "It's too bad that you've been done out of your vacation. Well! That's the way life is!" Michaels murmured a low good-by, picked up the bag and departed. A moment later Piggott strolled out of the apartment.

Ellery threw back his head and laughed delightedly. "What a mannerly beggar! Lying in his teeth, Pater. . . . And what did he want here, do you think?"

"He came to get something, of course," mused the Inspector. "And that means there's something here of importance that we have apparently overlooked. . . ."

He grew thoughtful. The telephone bell rang.

"Inspector?" Sergeant Velie's voice boomed over the wire. "I called headquarters but you weren't there, so I guessed you were still at Field's place. . . . I've some interesting news for you from Browne Bros. Do you want me to come up to Field's?"

"No," returned Queen. "We're through here. I'll be at my office just as soon as I've paid a visit to Field's on Chambers Street. I'll be there if anything important comes up in the interim. Where are you now?"

"Fifth Avenue—I've just come out of Browne's."

"Then go back to headquarters and wait for me. And, Thomas—send a uniformed man up here right away."

Queen hung up and turned to Johnson.

"Stay here until a cop shows up—it won't be long," he grunted. "Have him keep a watch in the apartment and arrange for a relief. Then report back to the main office. . . . Come along, Ellery. This is going to be a busy day!"

Ellery's protests were in vain. His father fussily hustled him out of the building and into the street, where the roar of a taxicab's exhaust effectually drowned out his voice.

10

IN WHICH MR. FIELD'S TOPHATS BEGIN TO ASSUME PROPORTIONS

It was exactly ten o'clock win the morning when Inspector Queen and his son opened the frosted glass door marked:

MONTE FIELD

ATTORNEY-AT-LAW

The large waiting room they entered was decorated in just such a fashion as might have been expected from a man of Field's taste in clothes. It was deserted, and with a puzzled glance Inspector Queen pushed through the door, Ellery strolling behind, and went into the General Office. This was a long room filled with desks. It resembled a newspaper "city room" except for its rows of bookcases filled with ponderous legal tomes.

The office was in a state of violent upheaval. Stenographers chattered excitedly in small groups. A number of male clerks whispered in a corner; and in the center of the room stood Detective Hesse, talking earnestly to a lean saturnine man with grayed temples. It was evident that the demise of the lawyer had created something of a stir in his place of business.

At the entrance of the Queens the employees looked at each other in a startled way and began to slip back to their desks. An embarrassed silence fell. Hesse hurried forward. His eyes were red and strained.

"Good morning, Hesse," said the Inspector abruptly. "Where's Field's private office?"

The detective led them across the room to still another door, a large PRIVATE lettered on its panels. The three men went into a small office which was overwhelmingly luxurious.

"This chap went for atmosphere, didn't he?" Ellery chuckled, sinking into a red-leather armchair.

"Let's have it, Hesse," said the Inspector, following Ellery's suit.

Hesse began to talk rapidly. "Got here last night and found the door locked. No sign of a light inside. I listened pretty closely but couldn't hear a sound, so I took it for granted that there was no one inside and camped in the corridor all night. At about a quarter to nine this morning the office manager breezed in and I collared him. He was that tall bird I was talking to when you came in. Name's Lewin—Oscar Lewin."

"Office manager, eh?" remarked the old man, inhaling snuff.

"Yes, Chief. He's either dumb or else he knows how to keep his mouth shut," continued Hesse. "Of course, he'd already seen the morning papers and was upset by the news of Field's murder.

I could see he didn't like my questions any too well, either. . . . I didn't get a thing out of him. Not a thing. He said he'd gone straight home last night—it seems Field had left about four o'clock and didn't come back—and he didn't know anything about the murder until he read the papers. We've been sort of sliding along here all morning, waiting for you to come."

"Get Lewin for me."

Hesse returned with the lanky office manager in his wake. Oscar Lewin was physically unprepossessing. He had shifty black eyes and was abnormally thin. There was something predatory in his beaked nose and bony figure. The Inspector looked him over coldly.

"So you're the office manager," he remarked. "Well, what do you think of this affair, Lewin?"

"It's terrible—simply terrible," groaned Lewin. "I can't imagine how it happened or why. Good Lord, I was talking to him only four o'clock yesterday afternoon!" He seemed genuinely distressed.

"Did Mr. Field appear strange or worried when you spoke to him?"

"Not at all, sir," replied Lewin nervously. "In fact, he was in unusually good spirits. Cracked a joke about the Giants and said he was going to see a darned good show last night—'Gunplay.' And now I see by the papers that he was killed there!"

"Oh, he told you about the play, did he?" asked the Inspector. "He didn't happen to remark by any chance that he was going with anybody?"

"No, sir." Lewin shuffled his feet.

"I see." Queen paused. "Lewin, as manager you must have been closer to Field than any other of his employees. Just what do you know about him personally?"

"Not a thing, sir, not a thing," said Lewin hastily. "Mr. Field was not a man with whom an employee could become familiar. Occasionally he said something about himself, but it was always of a general nature and more jesting than serious. To us outside he was always a considerate and generous employer—that's all."

"What exactly was the caliber of the business he conducted, Lewin? You must certainly know something about that."

"Business?" Lewin seemed startled. "Why, it was as fine a practice as any I've encountered in the law profession. I've worked for Field only two years or so, but he had some high-and-mighty clients, Inspector. I can give you a list of them. . . ."

"Do that and mail it to me," said Queen. "So he had a flourishing and respectable practice, eh? Any personal visitors to your knowledge—especially recently?"

"No. I can't remember ever seeing any one up here except his clients. Of course, he may have known some of them socially. . . . Oh, yes! Of course his valet came here at times—tall, brawny fellow by the name of Michaels."

"Michaels? I'll have to remember that name," said the Inspector thoughtfully. He looked up at Lewin. "All right, Lewin. That will be all now. You might dismiss the force for the day. And—just stay around for a while. I expect one of Mr. Sampson's men soon, and undoubtedly he will need your help." Lewin nodded gravely and retired.

The moment the door closed Queen was on his feet. "Where's Field's private washroom, Hesse?" he demanded. The detective pointed to a door in a far corner of the room.

Queen opened it, Ellery crowding close behind. They were peering into a tiny cubicle spaced off in an angle of the wall. It contained a washbowl, a medicine chest and a small clothes closet. Queen looked into the medicine chest first. It held a bottle of iodine, a bottle of peroxide, a tube of shaving cream, and other shaving articles. "Nothing there," said Ellery. "How about the closet?" The old man pulled the door open curiously. A suit of street clothes hung there, a half-dozen neckties and a fedora hat. The Inspector carried the hat back into the office and examined it. He handed it to Ellery, who disdainfully returned it at once to its peg in the closet.

"Dang those hats!" exploded the Inspector. There was a knock on the door and Hesse admitted a bland young man.

"Inspector Queen?" inquired the newcomer politely.

"Right," snapped the Inspector, "and if you're a reporter you can say the police will apprehend the murderer of Monte Field within twenty-four hours. Because that's all I'm going to give you right now."

The young man smiled. "Sorry, Inspector, but I'm not a reporter. I'm Arthur Stoates, new man at District Attorney Sampson's office. The Chief couldn't reach me until this morning and I was busy on something else—that's why I'm a little late. Too bad about Field, isn't it?" He grinned as he threw his coat and hat on a chair.

"It's all in the point of view," grumbled Queen. "He's certainly causing a heap of trouble. Just what were Sampson's instructions?"

"Well, I'm not as familiar with Field's career as I might be, naturally, but I'm pinch-hitting for Tim Cronin, who's tied up this morning on something else. I'm to make a start until Tim gets untangled, which will be some time this afternoon. Cronin, you know, was the man after Field a couple of years ago. He's aching to get busy with these files."

"Fair enough. From what Sampson told me about Cronin—if there's anything incriminating in these records and files, he'll ferret it out. Hesse, take Mr. Stoates outside and introduce him to Lewin—that's the office manager, Stoates. Keep your eye on him—he looks like a wily bird. And, Stoates—remember you're looking not for legitimate business and clientele in these records, but for something crooked. . . . See you later."

Stoates gave him a cheery smile and followed Hesse out. Ellery and his father faced each other across the room.

"What's that you've got in your hand?" asked the old man sharply.

"A copy of 'What Handwriting Tells,' which I picked up in this bookcase," replied Ellery lazily. "Why?"

"Come to think of it now, El," declared the Inspector slowly, "there's something fishy about this handwriting business." He shook his head in despair and rose. "Come along, son, there isn't a blamed thing here."

On their way through the main office, now empty except for Hesse, Lewin and Stoates, Queen beckoned to the detective. "Go home, Hesse," he said kindly. "Can't have you coming down with the grippe." Hesse grinned and sped through the door.

In a few minutes Inspector Queen was sitting in his private office at Center Street. Ellery termed it "the star chamber." It was small and cozy and homelike. Ellery draped himself over a chair and began to con the books on handwriting which he had filched from Field's apartment and office. The Inspector pressed a buzzer and the solid figure of Thomas Velie loomed in the doorway.

"Morning, Thomas," said Queen. "What is this remarkable news you have for me from Browne Bros.?"

"I don't know how remarkable it is, Inspector," said Velie coolly, seating himself in one of the straight-backed chairs which lined the wall, "but it sounded like the real thing to me. You told me last night to find out about Field's tophat. Well, I've an exact duplicate of it on my desk. Like to see it?"

"Don't be silly, Thomas," said Queen. "On the run!" Velie departed and was back in a moment carrying a hatbox. He tore the string and uncovered a shining tophat, of such fine quality that Queen blinked. The Inspector picked it up curiously. On the inside was marked the size: 7⅛.

"I spoke to the clerk, an old-timer, down at Browne's. Been waiting on Field for years," resumed Velie. "It seems that Field bought every stitch of his clothing there—for a long time. And it happens that he preferred one clerk. Naturally the old buzzard knows quite a bit about Field's tastes and purchases.

"He says, for one thing, that Field was a fussy dresser. His clothes were always made to order by Browne's special tailoring department. He went in for fancy suits and cuts and the latest in underclothes and neckwear. . . ."

"What about his taste in hats?" interposed Ellery, without looking up from the book he was reading.

"I was coming to that, sir," continued Velie. "This clerk made a particular point of the hat business. For instance, when I questioned him about the tophat, he said: 'Mr. Field was almost a fanatic on the subject. Why, in the last six months he has bought no less than *three* of them!' I caught that up, of course—made him check back with the sales records. Sure enough, Field bought three silk toppers in the last half-year!"

Ellery and his father found themselves staring at each other, the same question on their lips.

"Three—" began the old man.

"Now . . . isn't that an extraordinary circumstance?" asked Ellery slowly, reaching for his pince-nez.

"Where in heaven's name are the other two?" continued Queen, in a bewildered manner.

Ellery was silent.

Queen turned impatiently toward Velie. "What else did you find out, Thomas?"

"Nothing much of value, except for this point"—answered Velie—"that Field was an absolute fiend when it came to clothes. So much so that last year he bought fifteen suits and no less than a dozen hats, including the toppers!"

"Hats, hats, hats!" groaned the Inspector. "The man must have been a lunatic. Look here—did you find out whether Field ever bought walking sticks at Browne's?"

A look of consternation spread over Velie's face. "Why—why, Inspector," he said ruefully, "I guess I slipped up there.

I never even thought of asking, and you hadn't told me last night—"

"Heck! We're none of us perfect," growled Queen. "Get that clerk on the wire for me, Thomas."

Velie picked up one of the telephones on the desk and a few moments later handed the instrument to his superior.

"This is Inspector Queen speaking," said the old man rapidly. "I understand that you served Monte Field for a good many years? . . . Well, I want to check up on a little detail. Did Field ever purchase canes or walking sticks from you people? . . . What? Oh, I see. . . . Yes. Now, another thing. Did he ever give special orders about the manufacture of his clothes—extra pockets, or things like that? . . . You don't think so. All right. . . . What? Oh, I see. Thank you very much."

He hung up the receiver and turned about.

"Our lamented friend," he said disgustedly, "seems to have had as great an aversion to sticks as he had a love for hats. This clerk said he tried many times to interest Field in canes, and Field invariably refused to buy. Didn't like 'em, he said. And the clerk just confirmed his own impression about the special pockets—nothing doing. So that leaves us up a blank alley."

"On the contrary," said Ellery coolly, "it does nothing of the kind. It proves fairly conclusively that *the only article of apparel* taken away by the murderer last night was the hat. It seems to me that simplifies matters."

"I must have a moron's intelligence," grunted his father. "It doesn't mean a thing to me."

"By the way, Inspector," put in Velie, scowling, "Jimmy

reported about the fingerprints on Field's flask. There are a few, but there's no question, he says, that they're all Field's. Jimmy got a print from the Morgue, of course, to check up."

"Well," said the Inspector, "maybe the flask has nothing to do with the crime at all. We'll have to wait, anyway, for Prouty's report on its contents."

"There's something else, Inspector," added Velie. "That junk—the sweepings of the theatre—that you told Panzer to send over to you this morning came a couple of minutes ago. Want to see it?"

"Sure thing, Thomas," said Queen. "And while you're out bring me the list you made last night containing the names of the people who had no stubs. The seat numbers are attached to each name, aren't they?"

Velie nodded and disappeared. Queen was looking morosely at the top of his son's head when the Sergeant returned with an unwieldy package and a typewritten list.

They spread the contents of the package carefully on the desk. For the most part the collected material consisted of crumpled programs, stray scraps of paper, chiefly from candy boxes, and many ticket stubs—those which had not been found by Flint and his searchers. Two women's gloves of different design; a small brown button, probably from a man's coat; the cap of a fountain pen; a woman's handkerchief and a few other scattered articles of the kind usually lost or thrown away in theatres came to light.

"Doesn't look as if there's much here, does it?" commented the Inspector. "Well, at least we'll be able to check up on the ticket-stub business."

Velie heaped the lost stubs in a small pile and began to read off their numbers and letters to Queen, who checked them off on the list Velie had brought him. There were not many of these and the checking-off process was completed in a few moments.

"That's all, Thomas?" inquired the Inspector, looking up.

"That's all, Chief."

"Well, there are about fifty people still unaccounted for according to this list. Where's Flint?"

"He's in the building somewhere, Inspector."

Queen picked up his telephone and gave a rapid order. Flint appeared almost at once.

"What did you find last night?" asked Queen abruptly.

"Well, Inspector," answered Flint sheepishly, "we practically dry-cleaned that place. We found quite a bit of stuff, but most of it was programs and things like that, and we left those for the cleaning women, who were working along with us. But we did pick up a raft of ticket stubs, especially out in the alleys." He brought forth from his pocket a package of pasteboards neatly bound with a rubber band. Velie took them and continued the process of reading off numbers and letters. When he was finished Queen slapped the typewritten list down on the desk before him.

"No fruit in the loom?" murmured Ellery, looking up from the book.

"Ding it, every one of those people who had no stubs is accounted for!" growled the Inspector. "There isn't a stub or a name left unchecked. . . . Well, there's one thing I can do." He searched through the pile of stubs, referring to the lists, until he found the stub which had belonged to Frances Ives-Pope. He fished from his pocket the four stubs he had collected Monday night and carefully tested the girl's stub with the one for Field's seat. The torn edges did not coincide.

"There's one consolation," the Inspector continued, stuffing the five tickets into his vest pocket, "we haven't found a trace of the six tickets for the seats next to and in front of Field's seat!"

"I didn't think you would," remarked Ellery. He put the book down and regarded his father with unwonted seriousness. "Have you ever stopped to consider, Dad, that we don't know definitely *why* Field was in the theatre last night?"

Queen knit his gray brows. "That particular problem has been puzzling me, of course. We know from Mrs. Russo and Michaels that Field did not care for the theatre—"

"You can never tell what vagary will seize a man," said Ellery decisively. "Many things might make a nontheatre-going man decide suddenly to go in for that sort of entertainment. The fact remains—he was there. But what I want to know is *why* he was there."

The old man shook his head gravely. "Was it a business appointment? Remember what Mrs. Russo said—that Field had promised to be back at 10 o'clock."

"I fancy the business appointment idea," applauded Ellery. "But consider how many probabilities there are—the Russo woman might be lying and Field said nothing of the sort; or if he did, he might have had no intention of keeping the appointment with her at 10 o'clock."

"I've quite made up my mind, Ellery," said the Inspector, "whatever the probabilities, that he didn't go the Roman Theatre last night to see the show. He went there with his eyes open—for business."

"I think that's correct, myself," returned Ellery, smiling. "But you can never be too careful in weighing possibilities. Now, if he went on business, he went to meet somebody. Was that somebody the murderer?"

"You ask too many questions, Ellery," said the Inspector.

"Thomas, let's have a look at the other stuff in that package."

Velie carefully handed the Inspector the miscellaneous articles one by one. The gloves, fountain-pen cap, button and handkerchief Queen threw to one side after a quick scrutiny. Nothing remained except the small bits of candy paper and the crumpled programs. The former yielding no clues, Queen took up the programs. And suddenly, in the midst of his examination, he cried delightedly: "See what I've found, boys!"

The three men leaned over his shoulder. Queen held a program in his hand, its wrinkles smoothed out. It showed evidences of having been crushed and thrown away. On one of the inside pages, bordering the usual article on men's wear, was a number of varied marks, some forming letters, some forming numbers, still others forming cabalistic designs such as a person scribbles in moments of idle thought.

"Inspector, it looks as if you've found Field's own program!" exclaimed Flint.

"Yes, sir, it certainly does," said Queen sharply. "Flint, look through the papers we found in the dead man's clothing last night and bring me a letter showing his signature." Flint hurried out.

Ellery was studying the scrawls intently. On the top margin of the paper appeared:

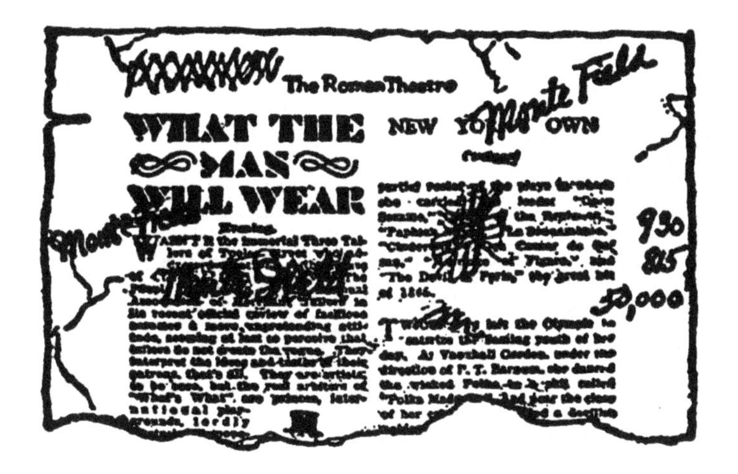

Flint returned with a letter. The Inspector compared the signatures—they were plainly by the same hand.

"We'll have them checked by Jimmie down in the laboratory," muttered the old man. "But I guess this is pretty authentic. It's Field's program, there can't be any doubt of that. . . . What do you make of it, Thomas?"

Velie grated: "I don't know what those other numbers refer to, but that '50,000' couldn't mean anything but dollars, Chief."

"The old boy must have been figuring his bank account," said Queen. "He loved the sight of his own name, didn't he?"

"That's not quite fair to Field," protested Ellery. "When a man is sitting idle, waiting for something to happen—as he will when he is in a theatre before the performance begins—one of his most natural actions is to scribble his initials or his name on the handiest object. In a theatre the handiest object would be the program. . . . The writing of one's own name is fundamental in psychology. So perhaps Field wasn't as egotistical as this seems to make him."

"It's a small point," said the Inspector, studying the scrawls with a frown.

"Perhaps," returned Ellery. "But to get back to a more pressing matter—I don't agree with you when you say the '50,000' probably refers to Field's bank account. When a man jots down his bank balance he will not do it in such round numbers."

"We can prove or disprove that easily enough," retorted the Inspector, picking up a telephone. He asked the police operator to get him the number of Field's office. When he had spoken to Oscar Lewin for some time, he turned back to Ellery with a crestfallen air.

"You were right, El," he said. "Field had an amazingly small personal account. All his accounts balance to less than six thousand dollars. And this despite the fact that he frequently made deposits of ten and fifteen thousand dollars. Lewin himself was surprised. He hadn't known, he said, how Field's personal finances stood until I asked him to look the matter up. . . . I'll bet dollars to doughnuts Field played the stock market or the horses!"

"I'm not particularly overwhelmed by the news," remarked Ellery. "It points to the probable reason for the '50,000' on the program. That number not only represents dollars, but more than that—it indicates a business deal in which the stakes were fifty thousand! Not a bad night's work, if he had come out of it alive."

"How about the other two numbers?" asked Queen.

"I'm going to mull over them a bit," replied Ellery, subsiding in his chair. "I *would* like to know what the business deal was that involved such a large financial consideration," he added, absently polishing his pince-nez.

"Whatever the business deal was," said the Inspector sententiously, "you may be sure, my son, it was an evil one."

"An evil one?" inquired Ellery in a serious tone.

"Money's the root of all evil," retorted the Inspector with a grin.

Ellery's tone did not change. "Not only the root, Dad—but the fruit, too."

"Another quotation?" mocked the old man.

"Fielding," said Ellery imperturbably.

11

IN WHICH THE PAST CASTS A SHADOW

The telephone bell tinkled.

"Q? Sampson speaking," came the District Attorney's voice over the wire.

"Good morning, Henry," said Queen. "Where are you and how do you feel this morning?"

"I'm at the office and I feel rotten," returned Sampson, chuckling. "The doctor insists I'll be a corpse if I keep this up and the office insists the City will go under unless I attend to business. So what's a feller to do? . . . I say, Q."

The Inspector winked at Ellery across the table, as if to say, "I know what's coming!"

"Yes, Henry?"

"There's a gentleman in my private office whom I think it would be greatly to your advantage to meet," continued Sampson in a subdued tone. "He wants to see you and I'm afraid you'll have to chuck whatever you're doing and hotfoot it up here. He"—Sampson's voice became a whisper—"he's a man I can't afford to antagonize unnecessarily, Q, old boy."

The Inspector frowned. "I suppose you're referring to Ives-Pope," he said. "Riled, is he, because we questioned the apple of his eye last night?"

"Not exactly," said Sampson. "He's really a decent old chap. Just—er—just be nice to him, Q, won't you?"

"I'll handle him with silk gloves," chuckled the old man. "If it will ease your mind any I'll drag my son along. He generally attends to our social obligations."

"That will be fine," said Sampson gratefully.

The Inspector turned to Ellery as he hung up. "Poor Henry's in something of a mess," he said quizzically, "and I can't say I blame him for trying to please. Sick as a dog and the politicians hopping on him, this Crœsus howling in his front office. . . . Come along, son, we're going to meet the celebrated Franklin Ives-Pope!"

Ellery groaned, stretching his arms. "You'll have another sick man on your hands if this continues." Nevertheless he jumped up and clamped his hat on his head. "Let's look over this captain of industry."

Queen grinned at Velie. "Before I forget, Thomas. . . . I want you to do a bit of sleuthing today. Your job is to find out why Monte Field, who did a rushing legal business and lived in princely style, had only six thousand dollars in his personal account. It's probably Wall Street and the racetrack but I want you to make sure. You might learn something from the cancelled vouchers—Lewin down at Field's office could help you there. . . . And while you're at it—this might be extremely important, Thomas—get a complete line-up on Field's movements all day yesterday."

The two Queens departed for Sampson's headquarters.

The office of the District Attorney was a busy place and even an Inspector of Detectives was treated with scant ceremony in the sacred chambers. Ellery was wroth, and his father smiled, and finally the District Attorney himself came rushing out of his sanctum with a word of displeasure to the clerk who had allowed his friends to cool their heels on a hard bench.

"Watch your throat, young man," warned Queen, as Sampson led the way to his office, muttering maledictions on the head of the offender. "Are you sure I look all right to meet the money-mogul?"

Sampson held the door open. The two Queens on the threshold saw a man, hands clasped behind his back, looking through the window on the uninteresting vista outside. As the District Attorney closed the door the occupant of the room wheeled about with astonishing agility for a man of his weight.

Franklin Ives-Pope was a relic of more virile financial days. He resembled the strong self-assertive type of magnate who like old Cornelius Vanderbilt had dominated Wall Street as much by force of personality as by extent of wealth. Ives-Pope had clear gray eyes, iron-gray hair, a grizzled mustache, a husky body still springy with youth and an air of authority unmistakably masterful. Standing against the light of the dingy window, he was a most impressive figure of a man and Ellery and Queen, stepping forward, realized at once that here was an individual whose intelligence required no patronage.

The financier spoke in a deep pleasant voice even before Sampson, slightly embarrassed, could make the introduction. "I suppose you're Queen, the manhunter," he said. "I've been anxious to meet you for a long time, Inspector." He offered a large square hand, which Queen took with dignity.

"It would be unnecessary for me to echo that statement, Mr. Ives-Pope," he said, smiling a little. "Once I took a flyer in Wall Street and I think you've got some of my money. This, sir, is my son Ellery, who is the brains and beauty of the Queen family."

The big man's eyes measured Ellery's bulk appreciatively. He shook hands, saying, "You've got a smart father there, son!"

"Well!" sighed the District Attorney, setting three chairs. "I'm glad that's over. You haven't the slightest idea, Mr. Ives-Pope, how nervous I've been about this meeting. Queen is the devil himself when it comes to the social amenities and I shouldn't have been surprised if he had clapped his handcuffs on you as you shook hands!"

The tension snapped with the big man's hearty chuckle.

The District Attorney came abruptly to the point. "Mr. Ives-Pope is here, Q, to find out for himself just what can be done in the matter of his daughter." Queen nodded. Sampson turned to the financier. "As I told you before, sir, we have every confidence in Inspector Queen—always have had. He generally works without any check or supervision from the District Attorney's office. In view of the circumstances, I thought I should make that clear."

"That's a sane method, Sampson," said Ives-Pope, with

approval. "I've always worked on that principle in my own business. Besides, from what I've heard about Inspector Queen, your confidence is well placed."

"Sometimes," said Queen gravely, "I have to do things that go against the grain. I will be frank to say that some things I did last night in the line of duty were extremely disagreeable to me. I suppose, Mr. Ives-Pope, your daughter is upset because of our little talk last night?"

Ives-Pope was silent for a moment. Then he raised his head and met the Inspector's gaze squarely. "Look here, Inspector," he said. "We're both men of the world and men of business. We've had dealings with all sorts of queer people, both of us; and we have, too, solved problems that presented enormous difficulties to others. So I think we can converse frankly. . . . Yes, my daughter Frances is more than a little upset. Incidentally, so is her mother, who is an ill woman at the best of times; and her brother Stanford, my son—but we needn't go into that. . . . Frances told me last night when she got home with—her friends—everything that happened. I know my daughter, Inspector, and I'd stake my fortune that there isn't the slightest connection between her and Field."

"My dear sir," returned the Inspector quietly, "I didn't accuse her of anything. Nobody knows better than I what peculiar things can happen in the course of a criminal investigation; therefore I never let the slightest blind spot escape my notice. All I did was to ask her to identify the bag. When she did so, I told her where it was found. I was waiting, of course, for an explanation. It did not come. . . . You must understand, Mr. Ives-Pope, that when a man is murdered and a woman's bag is found in his pocket it is the duty of the police to discover the owner of the bag and his or her connection with the crime. But of course—I do not have to convince you of that."

The magnate drummed on the arm of his chair. "I see your point of view, Inspector," he said. "It was obviously your duty, and it is still your duty to go to the bottom of the thing. In fact, I want you to make every effort to. My own personal opinion is that she is the victim of circumstances. But I don't want to plead her case. I trust you sufficiently to rely on your judgment after you've thoroughly probed the problem." He paused. "Inspector Queen, how would you like to have me arrange a little interview at my home tomorrow morning? I would not ask you to go to this trouble," he added apologetically, "except that Frances is quite ill, and her mother insists she stay at home. May we expect you?"

"Very good of you, Mr. Ives-Pope," remarked Queen calmly. "We'll be there."

The financier seemed indisposed to end the interview. He shifted heavily in his chair. "I've always been a fair man, Inspector," he said. "I feel somehow that I may be accused of using my position as a means of securing special privileges. That is not so. The shock of your tactics last night made it impossible for Frances to tell her story. At home, among the members of her family, I am sure she will be able to clear up her connection with the affair to your satisfaction." He hesitated for a moment, then continued in a colder tone. "Her fiancé will be there and perhaps his presence will help to calm her." His voice expressed the thought that he personally did not think so. “May we expect you, let us say, at ten-thirty?”

“That will be fine,” said Queen, nodding. “I should like to know more definitely, sir, just who will be present.”

“I can arrange it as you wish, Inspector,” replied Ives-Pope, “but I imagine Mrs. Ives-Pope will want to be there and I know that Mr. Barry will—my future son-in-law,” he explained dryly. “Perhaps a few of Frances’ friends—theatrical friends. My son Stanford may also grace us with his presence—a very busy young man, you know,” he added with a suspicion of bitterness.

The three men shifted embarrassedly. Ives-Pope rose with a sigh and Ellery, Queen and Sampson followed suit. “That’s all, I think, Inspector,” said the financier in a lighter tone. “Is there anything else I can do?”

“Not a thing.”

“Then I’ll be getting along.” Ives-Pope turned to Ellery and Sampson. “Of course, Sampson, if you can get away, I’d like you to be there. Do you think you can make it?” The District Attorney nodded. “And Mr. Queen”—the big man turned to Ellery—“will you come also? I understand that you have been following the investigation very closely at your father’s side. We shall be happy to have you.”

“I’ll be there,” said Ellery softly, and Ives-Pope left the office.

“Well, what do you think, Q?” asked Sampson, fidgeting in his swivel chair.

“A most interesting man,” returned the Inspector. “How fair-minded he is!”

“Oh, yes—yes,” said Sampson. “Er—Q, he asked me before

you came if you wouldn't go easy on the publicity. Sort of special favor, you know."

"He didn't have the nerve to come out with it to me, eh?" chuckled the Inspector. "He's quite human. . . . Well, Henry, I'll do my best, but if that young woman is implicated seriously, I won't vouch for hands off with the press."

"All right, all right, Q—it's up to you," said Sampson irritably. "Damn this throat of mine!" He took an atomizer from a desk drawer and sprinkled his throat wryly.

"Didn't Ives-Pope recently donate a hundred thousand dollars to the Chemical Research Foundation?" asked Ellery suddenly, turning to Sampson.

"I seem to remember something of that sort," said Sampson, gargling. "Why?"

Ellery mumbled an inaudible explanation that was lost in Sampson's violent gyrations with the sprayer. Queen, who was regarding his son speculatively, shook his head, consulted his watch and said, "Well, son, it's time we knocked off for lunch. What do you say—Henry, think you'd like to join us in a bite?"

Sampson grinned with an effort. "I'm full up to my neck with work, but even a District Attorney has to eat," he said. "I'll go on only one condition—that I pay the check. I owe you something, anyway."

As they donned their coats Queen picked up Sampson's telephone.

"Mr. Morgan? . . . Oh, hello, Morgan. I say, do you think you can find a little time this afternoon for a chat? . . . Right. Two-thirty will be fine. Good-by."

"That settles that," said the Inspector comfortably. "Always pays to be polite, Ellery—remember that."

At two-thirty promptly the two Queens were ushered into the quiet law office of Benjamin Morgan. It was noticeably different from Field's lavish suite—richly furnished but with a more businesslike simplicity. A smiling young woman closed the door after them. Morgan greeted them with some reserve. He held out a box of cigars as they sat down.

"No thanks—my snuff will do," said the Inspector genially, while Ellery after being introduced lit a cigarette and blew smoke rings. Morgan lit a cigar with shaking fingers.

"I suppose you're here to continue that talk of ours last night, Inspector?" said Morgan.

Queen sneezed, replaced his snuffbox, and leaned back in the chair. "Look here, Morgan old man," he said evenly. "You haven't been quite on the up-and-up with me."

"What do you mean?" asked Morgan, coloring.

"You told me last night," said the Inspector reflectively, "you told me last night that you parted amicably with Field two years ago, when you dissolved the firm of Field & Morgan. Did you say that?"

"I did," said Morgan.

"How, then, my dear fellow," asked Queen, "do you explain the little incident of the quarrel at the Webster Club? I certainly would not call a threat against another man's life an 'amicable' way of dissolving a partnership!"

Morgan sat quietly for several minutes while Queen stared patiently at him and Ellery sighed. Then he looked up and began to speak in a passionate undertone.

"I'm sorry, Inspector," he muttered, glancing away. "I might have known that a threat like that would be remembered by somebody. . . . Yes, it's true enough. We had lunch one day in the Webster Club at Field's suggestion. As far as I was concerned, the less I had to do with him socially the better I liked it. But the purpose of the luncheon was to go over some last details of the dissolution, and of course I had no choice. . . . I'm afraid I lost my temper. I did make a threat against his life, but it was—well, it was said in the heat of an angry moment. I forgot the whole thing before the week was over."

The Inspector nodded sagely. "Yes, things do happen like that sometimes. But"—and Morgan licked his lips in despairing anticipation—"a man doesn't threaten another man's life, even if he doesn't mean it, merely over a matter of business detail." He leveled his finger at Morgan's shrinking body. "Come on now, man—out with it. What are you holding back?"

Morgan's entire body had gone flaccid. His lips were ashy as he turned from one Queen to the other, mute appeal in his eyes. But their glances were inexorable and Ellery, who was regarding him much as a vivisectionist regards a guinea pig, interrupted.

"My dear Morgan," he said coldly, "Field had something on you, and he thought that that was a good time to tell you about it. It's as obvious as the red in your eye."

"You've guessed it in part, Mr. Queen. I've been one of the most unfortunate men God ever created. That devil Field—whoever killed him deserves to be decorated for his service to humanity. He was an octopus—a soulless beast in human form. I can't tell you how happy—yes, happy!—I am that he is dead!"

"Softly there, Morgan," said Queen. "Although I gather our mutual friend was a good deal of a skunk, your remarks might be overheard by a less sympathetic audience. And—?"

"Here's the whole story," mumbled Morgan, his eyes fixed on the desk blotter. "It's a hard one to tell. . . . When I was a kid at college I got into some trouble with a girl—a waitress in the college restaurant. She was not bad—just weak, and I suppose I was wild in those days. At any rate she had a child—my child. . . . I suppose you know that I come from a straitlaced family. If you don't, you would find out soon enough on investigation. They had great plans for me, they were socially ambitious—to cut it short, I couldn't very well marry the girl and bring her to father's house as my wife. It was a caddish thing to do. . . ."

He paused.

"But it was done, and that's all that matters. I've—I've always loved her. She was sensible enough about the arrangements. . . . I managed to provide for her out of my generous allowance. No one—I'll swear not a soul in this world with the exception of her widowed mother, a fine old lady—knew about the affair. I'll swear to that, I say. And yet—" His fist clenched, but he resumed with a sigh. "Eventually, I married the girl whom my family had selected for me." There was a painful silence as he stopped to clear his throat. "It was a *mariage de convenance*—just that and nothing else. She came from an old aristocratic family, and I had the money. We have lived fairly happily together. . . . And then I met Field. I curse the day I ever consented to go into partnership with him—but my own business was not exactly all it might have been and Field, if nothing else, was an aggressive and clever lawyer."

The Inspector took a pinch of snuff.

"Everything went smoothly at first," continued Morgan in the same low tone. "But by degrees I began to suspect that my partner was not everything he should have been. Queer clients—queer clients indeed—would enter his private office after hours; he would evade my questions about them; things began to look peculiar. Finally I decided my own reputation would suffer if I continued to be linked with the man, and I broached the subject of dissolution. Field objected strenuously, but I was stubborn and after all he could not dominate my desires. We dissolved."

Ellery's fingers tapped an absent tattoo on the handle of his stick.

"Then the affair at the Webster. He insisted we have lunch together for the settlement of the last few details. That wasn't his purpose at all, of course. You can guess, I suppose, his intentions. . . . He came out quite suavely with the overwhelming statement that he knew I was supporting a woman and my illegitimate child. He said that he had some of my letters to prove it, and a number of cancelled vouchers of checks I had sent her. . . . He admitted he had stolen them from me. I hadn't looked at them for years, of course. . . . Then he blandly announced that he meant to make capital out of this evidence!"

"Blackmail!" muttered Ellery, a light creeping into his eyes.

"Yes, blackmail," retorted Morgan bitterly. "Nothing less. He described in very graphic terms what would happen if the story should come out. Oh, Field was a clever crook! I saw the entire structure of social position I had built up—a process which took years—destroyed in an instant. My wife, her family, my own family—and more than that, the circle in which we moved—I shouldn't have been able to lift my head out of the muck. And as for business—well, it doesn't take much to make important clients go elsewhere for their legal work. I was trapped—I knew it and he knew it."

"Just how much did he want, Morgan?" asked Queen.

"Enough! He wanted twenty-five thousand dollars—just to keep quiet. I didn't even have any assurances that the affair would end there. I was caught and caught properly. Because, remember, this was not an affair which had died years before. I was still supporting that poor woman and my son. I am supporting them now. I will—continue to support them." He stared at his fingernails.

"I paid the money," he resumed morosely. "It meant stretching a bit but I paid it. But the harm was done. I saw red there at the Club, and—but you know what happened."

"And this blackmail has continued all the while, Morgan?" asked the Inspector.

"Yes, sir—for two solid years. The man was insatiable, I tell you! Even today I can't completely understand it. He must have been earning tremendous fees in his own practice, and yet he always seemed to be needing money. No small change, either—I have never paid him less than ten thousand dollars at one time!"

Queen and Ellery looked at each other fleetingly. Queen said, "Well, Morgan, it's a pretty kettle of fish. The more I hear about Field the more I dislike putting the irons on the fellow who did away with him. However! In the light of what you've told me, your statement last night that you hadn't seen Field for two years is patently untrue. When *did* you see him last?"

Morgan appeared to be racking his memory. "Oh, it was about two months ago, Inspector," he said at last.

The Inspector shifted in his chair. "I see. . . . I'm sorry you didn't tell me all this last night. You understand, of course, that your story is perfectly safe with the police. And it's mighty vital information. Now then—do you happen to know a woman by the name of Angela Russo?"

Morgan stared. "Why, no, Inspector. I've never heard of her."

Queen was silent for a moment. "Do you know a gentleman called 'Parson Johnny'?"

"I think I can give you some information there, Inspector. I'm certain that during our partnership Field was using the little thug for some shady business of his own. I caught him sneaking up into the office a number of times after hours, and when I asked Field about him, he would sneer and say, 'Oh, that's only Parson Johnny, a friend of mine!' But it was sufficient to establish the man's identity. What their connection was I can't tell you, because I don't know."

"Thanks, Morgan," said the Inspector. "I'm glad you told me that. And now—one last question. Have you ever heard the name Charles Michaels?"

"To be sure I have," responded Morgan grimly. "Michaels was Field's so-called valet—he acted in the capacity of bodyguard and was really a blackguard, or I'm greatly mistaken in my judgment of men. He came to the office once in a while. I can't think of anything else about him, Inspector."

"He knows you, of course?" asked Queen.

"Why—I suppose so," returned Morgan doubtfully. "I never spoke to him, but undoubtedly he saw me during his visits to the office."

"Well, now, that's fine, Morgan," grunted Queen, rising. "This has been a most interesting and informative chat. And—no, I don't think there's anything else. That is, at the moment. Just ride along, Morgan, and keep in town—available if we need you for anything. Remember that, won't you?"

"I'm not likely to forget it," said Morgan dully. "And—of course the story I told you—about my son—it won't come out?"

"You needn't have the slightest fear—about that, Morgan," said Queen, and a few moments later he and Ellery were on the sidewalk.

"So it was blackmail, Dad," murmured Ellery. "That gives me an idea, do you know?"

"Well, son, I've a few ideas of my own!" chuckled Queen, and in a telepathic silence they walked briskly down the street in the direction of headquarters.

12

IN WHICH THE QUEENS INVADE SOCIETY

Wednesday morning found Djuna pouring the coffee before a bemused Inspector and a chattering Ellery. The telephone bell rang. Both Ellery and his father jumped for the instrument.

"Here! What are you doing?" exclaimed Queen. "I'm expecting a call and that's it!"

"Now, now, sir, allow a bibliophile the privilege of using his own telephone," retorted Ellery. "I have a feeling that that's my friend the bookdealer calling me about the elusive Falconer."

"Look here, Ellery, don't start—" While they were chaffing each other good-naturedly across the table, Djuna picked up the telephone.

"The Inspector—the Inspector, did you say? Inspector," said Djuna, grinning as he held the mouthpiece to his thin chest, "it's for you."

Ellery subsided in his chair while Queen, with an air of triumph, snatched the instrument

"Yes?"

"Stoates calling from Field's office, Inspector," came a fresh cheery young voice. "I want to put Mr. Cronin on the wire."

The Inspector's brow wrinkled in anticipation. Ellery was listening intently, and even Djuna, with the monkeylike eagerness of his sharp features, had become rooted to his corner, as if he, too, awaited important news. Djuna in this respect resembled his brother anthropoid—there was an alertness, a bright inquisitiveness in his attitude and mien which delighted the Queens eternally.

Finally a high-pitched voice came over the wire. "This is Tim Cronin speaking, Inspector," came Cronin's excited tones. "As you know, I've been watching this bird Field for years. He's been my pet nightmare for as long as I can remember. The D. A. tells me that he gave you the story night before last, so I needn't go into it. But in all these years of watching and waiting and digging I've never been able to find a solitary piece of evidence against that crook that I could bring into a courtroom. And he was a crook, Inspector—I'd stake my life on that. . . . Anyway, it's the old story here. I really shouldn't have hoped for anything better, knowing Field as I did. And yet—well, I couldn't help praying that somewhere, somehow, he would slip up, and that I'd nail it when I could get my hands on his private records. Inspector—there's nothing doing."

Queen's face reflected a fleeting disappointment, which Ellery interpreted with a sigh, rising as he did so to walk restlessly up and down the room.

"I guess we can't help it, Tim," returned Queen, with an effort at heartiness. "Don't worry—we've other irons in the fire."

"Inspector," said Cronin abruptly, "you've got your hands full. Field was a really slick article. And from the way it looks to me, the genius who could get past his guard and put him away is a really slick article, too. He couldn't be anything else. Incidentally, we're not halfway through with the files and maybe what we've looked over isn't as unpromising as I made it sound. There's plenty here to suggest shady work on Field's part—it's just that there's no direct incriminating evidence. We're hoping that we find something as we go on."

"All right, Tim—keep up the good work," muttered the Inspector. "And let me know how you make out. . . . Is Lewin there?"

"You mean the office manager?" Cronin's voice lowered. "He's around somewhere. Why?"

"You want to keep your eye peeled," said Queen. "I have a sneaking suspicion he's not as stupid as he sounds. Just don't let him get too familiar with any records lying around. For all we know, he may have been in on Field's little sideline."

"Right, Inspector. Call you sometime later," and the receiver clicked as Cronin hung up.

At ten-thirty Queen and Ellery pushed open the high gate at the entrance to the Ives-Pope residence on Riverside Drive. Ellery was moved to remark that the atmosphere was a perfect invitation to formal morning dress and that he was going to feel extremely uncomfortable when they were admitted through the stone portals.

In truth, the house which concealed the destinies of the Ives-Popes was in many respects awe-inspiring to men of the modest tastes of the Queens. It was a huge rambling old stone house, set far back from the Drive, hunched on the greensward of a respectable acreage. "Must have cost a pretty penny," grunted the Inspector as his eyes swept the rolling lawns surrounding the building. Gardens and summer-houses; walks and bowered nooks—one would have thought himself miles away from the city which roared by a scant few rods away, behind the high iron palings which circled the mansion. The Ives-Popes were immensely wealthy and brought to this not uncommon possession a lineage stretching back into the dim recesses of American colonization.

The front door was opened by a whiskered patrician whose back seemed composed of steel and whose nose was elevated at a perilous angle toward the ceiling. Ellery lounged in the doorway, surveying this uniformed nobleman with admiration, while Inspector Queen fumbled in his pockets for a card. He was a long time producing one; the stiff-backed flunkey stood graven into stone. Red-faced, the Inspector finally discovered a battered card. He placed it on the extended salver and watched the butler retreat to some cavern of his own.

Ellery chuckled as his father drew himself up at the sight of Franklin Ives-Pope's burly figure emerging from a wide carved doorway.

The financier hurried toward them.

"Inspector! Mr. Queen!" he exclaimed in a cordial tone. "Come right in. Have you been waiting long?"

The Inspector mumbled a greeting. They walked through a high-ceilinged shining-floored hall, decorated with austere old furniture.

"You're on the dot, gentlemen," said Ives-Pope, standing aside to allow them to pass into a large room. "Here are some additional members of our little board meeting. I think you know all of us present."

The Inspector and Ellery looked about. "I know everybody, sir, except that gentleman—I presume he is Mr. Stanford Ives-Pope," said Queen. "I'm afraid my son has still to make the acquaintance of—Mr. Peale, is it?—Mr. Barry—and, of course, Mr. Ives-Pope."

The introductions were made in a strained fashion. "Ah, Q!" murmured District Attorney Sampson, hurrying across the room. "I wouldn't have missed this for the world," he said in a low tone. "First time I've met most of the people who'll be present at the inquisition."

"What is that fellow Peale doing here?" muttered Queen to the District Attorney, while Ellery crossed the room to engage the three young men on the other side in conversation. Ives-Pope had excused himself and disappeared.

"He's a friend of young Ives-Pope, and, of course, he's chummy with Barry there, too," returned the District Attorney. "I gathered from the chitchat before you came that Stanford, Ives-Pope's son, originally introduced these professional people to his sister Frances. That's how she met Barry and fell in love with him. Peale seems on good terms with the young lady, too."

"I wonder how much Ives-Pope and his aristocratic spouse

like the bourgeois company their children keep," said the Inspector, eyeing the small group on the other side of the room with interest.

"You'll find out soon enough," chuckled Sampson. "Just watch the icicles dripping from Mrs. Ives-Pope's eyebrows every time she sees one of these actors. I imagine they're about as welcome as a bunch of Bolsheviks."

Queen put his hands behind his back and stared curiously about the room. It was a library, well stocked with rich and rare books, catalogued carefully and immaculate behind shining glass. A desk dominated the center of the room. It was unpretentious for a millionaire's study, the Inspector noted with approval.

"Incidentally," resumed Sampson, "Eve Ellis, the girl who you said was with Miss Ives-Pope and her fiancé at the Roman Theatre Monday night is here, too. She's upstairs keeping the little heiress company, I imagine. Don't think the old lady likes it much. But they're both charming girls."

"What a pleasant place this must be when the Ives-Popes and the actors get together in private!" grunted Queen.

The four young men strolled towards them. Stanford Ives-Pope was a slender, well-manicured young man, fashionably dressed. There were deep pouches under his eyes. He wore a restless air of boredom that Queen was quick to note. Both Peale and Barry, the actors, were attired faultlessly.

"Mr. Queen tells me that you've got a pretty problem on your hands, Inspector," drawled Stanford Ives-Pope. "We're all uncommonly sorry to see poor Sis dragged into it. How in the world did her purse ever get into that chap's pocket? Barry hasn't slept for days over Frances' predicament, I give you my word!"

"My dear young man," said the Inspector, with a twinkle in his eye, "if I knew how Miss Ives-Pope's purse found its way into Monte Field's pocket, I wouldn't be here this morning. That's just one of the things that make this case so infernally interesting."

"The pleasure's all yours, Inspector. But you certainly can't think Frances had the slightest connection with all this?"

Queen smiled. "I can't think anything yet, young man," he protested. "I haven't heard what your sister has to say about it."

"She'll explain all right, Inspector," said Stephen Barry, his handsome face drawn into lines of fatigue. "You needn't worry about that. It's the damnable suspicion that she's open to that makes me angry—the whole thing is ridiculous!"

"I know just how you feel, Mr. Barry," said the Inspector kindly. "And I want to take this opportunity of apologizing for my conduct the other night. I was perhaps a little—harsh."

"I suppose I ought to apologize, too," returned Barry, with a wan smile. "I guess I said a few things I didn't mean in that office. In the heat of the moment—seeing Frances—Miss Ives-Pope go off in a faint—" He paused awkwardly.

Peale, a massive giant, ruddy and wholesome in his morning clothes, put his arm affectionately about Barry's shoulders. "I'm sure the Inspector understood, Steve old boy," he said cheerfully. "Don't take it so much to heart—everything's bound to come out all right."

"You can leave it to Inspector Queen," said Sampson, nudging the Inspector jovially in the ribs. "He's the only bloodhound

I've ever met who has a heart under his badge—and if Miss Ives-Pope can clear this thing up to his satisfaction, even to a reasonable extent, that will be the end of it."

"Oh, I don't know," murmured Ellery thoughtfully. "Dad's a great one for surprises. As for Miss Ives-Pope"—he smiled ruefully and bowed to the actor—"Mr. Barry, you're a deucedly lucky fellow."

"You wouldn't think so if you saw the mater," drawled Stanford Ives-Pope. "If I'm not mistaken, here she barges in now."

The men turned toward the door. An enormously stout woman was waddling in. A uniformed nurse supported her carefully under one huge arm, holding a large green bottle in her other hand. The financier followed briskly, by the side of a white-haired youngish looking man, wearing a dark coat and holding a black bag in his hand.

"Catharine, my dear," said Ives-Pope in a low voice to the stout woman as she sank into a greatchair, "these are the gentlemen whom I told you about—Inspector Richard Queen and Mr. Ellery Queen."

The two Queens bowed, receiving a stony glance from the myopic eyes of Mrs. Ives-Pope. "Charmed, I'm sure," she shrilled. "Where's Nurse? Nurse! I feel faint, please."

The uniformed girl hurried to her side, the green bottle ready. Mrs. Ives-Pope closed her eyes and inhaled, sighing with relief. The financier hurriedly introduced the white-haired man, Dr. Vincent Cornish, the family physician. The physician made swift apologies and disappeared behind the butler. "Great chap, this Cornish," whispered Sampson to Queen. "Not only the most fashionable doctor on the Drive, but a genuine scientist as well." The Inspector elevated his brows, but said nothing.

"The mater's one reason why I never cared for the medical profession," Stanford Ives-Pope was saying in a loud whisper to Ellery.

"Ah! Frances, my dear!" Ives-Pope hurried forward, followed by Barry, who dashed for the door. Mrs. Ives-Pope's fishy stare enveloped his back with cold disapproval. James Peale coughed embarrassedly and made a mumbled remark to Sampson.

Frances, attired in a filmy morning gown, her face pale and drawn, entered the room leaning heavily on the arm of Eve Ellis, the actress. Her smile was somewhat forced as she murmured a greeting to the Inspector. Eve Ellis was introduced by Peale and the two girls seated themselves near Mrs. Ives-Pope. The old lady was sitting squarely in her chair, glaring about her like a lioness whose cub has been threatened. Two servants appeared silently and set chairs for the men. At Ives-Pope's urgent request Queen sat down at the big desk. Ellery refused a chair, preferring to lean against a bookcase behind and to the side of the company.

When the conversation had died away the Inspector cleared his throat and turned toward Frances, who after a startled flutter of the eyelids returned his glance steadily.

"First of all Miss Frances—I hope I may call you that," began Queen in a fatherly tone, "allow me to explain my tactics of Monday night and to apologize for what must have seemed to you a totally unwarranted severity. From what Mr. Ives-Pope has told me, you can explain your actions on the night of the murder of Monte Field. I take it, therefore, that as far as you are concerned our little chat this morning will effectually remove you from the investigation. Before we have that chat, please believe me when I say that Monday night you were to me merely one of a number of suspicious characters. I acted in accordance with my habits in such cases. I see now how, to a woman of your breeding and social position, a grilling by a policeman under such tense circumstances would cause sufficient shock to bring on your present condition."

Frances smiled wearily. "You're forgiven, Inspector," she said in a clear, low voice. "It was my fault for being so foolish. I'm ready to answer any questions you may care to ask me."

"In just a moment, my dear." The Inspector shifted a bit to include the entire silent company in his next remark. "I should like to make one point, ladies and gentlemen," he said gravely. "We are assembled here for a definite purpose, which is to discover a possible connection, and there must be one, between the fact that Miss Ives-Pope's bag was found in the dead man's pocket, and the fact that Miss Ives-Pope apparently was unable to explain this circumstance. Now, whether this morning's work bears fruit or not, I must ask you all to keep whatever is said a profound secret. As District Attorney Sampson knows very well, I do not generally conduct an investigation with such a large audience. But I am making this exception because I believe you are all deeply concerned in the unfortunate young lady who has been drawn into this crime. You cannot, however, expect any consideration at my hands if one word of today's conversation reaches outside ears. Do we understand each other?"

"I say, Inspector," protested young Ives-Pope, "that's putting it a bit strong, don't you think? We all of us know the story, anyway."

"Perhaps, Mr. Ives-Pope," retorted the Inspector with a grim smile, "that is the reason I have consented to have all of you here."

There was a little rustle and Mrs. Ives-Pope opened her mouth as if to burst into wrathful speech. A sharp look from her husband made her lips droop together, with the protest unuttered. She transferred her glare to the actress sitting by Frances' side. Eve Ellis blushed. The nurse stood by Mrs. Ives-Pope with the smelling salts, like a setter dog about to point.

"Now, Miss Frances," resumed Queen kindly, "this is where we stand. I examine the body of a dead man named Monte Field, prominent lawyer, who was apparently enjoying an interesting play before he was so unceremoniously done away with, and find, in the rear coattail pocket of his full-dress suit, an evening bag. I identify this as yours by a few calling cards and some personal papers inside. I say to myself, 'Aha! A lady enters the problem!'—naturally enough. And I send one of my men to summon you, with the idea of allowing you to explain a most suspicious circumstance. You come—and you faint on being confronted with your property and the news of its place of discovery. At the time, I say to myself, 'This young lady knows something!'—a not unnatural conclusion. Now, in what way can you convince me that you know nothing—and that your fainting was caused only by the shock of the thing? Remember, Miss Frances—I am putting the problem not as Richard Queen but as a policeman looking for the truth."

"My story is not as illuminating, perhaps, as you might like it to be, Inspector," answered Frances quietly, in the deep hush that followed Queen's peroration. "I don't see how it is going to help you at all. But some facts which I think unimportant may be significant to your trained mind. . . . Roughly, this is what happened.

"I came to be in the Roman Theatre Monday night in a natural way. Since my engagement to Mr. Barry, although it has been a very quiet affair"—Mrs. Ives-Pope sniffed; her husband looked steadfastly at a point beyond his daughter's dark hair—"I have often dropped into the theatre, following a habit of meeting my fiancé after the performance. At such times he would either escort me home or take me to some place in the neighborhood for supper. Generally we make arrangements beforehand for these theatre meetings; but sometimes I drop in unexpectedly if the opportunity presents itself. Monday night was one of those times. . . ."

"I got to the Roman a few minutes before the end of the first act, since I have of course seen 'Gunplay' any number of times. I had my regular seat—arranged for me many weeks ago by Mr. Barry through Mr. Panzer—and had no more than settled myself to watch the performance when the curtain came down for the first intermission. I was feeling a little warm; the air was none too good. . . . I went first to the ladies' restroom downstairs off the general lounge. Then I came up again and went out into the alley through the open door. There was quite a crowd of people there, enjoying the air."

She paused for a moment and Ellery, leaning against the

bookcase, sharply surveyed the faces of the little audience. Mrs. Ives-Pope was looking about in her leviathan manner: Ives-Pope was still staring at the wall above Frances' head; Stanford was biting his fingernails; Peale and Barry were both watching Frances with nervous sympathy, looking furtively at Queen as if to gauge the effect of her words upon him; Eve Ellis' hand had stolen forward to clasp Frances' firmly.

The Inspector cleared his throat once more.

"Which alley was it, Miss Frances—the one on the left or the one on the right?" he asked.

"The one on the left, Inspector," she answered promptly. "You know I was sitting in M8 Left, and I suppose it was natural for me to go to the alley on that side."

"Quite so," said Queen smiling. "Go on, please."

"I stepped out into the alley," she resumed, less nervously, "and, not seeing any one I knew, stood close to the brick wall of the theatre, a little behind the open iron door. The freshness of the night air after the rain was delightful. I hadn't been standing there more than two minutes when I felt somebody brush up against me. I naturally moved a little to one side, thinking the person had stumbled. But when he—it was a man—when he did it again, I became a little frightened and started to walk away. He—he grasped my wrist and pulled me back. We were halfway behind the iron door, which was not pushed back completely and I doubt if anyone noticed his action."

"I see—I see," murmured the Inspector sympathetically. "It seems an unusual thing for a total stranger to do in a public place."

"It seemed as if he wanted to kiss me, Inspector. He leaned over and whispered, 'Good evening, honey!' and—well, of course, I jumped to that conclusion. I drew back a little and said as coldly as I could, 'Please let me go, or I will call for help.' He just laughed at that and bent closer. The reek of whisky on his breath was overpowering. It made me ill."

She stopped. Eve Ellis patted her hand reassuringly. Peale nudged Barry forcibly as the young man half-rose to his feet in muttered protest "Miss Frances, I'm going to ask you a peculiar question—it's almost ridiculous when you come to think of it," said the Inspector, leaning back in his chair. "Did the reek on his breath suggest good liquor or bad liquor? . . . There! I knew you'd smile." And the entire company tittered at the whimsical expression on Queen's face.

"Well, Inspector—it's hard to answer that," returned the girl freely. "I'm afraid I'm not on intimate terms with spirits. But from what I can remember, it had the odor of rather fine liquor. Fine liquor—but plenty of it!" she concluded with a grim little toss of her head.

"I would've spotted the vintage in a minute if I'd been there!" muttered Stanford Ives-Pope.

His father's lips tightened, but after a moment they relaxed into the suspicion of a grin. He shook his head warningly at his son.

"Go ahead, Miss Frances," said the Inspector.

"I was terribly frightened," the girl confessed, with a tremor of her red lips. "And feeling nauseated and all—I wrenched away from his outstretched hand and stumbled blindly into the theatre. The next thing I remember is sitting in my seat listening to the warning ring of the backstage bell, announcing the beginning of the second act. I really don't remember how I got there. My heart was in my throat and now I distinctly recall thinking that I would not tell Stephen—Mr. Barry—anything about the incident for fear he would want to look up this man and punish him. Mr. Barry is terribly jealous, you know." She smiled tenderly at her fiancé, who suddenly smiled back at her.

"And that, Inspector, is all I know about what happened Monday night," she resumed. "I know you're going to ask me where my purse comes into it. Well—it doesn't at all, Inspector. Because on my word of honor I can't remember a thing about it!"

Queen shifted in his chair. "And how is that, Miss Frances?"

"Actually, I didn't even know I had lost it until you showed it to me in the manager's office," she answered bravely. "I recall taking it with me when I rose at the end of the first act to go to the restroom; and also opening it there to use my powderpuff. But whether I left it there or dropped it later, somewhere else, I don't know to this minute."

"Don't you think, Miss Frances," interposed Queen, reaching for his snuffbox and then guiltily dropping it back into his pocket as he met the icy gaze of Mrs. Ives-Pope, "that you might have dropped it in the alley after this man accosted you?"

A look of relief spread over the girl's face, and it became almost animated. "Why, Inspector!" she cried. "That was just what I have thought about it all the time, but it seemed such a lame explanation—and I was so horribly afraid that I might be caught in a sort of—of spider's web. . . . I just couldn't bring myself to tell you that! While I don't actually remember, it seems logical, doesn't it?—that I dropped it when he grasped my wrist and entirely forgot about it afterward."

The Inspector smiled. "On the contrary, my dear," he said, "it is the only explanation which seems to cover the facts. In all probability this man found it there—picked it up—and in a moment of half-drunken amorousness put it into his pocket, probably intending to return it to you later. In this way he would have had another opportunity to meet you. He seems to have been quite smitten by your charms, my dear—and no wonder." And the Inspector bowed a little stiffly while the girl, the color in her face now completely restored, favored him with a dazzling smile.

"Now—a few things more, Miss Frances, and this little inquisition will be over," continued Queen. "Can you describe his physical appearance?"

"Oh, yes!" Frances returned quickly. "He made a rather forcible impression on me, as you can imagine. He was a trifle taller than I—that would make him about five feet eight—and inclined to corpulence. His face was bloated and he had deep leaden-colored pouches under his eyes. I've never seen a more dissipated-looking man. He was clean-shaven. There was nothing remarkable about his features except perhaps a prominent nose."

"That would be our friend Mr. Field, all right," remarked the Inspector grimly. "Now—think carefully, Miss Frances. Did you ever meet this man anywhere before—did you recognize him at all?"

The girl responded instantly. "I don't have to think much about that, Inspector. I can answer positively that I never saw the man before in my life!"

The pause which ensued was broken by the cool, even tones of Ellery. All heads turned toward him in a startled manner as he spoke.

"I beg your pardon, Miss Ives-Pope, for interrupting," he said affably. "But I am curious to know whether you noticed how the man who accosted you was dressed."

Frances turned her smile upon Ellery, who blinked quite humanly. "I didn't take particular notice of his clothes, Mr. Queen," she said, displaying white, brilliant teeth. "But I seem to remember his wearing a full-dress suit—his shirt bosom was a little stained—they were like liquor stains—and a tophat. From what I recall of his attire, it was rather fastidious and in good taste, except, of course, for the stains on his shirt."

Ellery murmured a fascinated thanks and subsided against the bookcase. With a sharp look at his son, Queen rose to his feet.

"Then that will be all, ladies and gentlemen. I think we may safely consider the incident closed."

There was an instantaneous little burst of approval and everybody rose to press in on Frances, who was radiant with happiness. Barry, Peale and Eve Ellis bore Frances off in triumphal march, while Stanford, with a lugubrious smile, offered his mother a carefully elbowed arm.

"Thus endeth the first lesson," he announced gravely. "Mater, my arm before you faint!" A protesting Mrs. Ives-Pope departed, leaning ponderously on her son.

Ives-Pope shook Queen's hand vigorously. "Then you think it's all over as far as my girl is concerned?" he asked.

"I think so, Mr. Ives-Pope," answered the Inspector. "Well, sir, thank you for your courtesy. And now we must be going—lots of work to do. Coming, Henry?"

Five minutes later Queen, Ellery and District Attorney Sampson were striding side by side down Riverside Drive toward 72nd Street, earnestly discussing the events of the morning.

"I'm glad that line of investigation is cleared up with no result," said Sampson dreamily. "By the Lord Harry, I admire that girl's pluck, Q!"

"Good child," said the Inspector. "What do you think, Ellery?" he asked suddenly, turning on his son, who was walking along staring at the River.

"Oh, she's charming," Ellery said at once, his abstracted eyes brightening.

"I didn't mean the girl, my son," said his father irritably. "I meant the general aspect of the morning's work."

"Oh, that!" Ellery smiled a little. "Do you mind if I become Æsopian?"

"Yes," groaned his father.

"A lion," said Ellery, "may be beholden to a mouse."

13

QUEEN TO QUEEN

Djuna had just cleared the table of the dinner dishes and was serving coffee to the two Queens at six-thirty that evening when the outer doorbell rang. The little man-of-all-work straightened his tie, pulled down his jacket (while the Inspector and Ellery eyed him in twinkling amusement), and marched gravely into the foyer. He was back in a moment bearing a silver tray upon which lay two calling cards. The Inspector picked them up with beetling brows.

"Such ceremony, Djuna!" he murmured. "Well, well! So 'Doc' Prouty's bringing a visitor. Show 'em in, you imp!"

Djuna marched back and returned with the Chief Assistant Medical Examiner and a tall, thin, emaciated man, entirely bald and wearing a closely clipped beard. Queen and Ellery rose.

"I've been expecting to hear from you, Doc!" Queen grinned, shaking hands with Prouty. "And if I'm not mistaken, here's

Professor Jones himself! Welcome to our castle, Doctor." The thin man bowed.

"This is my son and keeper of my conscience, Doctor," Queen added, presenting Ellery. "Ellery—Dr. Thaddeus Jones."

Dr. Jones offered a large limp hand. "So you're the chap Queen and Sampson keep prattling about!" he boomed. "Certainly happy to meet you, sir."

"I've been fairly itching to be introduced to New York City's Paracelsus and eminent Toxicologist," smiled Ellery. "The honor of rattling the city's skeletons is all yours." He shuddered elaborately and indicated some chairs. The four men sat down.

"Join us in some coffee, gentlemen," urged Queen, and shouted to Djuna, whose bright eyes were visible from behind the kitchenette door. "Djuna! You rascal! Coffee for four!" Djuna grinned and disappeared, to pop out a moment later like a jack-in-the-box, bearing four cups of steaming coffee.

Prouty, who resembled the popular conception of Mephistopheles, whipped from his pocket one of his black, dangerous-looking cigars and began to puff away furiously.

"This chitter-chatter may be all right for you men of leisure," he said briskly, between puffs, "but I've been working like a beaver all day analyzing the contents of a lady's stomach, and I want to get home for some sleep."

"Hear, hear!" murmured Ellery, "I gather from your soliciting the aid of Professor Jones that you met with some obstruction in your analysis of Mr. Field's corporeal remains. Lay on, Æsculapius!"

"I'll lay on," returned Prouty grimly. "You're right—I met

with a violent obstruction. I've had some little experience, if you'll pardon the professional modesty, in examining the innards of deceased ladies and gentlemen, but I'll confess I never saw 'em in such a mess as this chap Field's. Seriously, Jones will attest to the truth of *that.* His æsophagus, for example, and the entire tracheal tract looked as if some one had taken a blowtorch and played it gently over his insides."

"What was it—couldn't have been bichloride of mercury, could it, Doc?" asked Ellery, who prided himself on a complete ignorance of the exact sciences.

"Hardly," growled Prouty. "But let me tell you what happened. I analyzed for every poison on the calendar, and although this one had familiar petroleum components I couldn't place it exactly. Yes, sir—I was stumped good and proper. And to let you in on a secret—the Medical Examiner himself, who thought I was pie-eyed from overwork, made a stab at it with his own fine Italian hand. The net result in his case, my boys, was zero. And the M. E.'s not exactly a novice either when it comes to chemical analysis. So we surrendered the problem to our fountainhead of learning. Let him spout his own story."

Dr. Thaddeus Jones cleared his throat forbiddingly. "Thank you, my friend, for a most dramatic introduction," he said in his deep lumbering voice. "Yes, Inspector, the remains were turned over to me, and in all seriousness, I want to say here and now that my discovery was the most startling the Toxicologist's office has made in fifteen years!"

"My, my!" murmured Queen, taking a pinch of snuff. "I'm beginning to respect the mentality of our friend the murderer.

So many things point to the unusual lately! And what did you find, Doctor?"

"I took it for granted that Prouty and the Medical Examiner had done the preliminaries very well," began Dr. Jones, crossing his bony knees. "They generally do. And so, before anything else, I analayzed for the obscure poisons. Obscure, that is to say, from the standpoint of the criminal user. To show you how minutely I searched—I even thought of that favorite standby of our friends the fiction writers: *curare,* the South American toxin which makes the grade in four out of five detective stories. But even that sadly abused member of the toxic family disappointed me. . . ."

Ellery leaned back and laughed. "If you're referring in a mildly satirical way to my profession, Dr. Jones, let me inform you that I have never used *curare* in any of my novels."

The toxicologist's eyes twinkled. "So you're one of them, too, eh? Queen, old man," he added dolorously, turning to the Inspector, who was thoughtfully chewing on a piece of French pastry, "allow me to offer you my condolences. . . . At any rate, gentlemen, let me explain that in the case of rare poisons we can generally come to a definite conclusion without much trouble—that is, rare poisons that are in the pharmacopoeia. Of course, there are any number of rare poisons of which we have no knowledge whatever—Eastern drugs particularly.

"Well, to make a long story short, I found myself faced with the unpleasant conclusion that I was up a tree." Dr. Jones chuckled in reminiscence. "It wasn't a pleasant conclusion. The poison I analyzed had certain properties which were vaguely familiar, as

Prouty has said, and others which didn't jibe at all. I spent most of yesterday evening mulling over my retorts and testtubes, and late last night I suddenly got the answer."

Ellery and Queen sat up straight and Dr. Prouty relaxed in his chair with a sigh, reaching for a second cup of coffee. The toxicologist uncrossed his legs, his voice booming more terrifyingly than ever.

"The poison that killed your victim, Inspector, is known as tetra ethyl lead!"

To a scientist this announcement, in Dr. Jones's profoundest tones, might have carried a dramatic quality. To the Inspector it meant less than nothing. As for Ellery, he murmured, "Sounds like a mythological monster to me!"

Dr. Jones went on, smiling. "So it hasn't impressed you much, eh? But let me tell you a little about tetra ethyl lead. It is almost odorless—to be more exact, it resembles chloroform in physical appearance. Point number one. Point number two—it has an odor—faint, to be sure—but distinctly like that of ether. Point number three—it is fearfully potent. So potent—but let me illustrate just what this devilishly powerful chemical substance will do to living tissue."

By this time the toxicologist had gained the entire attention of his audience.

"I took a healthy rabbit, of the sort we use for experiment, and painted—just painted, mind you—the tender area behind the creature's ear with an undiluted dose of the stuff. Remember, this was not an internal injection. It was merely a painting of the skin. It would have to be absorbed through the dermis before it reached the bloodstream. I watched the rabbit for an hour—and after that I didn't have to watch him any more. He was as dead as any dead rabbit I ever saw."

"That doesn't seem so powerful to me, Doctor," protested the Inspector.

"It doesn't, eh? Well, take my word for it that it's extraordinary. For a mere daubing of whole, healthy skin—I tell you, I was astounded. If the skin had an incision of some sort, or if the poison were administered internally, that would be a different story. You can imagine, therefore, what happened to Field's insides when he *swallowed* the stuff—and he swallowed plenty!"

Ellery's brow was wrinkled in thought. He began to polish the lenses of his pince-nez.

"And that isn't all," resumed Dr. Jones. "As far as I know—and I have been in the service of the city for God knows how many years, and I've not kept uninformed about the progress of my science in other parts of the world, either—as far as I know, terra ethyl lead has never before been used for criminal purposes!"

The Inspector drew up, startled. "That's saying something, Doctor!" he muttered. "Are you sure?"

"Positive. That's why I'm so keenly interested."

"Just how long would it take for this poison to kill a man, Doctor?" asked Ellery slowly.

Dr. Jones grimaced. "That's something I can't answer definitely, for the very good reason that to my knowledge no human being has ever died of its effects before. But I can make a fairly good guess. I can't conceive of Field having lived more than fifteen to twenty minutes at the utmost after having taken the poison internally."

The silence that followed was broken by a cough from Queen. "On the other hand, Doctor, this very strangeness of the poison should make it fairly easy to trace. What, would you say, is its commonest source? Where does it come from? How would I go about getting it if I wanted some for a criminal purpose and didn't want to leave a trail?"

A gaunt smile lit up the features of the toxicologist. "The job of tracing this stuff, Inspector," he said fervently, "I'll leave to you. You can have it. Tetra ethyl lead, as far as I've been able to determine—remember, it is almost entirely new to us—occurs most commonly in certain petroleum products. I tinkered around quite a bit before I found the easiest way of making it in quantity. You'll never guess how it's done. It can be extracted from common, ordinary, everyday gasoline!"

The two Queens exclaimed under their breaths. "Gasoline!" cried the Inspector. "Why—how on earth could a man trace that?"

"That's the point," answered the toxicologist. "I could go to the corner gas station, fill up the tank of my car, run it home, extract some of the gasoline from the tank, go into my laboratory and distill the tetra ethyl lead in remarkably little-time with remarkably little effort!"

"Doesn't that imply, Doctor," put in Ellery hopefully, "that the murderer of Field had some laboratory experience—knew something about chemical analysis, and all that sort of rot?"

"No, it doesn't. Any man with a home-brew 'still' in his house could distill that poison without leaving a trace. The beauty of the process is that the tetra ethyl lead in the gasoline has a higher boiling point than any other of the fluid's constituents. All you have to do is distill everything out up to a certain temperature, and what's left is this poison."

The Inspector took a pinch of snuff with trembling fingers. "All I can say is—I take my hat off to the murderer," he muttered. "Tell me—Doctor—wouldn't a man have to know quite a bit about toxicology to possess such knowledge? How could he ever know this without some special interest—and therefore training—in the subject?"

Dr. Jones snorted. "Inspector, I'm surprised at you. Your question is already answered."

"How? What do you mean?"

"Haven't I just told you how to do it? And if you heard about the poison from a toxicologist, couldn't you make some provided you had the 'still'? You would require no knowledge except the boiling point of tetra ethyl lead. Get along with you, Queen! You haven't a chance in the world of tracing the murderer through the poison. In all probability he overheard a conversation between two toxicologists, or even between two medical men who had heard about the stuff. The rest was easy. I'm not saying this is so. The man might be a chemist, at that. But I'm concerned only in giving you the possibilities."

"I suppose it was administered in whisky, eh, Doctor?" asked Queen abstractedly.

"No doubt about it," returned the toxicologist. "The stomach, showed a large whisky content. Certainly, it would be an easy way for the murderer to slip it over on his victim. With the whisky you get nowadays, most of it smells etherized, anyway. And besides, Field probably had it down before he realized anything was wrong—if he did at all."

"Wouldn't he taste the stuff?" asked Ellery wearily.

"I've never tasted it, young man, so I can't say definitely," answered Dr. Jones, a trifle tartly. "But I doubt whether he would—sufficiently to alarm him, at any rate. Once he had it down it wouldn't make any difference."

Queen turned to Prouty, whose cigar had gone out. He had fallen into a hearty doze. "Say, Doc!"

Prouty opened his eyes sleepily. "Where are my slippers—I can't even seem to find my slippers, damn it!"

Despite the tension of the moment, there was a spontaneous roar of amusement at the expense of the Assistant Medical Examiner. When he had come to with sufficient thoroughness to understand what he had said, he joined the chuckling group and said, "Just goes to prove that I'd better be going home, Queen. What did you want to know?"

"Tell me," said Queen, still shaking, "what did you get from your analysis of the whisky?"

"Oh!" Prouty sobered instantly. "The whisky in the flask was as fine as any I've ever tested—and I've been doing nothing but testing booze for years now. It was the poison in the liquor on his breath that made me think at first that Field had drunk rotten booze. The Scotch and rye that you sent me in bottles from Field's apartment were also of the very highest quality. Probably the flask's contents came from the same place as the bottled stuff.

In fact, I should say that both samples were imported goods. I haven't come across domestic liquor of that caliber ever since the war—that is, except for the pre-war stuff that was stored away. . . . And I suppose Velie communicated my report to you that the ginger ale is okay."

Queen nodded. "Well, that seems to settle it," he said heavily. "It looks as if we're up against a blank wall on this tetra ethyl lead business. But just to make sure, Doc—work along with the professor here and try to locate a possible leak somewhere in the distribution of the poison. You fellows know more about that than anybody I could put on the case. It's just a stab in the dark and probably nothing will come of it."

"There's no question about it," murmured Ellery. "A novelist should stick to his last."

"I think," remarked Ellery eagerly, after the two doctors had gone, "that I'll amble down to my bookseller for that Falconer." He rose and began a hasty search for his coat.

"Here!" bellowed the Inspector, pulling him down into a chair. "Nothing doing. That blasted book of yours won't run away. I want you to sit here and keep my headache company."

Ellery nestled into the leather cushions with a sigh. "Just when I get to feeling that all investigations into the foibles of the human mind are useless and a waste of time, my worthy sire puts the onus of thought upon me again. Heigh-ho! What's on the menu?"

"I'm not putting any onus on you at all," growled Queen. "And stop using such big words. I'm dizzy enough. What I want you to do is help me go over this confounded mess of a case and see—well, what we can see."

"I might have suspected it," said Ellery. "Where do I start?"

"You don't," grunted his father. "I'm doing the talking tonight and you're going to listen. And you might make a few notes, too."

"Let's begin with Field. I think, in the first place, that we can take it for granted our friend went to the Roman Theatre Monday night not for pleasure but for business. Right?"

"No doubt about it in my mind," said Ellery. "What did Velie report about Field's movements Monday?,"

"Field got to his office at 9:30—his usual morning arrival hour. He worked until noon. He had no personal visitors all day. At twelve o'clock he lunched at the Webster Club alone, and at 1:30 returned to his office. He worked steadily until 4:00—and seems to have gone straight home, as the doorman and elevator-man both testify he arrived at the apartment about 4:30. Velie could get no further data except that Michaels arrived at 5:00 and left at 6:00. Field left at 7:30, dressed as we found him. I have a list of the clients whom he saw during the day, but it doesn't tell much."

"How about the reason for his small bank account?" asked Ellery.

"Just what I figured," returned Queen. "Field has been losing steadily on the stock market—and not chicken feed, either. Velie's just run a little tip to earth which makes Field out as a frequent visitor to the racetrack, where he's also dropped plenty. For a shrewd man, he certainly was an easy mark for the wiseacres. Anyway, that explains his having so little cash in his personal account. And more than that—it probably also explains more conclusively the item of '50,000' on the program we found. That meant money, and the money it referred to was in some way connected, I'm sure, with the person he was to meet at the theatre.

"Now, I think that we can pretty well conclude that Field knew his murderer rather intimately. For one thing, he accepted a drink obviously without suspicion, or at least question; for another, the meeting seems to have been definitely arranged for purposes of concealment—why, else, if that is not so, was the theatre chosen for the meeting at all?"

"All right. Let me ask you the same question," interposed Ellery, puckering his lips. "Why *should* a theatre be chosen as a meeting place to transact a secret and undoubtedly nefarious business? Wouldn't a park be more secret? Wouldn't a hotel lobby have its advantages? Answer that."

"Unfortunately, my son," said the Inspector mildly, "Mr. Field could have had no definite knowledge that he was going to be murdered. As far as he was concerned, all he was going to do was to take care of his part of the transaction. As a matter of fact, Field *himself* might have chosen the theatre as the place of meeting. Perhaps he wanted to establish an alibi for something. There's no way of telling yet just what he wanted to do. As for the hotel lobby—certainly he would run a grave risk of being seen. He might have been unwilling, further, to risk himself in such a lonely place as a park. And, lastly, he may have had some particular reason for not wanting to be seen in the company of the second party. Remember—the ticket stubs we found showed that the other person did not come into the theatre at the same time as Field. But this is all fruitless conjecture—"

Ellery smiled in a thoughtful manner, but said nothing. He was thinking to himself that the old man had not completely satisfied the objection, and that this was a strange thing in a man of Inspector Queen's direct habits of thought. . . .

But Queen was continuing. "Very well. We must always bear in mind the further possibility that the person with whom Field transacted his business was *not* his murderer. Of course, this is merely a possibility. The crime seems to have been too well planned for that. But if this *is* so, then we must look for *two* people in the audience Monday night who were directly connected with Field's death."

"Morgan?" asked Ellery idly.

The Inspector shrugged his shoulders. "Perhaps. Why didn't he tell us about it when we spoke to him yesterday afternoon? He confessed everything else. Well, maybe because he felt that a confession of having paid blackmail to the murdered man, together with the fact that he was found in the theatre, would be too damning a bit of circumstantial evidence."

"Look at it this way," said Ellery. "Here we find a man dead who has written on his program the number '50,000,' obviously referring to dollars. We know from what both Sampson and Cronin have told us about Field that he was a man of unscrupulous and probably criminal character. Further, we know from Morgan that he was also a blackmailer. I think, therefore, we can deduce safely that he went to the Roman Theatre on Monday night to collect or arrange for the payment of $50,000 in blackmail from some person unknown. Right so far?"

"Go ahead," grunted the Inspector noncommittally.

"Very well," continued Ellery. "If we conclude that the person blackmailed that night and the murderer were one and the same, we need look no further for a motive. There's the motive ready made—to choke off the blackmailing Field. *If*, however, we proceed on the assumption that the murderer and the person blackmailed were not the same, but two entirely different individuals, *then* we must still scrabble about looking for a motive for the crime. My personal opinion is that this is unnecessary—that the murderer and the blackmailed person are one. What do you think?"

"I'm inclined to agree with you, Ellery," said the Inspector. "I merely mentioned the other possibility—did not state my own conviction. Let us proceed, for the time being, then, on the assumption that Field's blackmail victim and his murderer were the same. . . .

"Now—I want to clear up the matter of the missing tickets."

"Ah—the missing tickets," murmured Ellery. "I was wondering what you made of that."

"Don't be funny, now, you rascal," growled Queen. "Here's what I make of it. All in all, we are dealing with eight seats—one in which Field sat, for which we have the stub found on Field's person; one in which the murderer sat, for which we have the stub found by Flint; and finally the six empty seats for which tickets were bought, as established by the box-office report, and for which stubs were not found, torn or whole, anywhere in the theatre or box office. First of all, it is barely possible that all of those six whole tickets were in the theatre Monday night, and went out of the theatre on somebody's person. Remember, the search of individuals was necessarily not so exhaustive as to include an examination for small things like tickets. This, however, is highly improbable. The best explanation is that either Field or his murderer bought all eight tickets at one time, intending to use two and reserving the other six to insure absolute privacy during the short time that the business was to be transacted. In this case, the most sensible thing to have done was to destroy the tickets as soon as they were bought; which was probably done by either Field or the murderer, according to who made the arrangements. We must, therefore, forget those six tickets—they're gone and we'll never get our hands on them.

"To proceed," continued the Inspector. "We know that Field and his victim entered the theatre separately. This may positively be deduced from the fact that when I put the two stubs back to front, the torn edges did not match. When two people enter together, the tickets are presented together and are invariably torn together. Now—this does not say that they did not come in at practically the same time, because for purposes of safety they may have come in one after the other, as if they did not know each other. However, Madge O'Connell claims no one sat in LL30 during Act I, and the orangeade boy, Jess Lynch, testified that ten minutes after Act II had started, there was still no one in LL30. This means that the murderer either had not yet entered the theatre, *or* he had come in before but was sitting in some other part of the orchestra, having a ticket necessarily for another seat."

Ellery shook his head. "I realize that as well as you, son," said the old man testily. "I'm just following the thought through. I was going to say that it doesn't seem likely the murderer had come into the theatre at the regular time. It's probable that he entered at least ten minutes after the second act started."

"I can give you proof of that," said Ellery lazily.

The Inspector took a pinch of snuff. "I know—those cabalistic figures on the program. How did they read?"

930
815
50,000

"We know what the fifty thousand represented. The other two figures must have referred not to dollars, but to time. Look at the '815.' The play started at 8:25. In all likelihood Field arrived about 8:15, or if he arrived sooner, he had some cause to refer to his watch at that time. Now, if he had an appointment with some one who, we assume, arrived much later, what more likely than that Field should have idly jotted down on his program—first, the '50,000,' which indicates that he was thinking about the impending transaction, which involved $50,000 in blackmail; then 8:15, the time he was thinking about it; and finally 9:30—the time the blackmail victim was due to arrive! It's the most natural thing in the world for Field to have done this, as it would be for anyone who is in the habit of scribbling in idle moments.

It's very fortunate for us, because it points to two things: first, to the exact time of the appointment with the murderer—9:30; and, second, it corroborates our conjecture as regards the actual time the murder was committed. At 9:25 Lynch saw Field alive and alone; at 9:30, by Field's written evidence, the murderer was due to arrive, and we take it for granted he did; according to Dr. Jones' statement it would take the poison from fifteen to twenty minutes to kill Field—and in view of Pusak's discovery at 9:55 of the dead body, we may say that the poison was administered about 9:35. If the tetra ethyl lead took at the most twenty minutes—that gives us 9:55. Much before then, of course, the murderer left the scene of the crime. Remember—he could not have known that our friend Mr. Pusak would suddenly desire to rise and leave his seat. The murderer was probably figuring that Field's body would not be discovered until the intermission, at 10:05, which would have been ample time for Field to have died without being able to murmur any message at all. Luckily for our mysterious murderer Field was discovered too late to gasp more than the information that he'd been murdered. If Pusak had walked out five minutes earlier we'd have our elusive friend behind the bars right now."

"Bravo!" murmured Ellery, smiling affectionately. "A perfect recitation. My congratulations."

"Oh, go jump in the bathtub," growled his father. "At this point I just want to repeat what you brought out Monday night in Panzer's office—the fact that although the murderer quitted the scene of the crime between 9:30 and 9:55, he was present in the theatre all the rest of the evening until we allowed everybody to go home. Your examination of the guards and the O'Connell girl, together with the doorman's evidence, Jess Lynch's presence in the alley, the usher's corroboration of this fact and all the rest of it, takes care of that. . . . He was there, all right.

"This leaves us momentarily up a tree. All we can do now is consider some of the personalities we've bumped into in the course of the investigation," went on the Inspector with a sigh. "First—did Madge O'Connell tell the truth when she said she had seen no one pass up or down the aisle during the second act? And that she had not seen, at anytime during the evening at all, the person who we know sat in LL30 from half-past nine until ten or fifteen minutes before the body was discovered?"

"It's a tricky question, Dad," remarked Ellery seriously, "because if she was lying about these things, we are losing a mine of information. If she *was* lying—good Lord!—she might be in a position at this moment either to describe, or identify, or possibly name the murderer! However, her nervousness and peculiar attitude might be ascribed to her knowledge that Parson Johnny was in the theatre, with a pack of policemen just aching to get their fingers on him."

"Sounds reasonable to me," grumbled Queen. "Well, what about Parson Johnny? How does he fit into this—or does he fit into it at all? We must always remember that, according to Morgan's statement, Cazzanelli was actively associated with Field. Field had been his lawyer, and perhaps had even bought the Parson's services for this shady business Cronin is nosing around about. If the Parson was not there by accident, was he there through Field or through Madge O'Connell, as she and he both say? I think, my son," he added with a fierce tug at his mustache, "that I'm going to give Parson Johnny a taste of the lash—it won't hurt his thick hide! And that snippy little O'Connell chit—won't do any harm to scare the wits out of her either. . . ."

He took an enormous pinch of snuff, sneezing to the tune of Ellery's sympathetic chuckles.

"And dear old Benjamin Morgan," continued the Inspector, "was he telling the truth about the anonymous letter which so conveniently gave him a mysterious source for his theatre ticket?

"And that most interesting lady, Mrs. Angela Russo. . . . Ah, the ladies, bless 'em! They always muddle a man's logic so. What did she say—that she came to Field's apartment at 9:30? Is her alibi perfectly sound? Of course, the doorman at the apartment house confirmed her statement. But it's easy to 'fix' doormen. . . . Does she know more than she had indicated about Field's business—particularly his private business? Was she lying when she said that Field told her he would be back at ten o'clock? Remember, we know that Field had an appointment in the Roman Theatre beginning at 9:30—did he really expect to keep it and be back at his rooms by ten o'clock? By cab it would be a fifteen or twenty-minute drive, through traffic, which would leave only ten minutes for the transaction—possible, of course. Couldn't do it much sooner by subway, either. We mustn't forget, too, that this woman was not in the theatre at any time during the evening."

"You'll have your hands full with that fair flower of Eve," remarked Ellery. "It's so beautifully evident that she's keeping back a story of some sort. Did you notice that brazen defiance?

Wasn't mere bravado. She knows something, Dad. I would certainly keep my eye on her—sooner or later she'll give herself away."

"Hagstrom will take care of her," said Queen abstractedly. "Now, how about Michaels? He has no supported alibi for Monday evening. But then it might not make any difference. He wasn't in the theatre. . . . There's something fishy about that fellow. Was he really looking for something when he came to Field's apartment Tuesday morning? We've made a thorough search of the premises—is it possible we've overlooked something? It's quite evident that he was lying when he spilled that story about the check, and not knowing that Field was dead. And consider this—he *must* have realized that he was running into danger in coming to Field's rooms. He'd read about the murder and couldn't have hoped that the police would delay going to the place. So he was taking a desperate chance—for what reason? Answer that one!"

"It might have had something to do with his imprisonment—by George, he looked surprised when I accused him, didn't he?" chuckled Ellery.

"Might at that," returned the Inspector. "By the way, I've heard from Velie about Michaels' term up in Elmira. Thomas reports that it was a hushed-up case—much more serious than the light sentence in the Reformatory indicates. Michaels was suspected of forgery—and it looked mighty black for him. Then Lawyer Field nicely got Mr. Michaels off on an entirely different count—something to do with petty larceny—and nothing was ever heard about the forgery business again. This boy Michaels looks like the real thing—have to step on his heels a bit."

"I have a little idea of my own about Michaels," said Ellery thoughtfully. "But let it go for the present."

Queen seemed not to hear. He stared into the fire roaring in the stone fireplace. "There's Lewin, too," he said. "Seems incredible that a man of Lewin's stamp should have been so confidentially associated with his employer without knowing a good deal more than he professes. Is he keeping something back? If he is, heaven help him—because Cronin will just about pulverize him!"

"I rather like that chap Cronin," sighed Ellery. "How on earth can a fellow be so set on one idea? . . . Has this occurred to you? I wonder if Morgan knows Angela Russo? Despite the fact that both of them deny a mutual acquaintance. Would be deucedly interesting if they did, wouldn't it?"

"'My son," groaned Queen, "don't go looking for trouble. We've a peck of it now without going out of our way for more. . . . By jingo!"

There was a comfortable silence as the Inspector sprawled in the light of the leaping flames. Ellery munched contentedly on a succulent piece of pastry. Djuna's bright eyes gleamed from the far corner of the room, where he had stolen noiselessly and squatted on his thin haunches on the floor, listening to the conversation.

Suddenly the old man's eyes met Ellery's in a spasmodic transference of thought.

"The hat . . ." muttered Queen. "We always come back to the hat."

Ellery's glance was troubled. "And not a bad thing to come back to, Dad. Hat—hat—hat! Where does it fit in? Just what do we know about it?"

The Inspector shifted in his chair. He crossed his legs, took another pinch of snuff and proceeded with a fresh vigor. "All right. We can't afford to be lazy in the matter of that blamed silk topper," he said briskly. "What do we know so far? First, that the hat did not leave the theatre. It seems funny, doesn't it? Doesn't seem possible that we would find no trace at all after such a thorough search. . . . Nothing was left in the cloakroom after everybody was gone; nothing was found in the sweepings that might indicate a hat torn to small pieces or burned; in fact, not a trace, not a thing for us to go on. Therefore, Ellery, the only sensible conclusion we can make at this point is *that we haven't looked for the hat in the right place!* And further, wherever it is, it's still there, due to our precaution of closing the theatre down since Monday night. Ellery, we've got to go back tomorrow morning and turn that place upside down. I won't sleep until we see light somewhere in this matter."

Ellery was silent. "I'm not at all satisfied with things as you've stated them, Dad," he muttered at last. "Hat—hat—there's something wrong somewhere!" He fell silent once more. "No! The hat is the focal point of this investigation—I cannot see any other way out of it. Solve the mystery of Field's hat and you will find the one essential clue that will point to the murderer. I'm so convinced of this that I'll be satisfied we're on the right track only when we're making progress in the explanation of the hat."

The old man nodded his head vigorously. "Ever since yesterday morning, when I had time to think over the hat business, I've felt that we had gone astray somewhere. And here it is Wednesday night—still no light. We've done necessary things—they've led nowhere. . . ." He stared into the fire. "Everything is so badly muddled. I've got all the loose ends at my fingertips, but for some blasted reason I can't seem to make them cohere—fit together—*explain* anything. . . . Undoubtedly, son, what is missing is the story of the top piece."

The telephone bell rang. The Inspector sprang for the instrument. He listened attentively to a man's unhurried tones, made a brisk comment and finally hung up.

"Who's the latest midnight babbler, O recipient of many confidences?" asked Ellery, grinning.

"That was Edmund Crewe," said Queen. "You may remember I asked him yesterday morning to go over the Roman. He spent all of yesterday and today at it. And he reports positively that there is no secret hiding place anywhere on the premises of the theatre. If Eddie Crewe, who is about the last word in architectural matters of this kind, says there's no hiding place there, you may rest assured it's so."

He jumped to his feet and espied Djuna squatting on his hams in the corner. "Djuna! Get the old bed ready," he roared. Djuna slipped through the room and disappeared with a silent grin. Queen wheeled on Ellery, who had already taken off his coat and was fumbling with his tie.

"The first thing we do tomorrow morning is go down to the Roman Theatre and start all over again!" the old man said decisively. "And let me tell you, son—I'm through fooling around! Somebody'd better watch out!"

Ellery affectionately encircled his father's shoulders with one great arm. "Come on to bed, you old fraud!" he laughed.

PART THREE

"A good detective is born, not made. Like all genius, he springs not from a carefully nurtured polizei but from all mankind. The most amazing detective I ever knew was a dirty old witch doctor who had never been out of the bush. . . . It is the peculiar gift of the truly great detective that he can apply to the inexorable rules of logic three catalyzers: an abnormal observation of events, a knowledge of the human mind and an insight into the human heart."

—*from* THE MANHUNTER'S MANUAL

by James Redix (the Younger)

14

IN WHICH THE HAT GROWS

On Thursday, September 27th, the third morning after the events of the crime in the Roman Theatre, Inspector Queen and Ellery rose at an early hour and dressed hastily. They repaired to a makeshift breakfast under the protesting eye of Djuna, who had been pulled bodily from his bed and thrust into the sober habiliments which he affected as major-domo of the Queen ménage.

While they were munching at anaemic pancakes, the old man asked Djuna to get Louis Panzer on the telephone. In a few moments the Inspector was speaking genially into the mouthpiece. "Good morning, Panzer. Please forgive me for hauling you out of bed at this ungodly time of the morning. . . . There's something important in the wind and we need your help."

Panzer murmured a sleepy reassurance.

"Can you come down to the Roman Theatre right away and open it for us?" went on the old man. "I told you that you wouldn't be shut down very long and now it looks as if you'll be able to cash in on the publicity the affair has been getting. I'm not sure when we can reopen, you understand, but it's barely possible that you'll be able to put your show on tonight. Can I count on you?"

"This is excellent!" Panzer's voice came over the wire in a tremulous eagerness. "Do you want me to come down to the theatre at once? I'll be there in a half-hour—I'm not dressed."

"That will be fine," returned Queen. "Of course, Panzer—no one is to be allowed inside yet. Wait for us on the sidewalk before you use your keys and don't notify anyone, either. We'll talk it all over at the theatre. . . . Just a moment."

He clamped the mouthpiece against his chest and looked up inquiringly at Ellery, who was gesturing frantically. Ellery formed his lips around the syllables of a name and the old man nodded approvingly. He spoke into the telephone again.

"There's one other thing you can do for me at present, Panzer," he continued. "Can you get hold of that nice old lady, Mrs. Phillips? I'd like to have her meet us at the theatre as soon as she can."

"Certainly, Inspector. If it's at all possible," said Panzer. Queen replaced the receiver on its hook.

"Well, that's that," he remarked, rubbing his hands together and delving into his pocket for the snuffbox. "Ah-h-h! Bless Sir Walter and all those hardy pioneers who championed the cause of the filthy weed!" He sneezed joyously. "One minute, Ellery, than we'll go."

He picked up the telephone once more and called detective

headquarters. He gave a few cheery orders, banged the instrument back on the table and hustled Ellery into his coat. Djuna watched them leave with a mournful expression: he had often pleaded with the Inspector to be allowed to accompany the Queens on their sporadic excursions into the byways of New York. The Inspector, who had his own ideas on the subject of rearing adolescents, invariably refused. And Djuna, who regarded his patron much as the Stone Age man regarded his amulets, accepted the inevitable and hoped for a more auspicious future.

It was a raw, wet day. Ellery and his father turned up their coat collars as they walked towards Broadway and the subway. Both were extraordinarily taciturn, but the keen anticipatory looks on their faces—so curiously alike and yet so different—portended an exciting and revealing day.

Broadway and its threaded canyons were deserted in the chill wind of the morning as the two men walked briskly down 47th Street towards the Roman Theatre. A drab-coated man lounged on the sidewalk before the closed glass doors of the lobby; another leaned comfortably against the high iron fence which cut off the left alley from the street. The dumpy form of Louis Panzer was visible standing before the central door of the theatre, in conversation with Flint.

Panzer shook hands excitedly. "Well, well!" he cried. "So the ban is to be lifted at last! . . . Exceedingly happy to hear that, Inspector."

"Oh, it isn't exactly lifted, Panzer," smiled the old man. "Have you the keys? Morning, Flint. Rest up any since Monday night?"

Panzer produced a heavy bunch of keys and unlocked the central door of the lobby. The four men filed in. The swarthy manager fumbled with the lock of the inside door and finally managed to swing it open. The dark interior of the orchestra yawned in their faces.

Ellery shivered. "With the possible exceptions of the Metropolitan Opera House and Titus' Tomb, this is the most dismal theatorium I've ever entered. It's a fitting mausoleum for the dear departed. . . ."

The more prosaic Inspector grunted as he pushed his son into the maw of the dark orchestra. "Get along with you! You'll be giving us all the 'willies.'"

Panzer, who had hurried ahead, turned on the main electric switch. The auditorium leaped into more familiar outlines by the light of the big arcs and chandeliers. Ellery's fanciful comparison was not so fantastic as his father had made it appear. The long rows of seats were draped with dirty tarpaulin; murky shadows streaked across the carpets, already dusty; the bare whitewashed wall at the rear of the empty stage made an ugly splotch in the sea of red plush.

"Sorry to see that tarpaulin there," grumbled the Inspector to Panzer. "Because it will have to be rolled up. We're going to conduct a little personal search of the orchestra. Flint, get those two men outside, please. They may as well do something to earn the city's money."

Flint sped away and returned shortly with the two detectives who had been on guard outside the theatre. Under the Inspector's direction they began to haul the huge sheets of rubberized seat covers to the sides, disclosing rows of cushioned chairs. Ellery, standing to one side near the extreme left aisle, withdrew from his pocket the little book in which he had scribbled notes and drawn a rough map of the theatre on Monday night. He was studying this and biting his under-lip. Occasionally he looked up as if to verify the layout of the theatre.

Queen bustled back to where Panzer was nervously pacing the rear. "Panzer, we're going to be mighty busy here for a couple of hours and I was too shortsighted to bring extra men with me. I wonder if I may impose upon you. . . . I have something in mind that requires immediate attention—it would take only a small part of your time and it would help me considerably."

"Of course, Inspector!" returned the little manager. "I'm only too glad to be of assistance."

The Inspector coughed. "Please don't feel that I'm using you as an errand boy or anything like that, old man," he explained apologetically. "But I need these fellows, who are trained in searches of this kind—and at the same time I must have some vital data from a couple of the District Attorney's men who are working downtown on another aspect of the case. Would you mind taking a note for me to one of them—name of Cronin—and bring back the parcel he gives you? I hate to ask you to do this, Panzer," he muttered. "But it's too important to trust to an ordinary messenger, and—ding it all! I'm in a hole."

Panzer smiled in his quick birdlike fashion. "Not another word, Inspector. I'm entirely at your service. I've the materials in my office if you care to write the note now."

The two men retired to Panzer's office. Five minutes later they re-entered the auditorium. Panzer held a sealed envelope in his hand and hurried out into the street. Queen watched him go, then turned with a sigh to Ellery, who had perched himself on the arm of the seat in which Field had been murdered and was still consulting the penciled map.

The Inspector whispered a few words to his son. Ellery smiled and clapped the old man vigorously on the back.

"What do you say we get a move on, son?" said Queen. "I forgot to ask Panzer if he had succeeded in reaching this Mrs. Phillips. I guess he did, though, or he would have said something about it. Where in thunder is she?"

He beckoned to Flint, who was helping the other two detectives in the back-breaking task of removing the tarpaulin.

"I've one of those popular bending exercises for you this morning, Flint. Go up to the balcony and get busy."

"What am I supposed to be looking for today, Inspector?" grinned the broad-shouldered detective. "Because I hope I have better luck than I did Monday night."

"You're looking for a hat—a nice, shiny top piece such as the swells wear, my boy," announced the Inspector. "But if you should come across anything else, use your lungs!" Flint trotted up the wide marble staircase towards the balcony. Queen looked after him, shaking his head. "I'm afraid the poor lad is doomed to another disappointment," he remarked to Ellery. "But I must make absolutely certain that there's nothing up there—and that the usher Miller who was guarding the balcony staircase Monday night was telling the truth. Come along, lazybones."

Ellery shed his topcoat reluctantly and tucked the little book away in his pocket. The Inspector wriggled out of his ulster and preceded his son down the aisle. Working side by side they began to search the orchestra pit at the extreme end of the auditorium. Finding nothing there, they clambered out into the orchestra again and, Ellery taking the right side and his father the left, began a slow, methodical combing of the theatre premises. They lifted the seats; probed experimentally into the plush cushions with long needles which the Inspector had produced mysteriously from his breast pocket; and kneeled to examine every inch of the carpet by the light of electric torches.

The two detectives who had by now completed the task of rolling up the tarpaulin began, on the Inspector's brief command, to work through the boxes, a man to each side of the theatre.

For a long time the four men proceeded in silence, unbroken except for the somewhat labored breathing of Inspector Queen. Ellery was working swiftly and efficiently, the old man more slowly. As they met near the center after completing the search of a row, they would regard each other significantly, shake their heads and continue afresh.

About twenty minutes after Panzer's departure the Inspector and Ellery, absorbed in their examination, were startled by the ringing of a telephone bell. In the silence of the theatre the clear trill of the bell rang out with astonishing sharpness. Father and son looked at each other blankly for an instant, then the old man laughed and plodded up the aisle in the direction of Panzer's office.

He returned shortly, smiling. "It was Panzer," he announced. "Got down to Field's office and found the place closed. No wonder—it's only a quarter of nine. But I told him to wait there until Cronin comes. It can't be long now."

Ellery laughed and they set to work again.

Fifteen minutes later, when the two men were almost finished, the front door opened and a small elderly woman dressed in black stood blinking in the brilliant arc lights. The Inspector sprang forward to meet her.

"You're Mrs. Phillips, aren't you?" he cried warmly. "It's mighty nice of you to come so soon, madam. I think you know Mr. Queen here?"

Ellery came forward, smiling one of his rare smiles and bowing with genuine gallantry. Mrs. Phillips was representative of a lovable old womanhood. She was short and of motherly proportions. Her gleaming white hair and air of kindliness endeared her immediately to Inspector Queen, who had a sentimental weakness for middle-aged ladies of presence.

"I certainly do know Mr. Queen," she said, extending her hand. "He was very nice to an old woman Monday night. . . . And I was so afraid you'd have to wait for me, sir!" she said softly, turning to the Inspector. "Mr. Panzer sent a messenger for me this morning—I haven't a telephone, you see. There was a time, when I was on the stage. . . . I came just as soon as I could."

The Inspector beamed. "For a lady it was remarkably prompt, *remark*ably prompt, Mrs. Phillips!"

"My father kissed the Blarney Stone several centuries ago, Mrs. Phillips," said Ellery gravely. "Don't believe a word av 'im. . . . I suppose it will be *au fait* if I leave you to tackle the rest of the orchestra, Dad? I'd like to have a little chat with Mrs. Phillips. Do you think you're physically able to complete the job alone?"

"Physically able—!" snorted the Inspector. "You plump right down that aisle and go about your business, son. . . . I should appreciate your giving Mr. Queen all the help you can, Mrs. Phillips."

The white-haired lady smiled and Ellery, taking her arm, led her off in the direction of the stage. Inspector Queen, looking after them wistfully, shrugged his shoulders after a moment and turned back to resume the search. A short time later, when he chanced to straighten up, he espied Ellery and Mrs. Phillips seated on the stage conversing earnestly, like two players rehearsing their roles. Queen proceeded slowly up and down the rows, weaving in and out among the empty seats, shaking his head dolefully as he approached the last few rows still empty-handed. When he looked up again the two chairs on the stage held no occupants. Ellery and the old lady had disappeared.

Queen came at last to LL32 Left—the seat in which Monte Field had died. He made a painstaking examination of the cushions, a light of resignation in his eyes. Muttering to himself he walked slowly across the carpet at the rear of the theatre and entered Panzer's office. A few moments later he reappeared, only to make his way to the cubicle which was used as an office by the publicity man, Harry Neilson. He was in this compartment for some time. He came out and visited the cashiers' offices. Shutting the door behind him when he had finished, he wended his way down the steps on the right of the theatre leading to the general lounge, on the floor below the orchestra. Here he took his time, delving into every corner, every niche in the wall, every waste container—all of which he found to be empty. He speculatively eyed the large bin standing directly under the water fountain. He peered into this receptacle and pottered away, finding nothing. Thereupon with a sigh he opened the door on which was gilt-lettered, LADIES' REST ROOM, and went inside. A few moments later he reappeared to push his way through the swinging doors marked GENTLEMEN.

When his meticulous search of the lower floor was completed he trudged up the steps again. In the orchestra he found Louis Panzer waiting, slightly flushed from his exertions but displaying a triumphant smile. The little manager was carrying a small parcel wrapped in brown paper.

"So you saw Cronin after all, Panzer?" said the Inspector, scurrying forward. "This is mighty nice of you, my boy—I appreciate it more than I can say. Is this the package Cronin gave you?"

"It is. A very nice chap, Cronin. I didn't have to wait long after I telephoned you. He came in with two other men named Stoates and Lewin. He didn't keep me more than ten minutes altogether. I hope it was important, Inspector?" Panzer continued, smiling. "I should like to feel that I've been instrumental in clearing up part of the puzzle."

"Important?" echoed the Inspector, taking the parcel from the manager's hand. "You have no idea how important it is. Some day I'll tell you more about it. . . . Will you excuse me a moment, Panzer?"

The little man nodded in a fleeting disappointment as the Inspector grinned, backing off into a dark corner. Panzer shrugged and disappeared into his office.

When he came out, hat and coat left behind, the Inspector was stuffing the parcel into his pocket.

"Did you get what you wanted, sir?" inquired Panzer.

"Oh, yes, yes, indeed!" Queen said, rubbing his hands. "And now—I see Ellery is still gone—suppose we go into your office for a few minutes and while away the time until he returns."

They went into Panzer's sanctum and sat down. The manager lit a long Turkish cigarette while the Inspector dipped into his snuffbox.

"If I'm not presuming, Inspector," said Panzer casually, crossing his short fat legs and emitting a cloud of smoke, "how are things going?"

Queen shook his head sadly. "Not so well—not so well. We don't seem to be getting anywhere with the main angles of the case. In fact, I don't mind telling you that unless we get on the track of a certain object we face failure. . . . It's pretty hard on me—I've never encountered a more puzzling investigation." He wore a worried frown as he snapped the lid of his snuffbox shut.

"That's too bad, Inspector," Panzer clucked in sympathy. "And I was hoping—Ah, well! We can't put our personal concerns above the demands of justice, I suppose! Just what is it you are seeking, Inspector, if you don't mind telling an outsider?"

Queen brightened. "Not at all. You've done me a good turn

this morning and—By jingo, how stupid of me not to think of this before!" Panzer leaned forward eagerly. "How long have you been manager of the Roman Theatre, Panzer?"

The manager raised his eyebrows. "Ever since it was built," he said. "Before that I managed the old Electra on 43rd Street—it is also owned by Gordon Davis," he explained.

"Oh!" The Inspector seemed to reflect deeply. "Then you would know this theatre from top to bottom—you would be as familiar with its construction as the architect, perhaps?"

"I have a rather thorough knowledge of it, yes," confessed Panzer, leaning back.

"That's excellent! Let me give you a little problem, then, Panzer. . . . Suppose you wished to conceal a—let us say, a tophat—somewhere in the building, in such a way that not even an exhaustive search of the premises would bring it to light. What would you do? Where would you hide it?"

Panzer scowled thoughtfully at his cigarette. "A rather unusual question, Inspector," he said at last, "and one which is not easy to answer. I know the plans of the theatre very well; I was consulted about them in a conference with the architect before the theatre was built. And I can positively state that the original blueprints did not provide for such medieval devices as concealed passageways, secret closets or anything of that sort. I could enumerate any number of places where a man might hide a comparatively small object like a tophat, but none of them would be proof against a really thorough search."

"I see." The Inspector squinted at his fingernails in an appearance of disappointment. "So that doesn't help. We've been over the place from top to bottom, as you know, and we can't find a trace of it. . . ."

The door opened and Ellery, a trifle begrimed but wearing a cheerful smile, entered. The Inspector glanced at him in eager curiosity. Panzer rose hesitantly with the evident intention of leaving father and son alone. A flash of intelligence shot between the Queens.

"It's all right, Panzer—don't go," said the Inspector peremptorily. "We've no secrets from you. Sit down, man!"

Panzer sat down.

"Don't you think, Dad," remarked Ellery, perching on the edge of the desk and reaching for his pince-nez, "that this would be an opportune moment to inform Mr. Panzer of tonight's opening? You remember we decided while he was gone that the theatre might be thrown open to the public this evening and a regular performance given. . . ."

"How could I have forgotten—!" said the Inspector without blinking, although this was the first time he had heard about the mythical decision. "I think we're about ready, Panzer, to lift the ban on the Roman. We find that we can do nothing further here, so there is no reason for depriving you of your patronage any longer. You may run a performance tonight—in fact, we are most anxious to see a show put on, aren't we Ellery?"

"'Anxious' is hardly the word," said Ellery, lighting a cigarette. "I should say we insist upon it."

"Exactly," murmured the Inspector severely. "We insist upon it, Panzer."

The manager had bobbed out of his chair, his face shining. "That's simply splendid, gentlemen!" he cried. "I'll telephone Mr. Davis immediately to let him know the good news. Of course"—his face fell—"it's terribly late to expect any sort of response from the public for tonight's performance. Such short notice . . ."

"You needn't worry about that, Panzer," retorted the Inspector. "I've caused your shutdown and I'll see that the theatre is compensated for it tonight. I'll get the newspaper boys on the wire and ask them to ballyhoo the opening in the next edition. It will mean a lot of unexpected publicity for you and undoubtedly the free advertising, combined with the normal curiosity of the public, will give you a sellout."

"That's sporting of you, Inspector," said Panzer, rubbing his hands. "Is there anything else I can do for you at the moment?"

"There's one item you've forgotten, Dad," interposed Ellery. He turned to the swart little manager. "Will you see that LL32 and LL30 Left are not sold tonight? The Inspector and I would enjoy seeing this evening's performance. We've not really had that pleasure yet, you know. And naturally we wish to preserve a stately incognito, Panzer—dislike the adulation of the crowd and that sort of thing. You'll keep it under cover, of course."

"Anything you say, Mr. Queen. I'll instruct the cashier to put aside those tickets," returned Panzer pleasantly. "And now, Inspector—you said you would telephone the press, I believe—?"

"Certainly." Queen took up the telephone and held pithy conversations with the city editors of a number of metropolitan newspapers. When he had finished Panzer bade them a hurried good-by to get busy with the telephone.

Inspector Queen and his son strolled out into the orchestra, where they found Flint and the two detectives who had been examining the boxes awaiting them.

"You men hang around the theatre on general principles," ordered the Inspector. "Be particularly careful this afternoon. . . . Any of you find anything?"

Flint scowled. "I ought to be digging clams in Canarsie," he said with a disgruntled air. "I fell down on the job Monday night, Inspector, and I'm blamed if I could find a thing for you today. That place upstairs is swept as clean as a hound's tooth. Guess I ought to go back to pounding a beat."

Queen slapped the big detective on the shoulder. "What's the matter with you? Don't be acting like a baby, lad. How on earth could you find anything when there wasn't anything to find? You fellows get something?" he demanded, swinging on the other two men.

They shook their heads in a gloomy negation.

A moment later the Inspector and Ellery climbed into a passing taxicab and settled back for the short drive to headquarters. The old man carefully closed the glass sliding window separating the driver's seat from the interior of the car.

"Now, my son," he said grimly, turning on Ellery, who was puffing dreamily at a cigarette, "please explain to your old daddy that hocus-pocus in Panzer's office!"

Ellery's lips tightened. He stared out of the window before replying. "Let me start this way," he said. "You have found nothing in your search today. Nor have your men. And although I scouted about myself, I was just as unsuccessful. Dad, make up your mind to this one primary point: The hat which Monte Field wore to the performance of 'Gunplay' on Monday night, in which he was seen at the beginning of the second act, and which presumably the murderer took away after the crime was committed, *is not in the Roman Theatre now and has not been there since Monday night.* To proceed." Queen stared at him with grizzled brows. "In all likelihood Field's tophat no longer exists. I would stake my Falconer against your snuffbox that it has fled this life and now enjoys a reincarnation as ashes in the City dumps. That's point number one."

"Go on," commanded the Inspector.

"Point number two is so elementary as to be infantile. Nevertheless, allow me the privilege of insulting the Queen intelligence. . . . If Field's hat is not in the Roman Theatre now and has not been in the Roman Theatre since Monday night, it must of necessity have been taken *out* of the Roman Theatre sometime during the course of that evening!"

He paused to gaze thoughtfully through the window. A traffic officer was waving his arms at the juncture of 42nd Street and Broadway.

"We have established therefore," he continued lightly, "the factual basis of a point which has been running us ragged for three days: to wit, did the hat for which we are looking leave the Roman Theatre. . . . To be dialectic—yes, it did. It left the Roman Theatre the night of the murder. Now we approach a greater problem—*how* did it leave and *when.*" He puffed at his cigarette and regarded the glowing tip. "We know that no person left the Roman Monday night with two hats or no hat at all. In no case was there anything incongruous in the attire of any person leaving the theatre. That is, a man wearing a full-dress costume did not go out with a fedora. In a similar way, no one wearing a silk topper was dressed in ordinary street clothes. Remember, we noticed nothing wrong from this angle in *anyone*. . . . This leads us inevitably, to my staggering mind, to the third fundamental conclusion: that Monte Field's hat left the theatre in the most natural manner in the world: *id est,* by way of some man's head, its owner being garbed in appropriate evening clothes!"

The Inspector was keenly interested. He thought over Ellery's statement for a moment. Then he said seriously, "That's getting us somewhere, son. But you say a man left the theatre wearing Monte Field's hat—an important and enlightening statement. But please answer this question: What did he do with his own hat, since no one left with two?"

Ellery smiled. "You now have your hand on the heart of our little mystery, Dad. But let it hold for the moment. We have a number of other points to mull over. For example, the man who departed wearing Monte Field's hat could have been only one of two things: either he was the actual murderer, or he was an accomplice of the murderer."

"I see what you're driving at," muttered the Inspector. "Go on."

"If he was the murderer, we have definitely established the sex and also the fact that our man was wearing evening clothes that night—perhaps not a very illuminating point, since there were scores of such men in the theatre. If he was only an accomplice, we must conclude that the murderer was one of two possibilities: either a man dressed in ordinary clothes, whose possession of a tophat as he left would be patently suspicious; or else a woman, who of course could not sport a tophat at all!"

The Inspector sank back into the leather cushions. "Talk about your logic!" he chortled. "My son, I'm almost proud of you—that is, I would be if you weren't so disgustingly conceited. . . . Things standing where they do, therefore, the reason you pulled your little drama in Panzer's office. . . ."

His voice lowered as Ellery leaned forward. They continued to converse in inaudible tones until the taxicab drew up before the headquarters building.

No sooner had Inspector Queen, who had proceeded blithely through the somber corridors with Ellery striding at his side, entered his tiny office than Sergeant Velie lumbered to his feet.

"Thought you were lost, Inspector!" he exclaimed. "That Stoates kid was in here not long ago with a suffering look on his face. Said that Cronin was tearing his hair at Field's office—that they still hadn't found a thing in the files of an incriminating nature."

"Go away, go away, Thomas my lad," gurgled the Inspector softly. "I can't bother myself with petty problems like putting a dead man behind bars. Ellery and I—"

The telephone bell rang. Queen sprang forward and snatched the instrument from the desk. As he listened the glow left his thin cheeks and a frown settled once more on his forehead. Ellery watched him with a strange absorption.

"Inspector?" came the hurried voice of a man. "This is Hagstrom reporting. Just got a minute—can't say much. Been tailing Angela Russo all morning and had a tough time. . . . Seems to be wise that I'm following her. . . . A half hour ago she thought she'd given me the slip—she hopped into a cab and beat it downtown. . . . And say, Inspector—just three minutes ago I saw her enter Benjamin Morgan's office!"

Queen barked, "Nail her the instant she comes out!" and slammed the receiver down. He turned slowly to Ellery and Velie and repeated Hagstrom's report. Ellery's face became a study in frowning astonishment. Velie appeared unmistakably pleased.

But the old man's voice was strained as he sat down weakly in his swivel chair. Finally he groaned, "What do you know about that!"

15

IN WHICH AN ACCUSATION IS MADE

Detective Hagstrom was a phlegmatic man. He traced his ancestry to the mountains of Norway, where stolidity was a virtue and stoicism the ultimate cult. Nevertheless, as he leaned against a gleaming marble wall on the twentieth floor of the Maddern Building, thirty feet to the side of the bronze-and-glass door marked:

BENJAMIN MORGAN

ATTORNEY AT LAW

his heart beat a trifle faster than usual. He shuffled his feet nervously as his jaw masticated a wad of chewing tobacco. If the truth were told Detective Hagstrom, a man of varied experience on the service of the police department, had never clamped his hand on the shoulder of a female with intent to arrest. He faced his coming assignment therefore in some trepidation, remembering with appalling clarity the fiery temperament of the lady for whom he was waiting.

His apprehension was well founded. When he had been lounging in the corridor some twenty minutes, and wondering whether his quarry had not slipped away through another exit, Benjamin Morgan's office door suddenly swung open and the large, curved figure of Mrs. Angela Russo garbed in a modish tweed ensemble, appeared. An unbecoming snarl distorted her carefully made-up features; she swung her purse menacingly as she strode toward the line of elevators. Hagstrom glanced quickly at his wrist watch. It was ten minutes to twelve. In a short time the offices would be disgorging their occupants for the lunch hour, and he was most desirous of making his arrest in the quiet of the deserted hall.

Accordingly he straightened up, adjusted his orange-and-blue necktie and stepped with a fair assumption of coolness into full view of the approaching woman. As she caught sight of him she slackened her stride perceptibly. Hagstrom hurried toward her, anticipating flight. But Mrs. Angela Russo was made of sterner stuff. She tossed her head and came on brazenly.

Hagstrom fixed his large red hand on her arm. "I guess you know what I want you for," he said fiercely. "Come along now, and don't make a fuss or I'll put the nippers on you!"

Mrs. Russo shook off his hand. "My, my—aren't you the big rough cop?" she murmured. "Just what do you think you're doing, anyway?"

Hagstrom glared. "None o' your lip, now!" His finger pressed savagely on the "Down" signal for the elevators. "You just shut up and come along!"

She faced him sweetly. "Are you trying to arrest me, by any chance?" she cooed. "Because you know, my big he-man, you've got to have a warrant to do that!"

"Aw, stow it!" he growled. "I'm not arresting you—I'm just inviting you to step down to headquarters for a little gab with Inspector Queen. You coming, or do I have to call the wagon?"

An elevator flashed to a stop. The elevatorman snapped, "Going down!" The woman glanced with momentary uncertainty at the car, peered slyly at Hagstrom and finally stepped into the elevator, the detective's hand firmly clasped on her elbow. They descended in silence under the curious scrutiny of several passengers.

Hagstrom, uneasy but determined, sensing somehow a storm brewing in the breast of the woman who strode so calmly by his side, was taking no chances. He did not relax his grasp until they sat side by side in a taxicab, bound for headquarters. Mrs. Russo's face had gone pasty under her rouge, despite the bold smile curving her lips. She turned suddenly to face her captor, leaning close to his rigidly official body.

"Mr. Cop, darling," she whispered, "do you think you could use a hundred-dollar bill?"

Her hand fumbled suggestively in her purse. Hagstrom lost his temper.

"Bribery, huh?" he sneered. "We'll have to chalk that one up for the Inspector!"

The woman's smile faded. For the rest of the journey she sat looking fixedly at the back of the driver's neck.

It was only when she was being marched, like a soldier on

parade, down the dark corridors of the big police structure that her poise returned. And when Hagstrom held open the door of Inspector Queen's office, she passed inside with an airy tilt to her head and a pleasant smile that would have deceived a police matron.

Inspector Queen's office was a cheery affair of sunlight and color. At the moment it resembled a clubroom. Ellery's long legs were stretched comfortably across the thick carpet, his eyes pleasantly absorbed in the contents of a small cheaply bound book entitled "The Complete Guide to Handwriting Analysis." The smoke of a cigarette curled from his slack fingers. Sergeant Velie was sitting stolidly in a chair against the far wall, engrossed in a contemplation of Inspector Queen's snuffbox, which was held lovingly between the thumb and forefinger of the old police official himself. Queen was seated in his comfortable armchair, smiling in hazy introspection at some secret thought.

"Ah! Mrs. Russo! Come in, come in!" exclaimed the Inspector, bouncing to his feet. "Thomas—a chair for Mrs. Russo, if you please." The Sergeant silently placed one of the bare wooden chairs by the side of the Inspector's desk and as silently retreated to his corner. Ellery had not even glanced in the woman's direction. He read on, the same pleasantly abstracted smile on his lips. The old man was bowing with hospitable courtesy to Mrs. Russo.

She looked about at the peaceful scene with bewilderment. She had been prepared for severity, harshness, brutality—the domestic atmosphere of the little office took her completely by surprise. Nevertheless she seated herself and, the instant of hesitation gone, she exhibited the same agreeable smile, the same ladylike demeanor that she had practiced so successfully in the corridors.

Hagstrom was standing inside the doorway, glaring with offended dignity at the profile of the seated woman.

"She tried to slip me a century note," he said indignantly. "Tried to bribe me, Chief!"

Queen's eyebrows instantly rose in shocked surprise. "My dear Mrs. Russo!" he exclaimed in a sorrowful voice. "You really didn't intend to make this excellent officer forget his duty to the city, did you? But of course not! How stupid of me! Hagstrom, certainly you must be mistaken, my dear fellow. A hundred dollars—" He shook his head dolefully sinking back into the leather swivel chair.

Mrs. Russo smiled. "Isn't it queer how these cops get the wrong impression?" she asked in a lovely voice. "I assure you, Inspector—I was just having a little fun with him. . . ."

"Exactly," said the Inspector, smiling again, as if this statement restored his faith in human nature. "Hagstrom, that'll be all."

The detective, who was staring open-mouthed from his superior to the smiling woman, recovered in time to intercept a wink which passed from Velie to Queen across the woman's head. He went out quickly, muttering to himself.

"Now, Mrs. Russo," began the Inspector, in a businesslike tone, "what can we do for you today?"

She stared at him. "Why—why, I thought you wanted to see me. . . ." Her lips tightened. "Cut the comedy, Inspector!" she said shortly. "I'm not paying any social calls on my own hook to this place and you know it. What did you pinch me for?"

The Inspector spread his sensitive fingers deprecatingly, his mouth pursed in protest. "But, my dear lady!" he said. "Certainly you have something to tell me. Because, if you are here—and we cannot evade that evident fact—you are here for a reason. Granted that you did not come exactly of your own free will—still you were brought here because you have something to say to me. Don't you see?"

Mrs. Russo stared fixedly into his eyes. "What the—Hey, look here, Inspector Queen, what are you driving at? What do you think I've got to tell you? I answered everything you asked me Tuesday morning."

"Well!" The old man frowned. "Let us say that you did *not* answer every question Tuesday morning with absolute veracity. For example—do you know Benjamin Morgan?"

She did not flinch. "All right. You take the cake on that one. Your bloodhound caught me coming out of Morgan's office—what of it?" She deliberately opened her purse and began to dab powder on her nose. As she did so she glanced slyly at Ellery from the corner of her eyes. He was still engrossed in his book, oblivious to her presence. She turned back to the Inspector with a toss of the head.

Queen was looking at her sadly. "My dear Mrs. Russo, you're not being fair to a poor old man. I wanted merely to point out that you had—shall I say—lied to me the last time I spoke to you. Now mat's a very dangerous procedure with police Inspectors, my dear—very dangerous."

"Listen here!" the woman said suddenly. "You're not going to get anywhere with this soft soap, Inspector. I *did* lie to you Tuesday morning. Because, you see, I didn't think you had anyone here who could follow me very long. Well, I took a gambler's chance and I lost. So you found out I was lying, and you want to know what it's all about. I'll tell you—and then maybe again I won't!"

"Oho!" exclaimed Queen softly. "So you feel you're in a safe enough position to dictate terms, eh? But Mrs. Russo—believe me you're putting your very charming neck into a noose!"

"Yeh?" The mask was fairly off now; the woman's face was stripped to its essential character of intrigue. "You got nothing on me and you know it damn well. All right—I did lie to you—what are you going to do about it? I'm admitting it now. And I'll even tell you what I was doing in that guy Morgan's office, if that'll help you any! That's tie kind of a squareshooter *I* am, Mr. Inspector!"

"My dear Mrs. Russo," returned the Inspector in a pained voice, a little puffed smile in his cheeks, "we know already what you were doing in Mr. Morgan's office this morning, so you won't be conferring such a great favor on us after all. . . . I'm really surprised that you should be willing to incriminate yourself to that extent, Mrs. Russo. Blackmail is a mighty serious offense!"

The woman grew deathly white. She half rose in the chair, gripping its arms.

"So Morgan squealed after all, the dirty dog!" she snarled. "And I thought he was a wise guy. I'll get him something to squeal about, take it from me!"

"Ah, now you're beginning to talk my language," murmured the Inspector, leaning forward. "And just what is it you know about our friend Morgan?"

"I know this about him—but look here, Inspector, I can give you a redhot tip. You wouldn't frame a poor lonely woman on a blackmail charge, would you?"

The Inspector's face lengthened. "Now, now, Mrs. Russo!" he said. "Is that a nice thing to say? Certainly I can't make any promises. . . ." He rose, his slender body deadly in its immobility. She shrank back a little. "You will tell me what you have on your mind, Mrs. Russo," he said deliberately, "on the bare chance that I may show my gratitude in the generally accepted fashion. You will please talk—truthfully, do you understand?"

"Oh, I know well enough you're a tough nut, Inspector!" she muttered. "But I guess you're fair, too. . . . What do you want to know?"

"Everything."

"Well, it isn't my funeral," she said, in a more composed voice. There was a pause while Queen examined her curiously. In accusing her of blackmailing Morgan he had made a successful stab in the dark; now a flash of doubt assailed him. She seemed much too sure of herself if all she knew were the details of Morgan's past, as the Inspector had taken for granted from the beginning of the interview. He glanced at Ellery and was apprehensively quick to note that his son's eyes were no longer on the book but riveted on the profile of Mrs. Russo.

"Inspector," said Mrs. Russo, a shrill triumph creeping into her voice, "I know who killed Monte Field!"

"What's that?" Queen jumped out of his seat, a flush suffusing his white features. Ellery had straightened convulsively in his chair, his sharp eyes boring into the woman's face. The book he had been reading slipped out of his fingers and dropped to the floor with a thud.

"I said I know who killed Monte Field," repeated Mrs. Russo, evidently enjoying the sensation she had caused. "It's Benjamin Morgan, and I heard him threaten Monte *the night before he was murdered!*"

"Oh!" said the Inspector, sitting down. Ellery picked up his book and resumed his interrupted study of "The Complete Guide to Handwriting Analysis." Quiet descended once more. Velie, who had been staring at father and son in struggling amazement, seemed at a loss to understand their suddenly changed manner.

Mrs. Russo grew angry. "I suppose you think I'm lying again, but I'm not!" she screamed. "I tell you I heard with my own ears Ben Morgan tell Monte Sunday night that he'd put him away!"

The Inspector was grave, but undisturbed. "I don't doubt your word in the least, Mrs. Russo. Are you sure it was Sunday night?"

"Sure?" she shrilled. "I'll say I'm sure!"

"And where did this happen?"

"Right in Monte Field's own apartment, that's where!" she said bitingly. "I was with Monte all evening Sunday, and as far as I know he wasn't expecting company, because we didn't usually have company when we spent the evening together. . . . Monte himself jumped when the doorbell rang about eleven o'clock and said, 'Who in hell could that be?' We were in the living room at the time. But he got up and went to the door, and right after that I heard a man's voice outside. I figured Monte wouldn't want me to be seen by anybody, so I went into the bedroom and closed the door, just leaving a crack open. I could hear Monte trying to stall the man off. Anyway, they finally came into the living room. Through the crack in the door I saw it was this fellow Morgan—I didn't know who he was at the time, but later on I got it during the talk they had. And afterward Monte told me."

She stopped. The Inspector listened imperturbably and Ellery was paying not the slightest attention to her words. She went on desperately.

"For about a half hour they talked till I could have howled. Morgan was sort of cold and set; he didn't get excited till the last. From what I gathered, Monte had asked Morgan not long before for a big wad of dough in return for some papers; and Morgan said he didn't have the money, couldn't raise it. Said he'd decided to drop into Monte's place for one last reckoning. Monte was kind of sarcastic and mean—he could be awfully mean when he wanted to. Morgan kept getting madder and madder, and I could see he was holding his temper in. . . ."

The Inspector interrupted. "Just what was the reason for Field's demand for money?"

"I wish I knew, Inspector," she returned savagely. "But both of 'em were mighty careful not to mention the reason. . . . Anyway, it was something about those papers that Monte wanted Morgan to buy. It wouldn't take much brains to guess that Monte had something on Morgan and was pushing it to the limit."

At the mention of the word "papers" Ellery's interest in Mrs.

Russo's story had revived. He had put the book down and begun to listen intently. The Inspector gave him a fleeting glance as he addressed the woman.

"Just how much money was Field demanding, Mrs. Russo?"

"You wouldn't believe me if I told you," she said, laughing disdainfully. "Monte was no piker. All he wanted was—fifty thousand dollars!"

The Inspector seemed unmoved. "Go on."

"So there they were," she continued, "jabbering back and forth, with Monte getting colder and Morgan getting madder. Finally Morgan picked up his hat and yelled, 'I'll be damned, you crook, if I'm going to be milked any more! You can do what you please—I'm through, do you understand? I'm through for good!' He was blue in the face. Monte didn't get up from his chair. He just said, 'You can do as you please, Benjamin my friend, but I give you exactly three days to hand that money over. And no bargaining, remember! Fifty thousand, or—but surely I don't have to remind you of the unpleasant consequences of refusal.' Monte sure was slick," she added admiringly. "Could sling the lingo like a professional.

"Morgan kept fiddling with his hat," she went on, "just as if he didn't know what to do with his hands. Then he exploded with, 'I told you where you get off, Field, and I mean every word of it. Publish those papers, and if it means ruin to me—I'll see to it that it's the last time you'll ever blackmail *anybody!*' He shook his fist under Monte's nose, and looked for a minute as if he was going to do him in then and there. Then all of a sudden he quieted down and without saying another word walked himself out of the apartment."

"And that's the story, Mrs. Russo?"

"Isn't it enough?" she flared. "What are you trying to do—protect that murdering coward? . . . But it isn't all. After Morgan left, Monte said to me, 'Did you hear what my friend said?' I made believe I didn't, but Monte was wise. He took me on his lap and said playfully, 'He'll regret it, Angel. . . .' He always called me Angel," she added coyly.

"I see. . . ." The Inspector mused. "And just what did Mr. Morgan say—that you took for a threat against Field's life?"

She stared at him incredulously. "Good gravy, are you dumb, or what?" she cried. "He said, 'I'll see to it it's the last time you'll ever blackmail *anybody!*' And then when my darling Monte was killed the very next night . . ."

"A very natural conclusion," smiled Queen. "Do I understand that you are preferring charges against Benjamin Morgan?"

"I'm not preferring anything except a little peace, Inspector," she retorted. "I've told you the story—now do what you want with it." She shrugged her shoulders and made as if to rise.

"One moment, Mrs. Russo." The Inspector held up a small and delicate finger. "You referred in your story to some 'papers' that Field was holding over Morgan's head. Did Field at any time during the quarrel between them actually bring out these papers?"

Mrs. Russo looked the old man coolly in the eye. "No, sir, he didn't. And make believe I'm not sorry he didn't, too!"

"A charming attitude of yours, Mrs. Russo. One of these days . . . I hope you understand that your skirts are not entirely—ah—clean in this matter, in a manner of speaking," said the Inspector. "So please consider very carefully before you answer my next question. Where did Monte Field keep his private documents?"

"I don't have to consider, Inspector," she snapped. "I just don't know. If there was any chance of my knowing I would, don't worry."

"Perhaps you made a few personal forays of your own when Field was absent from his apartment?" pursued Queen, smiling.

"Perhaps I did," she answered with a dimpling cheek. "But it didn't do any good. I'd swear they're not in those rooms. . . . Well, Inspector, anything else?"

The clear voice of Ellery seemed to startle her. But she coquettishly patted her hair as she turned towards him.

"As far as you know, Mrs. Russo," said Ellery icily, "from long and no doubt intimate association with your gallant Leander—how many different silk tophats did he possess?"

"You're the original crossword puzzle, aren't you?" she gurgled. "As far as I know, Mr. Man, he had only one. How many does a guy need?"

"You're certain of that, I suppose," said Ellery.

"Sure's you're born, Mr.—Queen." She contrived to slip a caress into her voice. Ellery stared at her as one stares at a strange zoological specimen. She made a little *moue* and turned about gayly.

"I'm not so popular around here so I'll beat it. . . . You're not going to put me in a nasty cell, are you, Inspector? I can go now, can't I?"

The Inspector bowed. "Oh yes—you may go, Mrs. Russo,

under a certain amount of surveillance. . . . But please understand that we may still require your delightful company at some not distant date. Will you remain in town?"

"Charmed, I'm sure!" she laughed and swept out of the room.

Velie snapped to his feet like a soldier and said, "Well, Inspector, I guess that settles it!"

The Inspector sank wearily into his chair. "Are you insinuating, Thomas, like some of Ellery's stupid fiction sergeants—which you are not—that Mr. Morgan be arrested for the murder of Monte Field?"

"Why—what else?" Velie seemed at a loss.

"We'll wait a while, Thomas," returned the old man heavily.

16

IN WHICH THE QUEENS GO TO THE THEATRE

Ellery and his father regarded each other across the length of the little office. Velie had resumed his seat with a puzzled frown. He sat quietly for a time in the growing silence, seemed suddenly to make a decision and asking permission left the room.

The Inspector grinned as he fumbled with the lid of his snuffbox.

"Did you get a scare, too, Ellery?"

Ellery, however, was serious. "That woman gives me a case of Wodehouse 'willies,'" he said, shuddering. "Scare is much too mild a word."

"I couldn't for the moment grasp the significance of her attitude," said Inspector Queen. "To think that she *knew,* while we have been fumbling around. . . . It scattered my wits."

"I should say the interview was highly successful," commented

Ellery. "Principally because I've been gathering a few interesting facts from this ponderous tome on chirography. But Mrs. Angela Russo does not measure up to my conception of perfect womanhood. . . ."

"If you ask me," chuckled the Inspector, "our beauteous friend has a crush on you. Consider the opportunities, my son—!"

Ellery made a grimace of profound distaste.

"Well!" Queen reached for one of the telephones on the desk. "Do you think we ought to give Benjamin Morgan another chance, Ellery?"

"Hanged if he deserves it," grumbled Ellery. "But I suppose it's the routine thing to do."

"You forget the papers, son—the papers," retorted the Inspector, a twinkle in his eye.

He spoke to the police operator in pleasant accents and a few moments later the buzzer sounded.

"Good afternoon, Mr. Morgan!" Queen said cheerfully. "And how are you today?"

"Inspector Queen?" asked Morgan after a slight hesitation. "Good afternoon to you, sir. How is the case progressing?"

"That's a fair question, Mr. Morgan," laughed the Inspector. "One, however, which I daren't answer for fear of being accused of incompetency. . . . Mr. Morgan, are you free this evening by any chance?"

Pause. "Why—not free exactly." The lawyer's voice was barely audible. "I am due at home, of course, for dinner, and I believe my wife has arranged a little bridge. Why, Inspector?"

"I was thinking of asking you to dine with my son and me

this evening," said the Inspector regretfully. "Could you possibly get away for the dinner hour?"

A longer paused. "If it's absolutely necessary, Inspector—?"

"I wouldn't put it that way exactly, Mr. Morgan. . . . But I would appreciate your accepting the invitation."

"Oh." Morgan's voice came more resolutely now. "In that case I'm at your command, Inspector. Where shall I meet you?"

"That's fine, that's fine!" said Queen. "How about Carlos', at six?"

"Very well, Inspector," returned the lawyer quietly and hung up the receiver.

"I can't help feeling sorry for the poor chap," murmured the old man.

Ellery grunted. He was not feeling inclined to sympathize. The taste of Mrs. Angela Russo was still strong in his mouth, and it was not a pleasant taste at all.

Promptly at six o'clock Inspector Queen and Ellery joined Benjamin Morgan in the convivial atmosphere of Carlos' restaurant foyer. He was sitting dejectedly in a red-leather chair, staring at the backs of his hands. His lips drooped sadly, his knees were widely separated in an instinctive attitude of depression.

He made a laudable attempt to smile as the two Queens approached. He rose with a firmness that indicated to his keen hosts a mind determined upon a fixed course of action. The Inspector was at his bubbling best, partly because he felt a genuine liking for the corpulent attorney and partly because it was his business. Ellery, as usual, was noncommittal.

The three men shook hands like old friends.

"Glad to see you're on time, Morgan," said the Inspector, as a stiff headwaiter conducted them to a corner table. "I really must apologize for taking you away from your dinner at home. There was a time once—" He sighed and they sat down.

"No apology necessary," said Morgan with a wan smile. "I suppose you know that every married man relishes a bachelor dinner at times. . . . Just what is it, Inspector, you wanted to talk to me about?"

The old man raised a warning finger. "No business now, Morgan," he said. "I have an idea Louis has something up his sleeve in the way of solid refreshment—right, Louis?"

The dinner was a culinary delight. The Inspector who was quite indifferent to the nuances of the art, had left the details of the menu to his son. Ellery was fanatically interested in the delicate subject of foods and their preparation. Consequently the three men dined well. Morgan was at first inclined to taste his food abstractedly, but he became more and more alive to the delightful concoctions placed before him, until finally he forgot his troubles altogether and chatted and laughed with his hosts.

With *café au lait* and excellent cigars, which Ellery smoked cautiously, the Inspector diffidently, and Morgan with enjoyment, Queen came to the point.

"Morgan, I'm not going to beat around the bush. I have an idea you know why I asked you here tonight. I'm going to be perfectly honest. I want the true explanation for your silence regarding the events of Sunday night, September the twenty-third—four nights ago."

Morgan had become grave immediately after the Inspector began to speak. He put the cigar on the ashtray and regarded the old man with an expression of ineffable weariness.

"It was bound to come," he said. "I might have known that you would find out sooner or later. I suppose Mrs. Russo told you out of spite."

"She did," confessed Queen frankly. "As a gentleman I refuse to listen to tales; as a policeman it is my duty. Why have you kept this from me, Morgan?"

Morgan traced a meaningless figure on the cloth with a spoon. "Because—well, because a man is always a fool until he is made to realize the extent of his folly," he said quietly, looking up. "I hoped and prayed—it is a human failing, I suppose—that the incident would remain a secret between a dead man and myself. And to find that that prostitute was hiding in the bedroom—listening to every word I said—it rather took the wind out of my sails."

He gulped down a glass of water, rushing ahead. "The God's honest truth, Inspector, is that I thought I was being drawn into a trap and I couldn't bring myself to furnish contributory evidence. There I found myself in the theatre, not so far away from my worst enemy found murdered. I could not explain my presence except by an apparently silly and unsubstantiated story; and I remembered in a bitter flash that I had actually quarreled with the dead man the night before. It was a tight position, Inspector—take my word for it."

Inspector Queen said nothing. Ellery was leaning far back in his chair, watching Morgan with gloomy eyes. Morgan swallowed hard and went on.

"That's why I didn't say anything. Can you blame a man for keeping quiet when his legal training warns him so decisively of the net of circumstantial evidence he is helping to manufacture?"

Queen was silent for a moment. Then—"We'll let that pass for the moment, Morgan. Why did you go to see Field Sunday night?"

"For a very good reason," answered the lawyer bitterly. "On Thursday, a week ago, Field called me up at my office and told me that he was making a last business venture that entailed his procuring fifty thousand dollars at once. Fifty thousand dollars!" Morgan laughed dryly. "After he had milked me until I was as flabby financially as an old cow. . . . And his 'business venture'—can you imagine what it was? If you knew Field as well as I did, you would find the answer on the race tracks and the stockmarket. . . . Perhaps I'm wrong. Perhaps he was hard pressed for money and was cleaning up his old 'accounts.' At any rate, he wanted the fifty thousand on a brand-new proposition—that he would actually return the original documents to me for that sum! It was the first time he had even suggested such a thing. Every time—before—he had insolently asked blackmail for silence. This time it was a buy-and-sell proposition."

"That's an interesting point, Mr. Morgan," put in Ellery, with a flicker of his eyes. "Did anything in his conversation definitely lead you to suspect that he was 'clearing up old accounts,' as you phrase it?"

"Yes. That is why I said what I did. He gave me the impression that he was hard up, meant to take a little vacation—vacation to him would be a three-year jaunt on the continent, nothing less—and was soliciting all his 'friends.' I never knew that he was in the blackmailing business on a large scale; but this time—!"

Ellery and the Inspector exchanged glances. Morgan forged ahead.

"I told him the truth. That I was in a bad way financially, chiefly through him, and that it would be absolutely impossible for me to raise the preposterous amount he demanded. He merely laughed—insisted on getting the money. I was most anxious to get the papers back, of course. . . ."

"Had you verified from your cancelled vouchers the fact that some were missing?" asked the Inspector.

"It wasn't necessary, Inspector," grated Morgan. "He actually exhibited the vouchers and letters for my benefit in the Webster Club two years ago—when we had the quarrel. Oh, there is no question about it. He was top man."

"Go on."

"He hung up on me with a thinly veiled threat last Thursday. I had tried desperately during the conversation to make him believe that I would in some way meet his demands, because I knew that he would have no scruples at all about publishing the papers once he realized he had sucked me dry. . . ."

"Did you ask him if you could see the documents?" asked Ellery.

"I believe I did—but he laughed at me and said I would see the color of my checks and letters when he saw the color of my money. He was nobody's fool, that crook—he was taking no chances on my doing him in while he brought out the damning evidence. . . . You see how frank I am. I will even admit that at times the thought of violence entered my head. What man could keep from thinking such thoughts under those circumstances? But I never entertained homicidal fancies seriously, gentlemen—for a very good reason." He paused.

"It wouldn't have done you any good," said Ellery softly. "You didn't know where the documents were!"

"Exactly," returned Morgan with a tremulous smile. "I didn't know. And with those papers liable to come to light at any time—to fall into anybody's hands—what good would Field's death have done me? I would probably have exchanged a bad taskmaster for a worse. . . . On Sunday night, after trying for three terrible days to get together the money he asked for—with no result—I decided to come to a final settlement with him. I went to his apartment and found him in a dressing gown, much surprised and not at all apprehensive at seeing me. The living room was upset—I did not know at the time that Mrs. Russo was hiding in the next room."

He relit the cigar with shaking fingers.

"We quarreled—or rather I quarreled and he sneered. He would listen to no argument, to no plea. He wanted the fifty thousand or he would send the story around—and the proofs. It sort of got on my nerves after a while. . . . I left before I lost control of myself utterly. And that's all, Inspector, on my word of honor as a gentleman and as an unfortunate victim of circumstances."

He turned his head away. Inspector Queen coughed and threw his cigar into the ashtray. He fumbled in his pocket for the brown snuffbox, took a pinch, inhaled deeply and leaned back in his chair. Ellery suddenly poured a glass of water for Morgan, who took it and drained it.

"Thank you, Morgan," said Queen. "And since you have been so frank in your story, please be honest and tell me whether you threatened Field's life Sunday night during your quarrel. It is only fair to let you know that Mrs. Russo flatly accused you of Field's murder because of something you said in the heat of the moment."

Morgan grew pale. His brows twitched and his eyes, glazed and worried, stared pitifully at the Inspector.

"She was lying!" he cried hoarsely. Several diners nearby looked around curiously, and Inspector Queen tapped Morgan's arm. He bit his lip and lowered his voice. "I did nothing of the sort, Inspector. I was honest with you a moment ago when I said that I had thought savagely from time to time of killing Field. It was a crippled, silly, pointless thought. I—I wouldn't have the courage to kill a man. Even at the Webster Club when I lost my temper completely and shouted that threat I didn't mean it. Certainly Sunday night—please believe me rather than that unscrupulous, money-grubbing harlot, Inspector—you must!"

"I merely want you to explain what you said. Because," said the Inspector quietly, "strange as it may seem, I do believe that you made the statement she attributes to you."

"What statement?" Morgan was in a sweat of fear; his eyes started from his head.

"'Publish those papers, and if it means ruin to me—I'll see to it that it's the last time you'll ever blackmail *anybody!*'" replied the Inspector. "Did you say that, Mr. Morgan?"

The lawyer stared incredulously at the Queens, then threw back his head and laughed. "Good heavens!" he gasped, at last. "Is that the 'threat' I made? Why, Inspector, what I meant was that if he published those documents, in the event that I couldn't meet his blackguard demands, that I'd make a clean breast of it to the police and drag him down with me. That's what I meant! And she thought I was threatening his life—" He wiped his eyes hysterically.

Ellery smiled, his finger summoning the waiter. He paid the check and lit a cigarette, looking sidewise at his father, who was regarding Morgan with a mixture of abstraction and sympathy.

"Very well, Mr. Morgan." The Inspector rose, pushed back his chair. "That's all we wanted to know." He stood aside courteously to allow the dazed, still trembling lawyer to precede them toward the cloakroom.

The sidewalk fronting the Roman Theatre was jammed when the two Queens strolled up 47th Street from Broadway. The crowd was so huge that police lines had been established. Traffic was at a complete standstill along the entire length of the narrow thoroughfare. The electric lights of the marquee blared forth the title "Gunplay" in vigorous dashes of light and in smaller lights the legend, "Starring—James Peale and Eve Ellis, Supported by an All-Star Cast." Women and men wielded frenzied elbows to push through the milling mob; policemen shouted hoarsely, demanding tickets for the evening's performance before they would allow anyone to pass through the lines.

The Inspector showed his badge and he and Ellery were hurled with the jostling crowd into the small lobby of the theatre. Beside the box office, his Latin face wreathed in smiles, stood Manager Panzer, courteous, firm and authoritative, helping to speed the long line of cash customers from the box office window to the ticket taker. The venerable doorman, perspiring mightily, was standing to one side, a bewildered expression on his face. The cashiers worked madly. Harry Neilson was huddled in a corner of the lobby, talking earnestly to three young men who were obviously reporters.

Panzer caught sight of the two Queens and hurried forward to greet them. At an imperious gesture from the Inspector he hesitated, then with an understanding nod turned back to the cashier's window. Ellery stood meekly in line and procured two reserved tickets from the box office. They entered the orchestra in the midst of a pushing throng.

A startled Madge O'Connell fell back as Ellery presented two tickets plainly marked LL32 Left and LL30 Left. The Inspector smiled as she fumbled with the pasteboards and threw him a half-fearful glance. She led them across the thick carpet to the extreme left aisle, silently indicated the last two seats of the last row and fled. The two men sat down, placed their hats in the wire holders below the seats and leaned back comfortably, for all the world like two pleasure-seekers contemplating an evening's gory entertainment.

The auditorium was packed. Droves of people being ushered down the aisles were rapidly consuming the empty seats. Heads twisted expectantly in the direction of the Queens, who became unwittingly the center of a most unwelcome scrutiny.

"Heck!" grumbled the old man. "We should have come in after the curtain went up."

"You're much too sensitive to public acclaim, *mon père,"* laughed Ellery. "I don't mind the limelight." He consulted his wrist watch and their glances met significantly. It was exactly 8:25. They wriggled in their seats and settled down.

The lights were blotted out, one by one. The chatter of the audience died in a responsive sympathy. In total darkness the curtain rose on a weirdly dim stage. A shot exploded the silence; a man's gurgling shout raised gasps in the theatre. "Gunplay" was off in its widely publicized and theatrical manner.

Despite the preoccupation of his father, Ellery, relaxed in the chair which three nights before had held the dead body of Monte Field, was able to sit still and enjoy the exceedingly mellow melodrama. The fine rich voice of James Peale, ushered onto the stage by a series of climactic incidents, rang out and thrilled him with its commanding art. Eve Ellis's utter absorption in her role was apparent—at the moment she was conversing in low throbbing tones with Stephen Barry, whose handsome face and pleasant voice were evoking admiring comment from a young girl seated directly to the Inspector's right. Hilda Orange was huddled in a corner, dressed flamboyantly as befitted her stage character. The old "character-man" pottered aimlessly about the stage. Ellery leaned toward his father.

"It's a well-cast production," he whispered. "Watch that Orange woman!"

The play stuttered and crackled on. With a crashing symphony of words and noise the first act came to an end. The Inspector consulted his watch as the lights snapped on. It was 9:05.

He rose and Ellery followed him lazily. Madge O'Connell, pretending not to notice them, pushed open the heavy iron doors across the aisle and the audience began to file out into the dimly lit alleyway. The two Queens sauntered out among the others.

A uniformed boy standing behind a neat stand covered with paper cups was crying his wares in a subdued, "refined" voice. It was Jess Lynch, the boy who had testified in the matter of Monte Field's request for ginger ale.

Ellery strolled behind the iron door—there was a cramped space between the door and the brick wall. He noticed that the wall of the building flanking the other side of the alley was easily six stories high and unbroken. The Inspector bought an orange-drink from the boy. Jess Lynch recognized him with a start and Inspector Queen greeted the boy pleasantly.

People were standing in small groups, their attitudes betokening a strange interest in their surroundings. The Inspector heard a woman remark, in a fearful, fascinated voice, "They say he was standing right out here Monday night, buying an orangedrink!"

The warning bell soon clanged inside the theatre, and those who had come outside for a breath of air hurried back into the orchestra. Before he sat down, the Inspector glanced over across the rear of the auditorium to the foot of the staircase leading to the balcony. A stalwart, uniformed young man stood alertly on the first step.

The second act exploded into being. The audience swayed and gasped in the approved fashion while the dramatic fireworks were shot off on the stage. The Queens seemed suddenly to have become absorbed in the action. Father and son leaned forward, bodies taut, eyes intent. Ellery consulted his watch at 9:30—and the two Queens settled back again while the play rumbled on.

At 9:50 exactly they rose, took their hats and coats and slipped out of the LL row into the clear space behind the orchestra. A number of people were standing—at which the Inspector smiled and blessed the power of the press beneath his breath. The white-faced usherette, Madge O'Connell, was leaning stiffly against a pillar, staring unseeingly ahead.

The Queens, espying Manager Panzer in the doorway of his office beaming deligntedly at the crowded auditorium, made their way towards him. The Inspector motioned him inside and rapidly stepped into the little anteroom, Ellery close behind. The smile faded from Panzer's face.

"I hope you've had a profitable evening?" he asked nervously.

"Profitable evening? Well—it depends upon what you mean by the word." The old man gestured briefly and led the way through the second door into Panzer's private office.

"Look here, Panzer," he said, pacing up and down in some excitement, "have you a plan of the orchestra handy which shows each seat, numbered, and all the exits?"

Panzer stared. "I think so. Just a moment." He fumbled in a filing cabinet, rummaged among some folders and finally brought out a large map of the theatre separated into two sections—one for the orchestra and the other for the balcony.

The Inspector brushed the second away impatiently as he

and Ellery bent over the orchestra plan.[2] They studied it for a moment. Queen looked up at Panzer, who was shifting from one foot to another on the rug, evidently at a loss to know what would be required of him next.

"May I have this map, Panzer?" asked the Inspector shortly. "I'll return it unharmed in a few days."

"Certainly, certainly!" said Panzer. "Is there anything else I can do for you now, Inspector? . . . I want to thank you for your consideration in the matter of publicity, sir—Gordon Davis is extremely pleased at the 'house' tonight. He asked me to relay his thanks."

"Not at all—not at all," grumbled the Inspector, folding the map and putting it in his breast pocket. "It was coming to you—what's right is right. . . . And now, Ellery—if you'll come along. . . . Good night, Panzer. Not a word about this, remember!"

The two Queens slipped out of Panzer's office while he was babbling his reassurances of silence.

They crossed the rear of the orchestra once more, in the direction of the extreme left aisle. The Inspector beckoned curtly to Madge O'Connell.

"Yes," she breathed, her face chalky.

"Just open those doors wide enough to let us through, O'Connell, and forget all about it afterward. Understand?" said the Inspector grimly.

She mumbled under her breath as she pushed open one of the

---

2 The plan illustrated in the frontispiece and drawn by Ellery Queen was designed from Manager Panzer's map. —THE EDITOR

big iron doors opposite the LL row. With a last warning shake of the head the Inspector slipped through, Ellery following—and the door came softly back into place again.

At 11 o'clock, as the wide exits were disgorging their first flocks of theatre-goers after the final curtain, Richard and Ellery Queen re-entered the Roman Theatre through the main door.

17

IN WHICH MORE HATS GROW

"Sit down, Tim—have a cup of coffee?"

Timothy Cronin, a keen-eyed man of medium height thatched plentifully with fire-red hair, seated himself in one of the Queens' comfortable chairs and accepted the Inspector's invitation in some embarrassment.

It was Friday morning and the Inspector and Ellery, garbed romantically in colorful dressing gowns, were in high spirits. They had retired the night before at an uncommonly early hour—for them; they had slept the sleep of the just; now Djuna had a pot of steaming coffee, of a variety which he blended himself, ready on the table; and indubitably all seemed right with the world.

Cronin had stalked into the cheery Queen quarters at an ungodly hour—disheveled, morose and unashamedly cursing. Not even the mild protests of the Inspector were able to stem the tide of profanity which streamed from his lips; and as for Ellery, he listened to the lawyer's language with an air of grave enjoyment, as an amateur harkens to a professional.

Then Cronin awoke to his environment, and blushed, and was invited to sit down, and stared at the unbending back of Djuna as that nimble man-of-affairs busied himself with the light appurtenances of the morning meal.

"I don't suppose you're in a mood to apologize for your shocking language, Tim Cronin, me lad," chided the Inspector, folding his hands Buddhalike over his stomach. "Do I have to inquire the reason for the bad temper?"

"Not much, you don't," growled Cronin, shifting his feet savagely on the rug. "You ought to be able to guess. I'm up against a blank wall in the matter of Field's papers. Blast his black soul!"

"It's blasted, Tim—it's blasted, never fear," said Queen sorrowfully. "Poor Field is probably roasting his toes over a sizzling little coalfire in Hell just now—and chortling to himself over your profanity. Exactly what is the situation—how do things stand?"

Cronin grasped the cup Djuna had set before him and drained its scalding contents in a gulp. "Stand?" he cried, banging down the cup. "They don't stand—they're nil, nit, not! By Christopher, if I don't get my hands on some documentary evidence soon I'll go batty! Why, Inspector—Stoates and I ransacked that swell office of Field's until I don't think there's a rat in the walls who dares show his head outside a ten-foot hole—and there's nothing. Nothing! Man—it's inconceivable. I'd stake my reputation that somewhere—the Lord alone knows where—Field's papers are hidden, just begging somebody to come along and carry them away."

"You seem possessed of a phobia on the subject of hidden papers, Cronin," remarked Ellery mildly. "One would think we are living in the days of Charles the First. There's no such thing as hidden papers. You merely have to know where to look."

Cronin grinned impertinently. "That's very good of you, Mr. Queen. Suppose you suggest the place Mr. Monte Field selected to hide *his* papers."

Ellery lit a cigarette. "All right. I accept the challenge to combat. . . . You say—and I don't doubt your word in the least—that the documents you suppose to be in existence are not in Field's office. . . . By the way, what makes you so sure that Field kept papers which would incriminate him in this vast clique of gangsters you told us about?"

"He must have," retorted Cronin. "Queer logic, but it works. . . . My information absolutely establishes the fact that Field had correspondence and written plans connecting him with men higher up in gangdom whom we're constantly trying to 'get' and whom we haven't been able to touch so far. You'll have to take my word for it; it's too complicated a story to go into here. But you mark my words, Mr. Queen—Field had papers that he couldn't afford to destroy. Those are the papers I'm looking for."

"Granted," said Ellery in a rhetorical tone. "I merely wished to make certain of the facts. Let me repeat, then, these papers are not in his office. We must therefore look for them farther afield. For example, they might be secreted in a safety-deposit vault."

"But, El," objected the Inspector, who had listened to the interplay between Cronin and Ellery in amusement, "didn't I tell you this morning that Thomas had run that lead to earth? Field did not have a box in a safety-deposit vault. That is established. He had no general delivery or private post-office box either—under his real name or any other name.

"Thomas has also investigated Field's club affiliations and discovered that the lawyer had no residence, permanent or temporary, besides the flat on 75th Street. Furthermore, in all Thomas' scouting around, he found not the slightest indication of a possible hiding place. He thought that Field might have left the papers in a parcel or bag in the keeping of a shopkeeper, or something of the sort. But there wasn't a trace. . . . Velie's a good man in these matters, Ellery. You can bet your bottom dollar that hypothesis of yours is false."

"I was making a point for Cronin's benefit," retorted Ellery. He spread his fingers on the table elaborately and winked. "You see, we must narrow the field of search to the point where we can definitely say: 'It must be here.' The office, the safety-deposit vault, the post-office boxes have been ruled out. Yet we know that Field could not afford to keep these documents in a place difficult of access. I cannot vouch for the papers *you're* seeking, Cronin; but it's different with the papers *we're* seeking. No, Field had them somewhere near at hand. . . . And, to go a step further, it's reasonable to assume that he would have kept all his important secret papers in the same hiding place."

Cronin scratched his head and nodded.

"We shall now apply the elementary precepts, gentlemen." Ellery paused as if to emphasize his next statement. "Since we have narrowed our area of inquiry to the exclusion of all possible hiding places save one—the papers must be in that one hiding place. . . . Nothing to that."

"Now that I pause to consider," interpolated the Inspector, his good humor suddenly dissipated into gloom, "perhaps we weren't as careful in that place as we might have been."

"I'm as certain we're on the right track," said Ellery firmly, "as that today is Friday and there will be fish suppers in thirty million homes tonight."

Cronin was looking puzzled. "I don't quite get it, Mr. Queen. What do you mean when you say there's only one possible hiding place left?"

"Field's apartment, Cronin," replied Ellery imperturbably. "The papers are there."

"But I was discussing the case with the D. A. only yesterday," objected Cronin, "and he said you'd already ransacked Field's apartment and found nothing."

"True—true enough," said Ellery. "We searched Field's apartment and found nothing. The trouble was, Cronin, that we didn't look in the right place."

"Well, by ginger, if you know now, let's get a move on!" cried Cronin, springing from his chair.

The Inspector tapped the red-haired man's knee gently and pointed to the seat. "Sit down, Tim," he advised. "Ellery is merely indulging in his favorite game of ratiocination. He doesn't know where the papers are any more than you do. He's guessing. . . . In detective literature," he added with a sad smile, "they call it the 'art of deduction.'"

"I should say," murmured Ellery, emitting a cloud of smoke, "that I am being challenged once more. Nevertheless, although I haven't been back to Field's rooms I intend, with Inspector Queen's kind permission, to return there and find the slippery documents."

"In the matter of these papers—" began the old man, when he was interrupted by the doorbell ringing. Djuna admitted Sergeant Velie, who was accompanied by a small, furtive young man so ill at ease as to be trembling. The Inspector sprang to his feet and intercepted them before they could enter the living room. Cronin stared as Queen said. "This the fellow, Thomas?" and the big detective answered with grim levity, "Large as life, Inspector."

"Think you could burgle an apartment without being caught, do you?" inquired the Inspector genially, taking the newcomer by the arm. "You're just the man I want."

The furtive young man seemed overcome by a species of terrified palsy. "Say, Inspector, yer not takin' me fer a ride, are ya?" he stammered.

The Inspector smiled reassuringly and led him out into the foyer. They held a whispered and one-sided conversation, with the stranger grunting assents at every second word uttered by the old man. Cronin and Ellery in the living room caught the flash of a small sheet of paper as it passed from the Inspector's hand into the clutching paw of the young man.

Queen returned, stepping spryly. "All right, Thomas. You

take care of the other arrangements and see that our friend here gets into no trouble. . . . Now, gentlemen—"

Velie made his adieu monosyllabically and led the frightened stranger from the apartment.

The Inspector sat down. "Before we go over to Field's rooms, boys," he said thoughtfully, "I want to make certain things plain. In the first place, from what Benjamin Morgan has told us, Field's business was law but his great source of income—blackmail. Did you know that, Tim? Monte Field sucked dozens of prominent men dry, in all likelihood to the tune of hundreds of thousands of dollars. In fact, Tim, we're convinced that the motive behind Field's murder was connected with this phase of his undercover activities. There is no doubt but that he was killed by somebody who was being taken in for huge sums of hush-money and could stand the gaff no longer.

"You know as well as I, Tim, that blackmail depends largely for its ugly life on the possession of incriminating documents by the blackmailer. That's why we're so sure that there are hidden papers about somewhere—and Ellery here maintains that they're in Field's rooms. Well, we'll see. If eventually we find those papers, the documents you've been hunting so long will probably come to light also, as Ellery pointed out a moment ago."

He paused reflectively. "I can't tell you, Tim, how badly I want to get my hands on those confounded documents of Field's. They mean a good deal to me. They'd clear up a lot of questions about which we're still in the dark. . . ."

"Well, then, let's get going!" cried Cronin, leaping from his chair. "Do you realize, Inspector, that I've worked for years on Field's tail for this one purpose? It will be the happiest day of my life. . . . Inspector—come on!"

Neither Ellery nor his father, however, seemed to be in haste. They retired to the bedroom to dress while Cronin fretted in the living room. If Cronin had not been so preoccupied with his own thoughts he would have noticed that the light spirits which had suffused the Queens when he arrived were now scattered into black gloom. The Inspector particularly seemed out of sorts, irritable and for once slow to push the investigation into an inevitable channel.

Eventually the Queens appeared fully dressed. The three men descended to the street. As they climbed into a taxicab Ellery sighed.

"Afraid you're going to be shown up, son?" muttered the old man, his nose buried in the folds of his topcoat.

"I'm not thinking of that," returned Ellery. "It's something else. . . . The papers will be found, never fear."

"I hope to Christmas you're right!" breathed Cronin fervently, and it was the last word spoken until the taxicab ground to a stop before the lofty apartment house on 75th Street.

The three men took the elevator to the fourth floor and stepped out into the quiet corridor. The Inspector peered about quickly, then punched the doorbell of the Field apartment. There was no answer, although they could hear the vague rustling of someone behind the door. Suddenly it swished open to reveal a red-faced policeman whose hand hovered uneasily in the region of his hip pocket.

"Don't be scared, man—we won't bite you!" growled the Inspector, who was completely out of temper for no reason that Cronin, nervous and springy as a racing colt, could fathom.

The uniformed man saluted. "Didn't know but it might be someone snoopin' around, Inspector," he said feebly.

The three men walked into the foyer, the slim, white hand of the old man pushing the door violently shut.

"Anything been happening around here?" snapped Queen, striding to the entrance to the living room and looking inside.

"Not a thing, sir," said the policeman. "I'm on four-hour shifts with Cassidy as relief and once in a while Detective Ritter drops in to see if everything is all right."

"Oh, he does, does he?" The old man turned back. "Anybody try to get into the place?"

"Not while I was here, Inspector—nor Cassidy neither," responded the policeman nervously. "And we've been alternating ever since Tuesday morning. There hasn't been a soul near these rooms except Ritter."

"Park out here in the foyer for the next couple of hours, officer," commanded the Inspector. "Get yourself a chair and take a snooze if you want to—but if anybody should start monkeying with the door tip us off pronto."

The policeman dragged a chair from the living room into the foyer, sat down with his back against the front door, folded his arms and unashamedly closed his eyes.

The three men took in the scene with gloomy eyes. The foyer was small but crowded with oddments of furniture and decoration. A bookcase filled with unused-appearing volumes; a small table on which perched a "modernistic" lamp and some carved ivory ashtrays; two Empire chairs; a peculiar piece of furniture which seemed half sideboard and half secretary; and a number of cushions and rugs were scattered about. The Inspector stood regarding this melange wryly.

"Here, son—I guess the best way for us to tackle the search is for the three of us to go through everything piece by piece, one checking up on the other. I'm not very hopeful about it. I'll tell you that."

"The gentleman of the Wailing Wall," groaned Ellery. "Grief is writ fine and large on his noble visage. You and I, Cronin—we're not such pessimists, are we?"

Cronin growled, "I'd say—less talk and more action, with all the respects in the world for these little family ructions."

Ellery stared at him with admiration. "You're almost insectivorous in your determination, man. More like an army ant than a human being. And poor Field's lying in the morgue, too. . . . *Allons, enfants!*"

They set to work under the nodding head of the policeman. They worked silently for the most part. Ellery's face reflected a calm expectancy; the Inspector's a doleful irritation; Cronin's a savage indomitability. Book after book was extracted from the case and carefully inspected—leaves shaken out—covers examined minutely—backboards pinched and pierced. There were over two hundred books and the thorough search took a long time. Ellery, after a period of activity, seemed inclined to allow his father and Cronin to do the heavier work of inspection while he devoted his attention more and more to the titles of the volumes.

At one point he uttered a delighted exclamation and held up to the light a thin, cheaply bound book. Cronin leaped forward immediately, his eyes blazing. The Inspector looked up with a flicker of interest. But Ellery had merely discovered another volume on handwriting analysis.

The old man stared at his son in silent curiosity, his lips puckered thoughtfully. Cronin turned back to the bookcase with a groan. Ellery, however, riffling the pages rapidly cried out again. The two men craned over his shoulder. On the margins of several pages were some penciled notations. The words spelled names: "Henry Jones," "John Smith," "George Brown." They were repeated many times on the margins of the page, as if the writer were practicing different styles of penmanship.

"Didn't Field have the most adolescent yen for scribbling?" asked Ellery, staring fascinatedly at the penciled names.

"As usual you have something up your sleeve, my son," remarked the Inspector wearily. "I see what you mean, but I don't see that it helps us any. Except for—By jinks, that's an idea!"

He bent forward and attacked the search once more, his body vibrant with fresh interest. Ellery, smiling, joined him. Cronin stared uncomprehendingly at both.

"Suppose you let me in on this thing, folks," he said in an aggrieved voice.

The Inspector straightened up. "Ellery's hit on something that, if it's true, is a bit of luck for us and reveals still another sidelight on Field's character. The blackhearted rascal! See here, Tim—if a man's an inveterate blackmailer and you find continual evidence that he has been practicing handwriting from textbooks on the subject, what conclusion would you draw?"

"You mean that he's a forger, too?" frowned Cronin. "I never suspected that in spite of all these years of hounding him."

"Not merely a forger, Cronin," laughed Ellery. "I don't think you will find Monte Field has penned somebody else's name to a check, or anything of that sort. He was too wily a bird to make such a grievous error. What he probably did do was secure original and incriminating documents referring to a certain individual, make copies of them and sell the *copies* back to the owner, retaining the originals for further use!"

"And in that case, Tim," added the Inspector portentously, "if we find this gold mine of papers somewhere about—which I greatly doubt—we'll also find, as like as not, the original or originals of the papers for which Monte Field was murdered!"

The red-haired Assistant District Attorney pulled a long face at his two companions. "Seems like a lot of 'if's'" he said finally, shaking his head.

They resumed the search in growing silence.

Nothing was concealed in the foyer. After an hour of steady, back-breaking work they were forced reluctantly to that conclusion. Not a square inch was left unexamined. The interior of the lamp and of the bookcase; the slender, thin-topped table; the secretary, inside and outside; the cushions; even the walls tapped carefully by the Inspector, who by now was aroused to a high pitch of excitement, suppressed but remarkable in his tight lips and color-touched cheeks.

They attacked the living room. Their first port-of-call was the wall, searching for signs of tampered woodwork. And still the big clothes closet inside the room directly off the foyer. Again the Inspector and Ellery went through the topcoats, overcoats and capes hanging on the rack. Nothing. On the shelf above were the four hats they had examined on Tuesday morning: the old Panama, the derby and the two fedoras. Still nothing. Cronin bumped down on his knees to peer savagely into the darker recesses of the closet, tapping the wall, searching for signs of tampered woodwork. And still nothing. With the aid of a chair the Inspector poked into the corners of the area above the shelf. He climbed down, shaking his head.

"Forget the closet, boys," he muttered. They descended upon the room proper.

The large carved desk which Hagstrom and Piggott had rifled three days before invited their scrutiny. Inside was the pile of papers, canceled bills and letters they had offered for the old man's inspection. Old Queen actually peered through these torn and ragged sheets as if they might conceal messages in invisible ink. He shrugged his shoulders and threw them down.

"Darned if I'm not growing romantic in my old age," he growled. "The influence of a fiction-writing rascal of a son."

He picked up the miscellaneous articles he himself had found on Tuesday in the pockets of the closet coats. Ellery was scowling now; Cronin was beginning to wear a forlorn, philosophical expression; the old man shuffled abstractedly among the keys, old letters, wallets, and then turned away.

"Nothing in the desk," he announced wearily. "I doubt if that clever limb of Satan would have selected anything as obvious as a desk for a hiding place."

"He would if he'd read Edgar Allen Poe," murmured Ellery. "Let's get on. Sure there is no secret drawer here?" he asked Cronin. The red head was shaken sadly but emphatically.

They probed and poked about in the furniture, under the carpets and lamps, in bookends, curtain rods. With each successive failure the apparent hopelessness of the search was reflected in their faces. When they had finished with the living room it looked as if it had innocently fallen in the path of a hurricane—a bare and comfortless satisfaction.

"Nothing left but the bedroom, kitchenette and lavatory," said the Inspector to Cronin; and the three men went into the room which Mrs. Angela Russo had occupied Monday night.

Field's bedroom was distinctly feminine in its accoutrements—a characteristic which Ellery ascribed to the influence of the charming Greenwich Villager. Again they scoured the premises, not an inch of space eluding their vigilant eyes and questing hands; and again there seemed nothing to do but admit failure. They took apart the bedding and examined the spring of the bed; they put it together again and attacked the clothes closet. Every suit was mauled and crushed by their insistent fingers—bathrobes, dressing gowns, shoes, cravats. Cronin halfheartedly repeated his examination of the walls and moldings. They lifted rugs and picked up chairs; shook out the pages of the telephone book in the bedside telephone table. The Inspector even lifted the metal disk which fitted around the steampipe at the floor, because it was loose and seemed to present possibilities.

From the bedroom they went into the kitchenette. It was so crowded with kitchen furnishings that they could barely move about. A large cabinet was rifled; Cronin's exasperated fingers dipped angrily into the flour and sugar bins. The stove, the dish closet, the pan closet—even the single marble washtub in a corner—was methodically gone over. On the floor to one side stood the half empty case of liquor bottles. Cronin cast longing glances in this direction, only to look guiltily away as the Inspector glared at him.

"And now—the bathroom," murmured Ellery. In an ominous silence they trooped into the tiled lavatory. Three minutes later they came out, still silently, and went into the living room where they disposed themselves in chairs. The Inspector drew out his snuffbox and took a vicious pinch; Cronin and Ellery lit cigarettes.

"I should say, my son," said the Inspector in sepulchral tones after a painful interval broken only by the snores of the policeman in the foyer, "I should say that the deductive method which has brought fame and fortune to Mr. Sherlock Holmes and his legions has gone awry. Mind you, I'm not scolding. . . ." But he slouched into the fastnesses of the chair.

Ellery stroked his smooth jaw with nervous fingers. "I seem to have made something of an ass of myself," he confessed. "And yet those papers are here somewhere. Isn't that a silly notion to have? But logic bears me out. When ten is the whole and two plus three plus four are discarded, only one is left. . . . Pardon me for being old-fashioned. I insist the papers are here."

Cronin grunted and expelled a huge mouthful of smoke.

"Your objection sustained," murmured Ellery, leaning back. "Let's go over the ground again. No, no!" he explained hastily, as Cronin's face lengthened in dismay—"I mean orally. . . . Mr. Field's apartment consists of a foyer, a living room, a kitchenette, a bedroom and a lavatory. We have fruitlessly examined a foyer, a living room, a kitchenette, a bedroom and a lavatory. Euclid would regretfully force a conclusion here. . . ." He mused, "How have we examined these rooms?" he asked suddenly. "We have gone over the obvious things, pulled the obvious things to pieces. Furniture, lamps, carpets—I repeat, the obvious things. And we have tapped floors, walls and moldings. It would seem that nothing has escaped the search. . . ."

He stopped, his eyes brightening. The Inspector threw off his look of fatigue at once. From experience he was aware that Ellery rarely grew excited over inconsequential things.

"And yet," said Ellery slowly, gazing in fascination at his father's face, "by the Golden Roofs of Seneca, we've overlooked something—actually overlooked something!"

"What!" growled Cronin. "You're kidding."

"Oh, but I'm not," chuckled Ellery, lounging to his feet "We have examined floors and we have examined walls, but have we examined—ceilings?"

He shot the word forth theatrically while the two men stared at him in amazement.

"Here, what are you driving at, Ellery?" asked his father, frowning.

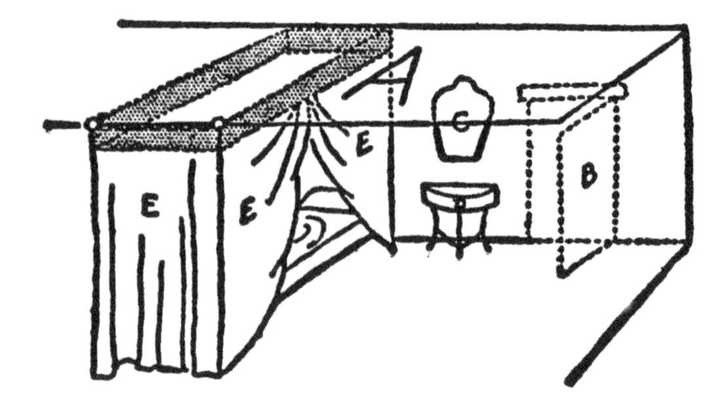

A—Ceiling
B—Door to Living Room
C—Mirror
D—Dressing Table

E—Damask curtains around bed, from ceiling to floor, concealing Shaded portino which represents panel containing hats.

Ellery briskly crushed his cigarette in an ashtray. "Just this," he said. "Pure reasoning has it that when you have exhausted every possibility but one in a given equation that one, no matter how impossible, no matter how ridiculous it may seem in the postulation—*must be the correct one*. . . . A theorem analogous to the one by which I concluded that the papers were in this apartment."

"But, Mr. Queen, for the love of Pete—ceilings!" exploded Cronin, while the Inspector looked guiltily at the living room ceiling. Ellery caught the look and laughed, shaking his head.

"I'm not suggesting that we call in a plasterer to maul these lovely middle-class ceilings," he said. "Because I have the answer already. What is it in these rooms somewhere that is on the ceiling?"

"The chandeliers," muttered Cronin doubtfully, gazing upward at the heavily bronzed fixture above their heads.

"By jinks—the canopy over the bed!" shouted the Inspector. He jumped to his feet and ran into the bedroom. Cronin pounded hard after him, Ellery sauntering interestedly behind.

They stopped at the foot of the bed and stared up at the canopy. Unlike the conventional canopies of American style, this florid ornament was not merely a large square of cloth erected on four posts, an integral part of the bed only. The bed was so constructed that the four posts, beginning at the four corners, stretched from floor to ceiling. The heavy maroon-colored damask of the canopy also reached from floor to ceiling, connected at the top by a ringed rod from which the folds of the damask hung gracefully.

"Well, if it's anywhere," grunted the Inspector, dragging one of the damask-covered bedroom chairs to the bed, "it's up here. Here, boys, lend a hand."

He stood on the chair with a fine disregard for the havoc his shoes were wreaking on the silken material. Finding upon stretching his arms above his head that he was still many feet short of touching the ceiling, he stepped down.

"Doesn't look as if you could make it either, Ellery," he muttered. "And Field was no taller than you. There must be a ladder handy somewhere by which Field himself got up here!"

Cronin dashed into the kitchenette at Ellery's nod in that direction. He was back in a moment with a six-foot stepladder. The Inspector, mounting to the highest rung, found that his fingers were still short of touching the rod. Ellery solved the difficulty by ordering his father down and climbing to the top himself. Standing on the ladder he was in a position to explore the top of the canopy.

He grasped the damask firmly and pulled. The entire fabric gave way and fell to the sides, revealing a wooden panel about twelve inches deep—a framework which the hangings had concealed. Ellery's fingers swept swiftly over the wooden reliefwork of this panel. Cronin and the Inspector were staring with varying expressions up at him. Finding nothing that at the moment presented a possibility of entrance, Ellery leaned forward and explored the damask directly beneath the floor of the panel.

"Rip it down!" growled the Inspector.

Ellery jerked violently at the material and the entire canopy of damask fell to the bed. The bare unornamented floor of the panel was revealed.

"It's hollow," announced Ellery, rapping his knuckles on the underside paneling.

"That doesn't help much," said Cronin. "It wouldn't be a solid chunk, anyway. Why don't you try the other side of the bed, Mr. Queen?"

But Ellery, who had drawn back and was again examining the side of the panel, exclaimed triumphantly. He had been seeking a complicated, Machiavellian "secret door"—he found now that the secret door was nothing more, subtle than a sliding panel. It was cleverly concealed—the juncture of sliding and stationary panels was covered by a row of wooden rosettes and clumsy decorations—but it was nothing that a student of mystery lore would have hailed as a triumph of concealment.

"It begins to appear as if I were being vindicated," Ellery chuckled as he peered into the black recesses of the hole he had uncovered. He thrust a long arm into the aperture. The Inspector and Cronin were staring at him with bated breath.

"By all the pagan gods," shouted Ellery suddenly, his lean body quivering with excitement. "Do you remember what I told you, Dad? Where would those papers be except in—hats!"

His sleeve coated with dust, he withdrew his arm and the two men below saw in his hand a musty silk tophat!

Cronin executed an intricate jig as Ellery dropped the hat on the bed and dipped his arm once more into the yawning hole. In a moment he had brought out another hat—and another—and still another! There they lay on the bed—two silk hats and two derbies.

"Take this flashlight, son," commanded the Inspector. "See if there's anything else up there."

Ellery took the proffered electric torch and flashed its beam into the aperture. After a moment he clambered down, shaking his head.

"That's all," he announced, dusting his sleeve, "but I should think it would be enough."

The Inspector picked up the four hats and carried them into the living room, where he deposited them on a sofa. The three men sat down gravely and regarded each other.

"I'm sort of itching to see what's what," said Cronin finally, in a hushed voice.

"I'm rather afraid to look," retorted the Inspector.

"Mene mene tekel upharsin," laughed Ellery. "In this case it

might be interpreted as 'the handwriting on the panel.' Examine on, Macduff!"

The Inspector picked up one of the silk hats. It bore on the rich satiny lining the chaste trademark of Browne Bros. Ripping out the lining and finding nothing beneath, he tried to tear out the leather sweatband. It resisted his mightiest efforts. He borrowed Cronin's pocket knife and with difficulty slashed away the band. Then he looked up.

"This hat, Romans and countrymen," he said pleasantly, "contains nothing but the familiar ingredients of hat-wear. Would you care to examine it?"

Cronin uttered a savage cry and snatched it from the Inspector's hand. He literally tore the hat to pieces in his rage.

"Heck!" he said disgustedly, throwing the remnants on the floor. "Explain that to my undeveloped brain, will you, Inspector?"

Queen smiled, taking up the second silk hat and regarding it curiously.

"You're at a disadvantage, Tim," he said. "We know why one of these hats is a blank. Don't we, Ellery?"

"Michaels," murmured Ellery.

"Exactly—Michaels," returned the Inspector.

"Charley Michaels!" exclaimed Cronin. "Field's strong-arm guy, by all that's holy! Where does he come into this?"

"Can't tell yet. Know anything about him?"

"Nothing except that he hung onto Field's coattails pretty closely. He's an ex-jailbird, did you know that?"

"Yes," replied the Inspector dreamily. "We'll have a talk

about that phase of Mr. Michaels some other time. . . . But let me explain that hat: Michaels on the evening of the murder laid out, according to his statement, Field's evening clothes, including a silk hat. Michaels swore that as far as he knew Field possessed only *one* topper. Now if we suppose that Field used hats for concealing papers, and was going to the Roman Theatre that night wearing a 'loaded' one he must necessarily have substituted the loaded hat for the empty one which Michaels prepared. Since he was so careful to keep only one silk hat in the closet, he realized that Michaels, should he find a topper, would be suspicious. So, in switching hats, he had to conceal the empty one. What more natural than that he should put it in the place from which he had taken the loaded hat—the panel above the bed?"

"Well, I'll be switched!" exclaimed Cronin.

"Finally," resumed the Inspector, "We can take it as gospel that Field, who was devilishly careful in the matter of his headgear, intended to restore the theatre hat to its hideaway when he got home from the Roman. Then he would have taken out this one which you've just torn up and put it back in the clothes closet. . . . But let's get on."

He pulled down the leather innerband of the second silk hat, which also bore the imprint of Browne Bros. "Look at this, will you!" he exclaimed. The two men bent over and saw on the inner surface of the band, lettered with painful clarity in a purplish ink, the words BENJAMIN MORGAN.

"I've got to pledge you to secrecy, Tim," said the Inspector immediately, turning to the red-haired man. "Never let on that you were a witness to the finding of papers in any way implicating Benjamin Morgan in this affair."

"What do you think I am, Inspector?" growled Cronin. "I'm as dumb as an oyster, believe me!"

"All right, then." Queen felt the lining of the hat. There was a distinct crackle.

"Now," remarked Ellery calmly, "we know for the first time definitely why the murderer *had* to take away the hat Field wore Monday night. In all likelihood the murderer's name was lettered in the same way—that's indelible ink, you know—and the murderer couldn't leave a hat with his own name in it at the scene of the crime."

"By gosh, if you only had that hat, now," cried Cronin, "you'd know who the murderer is!"

"I'm afraid, Tim," replied the Inspector dryly, "that hat is gone forever."

He indicated a row of careful stitches at the base of the inner band, where the lining was attached to the fabric. He ripped these stitches swiftly and inserted his fingers between the lining and the crown. Silently he drew out a sheaf of papers held together by a thin rubber Band.

"If I were as nasty as some people think I am," mused Ellery, leaning back, "I might with perfect justice say, 'I told you so.'"

"We know when we're licked, my son—don't rub it in," chortled the Inspector. He snapped off the rubber band, glanced hastily through the papers and with a satisfied grin deposited them in his breast pocket.

"Morgan's, all right," he said briefly, and attacked one of the derbies.

The inner side of the band was marked cryptically with an X. The Inspector found a row of stitches exactly as in the silk hat. The papers he drew out—a thicker bundle than Morgan's—he examined cursorily. Then he. handed them to Cronin, whose fingers were trembling.

"A stroke of luck, Tim," he said slowly. "The man you were angling for is dead, but there are a lot of big names in this. I think you'll find yourself a hero one of these days."

Cronin grasped the bundle and feverishly unfolded the papers, one by one. "They're here—they're here!" he shouted. He jumped to his feet, stuffing the sheaf into his pocket.

"I've got to beat it, Inspector," he said rapidly. "There's a lot of work to do at last—and besides, what you find in that fourth hat is none of my business. I can't thank you and Mr. Queen enough! So long!"

He dashed from the room, and a moment later the snores of the policeman in the foyer came to an abrupt end. The outer door banged shut.

Ellery and the Inspector looked at each other.

"I don't know what good this stuff is going to do us," grumbled the old man, fumbling with the inner band of the last hat, a derby. "We've found things and deduced things and run rings around our imaginations—well . . ." He sighed as he held the band up to the light.

It was marked: MISC.

18

STALEMATE

At Friday noon, while Inspector Queen, Ellery and Timothy Cronin were deep in their search of Monte Field's rooms, Sergeant Velie, sombre and unmoved as usual, walked slowly up 87th Street from Broadway, mounted the brownstone steps of the house in which the Queens lived and rang the bell. Djuna's cheery voice bade him ascend, which the good Sergeant did with gravity.

"Inspector's not home!" announced Djuna pertly, his slim body completely hidden behind an enormous housewife's apron. Odorous traces of an onion-covered steak pervaded the air.

"Get on with you, you imp!" growled Velie. He took from his inner breast pocket a bulky envelope sealed, and handed it to Djuna. "Give this to the Inspector when he comes home. Forget, and I'll dip you into the East River."

"You and who else?" breathed Djuna, with a remarkable twitching of his lips. Then he added decorously, "Yes, sir."

"All right, then." Velie deliberately turned about and descended to the street, where his broad back was visible in formidable proportions to the grinning Djuna from the fourth-story window.

When, at a little before six, the two Queens trudged wearily into their rooms, the alert eyes of the Inspector pounced upon the official envelope where it lay on his plate.

He tore off a corner of the envelope and pulled out a number of typewritten sheets on the stationery of the Detective Bureau.

"Well, well!" he muttered to Ellery, who was lazily pulling off his topcoat "The clans are gathering. . . ."

Sinking into an armchair, his hat forgotten on his head, his coat still buttoned, he set about reading the reports aloud.

The first slip read:

REPORT OF RELEASE

28 September 192–

John Cazzanelli, alias Parson Johnny, alias John the Wop, alias Peter Dominick, released from custody today on parole.

Undercover investigation of J. C.'s complicity in the robbery of the Bonomo Silk Mills (June 2, 192—) not successful. We are searching for "Dinky" Morehouse, police informer, who has disappeared from usual haunts, for further information.

Release effected under advice of District Attorney

Sampson. J. C. under surveillance and is available at any time.

T. V.

The second report which the Inspector picked up, laying aside the advices concerning Parson Johnny with a frown, read as follows:

REPORT ON WILLIAM PUSAK

September 28,192–

Investigation of the history of William Pusak reveals the following:

32 years old; born in Brooklyn, N.Y., of naturalized parents; unmarried; regular habits; socially inclined; has "dates" three or four nights a week; religious. Is bookkeeper at Stein & Rauch, clothing merchants, 1076 Broadway. Does not gamble or drink. No evil companions. Only vice seems fondness for girls.

Activities since Monday night normal. No letters sent, no money withdrawn from bank, hours fairly regular. No suspicious movements of any kind.

Girl, Esther Jablow, seems Pusak's "steadiest." Has seen E. J. twice since Monday—Tuesday at lunch, Wednesday evening. Went to movies and Chinese restaurant Wednesday evening.

Operative No. 4
OK'd: T. V.

The Inspector grunted as he threw the sheet aside. The third report was headed:

REPOT ON MADGE O'CONNELL

Friday, Sept. 28, '2–

O'Connell, lives at 1436 10th Avenue. Tenement, 4th floor. No father. Idle since Monday night, due to shutting down of Roman Theatre. Left theatre Monday night at general release of public. Went home, but stopped in drugstore corner 8th Avenue and 48th Street to telephone. Unable to trace call. Overheard reference to Parson Johnny in phone conversation. Seemed excited.

Tuesday did not leave house until 1 o'clock. No attempt to get in touch with Parson Johnny at Tombs. Went around theatre employment agencies looking for usherette position after finding out Roman Theatre was closed indefinitely.

Nothing new Wednesday all day or Thursday. Returned to work at Roman Thursday night after call from manager. No attempt see or communicate with Parson Johnny. No incoming calls, no visitors, no mail. Seemed suspicious—think she is "wise" to tailing.

Operative No. 11
OK'd: T. V.

"Hmph!" muttered the Inspector as he picked up the next sheet of paper. "Let's see what this one says. . . ."

REPORT ON FRANCES IVES-POPE

September 28, 192–

F. I.-P. left Roman Theatre Monday night directly after release from Manager's Office by Inspector Queen. Examined with other departing members of audience at main door. Left in company of Eve Ellis, Stephen Barry, Hilda Orange, of the cast. Took taxi to Ives-Pope house on Riverside Drive. Taken out in half-unconscious condition. Three actors left house soon after.

Tuesday she did not leave house. Learned from a gardener she was laid up in bed all day. Learned she received many calls during day.

Did not appear formally until Wednesday morning at interview in house with Inspector Queen. After interview, left house in company of Stephen Barry, Eve Ellis, James Peale, her brother Stanford. Ives-Pope limousine drove party out into Westchester. Outing revived F. Evening stayed at home with Stephen Barry. Bridge party on.

Thursday went shopping on Fifth Avenue. Met Stephen Barry for luncheon. He took her to Central Park; spent afternoon in open. S. B. escorted her home before five. S. B. stayed to dinner, leaving after dinner for work at Roman Theatre on call from stage manager. F. I.-P. spent evening at home with family.

No report Friday morning. No suspicious actions all

week. At no time accosted by strange persons. No communication from or to Benjamin Morgan.

Operative No. 39
OK'd: T. V.

"And that's that," murmured the Inspector. The next report he selected was extremely short.

REPORT ON OSCAR LEWIN

September 28, 192–

Lewin spent all day Tuesday, Wednesday, Thursday and Friday morning at office of Monte Field working with Messrs. Stoates and Cronin. Three men lunched together on each day.

Lewin married, lives in Bronx, 211 E. 156th Street. Spent every evening at home. No suspicious mail, no suspicious calls. No evil habits. Leads sober, modest life. Has good reputation.

Operative No. 16

NOTE: Full details of Oscar Lewin's history, habits, etc., available on request through Timothy Cronin, Assistant District Attorney.

T. V.

The Inspector sighed as he deposited the five sheets of paper on his plate, rose, doffed his hat and coat, flung them into

Djuna's waiting arms and sat down again. Then he picked up the last report from the contents of the envelope—a larger sheet to which was pinned a small slip marked: MEMORANDUM TO R. Q.

This slip read:

> Dr. Prouty left the attached report with me this morning for transmission to you. He is sorry he could not report in person, but the Burbridge poison case is taking all his time.

It was signed with Velie's familiar scrawling initials.

The attached sheet was a hastily typewritten message on the letterhead of the Chief Medical Examiner's office.

> Dear Q [the message ran]: Here's the dope on the tetra ethyl lead. Jones and I have been superintending an exhaustive probe of all possible sources of dissemination. No success, and I think you can resign yourself to your fate in this respect. You'll never trace the poison that killed Monte Field. This is the opinion not merely of your humble servant but of the Chief and of Jones. We all agree that the most logical explanation is the gasoline theory. Try to trace *that,* Sherlocko!

A postscript in Dr. Prouty's handwriting ran:

> Of course, if anything turns up, I'll let you know immediately. Keep sober.

"Fat lot of good *that* is!" mumbled the Inspector, as Ellery without a word attacked the aromatic and tempting meal that the priceless Djuna had prepared. The Inspector dug viciously into the fruit salad. He looked far from happy. He grumbled beneath his breath, cast baleful glances at the sheaf of reports by his plate, peered up at Ellery's tired face and heartily munching jaws and finally threw down his spoon altogether.

"Of all the useless, exasperating, empty bunch of reports I ever saw—!" he growled.

Ellery smiled. "You remember Periander, of course. . . . Eh? You might be polite, sir. . . . Periander of Corinth, who said in a moment of sobriety, 'To industry nothing is impossible!'"

With the fire roaring, Djuna curled up on the floor in a corner, his favorite attitude. Ellery smoked a cigarette and stared comfortably into the flames while old Queen crammed his nose vengefully with the contents of his snuffbox. The two Queens settled down to a serious discussion. To be more exact—Inspector Queen settled down and lent the tone of seriousness to the conversation, since Ellery seemed in a sublimely dreamy mood far removed from the sordid details of crime and punishment.

The old man brought his hand down on the arm of his chair with a sharp slap. "Ellery, did you ever in your born days see a case so positively nerve-racking?"

"On the contrary," commented Ellery, staring with half-closed eyes into the fire. "You are developing a natural case of nerves. You allow little things like apprehending a murderer to upset you unduly. Pardon the hedonistic philosophy. . . . If you will recall, in my story entitled 'The Affair of the Black Widow,' my good sleuths had no difficulty at all in laying their hands on the criminal. And why? Because they kept their heads. Conclusion: Always keep your head. . . . I'm thinking of tomorrow. Glorious vacation!"

"For an educated man, my son," growled the Inspector petulantly, "you show a surprising lack of coherence. You say things that mean nothing and mean things when you say nothing. No—I'm all mixed up—"

Ellery burst into laughter. "The Maine woods—the russet—the good Chauvin's cabin by the lake—a rod—air—Oh, Lord, won't tomorrow ever come?"

Inspector Queen regarded his son with a pitiful eagerness. "I—I sort of wish . . . Well, never mind." He sighed. "All I do say, El, is that if my little burglar fails—it's all up with us."

"To the blessed Gehenna with burglars!" cried Ellery. "What has Pan to do with human tribulation? My next book is as good as written, Dad."

"Stealing another idea from real life, you rascal," muttered the old man. "If you're borrowing the Field case for your plot, I'd be extremely interested to read your last few chapters!"

"Poor Dad!" chuckled Ellery. "Don't take life so seriously. If you fail, you fail. Monte Field wasn't worth a hill of legumes, anyway."

"That's not the point," said the old man. "I hate to admit defeat. . . . What a queer mess of motives and schemes this case is, Ellery. This is the first time in my entire experience that I have had such a hard nut to crack. It's enough to give a man apoplexy!

I know WHO committed the murder—I know WHY the murder was committed—I even know HOW the murder was committed! And where am I? . . ."He paused and savagely took a pinch of snuff. "A million miles from nowhere, that's where!" he growled, and subsided.

"Certainly a most unusual situation," murmured Ellery. "Yet—more difficult things have been accomplished. . . . Heigh-ho! I can't wait to bathe myself in that Arcadian stream!"

"And get pneumonia, probably," said the Inspector anxiously. "You promise me now, young man, that you don't do any back-to-Nature stunts out there. I don't want a funeral on my hands—I . . ."

Ellery grew silent suddenly. He looked over at his father. The Inspector seemed strangely old in the flickering light of the fire. An expression of pain humanized the deeply sculptured lines of his face. His hand, brushing back his thick gray hair, looked alarmingly fragile.

Ellery rose, hesitated, colored, then bent swiftly forward and patted his father on the shoulder.

"Brace up, Dad," he said in a low voice. "If it weren't for my arrangements with Chauvin . . . Everything will be all right—take my word for it. If there were the slightest way in which I could help you by remaining. . . . But there isn't. It's your job now, Dad—and there's no man in the world who can handle it better than you. . . ." The old man stared up at him with a strange affection. Ellery turned abruptly away. "Well," he said lightly, "I'll have to pack now if I expect to make the 7:45 out of Grand Central tomorrow morning."

He disappeared into the bedroom. Djuna, who had been sitting Turkishwise in his corner, got quickly to his feet and crossed the room to the Inspector's chair. He slipped to the floor, his head resting against the old man's knees. The silence was punctuated by the snapping of wood in the fireplace and the muffled sounds of Ellery moving about in the next room.

Inspector Queen was very tired. His face, worn, thin, white, lined, was like a cameo in the dull red light His hand caressed Djuna's curly head.

"Djuna, lad," he muttered, "never be a policeman when you grow up."

Djuna twisted his neck and stared gravely at the old man. "I'm going to be just what you are," he announced. . . .

The old man leaped to his feet as the telephone bell rang. He snatched the instrument from its table, his face livid, and said in a choked voice: "Queen speaking. Well?"

After a time he put down the phone and trudged across the room toward the bedroom. He leaned against the lintel heavily. Ellery straightened up from his suitcase—and jumped forward.

"Dad!" he cried. "What's the matter?"

The Inspector essayed a feeble smile. "Just—a—little tired, son, I guess," he grunted. "I just heard from our housebreaker. . . ."

"And—?"

"He found absolutely nothing."

Ellery gripped his father's arm and led him to the chair by the bed. The old man slumped into it, his eyes ineffably weary. "Ellery, old son," he said, "the last shred of evidence is gone. It's maddening! Not a morsel of physical, tangible evidence that would convict the murderer in court. What have we? A series of perfectly sound deductions—and that's all. A good lawyer would make Swiss cheese out of our case. . . . Well! The last word hasn't been spoken yet," he added with a sudden grimness as he rose from the chair. He pounded Ellery's broad back in returning vigor.

"Get to bed, son," he said. "You've got to get up early tomorrow morning. I'm going to sit up and think."

INTERLUDE

IN WHICH THE READER'S ATTENTION IS RESPECTFULLY REQUESTED

The current vogue in detective literature is all for the practice of placing the reader in the position of chief sleuth. I have prevailed upon Mr. Ellery Queen to permit at this point in THE ROMAN HAT MYSTERY the interpolation of a challenge to the reader. . . . "Who killed Monte Field?" "How was the murder accomplished?" . . . Mr. Queen agrees with me that the alert student of mystery tales, now being in possession of all the pertinent facts, should at this stage of the story have reached definite conclusions on the questions propounded. The solution—or enough of it to point unerringly to the guilty character—may be reached by a series of logical deductions and psychological observations. . . . In closing my last personal appearance in the tale let me admonish the reader with a variation of the phrase *Caveat Emptor:* "Let the reader beware!"

J. J. McC.

PART FOUR

"The perfect criminal is a superman. He must be meticulous in his techniques: unseen, unseeable, a Lone Wolf. He must have neither friends nor dependents. He must be careful to a fault, quick of brain, hand and foot. . . . But these are nothing. There have been such men. . . . On the other hand, he must be a favored child of Fate—for circumstances over which he cannot have the remotest control must never contrive his downfall. This, I think, is more difficult to achieve. . . . But the last is most difficult of all. He must never repeat his crime, his weapon or his motive! . . . In all my two-score years as an official of the American police I have not once encountered the perfect criminal nor investigated the perfect crime."

—*from* AMERICAN CRIME AND METHODS OF DETECTION by Richard Queen

19

IN WHICH INSPECTOR QUEEN CONDUCTS MORE LEGAL CONVERSATIONS

It was notable, particularly to District Attorney Sampson, that on Saturday evening Inspector Richard Queen was far from being himself. The old man was irritable, snappish and utterly uncongenial. He paced fretfully across the carpet of Manager Louis Panzer's office, biting his lips and muttering beneath his breath. He seemed oblivious to the presence of Sampson, Panzer and a third person who had never been in that theatrical sanctum before and was seated, mouselike, in one of Panzer's big chairs, his eyes like saucers. This was bright-eyed Djuna, granted the unprecedented privilege of accompanying his gray patron on this last incursion into the Roman Theatre.

In truth, Queen was singularly depressed. He had many times in his official life been confronted by apparently insoluble problems; he had as many times brought triumph out of failure. The Inspector's strange manner therefore was doubly inexplicable to

Sampson, who had been associated with the old man for years and had never seen him so completely unstrung.

The old man's moodiness was not due to the progress of the Field investigation, as Sampson worriedly thought. Wiry little Djuna, sitting open-mouthed in his corner, was the only spectator to the Inspector's mad pacing who could have put his finger on the truth. Djuna, wise by virtue of *gamin* perspicacity, observant by nature, familiar with Queen's temperament through a loving association, knew that his patron's manner was due solely to Ellery's absence from the scene. Ellery had left New York on the 7:45 express that morning, having been gloomily accompanied to the station by his father. At the last moment the younger man had changed his mind, announcing his decision to forego the trip to Maine and abide in New York by his father's side until the case was concluded. The old man would have none of it. With his shrewd insight into Ellery's nature, he realized how keenly his highly strung son had been looking forward to this first vacation in over a year. It was not in his heart, impatient as he was for the constant presence of his son, to deprive him of this long contemplated pleasure trip.

Accordingly, he had swept aside Ellery's proposal and pushed him up the steps of the train, with a parting clap and a wan smile. Ellery's last words, shouted from the platform as the train glided out of the station, were: "I'm not forgetting you, Dad. You'll hear from me sooner than you expect!"

Now, torturing the nap of Manager Panzer's rug, the Inspector was feeling the full impact of their separation. His brain was addled, his constitution flabby, his stomach weak, his eyes dim.

He felt completely out of tune with the world and its denizens, and he made no attempt to conceal his irritation.

"Should be about time now, Panzer," he growled to the stout little manager. "How long does this infernal audience take to clear out, anyway?"

"In a moment, Inspector, in a moment," replied Panzer. The District Attorney sniffed away the remnants of his cold. Djuna stared in fascination at his god.

A rap on the door twisted their heads about. Tow-headed Harry Neilson, the publicity man, poked his rugged face into the room. "Mind if I join the little party, Inspector?" he inquired cheerfully. "I was in at the birth, and if there's going to be a death—why, I'm aiming to stick around, with your permission!"

The Inspector shot him a dour glance from beneath his shaggy eyebrows. He stood in a Napoleonic attitude, his every hair and muscle bristling with ill-nature. Sampson regarded him in surprise. Inspector Queen was showing an unexpected side to his temper.

"Might's well," he barked. "One more won't hurt. There's an army here as it is."

Neilson reddened slightly and made a move as if to withdraw. The Inspector's eye twinkled with a partial return to good spirits.

"Here—sit down, Neilson," he said, not unkindly. "Mustn't mind an old fogey like me. I'm just frazzled a bit. Might need you tonight at that."

"Glad to be let in on it, Inspector," grinned Neilson. "What's the idea—sort of Spanish Inquisition?"

"Just about." The old man bent his brows. "But—well see."

At this moment the door opened and the tall, broad figure of Sergeant Velie stepped quickly into the room. He was carrying a sheet of paper which he handed to the Inspector.

"All present, sir," he said.

"Everybody out?" snapped Queen.

"Yes, sir. I've told the cleaning women to go down into the lounge and hang around until we're through. Cashiers have gone home, so have the ushers and usherettes. Cast is backstage, I guess, getting dressed."

"Right. Let's go, gentlemen." The Inspector stalked out of the room followed closely by Djuna, who had not opened his mouth all evening except to emit noiseless gasps of admiration, for no reason that the amused District Attorney could see. Panzer, Sampson and Neilson also followed, Velie bringing up the rear.

The auditorium was again a vast and deserted place, the empty rows of seats stark and cold. The lights of the theatre had been switched on in full and their cold radiance lit up every corner of the orchestra.

As the five men and Djuna swung toward the extreme left aisle, there was a concerted bobbing of heads from the left section of seats. It was apparent now that a small group of people were awaiting the arrival of the Inspector, who walked heavily down the aisle and took up a position in front of the left boxes, so that all the seated people faced him. Panzer, Neilson and Sampson stood at the head of the aisle with Djuna at one side, a feverish spectator.

The assembled party was placed peculiarly. From the row nearest the Inspector, who stood about halfway down the orchestra, and proceeding towards the rear the only seats occupied were those directly on the left aisle. The end two seats of the dozen rows were filled by a motley aggregation—men and women, old and young. They were the same people who had occupied these chairs on the night of the fatal performance and whom Inspector Queen had personally examined after the discovery of the body. In the section of eight seats—Monte Field's and the empty ones which had surrounded it—were grouped William Pusak, Esther Jablow, Madge O'Connell, Jess Lynch and Parson Johnny—the Parson furtive-eyed, uneasy and whispering to the usherette behind nicotined fingers.

At the Inspector's sudden gesture all became silent as the grave. Sampson, looking about him at the bright chandeliers and lights, the deserted theatre, the lowered curtain, could not help feeling that the stage was being set for dramatic revelations. He leaned forward interestedly. Panzer and Neilson were quiet and watchful. Djuna kept his eyes fixed on the old man.

"Ladies and gentlemen," Queen announced curtly, staring at the assembled company, "I've brought you here for a definite purpose. I will not keep you any longer than is absolutely necessary, but what is necessary and what is not necessary is entirely up to me. If I find that I do not receive what I consider truthful answers to my questions, everybody will stay here until I am satisfied. I want that thoroughly understood before we proceed."

He paused and glared about. There was a ripple of apprehension, a sudden crackle of conversation which died as quickly as it was born.

"On Monday night," continued the Inspector frostily, "you

people attended the performance at this theatre and, with the exception of certain employees and others now seated at the rear, occupied the seats in which you now find yourselves." Sampson grinned as he noticed the stiffening of backs at these words, as if each individual felt his seat grow suddenly warm and uncomfortable beneath him.

"I want you to imagine that this is Monday night. I want you to think back to that night and try to remember everything that happened. By everything I mean any occurrence, no matter how trivial or apparently unimportant, that might have left an impression on your memory. . . ."

As the Inspector warmed to his words, a number of people drifted into the orchestra at the rear. Sampson greeted them in whispers. The little party was composed of Eve Ellis, Hilda Orange, Stephen Barry, James Peale and three or four other members of the cast of "Gunplay." They were dressed in their street clothes. Peale whispered to Sampson that they had just come from their dressing rooms and had dropped into the auditorium on hearing voices.

"Queen's holding a little powwow," whispered Sampson in return.

"Do you think the Inspector has any objections to our staying a while and listening?" asked Barry in a low tone, with an apprehensive glance toward the Inspector, who had stopped and was staring icily in their direction.

"Don't see why—" began Sampson worriedly, when Eve Ellis murmured, "Shhh!" and they all became silent.

"Now—" said the Inspector venomously, when the flurry had

subsided, "this is the situation. Remember, you are now back in Monday evening. The curtain has gone up on the second act and the theatre is dark. There is a lot of noise from the stage and you are intent on the exciting sequences of the play. . . . Did any of you, especially those sitting in the aisle seats, notice anything peculiar, unusual or disturbing around or near you at that time?"

He paused expectantly. There were puzzled, fearful shakings of the head. No one answered.

"Think hard," growled the Inspector. "You remember on Monday night I went down this aisle and questioned all of you in the same vein. Naturally I don't want lies, and I can't reasonably expect that you will tell me something startling now when you could remember nothing Monday night. But this is a desperate situation. A man was murdered here and we are frankly up against it. One of the most difficult cases we have ever encountered! In the light of such a condition, when we find ourselves against a blank wall with not the slightest idea where to turn—I am being honest with you as I expect you to be with me—I *must* turn to you as the only members of the audience five nights ago who were in a position to see something important, if anything important occurred. . . . It has been my experience that often, under stress of nervousness and excitement, a man or woman will forget a little detail that returns to memory after a few hours, days, weeks of normalcy. It is my hope that something of the sort has taken place with you. . . ."

As Inspector Queen spoke, the words dropping acidly from his lips, the company lost its nervousness in its fascinated interest. When he paused, people put their heads together and whispered excitedly, shaking their heads at times, arguing in fierce, low tones at others. The Inspector waited in a resigned patience.

"Raise your hands if you have something to tell me . . ." he said.

A woman's timid white hand fluttered aloft.

"Yes, madam?" commanded Queen, pointing his finger. "Do you recall anything unusual?"

A withered old lady rose embarrassedly to her feet and began to stammer in a squeaking voice. "I don't know whether it's important or not, sir," she said tremulously. "But I do remember some time during the second act a woman, I think it was, walking down the aisle and a few seconds later walking up again."

"Yes? That's interesting, madam," commented the Inspector. "About what time was this—can you recall?"

"I don't remember the time, sir," shrilled the old lady, "but it was about ten minutes or so after the beginning of the act."

"I see. . . . And do you recall anything of her appearance? Was she young or old? What did she wear?"

The old lady looked troubled. "I don't exactly remember, sir," she quavered. "I wasn't paying—"

A high, clear voice interrupted from the rear. Heads twisted about. Madge O'Connell had jumped to her feet.

"You don't have to mess around with that any more, Inspector," she announced coldly. "That lady saw *me* walking down the aisle and back again. That was before I—you know." She winked pertly in the Inspector's direction.

People gasped. The old lady stared with pitiful bewilderment at the usherette, then at the Inspector and finally sat down.

"I'm not surprised," said the Inspector quietly. "Well, anybody else?"

There was no answer. Realizing that the company might feel shy of announcing their thoughts in public Queen started up the aisle, working from row to row, questioning each person separately in tones inaudible to the rest. When he had finished he returned slowly to his original position.

"I see that I must allow you ladies and gentlemen to return to your peaceful firesides. Thank you very much for your help. . . . Dismissed!"

He flung the word at them. They stared at him dazedly, then rose in muttering groups, took up their coats and hats and under Velie's stern eye began to file out of the theatre. Hilda Orange, standing in the group behind the last row, sighed.

"It's almost embarrassing to see that poor old gentleman's disappointment," she whispered to the others. "Come on, folks, let's be going, too."

The actors and actresses left the theatre among the departing company.

When the last man and woman had disappeared, the Inspector marched back up the aisle and stood gloomily staring at the little group who were left. They seemed to sense the seething fire in the old man and they cowered. But the Inspector, with a characteristic lightning change of front, became human again.

He sat down in one of the seats and folded his arms over the back, surveying Madge O'Connell, Parson Johnny and the others.

"All right, folks," he said in a genial tone. "How about you,

Parson? You're a free man, you don't have to worry about silks any more and you can speak up now like any self-respecting citizen. Can you give us any help in this affair?"

"Naw," grunted the little gangster. "I told you all I knew. Ain't got a thing to say."

"I see. . . . You know, Parson, that we're interested in your dealings with Field." The gangster looked up in shocked surprise. "Oh, yes," continued the Inspector. "We want you to tell us sometime about your business with Mr. Field in the past. You'll keep that in mind, won't you? . . . Parson," he said sharply, "who killed Monte Field? Who had it in for him? If you know—out with it!"

"Aw, Inspector," the Parson whined, "you ain't pullin' that stuff on me again, are you? How should I know? Field was one slick guy—he didn't go around welching on his enemies. No, sir! *I* wouldn't know. . . . He was pretty good to me—got me off on a couple of charges," he admitted unblushingly. "But I didn't have no more idea he was here Monday night than—hell, than anything."

The Inspector turned to Madge O'Connell.

"How about you, O'Connell?" he asked softly. "My son, Mr. Queen, tells me that on Monday night you confided in him about closing the exit doors. You didn't say anything to me about that. What do *you* know?"

The girl returned his stare coolly. "I told you once, Inspector. I haven't a thing to say."

"And you, William Pusak—" Queen turned to the wizened little bookkeeper. "Do you remember anything now that you forgot Monday night?"

Pusak wiggled uncomfortably. "Meant to tell you, Inspector," he mumbled. "And when I read about it in the papers it came back to me. . . . As I bent over Mr. Field Monday night I smelled a terrible smell of whisky. I don't remember if I told you that before."

"Thank you," remarked the Inspector dryly, rising. "A very important contribution to our little investigation. You may go, the whole lot of you. . . ."

The orangeade boy, Jess Lynch, looked disappointed. "Don't you want to talk to me, too, sir?" he asked anxiously.

The Inspector smiled despite his abstraction. "Ah, yes. The helpful purveyor of orangeade. . . . And what have you to say, Jess?"

"Well, sir, before this fellow Field came over to my stand to ask for the ginger ale, I happened to notice that he picked up something in the alleyway," said the boy eagerly. "It was shiny, sort of, but I couldn't see it clear enough. He put it in his hip pocket right away."

He concluded triumphantly, glancing about him as if to invite applause. The Inspector seemed interested enough.

"What was this shiny object like, Jess?" he inquired. "Might it have been a revolver?"

"Revolver? Gosh, I don't think so," said the orangeade boy doubtfully. "It was square, like. . . ."

"Might it have been a woman's purse?" interrupted the Inspector.

The boy's face brightened. "That's it!" he cried. "I'll bet that's what it was. Shined all over, like colored stones."

Queen sighed. "Very good, Lynch," he said. "You go home now like a good boy."

Silently the gangster, the usherette, Pusak and his feminine charge, and the orangeade boy rose and departed. Velie accompanied them to the outer door.

Sampson waited until they had gone before he took the Inspector to one side.

"What's the matter, Q?" he demanded. "Aren't things going right?"

"Henry, my boy," smiled the Inspector, "we've done as much as mortal brains could. Just a little more time. . . . I wish—" He did not say what he wished. He grasped Djuna firmly by the arm and bidding Panzer, Neilson, Velie and the District Attorney a placid good night, left the theatre.

At the apartment, as the Inspector wielded his key and the door swung open, Djuna pounced on a yellow envelope lying on the floor. It had evidently been stuck through the crack at the bottom of the door. Djuna flourished it in the old man's face.

"It's from Mr. Ellery, I'll bet!" he cried. "I knew he wouldn't forget!" He seemed more extraordinarily like a monkey than ever as he stood grinning, the telegram in his hand.

The Inspector snatched the envelope from Djuna's hand and, not pausing to take off his hat or coat, switched on the lights in the living room and eagerly extracted the yellow slip of paper.

Djuna had been correct.

ARRIVED SAFELY [it ran] CHAUVIN WILD WITH DELIGHT FISHING PROSPECT EXCEPTIONAL Stop

> THINK I HAVE SOLVED YOUR LITTLE PROBLEM Stop JOIN DISTINGUISHED COMPANY OF RABELAIS CHAUCER SHAKESPEARE DRYDEN WHO SAID MAKE A VIRTUE OF NECESSITY Stop WHY NOT GO INTO BLACKMAILING BUSINESS YOURSELF Stop DON'T GROWL DJUNA TO DEATH AFFECTIONATELY ELLERY

The Inspector stared down at the harmless yellow slip, a startled comprehension transmuting the harsh lines of his face.

He whirled on Djuna, clapped that young gentleman's cap on his tousled head and pulled his arm purposefully.

"Djuna, old son," he said gleefully, "let's go around the corner and celebrate with a couple of ice-cream sodas!"

20

IN WHICH MR. MICHAELS WRITES A LECTURE

For the first time in a week, Inspector Queen was genuinely himself as he strode cheerfully into his tiny office at the headquarters building and shied his coat at a chair.

It was Monday morning. He rubbed his hands, hummed "The Sidewalks of New York," as he plumped down at his desk and briskly ran through his voluminous mail and reports. He spent a half-hour issuing instructions by word of mouth and telephone to subordinates in various offices of the Detective Bureau, studied briefly a number of reports which a stenographer placed before him and finally pressed one of a row of buttons on his desk.

Velie appeared at once.

"Howdy, Thomas," said the Inspector heartily. "How are you this fine Fall morning?"

Velie permitted himself a smile. "Well enough, Inspector," he said. "And you? You seemed a little under the weather Saturday night."

The Inspector chuckled. "Let bygones be bygones, Thomas, my lad. Djuna and I visited the Bronx Zoo yesterday and spent a delightful four hours among our brethren, the animals."

"That imp of yours was in his element, I'll bet," growled Velie, "among the monkeys especially."

"Now, now, Thomas," chided the Inspector. "Don't be mistaken about Djuna. He's a smart little whippersnapper. Going to be a great man some day, mark my words!"

"Djuna?" Velie nodded gravely. "Guess you're right, Inspector. I'd give my right paw for that kid. . . . What's the program today, sir?"

"There's a lot on the program today, Thomas," Queen said mysteriously. "Did you get hold of Michaels after I telephoned you yesterday morning?"

"Sure thing, Inspector. He's been waiting outside for an hour. Came in early, with Piggott hanging on his heels. Piggott's been tailing him all over creation and he's pretty disgusted."

"Well, I always said a man's a fool to become a policeman," chuckled Queen. "Bring in the lamb."

Velie went out, to reappear a moment later with the tall, portly Michaels. Field's valet was dressed sombrely. He seemed nervous and ill at ease.

"Now, Thomas, my lad," said the Inspector after he had motioned Michaels to the chair beside his desk, "you go out and lock that door and don't let the Commissioner himself disturb me. Get that?"

Velie repressed a curious glance, grunted and departed. A few moments later a bulky figure was dimly discernible in silhouette through the frosted glass of the door.

At the expiration of a half-hour Velie was summoned by telephone to his superior's office. He unlocked the door. On the desk before the Inspector reposed a cheap square envelope unsealed, a sheet of notepaper partly visible as it lay inside. Michaels was on his feet, pale and trembling, his hat crushed in two beefy hands. Velie's sharp eyes noticed a generous ink stain on the fingers of the man's left hand.

"You are going to take *very* good care of Mr. Michaels, Thomas," said the Inspector genially. "Today, for instance, I want you to entertain him. I have no doubt you'll find something to do—go to a movie—there's an idea! In any event be friendly with the gentleman until you hear from me. . . . No communication with anybody, Michaels, do you hear?" he added brusquely, turning to the big man. "Just you tag along with Sergeant Velie and play nicely."

"You know I'm on the square, Inspector," mumbled Michaels sullenly. "You don't have to—"

"Just a precaution, Michaels—just an elementary precaution," interrupted the Inspector, smiling. "Have a nice time, boys!"

The two men left. Seated at his desk, Queen tilted his swivel chair, picked up the envelope before him reflectively, took out the slip of cheap white paper and read it over with a little smile.

The note bore neither date nor salutation. The message began abruptly.

"The writer is Chas. Michaels, I think you know me. I have been Monte Field's right-hand man for over two years."

I won't beat around the bush. Last Monday night you killed Field in the Roman Theatre. Monte Field told me Sunday he had an appointment with you at the Theatre. And I am the only one who does know this.

Another thing. I also know *why* you killed him. You put him away to get hold of the papers in Field's hat. But you do not know that the papers you stole from him *are not the originals.* To prove this to you, I am enclosing one sheet from the testimony of Nellie Johnson which was in Field's possession. If the papers you took from Field's hat are still in existence, compare what you have with this one. You will soon see that I am giving you the straight goods. And I have the rest of the originals safely put away where you will never lay hands on them. I might say that the police are looking for them with their tongues hanging out. Wouldn't it be nice if I stepped into Inspector Queen's office with the papers and my little story?

I will give you a chance to buy these papers. You can bring $25,000 in cold cash to the place I describe, and I will hand them over to you. I need money and you need the papers and my silence.

Meet me tomorrow, Tuesday night, at twelve o'clock, at the seventh bench on the right-hand side of the paved path in Central Park which starts at the northwest corner of 59th Street and 5th Avenue. I will be dressed in a gray overcoat and a gray slouch hat. Just say the word Papers to me.

"This is the only way you can get the papers. Don't look for me before the appointment. If you are not there, I know what I have to do."

The scrawl, closely and painfully written, was signed: "Charles Michaels."

Inspector Queen sighed, licked the flap of the envelope and sealed it. He stared steadily at the name and address written in the same handwriting on the envelope. Unhurriedly he affixed a stamp on one corner.

He pressed another button. The door opened to admit Detective Ritter.

"Good morning, Inspector."

"Morning, Ritter." The Inspector weighed the envelope reflectively in his hand. "What are you working on now?"

The detective shuffled his feet. "Nothing special, Inspector. I was helping Sergeant Velie up to Saturday, but I haven't had any work yet on the Field case this morning."

"Well, then, I'll give you a nice little job." The Inspector suddenly grinned, holding out the envelope. Ritter took it with a bewildered air. "Here, son, go to the corner of 149th Street and Third Avenue and post this letter in the nearest mailbox!"

Ritter stared, scratched his head, looked at Queen and finally went out, depositing the letter in his pocket.

The Inspector tilted his chair and took a pinch of snuff with every evidence of satisfaction.

21

IN WHICH INSPECTOR QUEEN MAKES A CAPTURE

On Tuesday evening, October second, promptly at 11:30 P.M., a tall man wearing a soft black hat and a black overcoat, the collar pulled up around his face to keep out the raw night air, sauntered out of the lobby of a small hotel on 53rd Street near Seventh Avenue and proceeded at a sharp pace up Seventh Avenue toward Central Park.

Arrived at 59th Street he turned to the east and made his way along the deserted thoroughfare in the direction of Fifth Avenue. When he reached the Fifth Avenue entrance to Central Park, off the Plaza circle, he stopped in the shadow of one of the big concrete corner posts and leaned back idly. As he lit a cigarette the flare from a match illumined his face. It was that of an elderly man, a trifle lined. A grizzled mustache drooped in a straggling line from his upper lip. Under his hat a gray patch of hair was visible. Then the light from the match flickered out.

He stood quietly against the concrete post, hands jammed into his overcoat pockets, puffing away at his cigarette. An observer would have noticed, had he been keen, that the man's fingers trembled slightly and that his black-shod feet tapped the sidewalk in an unsteady tattoo.

When his cigarette burned down, he threw it away and glanced at a watch on his wrist. The hands stood at 11:50. He swore impatiently and stepped past the portals of the Park entrance.

The light from the overhead arcs bordering the Plaza dimmed as he walked up the stone lane. Hesitating, as if he were undecided as to his course of action, he looked about him, considered for a moment, then crossed over to the first bench and sat down heavily—like a man tired from his day's work and contemplating a restful quarter of an hour in the silence and darkness of the Park.

Slowly his head dropped; slowly his figure grew slack. He seemed to have fallen into a doze.

The minutes ticked away. No one passed the quiet figure of the black-clad man as he sat on his bench. On Fifth Avenue the motors roared past. The shrill whistle of the traffic officer in the Plaza pierced the chill air periodically. A cold wind soughed through the trees. From somewhere in the Stygian recesses of the Park came a girl's clear laugh—soft and far-off, but startlingly distinct. The minutes drowsed on; the man was falling into a deeper sleep.

And yet, just as the bells of the neighborhood churches began to toll the hour of twelve, the figure tensed, waited an instant and then rose determinedly.

Instead of heading toward the entrance he turned and plodded farther up the walk, his eyes bright and inquisitive in the gloomy depths created by his hat brim and coat collar. He seemed to be counting the benches as he proceeded in a steady, unhurried gait. Two—three—four—five—He stopped. In the semidarkness ahead he could barely make out a still gray figure seated on a bench.

The man walked slowly on. Six—seven—He did not pause, but went straight ahead. Eight—nine—ten. . . . Only then did he wheel and retrace his steps. This time his gait was brisker, more definite. He approached the seventh bench rapidly, then stopped short. Suddenly, as if he had made up his mind, he crossed over to the spot where the indistinctly looming figure rested quietly and sat down. The figure grunted and moved over a trifle to give the newcomer more room.

The two men sat in silence. After a time the black-garbed man dipped into the folds of his coat and produced a packet of cigarettes. He lit one and held the match for a moment after the tip of the cigarette glowed red. In the ray of the match light he covertly examined the quiet man at his side. The brief moment told him little—the occupant of the bench was as well muffled and concealed as himself. Then the light puffed out and they were in darkness once more.

The black-coated man seemed to come to a decision. He leaned forward, tapped the other man sharply on the knee and said in a low, husky voice the one word:

"Papers!"

The second man came to life immediately. He half-shifted his position, scrutinized his companion and grunted as if in satisfaction. He carefully leaned away from the other man on the bench and with his right gloved hand dug into his right overcoat pocket. The first man bent eagerly forward, his eyes bright. The gloved hand of his companion came out of the pocket, holding something tightly.

Then the owner of the hand did a surprising thing. With a fierce bunching of muscles he sprang from the bench and leaped backward, away from the first man. At the same time he leveled his right hand straight at the crouched frozen figure. And a fragmentary gleam of light from an arc lamp far off revealed the thing he held in his hand—a revolver.

Crying out hoarsely, the first man sprang to his feet with the agility of a cat. His hand plunged with a lightning-like movement into his overcoat pocket. He darted, reckless of the weapon pointed at his heart, straight forward at the tense figure before him.

But things were happening. The peaceful tableau, so suggestive a bare instant before of open spaces and dark country silence, was transformed magically into a scene of intense activity—a writhing, yelling pandemonium. From a cluster of bushes a few feet behind the bench a swiftly moving group of men with drawn guns materialized. At the same time, from the farther side of the walk, a similar group appeared, running toward the pair. And from both ends of the walk—from the entrance about a hundred feet away and from the opposite direction, in the blackness of the Park—came several uniformed policemen, brandishing revolvers. The groups converged almost as one.

The man who had drawn his gun and leaped from the bench

did not await the arrival of reinforcements. As his companion of a moment before plunged his hand into his coat pocket the gun-wielder took careful aim and fired. The weapon roared, awakening echoes in the Park. An orange flame streaked into the body of the black-coated man. He lurched forward, clutching his shoulder spasmodically. His knees buckled and he fell to the stone walk. His hand still fumbled in his coat.

But an avalanche of men's bodies kept him from whatever furious purpose was in his mind. Ungentle fingers gripped his arms and pinned them down, so that he could not withdraw his hand from his pocket. They held him in this way, silently, until a crisp voice behind them said, "Careful, boys—watch his hands!"

Inspector Richard Queen wriggled into the hard-breathing group and stood contemplatively above the writhing figure on the pavement.

"Take his hand out, Velie—easy, now! Hold it stiff, and—stiff, man stiff! He'd jab you in a flash!"

Sergeant Thomas Velie, who was straining at the arm, gingerly pulled it from the pocket despite the violent flounderings of the man's body. The hand appeared—empty, muscles loosened at the last moment. Two men promptly fastened it in a vise.

Velie made a movement as if to explore the pocket. The Inspector stopped him with a sharp word and himself bent over the threshing man on the walk.

Carefully, delicately, as if his life depended upon caution, the old man lowered his hand into the pocket and felt about its exterior. He gripped something and just as cautiously withdrew it, holding it up to the light.

It was a hypodermic needle. The light of the arc lamp made its pale limpid contents sparkle.

Inspector Queen grinned as he knelt by the wounded man's side. He jerked off the black felt hat.

"Disguised and everything," he murmured.

He snatched at the gray mustache, passed his hand rapidly over the man's lined face. A smudge immediately appeared on the skin.

"Well, well!" said the Inspector softly, as the man's feverish eyes glared up at him. "Happy to meet you again, Mr. Stephen Barry, and your good friend, Mr. Tetra Ethyl Lead!"

22

— AND EXPLAINS

Inspector Queen sat at the writing desk in his living room scribbling industriously on a long narrow sheet of notepaper headed THE QUEENS.

It was Wednesday morning—a fair Wednesday morning, with the sun streaming into the room through the dormer windows and the cheerful noises of 87th Street faintly audible from the pavements below. The Inspector wore his dressing gown and slippers. Djuna was busy at the table clearing away the breakfast dishes.

The old man had written:

DEAR SON: As I wired you late last night, the case is finished. We got Stephen Barry very nicely by using Michaels' name and handwriting as bait. I really ought to congratulate myself on the psychological soundness of the plan. Barry was desperate and like so many other criminals thought he could duplicate his crime without being caught.

I hate to tell you how tired I am and how unsatisfying spiritually the job of manhunter is sometimes. When I think of that poor lovely little girl Frances, having to face the world as the sweetheart of a murderer. . . . Well, El, there's little justice and certainly no mercy in this world. And, of course, I'm more or less responsible for her shame. . . . Yet Ives-Pope himself was quite decent a while ago when he telephoned me on hearing the news. I suppose in one way I did him and Frances a service. We—

The doorbell rang and Djuna, drying his hands hastily on a kitchen towel, ran to the door. District Attorney Sampson and Timothy Cronin walked in—excited, happy, both talking at once. Queen rose, covering the sheet of paper with a blotter.

"Q, old man!" cried Sampson, extending both hands. "My congratulations! Have you seen the papers this morning?"

"Glory to Columbus!" grinned Cronin, holding up a newspaper on which in screaming headlines New York was apprised of the capture of Stephen Barry. The Inspector's photograph was displayed prominently and a rhapsodic story captioned "Queen Adds Another Laurel!" ran two full columns of type down the sheet.

The Inspector, however, seemed singularly unimpressed. He waved his visitors to chairs, and called for coffee, and began to talk about a projected change in the personnel of one of the city departments as if the Field case interested him not at all.

"Here, here!" growled Sampson. "What's the matter with

you? You ought to be throwing out your chest, Q. You act as if you'd pulled a dud rather than succeeded."

"It's not that, Henry," said the Inspector with a sigh. "I just can't seem to be enthusiastic about anything when Ellery isn't by my side. By jingo, I wish he were here instead of in those blamed Maine woods!"

The two men laughed. Djuna served the coffee and for a time the Inspector was too occupied with his pastry to brood. Over his cigarette Cronin remarked: "I for one merely dropped in to pay my respects, Inspector, but I'm curious about some aspects of this case. . . . I don't know much about the investigation as a whole, except what Sampson told me on the way up."

"I'm rather at sea myself, Q," put in the District Attorney. "I imagine you have a story to tell us. Let's have it!"

Inspector Queen smiled sadly. "To save my own face I'll have to relate it as if I did most of the work. As a matter of fact, the only really intelligent work in the whole sordid business was Ellery's. He's a sharp lad, that son of mine."

Sampson and Cronin relaxed as the Inspector took some snuff and settled back in his armchair. Djuna folded himself quietly in a corner, ears cocked.

"In going over the Field case," began the Inspector, "I will have to refer at times to Benjamin Morgan, who is really the most innocent victim of all.[3] I want you to bear in mind, Henry, that

3 Inspector Queen's statement here is not altogether true. Benjamin Morgan was far from "innocent." But the Inspector's sense of justice compelled him to shield the lawyer and keep his word regarding silence. —E.Q.

whatever I say about Morgan is to go no further, either professionally or socially. I already have Tim's assurance of silence. . . ."

Both men nodded wordlessly. The Inspector continued:

"I needn't explain that most investigations of crime begin with a search for the motive. Many times you can discard suspect after suspect when you know the reason behind the crime. In this case the motive was obscure for a long time. There were certain indications, like Benjamin Morgan's story, but these were inconclusive. Morgan had been blackmailed by Field for years—a part of Field's activities of which you gentlemen were ignorant, despite your knowledge of his other social habits. This seemed to point to blackmail as a possible motive—or rather the choking off of blackmail. But then any number of things could have been the motive—revenge, by some criminal whom Field had been instrumental in 'sending up.' Or by a member of his criminal organization. Field had a host of enemies, and undoubtedly a host of friends who were friends only because Field held the whiphand. Any one of scores of people—men and women both—might have had a *motive* for killing the lawyer. So that, since we had so many other pressing and immediate things to think about and do that night at the Roman Theatre, we did not bother much with motive. It was always in the background, waiting to be called into service."

"But mark this point. If it was blackmail—as Ellery and I eventually decided, since it seemed the most likely possibility—there were most certainly some papers floating about in Field's possession which would be enlightening, to say the least. We knew that Morgan's papers existed. Cronin insisted that the papers for which *he* was looking were about somewhere. So we had to keep our eyes constantly on the alert for papers—tangible evidence which might or might not make clear the essential circumstances behind the crime."

"At the same time, in the matter of documents, Ellery was piqued by the great number of books on handwriting analysis he found among Field's effects. We concluded that a man like Field, who had blackmailed once to our knowledge (in the case of Morgan) and many times to our suspicions; and who was keenly interested in the science of handwriting, might have been a forger to boot. If this were true, and it seemed a plausible explanation, then it probably meant that Field made a habit of forging the original blackmail papers. The only reason he could have for doing this, of course, would be to sell the forgeries and keep the originals for further extortion. His association with the underworld undoubtedly helped him master the tricks of the trade. Later, we discovered that this hypothesis was true. And by that time we had definitely established blackmail as the motive of the crime. Remember, though, that this led us nowhere, since any one of our suspects might have been the blackmail victim and we had no way of telling who it was."

The Inspector frowned, settled back into his seat more comfortably.

"But I'm tackling this explanation the wrong way. It just goes to show you how habit will take hold of a man. I'm so accustomed to beginning with motive. . . . However! There is only one important and central circumstance which stands out in the investigation. It was a confounding clue—rather, the lack of a clue. I refer to the missing hat. . . ."

"Now the unfortunate thing about the missing hat was that we were so busy pressing the immediate inquiry at the Roman Theatre on Monday night we couldn't grasp the full significance of its absence. Not that we weren't bothered by it from the beginning—far from it. It was one of the first things I noticed when I examined the body. As for Ellery, he caught it as soon as he entered the theatre and bent over the dead man. But what could we do? There were a hundred details to take care of—questions to ask, orders to give, discrepancies and suspicious discoveries to clean up—so that, as I say, we inadvertently missed our great opportunity. If we had analyzed the meaning of the hat's disappearance then and there—we might have clinched the case that very night."

"Well, it hasn't taken so long after all, you growler," laughed Sampson. "This is Wednesday and the murder was committed a week ago Monday. Only nine days—what are you kicking about?"

The Inspector shrugged. "But it would have made a considerable differencc," he said. "If only we had reasoned it out—Well! When finally we did get around to dissecting thc problem of the hat, we asked ourselves first of all: Why was the hat taken? Only two answers seemed to make sense: one, that the hat was incriminating in itself; two, that it contained something which the murderer wanted and for which the crime was committed. As it turned out, both were true. The hat was incriminating in itself because on the underside of the leather sweatband was Stephen Barry's name, printed in indelible ink; and the hat contained something which the murderer very emphatically wanted—the blackmail papers. He thought at the time, of course, that they were the originals.

"This did not get us very far, but it was a starting point. By the time we left Monday night with the command to shut down the theatre, we had not yet found the missing hat despite a sweeping search. However, we had no way of knowing whether the hat had managed in some mysterious manner to leave the theatre, or whether it was still there though unrevealed by our search. When we returned to the theatre on Thursday morning we settled once and for all the question of the location of Monte Field's pesky topper—that is, negatively. It was *not* in the theatre—that much was certain. And since the theatre had been sealed since Monday night, it follows that the hat must have left that same evening."

"Now everybody who left Monday night left with only one hat. In the light of our second search, therefore, we were compelled to conclude that somebody had walked out that night with Monte Field's hat in his hand or on his head, necessarily leaving his own in the theatre."

"He could not have disposed of the hat outside the theatre except when he left at the time the audience was allowed to leave; for up to that time all exits were guarded or locked, and the left-hand alley was blocked first by Jess Lynch and Elinor Libby, next by John Chase, the usher, and after that by one of my policemen. The right-hand alley, having no exit other than the orchestra doors, which were guarded all night, offered no avenue of disposal."

"To go on with the thought—since Field's hat was a tophat, and since nobody left the theatre dressed in a tophat who was not wearing evening clothes—this we watched for very closely—therefore the man who took away the missing hat *must* have been garbed in full dress. You might say that a man planning such a crime in advance would have come to the theatre without a hat, and therefore would have none to dispose of. But if you will stop to think, you must see that this is highly improbable. He would have been quite conspicuous, especially while entering the theatre, if he went in minus a tophat. It was a possibility, of course, and we kept it in mind; but we reasoned that a man working out such a consummate crime as this would have shied from taking any unnecessary chance of being identified. Also, Ellery had satisfied his own mind that the murderer had no foreknowledge of the Field hat's importance. This made still more improbable the possibility that the murderer arrived without a hat of his own. Having a hat of his own, he might have disposed of it, we thought, during the first intermission—which is to say, before the crime was committed. But Ellery's deductions proving the murderer's lack of foreknowledge made this impossible, since he would not have known at the first intermission of the *necessity* of doing away with his own hat. At any rate, I think we were justified in assuming that our man had to leave his own hat in the theatre and that it must have been a tophat. Does it follow so far?"

"It seems logical enough," admitted Sampson, "though very complicated."

"You have no idea how complicated it was," said the Inspector grimly, "since at the same time we had to bear in mind the other possibilities—such as the man walking out with Field's hat being not the murderer but an accomplice. But let's get on.

"The next question we asked ourselves was this: what *happened* to the tophat which the murderer left behind in the theatre? What did he do with it? Where did he leave it? . . . I can tell you that was a puzzler. We had ransacked the place from top to bottom. True, we found several hats backstage which Mrs. Phillips, the wardrobe mistress, identified as the personal property of various actors. But none of these was a personally owned tophat. Where then was the tophat which the murderer had left behind in the theatre? Ellery with his usual acumen struck right at the heart of the truth. He said to himself, 'The murderer's tophat must be here. We have not found any tophat whose presence is remarkable or out of the ordinary. Therefore the tophat we are seeking must be one whose presence is *not* out of the ordinary.' Fundamental? Almost ridiculously so. And yet I myself did not think of it."

"What tophats were there whose *presence* was not out of the ordinary—so natural and in so natural a place that they were not even questioned? In the Roman Theatre, where all the costumes were hired from Le Brun, the answer is simple: the rented tophats being used for purposes of the play. Where would such tophats be? Either in the actors' dressing rooms or in the general wardrobe room backstage. When Ellery had reached this point in his reasoning he took Mrs. Phillips backstage and checked up on every tophat in the actors' rooms and the wardrobe room. Every tophat there—and all were accounted for, none being missing—was a property tophat bearing on its lining the Le Brun insignia. Field's hat, which we had proved to be a Browne Bros, topper, was not among the property tophats or anywhere backstage."

"Since no one left the theatre Monday night with more than one tophat, and since Monte Field's hat was unquestionably taken out of the theatre that same night, it was positively established that the murderer's own tophat must have been in the Roman all the time the house was sealed, and was still there at the time of our second search. Now, the only tophats remaining in the theatre were property tophats. It therefore follows that the murderer's own tophat (which he was forced to leave behind because he walked out with Field's) *must* have been one of the property hats backstage, since let me repeat, these were the only tophats of which it could physically have been one."

"In other words—one of these property tophats backstage belonged to the man who left the theatre Monday night in full dress wearing Field's silk topper."

"If this man were the murderer—and he could scarcely be anyone else—then our field of inquiry was narrowed to a considerable degree. He could only have been either a male member of the cast who left the theatre in evening clothes, or somebody closely connected with the theatre and similarly dressed. In the latter case, such a person would have had to have, first, a property tophat to leave behind; second, undisputed access to the wardrobe and dressing rooms; and, third, the opportunity to leave his property tophat in either place."

"Now let us examine the possibilities in the latter case—that the murderer was closely connected with the theatre, yet not an actor." The Inspector paused to sniff deeply of the snuff in his treasured box. "The workmen backstage could be discarded because none of them wore the evening clothes which were necessary in order to take away Field's tophat. The cashiers, ushers, doormen and other minor employees were eliminated for the same reason. Harry Neilson, the publicity man, was also dressed in ordinary street clothes. Panzer, the manager, was attired in full dress, it is true, but I took the trouble to check up his head size and found it to be 6 ¾—an unusually small size. It would be virtually impossible for him to have *worn* Field's hat, which was 7 ⅛. It is true that we left the theatre before he did. On my way out, however, I definitely instructed Thomas Velie to make no exception in Panzer's case, but to search him as the others had been searched. I had examined Panzer's hat merely from a sense of duty while in his office earlier in the evening, and found it to be a derby. Velie subsequently reported that Panzer walked out with this derby on his head and no other hat in his possession. Now—if Panzer had been the man we were looking for, he might have walked out with Field's hat despite its larger size by merely holding it in his hand. But when he left with a derby, that was conclusive that he could not have taken away Field's hat, since the theatre was shut down immediately after his departure and no one—my men on duty saw to that—no one entered the premises until Thursday morning under my own eye. Theoretically it was possible for Panzer, or anyone else in the Roman personnel, to have been the murderer had he been able to secrete Field's tophat in the theatre. But this last hypothesis was dissipated by the report of Edmund Crewe, our official architectural expert, who definitely stated that there was no secret hiding place anywhere in the Roman Theatre.

"The elimination of Panzer, Neilson and the employees left only the cast as possibilities. How we finally narrowed down the field of inquiry until we got to Barry, let's leave for the moment. The interesting part of this case is really the startling and complex series of deductions which gave us the truth purely through logical reasoning. I say 'us'—I should say Ellery. . . ."

"For a police Inspector you are certainly a shrinking violet," chuckled Cronin. "By gee, this is better than a detective story. I ought to be working now, but since my boss seems to be as interested as I am—keep going, Inspector!"

Queen smiled, forging ahead.

"The fact that the murderer was traced to the cast," he continued, "answers a question which has probably occurred to you and which certainly troubled us in the beginning. We could not at first understand why the theatre should have been chosen as a meeting place for the transaction of secret business. When you stop to think about it, a theatre presents enormous disadvantages under ordinary circumstances. Extra tickets, to mention only one thing, have to be bought to insure privacy through empty seats in the vicinity. What a silly tangle to get into when other meeting places are so much more convenient! A theatre is dark most of the time and disturbingly quiet. Any untoward noise or conversation is remarked. The crowds present a constant danger—one of recognition. However, all this is automatically explained when you realize that Barry was a member of the cast. From his standpoint the theatre was ideal—for who would dream of suspecting an actor of murder when the victim is found dead in the orchestra? Of course Field acquiesced, never suspecting what was in Barry's mind and that he was conniving his own death. Even if he were a little suspicious, you must remember that he was accustomed to dealing with dangerous people and probably felt capable of taking care of himself. This may have made him a little overconfident—we have no way, of course, of knowing.

"Let me get back to Ellery again—my favorite subject," continued the Inspector, with one of his recurrent dry chuckles. "Aside from these deductions about the hat—as a matter of fact, before the deductions were completely worked out—Ellery got his first indication of which way the wind blew during the meeting at the Ives-Pope house. It was clear that Field had not accosted Frances Ives-Pope in the alleyway between acts with merely flirtatious intentions. It seemed to Ellery that some connection existed between the two widely separated individuals. Now, this does not mean that Frances had to be aware of the connection. She was positive that she had never heard of or seen Field before. We had no reason to doubt her and every reason to believe her. That possible connection might have been Stephen Barry, provided Stephen Barry and Field knew each other without Frances' knowledge. If, for example, Field had an appointment at the theatre Monday night with the actor and suddenly saw Frances, it was possible that in his half-drunken mood he would venture to approach her, especially since the subject he and Barry had in common concerned her so deeply. As for recognizing her—thousands of people who read the daily papers know every line of her features—she is a much-photographed young society lady. Field certainly would have acquainted himself with her description and appearance out of sheer thoroughness of business method. . . . But to return to the triangle connection—Field, Frances, Barry—which I will go into detail later. You realize that no one else in the cast except Barry, who was engaged to Frances and had been publicly announced as her fiancé, with pictures and all the rest of the journalistic business, could have satisfied so well the question: Why did Field accost Frances?

"The other disturbing factor concerning Frances—the discovery of her bag in Field's clothes—was plausibly explained by her dropping it in the natural excitement of the moment when the drunken lawyer approached her. This was later confirmed by Jess Lynch's testimony to the effect that he saw Field pick up Frances' bag. Poor girl—I feel sorry for her." The Inspector sighed.

"To get back to the hat—you'll notice we always return to that blasted top piece," resumed Queen, after a pause. "I never knew of a case in which a single factor so dominated every aspect of the investigation. . . . Now mark this: Of the entire cast Barry was *the only one* who left the Roman Theatre Monday night dressed in evening clothes and tophat. As Ellery watched at the main door Monday night while the people were filing out, his mind characteristically registered the fact that the entire cast, except Barry, left the theatre wearing street clothes; in fact, he even mentioned this to Sampson and me in Panzer's office later, although at the time neither of us realized its full significance. . . . Barry was therefore the only member of the cast who could have taken away Field's tophat. Think this over a moment and you will see that, in view of Ellery's hat deductions, we could now pin the guilt to Barry's shoulders beyond the shadow of a doubt.

"Our next step was to witness the play, which we did the evening of the day on which Ellery made the vital deductions—Thursday. You can see why. We wanted to confirm our conclusion by seeing whether Barry had the *time* during the second act to commit the murder. And, amazingly enough, of all the members of the cast, Barry was the only one who did have the time. He was absent from the stage from 9:20—he opened the business of the act and left almost at once—until 9:50, when he returned to the stage to remain there until the act ended. This was incontrovertible—part of a fixed and unchanging time schedule. Every other player was either on the stage all the time or else went on and off at extremely short intervals. This means that last Thursday night, more than five days ago—and the whole case took only nine days to consummate—we had solved our mystery. But solving the mystery of the murderer's identity was a far cry from bringing him to justice. You'll see why in a moment."

"The fact that the murderer could not enter until 9:30 or thereabouts explains why the torn edges of LL32 Left and LL30 Left did not coincide. It was necessary for Field and Barry, you see, to come in at different times. Field could not very well enter with Barry or even at a noticeably later hour—the matter of secrecy was too important to Barry, and Field understood, or thought he did, how necessary it was for him to play the secret game."

"When we pinned the guilt on Barry Thursday night, we resolved to question subtly the other members of the cast as well as workmen backstage. We wanted to find out, of course, whether any one had actually seen Barry leave or return. As it happened, no one had. Everybody was busy either acting, redressing, or working backstage. We conducted this little investigation after the performance that night, when Barry had already left the theatre. And it was checkmate, right enough."

"We had already borrowed a seating plan from Panzer. This map, together with the examination of the alleyway on the left and the dressing-room arrangement backstage—an examination made directly after the second act Thursday night—showed us how the murder was committed."

Sampson stirred. "I've been puzzling my wits about that," he confessed. "After all, Field was no babe-in-the-woods. This Barry must be a wizard, Q. How did he do it?"

"Every riddle is simple when you know the answer," retorted the Inspector. "Barry, whose freedom began at 9:20, immediately returned to his dressing room, slapped on a quick but thorough facial disguise, donned an evening cloak and the tophat which was part of his costume—you'll remember he was already dressed in evening clothes—and slipped out of his room into the alley.

"Of course you can't be expected to know the topography of the theatre. There is a series of tiers in a wing of the building backstage, facing the left alley, which is made up of dressing rooms. Barry's room is on the lowest tier, the door opening into the alleyway. There is a flight of iron steps leading down to the pavement."

"It was through this door that he quitted the dressing room, walking through the dark alley while the side doors of the theatre were shut during Act II. He sneaked out into the street, since there was no guard at the head of the alley at that time—and he knew it—nor had Jess Lynch and his 'girl' arrived, luckily for him; and entered the theatre brazenly through the regular front entrance, as if he were a latecomer. He presented his ticket—LL30 Left—at the door, muffled in his cloak and of course well disguised. As he passed into the theatre he deliberately threw away his ticket stub. This appeared to him to be a wise move, since he figured that if the ticket stub were found there, it would point to a member of the audience and directly away from the stage. Also, if his plans fell through and he were later searched carefully, the finding of the stub on his person would be damning evidence. All in all, he thought his move not only misleading but protective."

"But how did he plan to get to the seat without being ushered to it—and therefore seen?" objected Cronin.

"He hadn't planned to evade the usher," returned the Inspector. "Naturally, he had hoped, since the play was well on and the theatre dark, to gain the last row, the nearest to the door, before the usher could approach. However, even if the usher forestalled him and escorted him to the seat he was well disguised and the blackness of the theatre was proof enough against recognition. So that, if things turned out as badly as possible for him, the most that would be remembered was that some man, unknown, barely describable in general contour, arrived during the second act. As it happened he was not accosted, since Madge O'Connell was luckily seated with her lover. He managed to slip into the seat next to Field without being noticed.

"Remember, what I've just told you," went on the Inspector, clearing his dry throat, "is not the result of deduction or investigation. We could have no means of discovering such facts. Barry made his confession last night and cleared up all these points. . . . Knowing the culprit was Barry, of course, we might have reasoned out the entire procedure—it follows simply and is the natural situation if you know the criminal. It wasn't necessary, however. Does that sound like an alibi for Ellery or myself? Hmph!" The old man barely smiled.

"When he sat down next to Field he had a carefully planned idea of his course of action. Don't forget that he was on a strict time schedule and could not afford to waste a minute. On the other hand, Field, too, knew that Barry had to get back so he made no unnecessary delays. The truth of the matter, as Barry has told us, is that he expected to have a more difficult time with Field than he actually did have. But Field was sociably amenable to Barry's suggestions and conversation, probably because he was quite drunk and expected to receive a huge sum of money within a short time."

"Barry first requested the papers. When Field cannily asked for the money before he produced the documents, Barry showed him a wallet bulging with apparently genuine bills. It was quite dark in the theatre and Barry did not take the bills apart. Actually they were stage money. He patted them suggestively and did what Field must have expected: refused to hand over the money until he had checked the documents. Bear in mind that Barry was an accomplished actor and could handle the difficult situation with the confidence imparted to him by his stage training. . . . Field reached under his seat and to Barry's utter astonishment and consternation produced his tophat. Barry says that Field remarked: 'Never thought I'd keep the papers in this, did you? As a matter of fact, I've dedicated this hat to your history quite exclusively. See—it has your name in it.' And with this astounding statement he turned back the band! Barry used his pocket pencil flashlight and saw his name inked in on the underside of the leather sweatband."

"Just imagine what went through his mind at this moment. Here he saw what seemed at the moment a ruinous accident to his careful plans. Should Field's hat be examined—and of course it would be—at the time of the discovery of the body, then the name Stephen Barry on the band would be overwhelming evidence. . . . Barry had no time to rip out the band. In the first place he had no knife—unfortunately for him; and in the second place the hatband was closely and securely stitched to the tough fabric. Working on split-time, he saw at once that the only course open to him was to take the hat away after he killed Field. Since he and Field were of the same general physique, with Field wearing an average sized hat, 7 ⅛, he immediately decided to leave the theatre wearing or carrying Field's hat. He would deposit his own in the dressing room, where its presence was not out of the way, take Field's hat from the theatre with him and destroy it as soon as he reached his rooms. It also occurred to him that if the hat were by some chance examined as he was leaving the theatre, his name printed inside would certainly ward off suspicion. In all probability it was this fact that made Barry feel he was running into no particular danger, even though he had not foreseen the unexpected circumstance."

"Clever rogue," murmured Sampson.

"The quick brain, Henry, the quick brain," said Queen gravely. "It has run many a man's neck into the noose. . . . As he made the lightning decision to take the hat, he realized that he could not leave his own in its place. For one thing, his hat was a snapdown—an opera hat—but more important, it had the name of Le Brun, the theatrical costumer, stamped in it. You can see that this would immediately point to someone in the cast—just the thing he wished to avoid. He told me also that at the moment, and for quite some time thereafter, he felt that the most the police could deduce from the hat's being missing was that it was taken because it contained something valuable. He could not see how this investigatory guess would point the finger of suspicion anywhere near him. When I explained to him the series of deductions Ellery made from the mere fact that the tophat was missing, he was utterly astounded. . . . You can see, now, that the only really fundamental weakness of his crime was due not to an oversight or a mistake on his part, but to an occurrence which he could not possibly have foreseen. It forced his hand and the entire chain was started. Had Barry's name not been lettered in Field's hat, there is no question in my mind but that he would be a free and unsuspected man today. The police records would carry another unsolved murder on its pages.

"I need not state that this entire train of thought flashed through his brain in less time than it takes to describe. He saw what he had to do and his plans adjusted themselves instantly to the new development. . . . When Field extracted the papers from the hat, Barry examined them cursorily under the lawyer's watchful eye. He did this by the same pencil flashlight—a tiny streak of illumination quite obscured by their shielding bodies. The papers seemed in good order and complete. But Barry did not spend much time over the papers at the moment. He looked up with a rueful smile and said: 'Seem to be all here, damn you'—very naturally, as if they were enemies under a truce and he was being a good sport. Field interpreted the remark for what it was intended to convey. Barry dipped into his pocket—the light was out now—and, as if he was nervous, took a swig at a pocket-flask of good whisky. Then as if recollecting his manners, he asked Field pleasantly enough if he would not take a drink to bind the bargain. Field, having seen Barry drink from the flask, could have no suspicion of foul play. In fact, he probably never dreamed that Barry would try to do him in. Barry handed him a flask. . . ."

"But it wasn't the same flask. Under cover of the darkness he had taken out two flasks—the one he himself used coming from his left hip pocket. In handing it over to Field, he merely switched flasks. It was very simple—and made simpler because of the darkness and the fuddled condition of the lawyer. . . . The ruse of the flask worked. But Barry had taken no chances. He had in his pocket a hypodermic filled with the poison. If Field had refused to drink Barry was prepared to plunge the needle into the lawyer's arm or leg. He possessed a hypodermic needle which a physician had procured for him many years before. Barry had suffered from nervous attacks and could not remain under a doctor's care since he was traveling from place to place with a stock company. The hypodermic was untraceable, therefore, on a cold trail years old; and he was ready if Field refused to drink. So you see—his plan, even in this particular, was foolproof. . . ."

"The flask from which Field drank contained good whisky, all right, but mixed with tetra ethyl lead in a copious dose. The poison's slight ether smell was lost in the reek of the liquor; and

Field, drinking, gulped down a huge mouthful before he realized that anything was wrong, if he did at all."

"Mechanically he returned the flask to Barry, who pocketed it and said: 'I guess I'll look over these papers more carefully—there's no reason why I should trust you, Field. . . .' Field, who was feeling extremely disinterested by this time, nodded in a puzzled sort of way and slumped down in his seat. Barry really did examine the papers but he watched Field like a hawk out of the corner of his eye all the time. In about five minutes he saw that Field was out—out for good. He was not entirely unconscious but well under way; his face was contorted and he was gasping for breath. He seemed unable to make any violent muscular movement or outcry. Of course, he'd utterly forgotten Barry—in his agony—perhaps didn't remain conscious very long. When he groaned those few words to Pusak it was the superhuman effort of a practically dead man. . . ."

"Barry now consulted his watch. It was 9:40. He had been with Field only ten minutes. He had to be back on the stage at 9:50. He decided to wait three minutes more—it had taken less time than he had figured—to make sure that Field would not raise a rumpus. At 9:43 exactly, with Field terribly inanimate in his internal agonies, Barry took Field's hat, snapped down his own and slipped it under his cloak, and rose. The way was clear. Hugging the wall, walking down the aisle as carefully and unobtrusively as possible, he gained the rear of the leftside boxes without anyone noticing him. The play was at its highest point of tension. All eyes were riveted on the stage."

"In the rear of the boxes he ripped off the false hair, rapidly adjusted his make-up and passed through the stage door. The door leads into a narrow passageway which in turn leads into a corridor, branching out to various parts of the backstage area. His dressing room is a few feet from the entrance to the corridor. He slipped inside, threw his stage hat among his regular effects, dashed the remaining contents of the death flask into the wash bowl and cleaned out the flask. He emptied the contents of the hypodermic into the toilet drain and put away the needle, cleaned. If it was found—what of it? He had a perfectly sound excuse for owning it and besides the murder had not been committed by such an instrument at all. . . . He was now ready for his cue, calm, debonair, a little bored. The call came at exactly 9:50, he went on the stage and was there until the hue-and-cry was raised at 9:55 in the orchestra. . . ."

"Talk about your complicated plots!" ejaculated Sampson.

"It is not so complicated as it seems at first hearing," returned the Inspector. "Remember that Barry is an exceptionally clever young man and above all an excellent actor. No one *but* an accomplished actor could have carried off such a plan. The procedure was simple, after all; his hardest job was to keep to his time schedule. If he was seen by any one he was disguised. The only dangerous part of his scheme was the getaway—when he walked down the aisle and went backstage through the box stage-door. The aisle he took care of by keeping an eye out for the usher while he sat next to Field. He had known beforehand, of course, that the ushers, due to the nature of the play, kept their stations more or less faithfully, but he counted on his disguise and hypodermic to help him through any emergency that might arise. However, Madge O'Connell was lax in her duty and so even this was in his favor. He told me last night, not without a certain pride, that he had prepared for every contingency. . . . As for the stagedoor, he knew from experience that at that period in the play's progress practically every one was on the stage. The technical men were busy at their stations, too. . . . Remember that he planned the crime knowing in advance the exact conditions under which he would have to operate. And if there was an element of danger, of uncertainty—well, it was all a risky business, wasn't it?—he asked me last night, smiling; and I had to admire him for his philosophy if for nothing else."

The Inspector shifted restlessly. "This makes clear, I hope, just how Barry did the job. As for our investigation. . . . With the hat deductions made and our knowledge of the murderer's identity, we still had no inkling of the exact circumstances behind the crime. If you've been keeping in mind the material evidence which we had collected on Thursday night, you will see that we had nothing at all with which to work. The best thing we could hope for was that somewhere among the papers for which all of us were looking was a clue which would tie up to Barry. Even that would not be enough, but. . . . So the next step," said the Inspector, after a sigh, "was the discovery of the papers in Field's neat hiding place at the top of the bed canopy in his apartment. This was Ellery's work from start to finish. We had found out that Field had no safety-deposit box, no post-office box, no outside residence, no friendly neighbor or tradesman, and that the documents were not in his office. By a process of elimination Ellery insisted that they must be somewhere in Field's rooms.

You know how this search ended—an ingenious bit of pure reasoning on Ellery's part We found Morgan's papers; we found Cronin's stuff relating to the gang activities—and by the way, Tim, I'm going to be keenly alive to what happens when we start on the big clean-up—and we found finally a wad of miscellaneous papers. Among these were Michaels' and Barry's. . . . You'll remember, Tim, that Ellery, from the handwriting analysis business, deducted that possibly we would find the originals of Barry's papers—and so we did.

"Michaels' case was interesting. That time he went to Elmira on the 'petty larceny' charge, it was through Field's clever manipulations with the law. But Field had the goods on Michaels and filed the documentary evidence of the man's real guilt away in his favorite hiding place, in the event that he might wish to use it at some future date. A very saving person, this Field. . . . When Michaels was released from prison Field used him unscrupulously for his dirty work, holding the threat of those papers over the man's head."

"Now Michaels had been on the lookout for a long time. He wanted the papers badly, as you may imagine. At every opportunity he searched the apartment for them. And when he didn't find them time after time, he became desperate. I don't doubt that Field, in his devilishly sardonic way, enjoyed the knowledge that Michaels was ransacking the place day after day. . . . On Monday night Michaels did what he said he did—went home and to bed. But early Tuesday morning, when he read the papers and learned that Field had been killed, he realized that the jig was up. He had to make one last search for the papers—if he didn't find them, the police might and he would be in hot water. So he risked running into the police net when he returned to Field's rooms Tuesday morning. The story about the check was nonsense, of course."

"But let's get on to Barry. The original papers we found in the hat marked 'Miscellaneous' told a sordid story. Stephen Barry, to make it short and ugly, has a strain of negroid blood in his veins. He was born in the South of a poor family and there was definite documentary evidence—letters, birth records and the like—to prove that his blood had the black taint. Now Field, as you know, made it his business to run things like this to earth. In some way he got hold of the papers, how long ago we can't say, but certainly quite a while back. He looked up Barry's status at the time and found him to be a struggling actor, on his uppers more often than he was in funds. He decided to let the fellow alone for the time. If ever Barry came into money or in the limelight, there would be time enough to blackmail him. . . . Field's wildest dreams could not have foreseen Barry's engagement to Frances Ives-Pope, daughter of a multi-millionaire and blue-blood society girl. I needn't explain what it would have meant to Barry to have the story of his mixed blood become known to the Ives-Popes. Besides—and this is quite important—Barry was in a constant state of impoverishment due to his gambling. What money he earned went into the pockets of the bookmakers at the racetrack and in addition he had contracted enormous debts which he could never have wiped out unless his marriage to Frances went through. So pressing was his need, in fact, that it was he who subtly urged an early marriage. I have been wondering just how he regarded Frances sentimentally. I don't think, in all fairness to him, that he was marrying wholly because of the money involved. He really loves her, I suppose—but then, who wouldn't?"

The old man smiled reminiscently and went on. "Field approached Barry some time ago with the papers—secretly, of course. Barry paid what he could, but it was woefully little and naturally did not satisfy the insatiable blackmailer. He kept putting Field off desperately. But Field himself was getting into hot water because of his own gambling and was 'calling in' his little business deals one by one. Barry, pushed to the wall, realized that unless Field were silenced everything would be lost. He planned the murder. He saw that even if he did manage to raise the $50,000 Field demanded—a palpable impossibility—and even if he did get the original papers, yet Field might still wreck his hopes by merely circulating the story. There was only one thing to do—kill Field. He did it."

"Black blood, eh?" murmured Cronin. "Poor devil."

"You would scarcely guess it from his appearance," remarked Sampson. "He looks as white as you or I."

"Barry isn't anywhere near a full-blooded Negro," protested the Inspector. "He has just a drop in his veins—just a drop, but it would have been more than enough for the Ives-Popes. . . . To get on. When the papers had been discovered and read—we knew everything. Who—how—why the crime was committed. So we took stock of our evidence to bring about a conviction. You can't hale a man into court on a murder charge without evidence. . . . Well, what do you think we had? Nothing!

"Let me discuss the clues which might have been useful as evidence. The lady's purse—that was out. Valueless, as you know. . . . The source of the poison—a total failure. Incidentally, Barry did procure it exactly as Dr. Jones suggested—Jones, the toxicologist. Barry bought ordinary gasoline and distilled the tetra ethyl lead from it. There was no trace left. . . . Another possible clue—Monte Field's hat. It was gone. . . . The extra tickets for the six vacant seats—we had never seen them and there seemed little chance that we ever would. . . . The only other material evidence—the papers—indicated motive but proved nothing. By this token Morgan might have committed the crime, or any member of Field's criminal organization."

"Our only hope for bringing about a conviction depended upon our scheme to have Barry's apartment burglarized in the hope that either the hat, or the tickets, or some other clue like the poison or the poison apparatus, would be found. Velic got me a professional housebreaker and Barry's apartment was rifled Friday night while he was acting his role in the theatre. Not a trace of any of these clues came to light. The hat, the tickets, the poison—everything had been destroyed. Obviously, Barry would have done that; we could only make sure."

"In desperation, I called a meeting of a number of the Monday night audience, hoping that I would find someone who remembered seeing Barry that night. Sometimes, you know, people recall events later which they forgot completely in the excitement of a previous quizzing. But this too, as it happened, was a failure. The only thing of value that turned up was the orangeade boy's testimony about seeing Field pick up an evening bag in the alley. This got us nowhere as far as Barry was concerned, however. And remember that when we questioned the cast Thursday night we got no direct evidence from them."

"So there we were with a beautifully hypothetical statement of facts for a jury, but not a shred of genuine evidence. The case we had to present would have offered no difficulties to a shrewd defending attorney. It was all circumstantial evidence, based chiefly on reasoning. You know as well as I do what a chance such a case would have in court. . . . Then my troubles really began, for Ellery had to leave town."

"I racked my brains—the few I have." Queen scowled at his empty coffee cup. "Things looked black enough; How could I convict a man without evidence? It was maddening. And then Ellery did me the final service of wiring me a suggestion."

"A suggestion?" asked Cronin.

"A suggestion that I do a little blackmailing myself. . . ."

"Blackmailing yourself?" Sampson stared. "I don't see the point."

"Trust Ellery to make a point that on the surface is obscure," retorted the Inspector. "I saw at once that the only course left open to me was to *manufacture* evidence!"

Both men frowned in puzzlement.

"It's simple enough," said Queen. "Field was killed by an unusual poison. And Field was killed because he was blackmailing Barry. Wasn't it fair for me to assume that if Barry were suddenly blackmailed on the identical score, he would again use poison—and in all likelihood the *same* poison? I don't have to tell you that 'Once a poisoner always a poisoner.' In the case of

Barry, if I could only get him to try to use that tetra ethyl lead on somebody else, I'd have him! The poison is almost unknown—but I needn't explain further. You can see that if I caught him with tetra ethyl lead, that would be all the evidence I needed.

"How to accomplish the feat was another matter. . . . The blackmail opportunity fitted the circumstances perfectly. I actually had the original papers pertaining to Barry's parentage and tainted blood. Barry thought these destroyed—he had no reason to suspect that the papers he took from Field were clever forgeries. If I blackmailed him he was in the same boat as before. Consequently he would have to take the same action."

"And so I used our friend Charley Michaels. The only reason I utilized him was that to Barry it would seem logical that Michaels, Field's crony and bully and constant companion, should be in possession of the original papers. I got Michaels to write a letter, dictated by me. The reason I wanted Michaels to write it was that possibly Barry, through association with Field, was familiar with the man's handwriting. This may seem a small point but I couldn't take any chances. If I slipped up on my ruse, Barry would see through it at once and I'd never get him again."

"I enclosed a sheet of the original papers in the letter, to show that the new blackmailing threat had teeth. I stated that Field had brought Barry copies—the sheet enclosed proved my statement. Barry had no reason in the world to doubt that Michaels was milking him as his master had done before. The letter was so worded as to be an ultimatum. I set the time and the place and, to make a long story short, the plan worked. . . ."

"I guess that's all, gentlemen. Barry came, he had his trusty little hypodermic filled with tetra ethyl lead, also a flask—an exact replica, you see, of the Field crime except for locale. My man—it was Ritter—was instructed to take no chances. As soon as he recognized Barry he covered him and raised the alarm. Luckily we were almost at their elbows behind the bushes. Barry was desperate and would have killed himself and Ritter, too, if he'd had half a chance."

There was a significant silence as the Inspector finished, sighed, leaned forward and took some snuff.

Sampson shifted in his chair. "Listens like a thriller, Q," he said admiringly. "But I'm not clear on a few points. For example, if this tetra ethyl lead is so little known, how on earth did Barry ever find out about it—to the degree of actually making some himself?"

"Oh." The Inspector smiled. 'That worried me from the moment Jones described the poison. I was in the dark even after the capture. And yet—it just goes to show how stupid I am—the answer was under my nose all the time. You will remember that at the Ives-Pope place a certain Dr. Cornish was introduced. Now Cornish is a personal friend of the old financier and both of them are interested in medical science. In fact, I recall Ellery's asking at one time: "Didn't Ives-Pope recently donate $100,000 to the Chemical Research Foundation?" That was true. It was on the occasion of a meeting in the Ives-Pope house one evening several months ago that Barry accidentally found out about tetra ethyl lead. A delegation of scientists had called upon the magnate, introduced by Cornish, to request his financial aid in the Foundation. In the course of the evening, the talk naturally turned to medical gossip and the latest scientific discoveries. Barry admitted that he overheard one of the directors of the Foundation, a famous toxicologist, relate to the group the story of the poison. At this time Barry had no idea that he would put the knowledge to use; when he decided to kill Field, he saw the advantages of the poison and its untraceable source immediately."

"What the deuce was the significance of that message you sent to me by Louis Panzer Thursday morning, Inspector?" inquired Cronin curiously. "Remember? Your note requested that I watch Lewin and Panzer when they met to see if they knew each other. As I reported to you, I asked Lewin later and he denied any acquaintance with Panzer. What was the idea?"

"Panzer," repeated the Inspector softly. "Panzer has always intrigued me, Tim. At the time I sent him to you, remember the hat deductions which absolved him had not yet been made. . . . I sent him to you merely out of a sense of curiosity. I thought that if Lewin recognized him, it might point to a connection between Panzer and Field. My thought was not borne out; it wasn't too hopeful to begin with. Panzer might have been acquainted with Field on the outside without Lewin's knowledge. On the other hand, I didn't particularly want Panzer hanging around the theatre that morning; so the errand did both of us a lot of good."

"Well, I hope you were satisfied with that package of newspapers I sent you in return, as you instructed," grinned Cronin.

"How about the anonymous letter Morgan received? Was that a blind, or what?" demanded Sampson.

"It was a sweet little frame-up," returned Queen grimly. "Barry explained that to me last night. He had heard of Morgan's threat against Field's life. He didn't know, of course, that Field was blackmailing Morgan. But he thought it might plant a strong false trail if he got Morgan to the theatre on a thin story Monday night. If Morgan didn't come, there was nothing lost. If he did—He worked it this way. He chose ordinary cheap notepaper, went down to one of the typewriter agencies and, wearing gloves, typed the letter, signed it with that useless scrawled initial, and mailed the thing from the general post-office. He was careful about fingerprints and certainly the note could never be traced to him. As luck would have it, Morgan swallowed the bait and came. The very ridiculousness of Morgan's story and the obvious falsity of the note, as Barry figured, made Morgan a strong suspect. On the other hand, Providence seems to provide compensations. For the information we got from Morgan about Field's blackmailing activities did Mr. Barry a heap of harm. He couldn't have foreseen that, though."

Sampson nodded. "I can think of only one other thing. How did Barry arrange for the purchase of the tickets—or did he arrange for it at all?"

"He certainly did. Barry convinced Field that as a matter of fairness to himself, the meeting and the transfer of papers should take place in the theatre under a cloak of absolute secrecy. Field was agreeable and was easily persuaded to purchase the eight tickets at the box office. He himself realized that the six extra tickets were needed to insure privacy. He sent Barry seven and Barry promptly destroyed them all except LL30 Left."

The Inspector rose, smiling tiredly. "Djuna!" he said in a low voice. "Some more coffee."

Sampson stopped the boy with a protesting hand. "Thanks, Q, but I've got to be going. Cronin and I have loads of work on this gang affair. I couldn't rest, though, until I got the whole story from your own lips. . . . Q, old man," he added awkwardly, "I'm really sincere when I say that I think you've done a remarkable piece of work."

"I never heard of anything like it," put in Cronin heartily. "What a riddle, and what a beautiful piece of clear reasoning, from beginning to end!"

"Do you really think so?" asked the Inspector quietly. "I'm so glad, gentlemen. Because all the credit rightfully belongs to Ellery. I'm rather proud of that boy of mine. . . ."

When Sampson and Cronin had departed and Djuna had retired to his tiny kitchen to wash the breakfast dishes, the Inspector turned to his writing desk and took up his fountain pen. He rapidly read over what he had written to his son. Signing, he put pen to paper once more.

> Let's forget what I just wrote. More than an hour has passed since then. Sampson and Tim Cronin came up and I had to crystallize our work on the case for their benefit. I never saw such a pair! Kids, both of 'em. Gobbled the story as if it were a fairy tale. . . . As I talked, I saw with appalling clarity how little I actually did and how much you did. I'm pining for the day when you will pick out some nice girl and be married, and then the whole darned Queen family can pack off to Italy and settle down to a life of peace. . . . Well, El, I've got to dress and go down

to headquarters. A lot of routine work has collected since last Monday and my job is just about cut out for me. . . .

When are you coming home? Don't think I want to rush you, but it's so gosh-awful lonesome, son. I—No, I guess I'm selfish as well as tired. Just a doddering old fogey who needs coddling. But you *will* come home soon, won't you? Djuna sends his regards. The rascal is taking my ears off with the dishes in the kitchen.

Your loving
FATHER

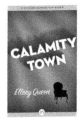

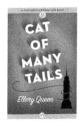

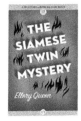